Unchained

MARIE ALLEN

Unchained Love Series
Book One

For the girls who were taught that love was a debt. May you find the one who spends a lifetime proving you are the prize.
Until then, he's waiting inside.

Content Warning

Dear Reader,

Thank you for picking up *Unchained*. This is a story with a hard-won happily ever after, but the journey to get there explores some deep and emotionally intense themes. I believe in allowing readers to make informed choices, so please find a list of specific content warnings below.

<u>This book contains:</u>

-Explicit sexual content and open door spice.

-On-page depiction of grief and loss related to an overdose

-Themes of addiction, emotional abuse, and neglect

-Discussions and memories of past domestic violence (not depicted in the present)

-Brief violence/fighting

Please take care of yourselves and your hearts while reading.

Playlist

1. Lovely- Billie Eilish & Khalid
2. Youth- Daughter
3. Liability- Lorde
4. Mice- Billie Marten
5. Bad Apple- Billie Marten
6. C-side- Khruangbin & Leon Bridges
7. Love Interruption- Jack White
8. Corcovado- Stan Getz & Joao Gilberto
9. Can I Call You Rose?- Thee Sacred Soul
10. Wicked Games- Chris Isaak
11. Glory Box- Portishead
12. My Love Mine All Mine- Evan Jacobson
13. All I Need- Radiohead
14. Can't Help Falling In Love- Haley Reinhart
15. Hope Is A Dangerous Thing- Lana Del Rey
16. A Love International- Khruangbin
17. Smooth Operator- Sade
18. No Ordinary Love- Sade
19. Clair de Lune - Claude Debussy
20. Dark Minuet - Nicholas Britell
21. Wicked Games Live - James Vincent McMorrow
22. Wicked Games Live - James Vincent McMorrow
23. Midnight in Harlem - Tedeschi Trucks Band
24. Belong to You - Sabrina Claudio
25. La Vie En Rose - Daniela Andrade
26. Unchained Melody- Righteous Brothers
27. Nothings Gonna Hurt You Baby - Cigarettes After Sex
28. Fade into You - Mazzy Star
29. Fly Me to the Moon- The Macarons Project
30. Take Me to Church- Hoizer
31. The Way That You Feel- Leif Vollebekk
32. By Your Side- Sade
33. Anyone Who Knows What Love is- Irma Thomas
34. Dark F**king Spirit- Chris Benstead
35. Promise- Ben Howard
36. Sea of Love- Cat Power
37. First Day of My Life - Bright Eyes
38. Blood Is Blue - Billie Marten
39. Et si tu n'existais pas- Joe Dassin
40. I Only Have Eyes For You - The Flamingos

Reader Note:

To fully immerse yourself in Alana and Kais's world, I invite you to listen along with the official *Unchained* playlist. Each chapter header features a music note (♫) and a track number. For the most emotional impact, play the corresponding song on repeat as you read. Let the melody guide you through their love, heartbreak, and every moment in between.

Prologue

♫ 1 &2

TRUTH DOESN'T MATTER IN A ROOM LIKE THIS. NEITHER does love. Nor sacrifice.

"If there is nothing further, I will now proceed to deliver my judgment," the judge's voice rang out across the courtroom.

One last chance to fight for her. One last chance to be heard.

"I'd like to say something, if that's okay?" I stood from the front row of the gallery, my heart pounding.

Across the room, my mother's eyes snapped to mine. The same wordless threat to stay silent she's given me my whole life. Not today.

"Approach the witness stand and state your name, please," Judge Simons said, as if my sister's future wasn't hanging on every word said in this courtroom today.

I clasped my shaking hands together as I walked to the podium.

"Alana Cameron," I said, clearing my throat. "I'm the defendant's daughter and Macy's sister."

"Half-sister," Lisa Estepp called from behind me, like that made me matter less.

"I suggest you hold your tongue, Mrs. Estepp," the judge didn't even look at her.

"How old are you, Ms. Cameron?" she asked, her gaze settling on mine.

"Eighteen, ma'am. I just graduated high school last week."

I don't know why I added that—maybe I thought if she knew I wasn't just some kid, she might actually hear me.

Her face softened slightly but her eyes remained impassive.

"Go on, Ms. Cameron. But be brief."

I could feel the weight of every eye on me. Especially hers. My mother, seething in silence. I cleared my throat, even though it did nothing to settle the fear clawing up my spine.

"I just wanted to say... I don't think Macy should stay with my mom."

A hiss cut through the room. My mother scoffed, loud enough for everyone to hear, as if that would make her lies more believable next to the truth I was finally offering.

"And why is that, Ms. Cameron?" Judge Simons asked, regarding me like some unruly teenager. "Her drug tests are clean, and she's done everything this court has asked her to do. Our goal is not to separate families here."

She sounded just as offended as my mother. Like I was the one breaking something that could still be fixed. That was enough to let my defensiveness overtake my fear.

"Because she's not doing any of that. I am." I hesitated, just for a second, but I couldn't stop now. "I've been the one taking care of Macy since the day she was born and Victor—her dad—went to jail. I had to switch to online classes so I could stay home with her because my mom would disappear for days. And when she came back, she was still high."

My throat went dry but I pushed on.

"I'm the only one who was there when Macy was in the hospital, when she was born addicted. I had to watch her cry until her whole face turned red. I was the one waking up in the middle of the night to give her morphine because she was in so much pain."

My voice cracked. My tears burned hot and fast, but I didn't stop. I looked over at my mother, searching her face for anything—remorse, guilt. But there was nothing. Just a twitch of her brow, that self-righteous expression like I was the one who'd wronged her. I wiped my face hard, rolled my shoulders back. I had to get through this. I had to finish.

"And she's been using my urine for your tests," I said ashamed of myself, but the truth was the truth. "She puts it in a condom, tapes it to her leg, wraps it in hot hands so it passes as fresh."

A gasp from behind me—Lisa. I don't have to see her to picture her frowning under her blue-rinse perm.

"That is not true!" My mother shot up, yelling now, hands clenched at her sides.

Judge Simons banged her gavel. "Order. Ms. Assad, I suggest you have a seat before I hold you in contempt." Judge Simons turned her gaze to me. "Ms. Cameron, if what you're saying is true —aside from the fact that it's a crime—why didn't you come forward sooner?"

"I was afraid, I guess." My fingers twisted together, my shoulders hunched tight with stress. "At first, I was mostly afraid of Victor. Being punched and choked by him wasn't exactly my favorite pastime." I let out a dry, humorless laugh. "But then when he got locked up and it was just the three of us—my mom, Macy, and me—I thought things would get better. I thought she'd finally get help."

I paused, trying to swallow the emotion threatening to choke me.

"But she didn't. And I knew if I said anything, I'd lose—Macy. I wouldn't be allowed to see her again." My voice cracked. "And she's the only family I've ever had. I love her like she's my own daughter. I just didn't want to lose her." A sob slipped out before I could stop it. "I thought if I graduated and got a job, I could get us out. I could save her. And maybe my mom would finally get better." I wiped at my eyes, struggling to finish. "I'm sorry." The words trailed off into nothing.

Judge Simons inhaled deeply. "Thank you, Ms. Cameron."

She looked down at the papers in front of her—not reading them, just thinking. She looked at my mother. Then back at me.

"Ms. Cameron," she said softly, her voice shifting—lower, almost kind now.

It caught me off guard.

"Look at me for a moment, please."

I lifted my eyes.

"You're eighteen years old. And you've been dealt an incredibly hard hand—a hand that would've broken most people. But you stepped up when your sister needed someone. That's an extraordinary thing." She offered a faint, almost reluctant smile. "But you've got your whole life ahead of you. And I can't, in good conscience, saddle you with the care of a three-year-old before you're emotionally and financially ready for it."

Panic shot through my chest.

"But—" I started desperately, leaning forward.

She held up a hand to silence me.

"I know what you're going to say, Ms. Cameron. That you can do it. That you'll work hard and sacrifice everything to make sure that little girl is okay. And I believe you."

Her eyes hardened a little, like she was preparing me for the blow.

"But this is bigger than you. Macy needs long-term stability. And the work that needs to be done to repair her relationship with your mother is... overwhelming. I'm sure Mr. and Mrs. Estepp will allow you to visit and maintain your relationship with her while you focus on healing and building your future."

My shoulders dropped. My chest ached like it had been cracked wide open. My entire body felt cold. I didn't say a word.

I had nothing to say. No lawyer. No money. No power. Just a broken story and a breaking heart. Nothing that said I was the better option—not on paper. Not to people like them.

"Please have a seat, Ms. Cameron," the judge said gently. "I'll read my decision now."

I moved as if underwater, my feet barely brushing the ground. Every step felt like failure. *This is why I don't speak up. Why I don't ask for help. Why I keep my head down and stay quiet. Because every time I open my mouth, it ends like this. With a slammed door. With disaster.*

"In the case of Macy Marlene Estepp," Judge Simons said, "I grant sole custody to James and Lisa Estepp, effective immediately, with supervised visitation twice a week granted to Melanie Assad. Case dismissed."

The sound of the gavel cracked across the room, echoing in my chest long after people began to shuffle out. Lisa clapped her hands together, like she'd just won a scratch-off ticket—not custody of a toddler who didn't understand her world had just been ripped apart. My mother stood and crossed the courtroom with that familiar angry click of her heels. She leaned in so closely her breath hit my ear.

"You're fucking dead to me," she whispered.

Then she walked off smiling, like she hadn't just tried to shatter me. But she didn't have to try. I was already in pieces. I didn't follow her. I didn't speak. I kept my eyes on the floor as I left the courtroom and moved down the hall, feet dragging toward the waiting room where the social worker sat with Macy. Her face lit up the second she saw me.

"Momma!" she squealed, squirming in the woman's lap, her arms reaching out.

My chest caved. She always called me that. I usually corrected her. But not today. I scooped her up, hugging her tight, breathing in the lavender-sweet scent of her curls. I didn't know how to let her go. I didn't want to.

"Are we going home now?" she asked, her voice small against my shoulder.

Before I could answer, Lisa chimed in behind me. "You're coming home with Grammy and Grandpa, Macy!"

She said it like it was a treat, like a toy or a trip to the zoo. Macy's face fell. Her little mouth turned down, her glassy hazel eyes lifting to mine with a question I couldn't answer.

"I don't want to," she said, and the sound of it cracked me open. She clung to me, tiny arms locked tight around my neck.

"I know, baby girl. I know." I rocked her gently, swallowing the lump in my throat. "It's just like a big sleepover, okay? Grammy's got lots of toys, and your favorite cookies and cream ice cream..."

"I don't want that," she cried. "I want you!" She held on tighter as Lisa stepped forward, arms out.

"I'll be back with you before you know it," I whispered, kissing her temple, trying to make myself believe the lie I was telling. "I promise."

I held her for one more breath. One more second. Then I forced myself to peel her off me and hand her over. Lisa reached for her with stiff arms.

"Oh, come on, Macy, settle down," she barked, as Macy flailed in her grip. "James, take her please."

Her husband stepped in, grabbed Macy from her arms, and left in a flash—her cries of "Momma! Momma!" echoing down the hallway until they disappeared. I stayed frozen in place. My arms felt empty in a way I knew would never leave me.

Lisa turned back, brushing invisible lint off her pants, smoothing her blouse like this was any other Tuesday. Her lips were pursed, not smiling. Not even now.

"I should bring over some of her stuff," I said, voice raw. "Or maybe... maybe I could watch her during the day while you guys are working or—"

"That won't be necessary, Alana." Her words devoid of any compassion for me.

"I'm sorry, but we think it's best for Macy if there's no contact for now—at least until things with your mother are... resolved."

My breath caught in my chest. Anger roared up in my throat. "What?" I snapped. "You can't do that."

She scoffed, cool and casual. "I absolutely can. And if you'd like to see her, you can arrange something through your mother."

She said it like she knew exactly what that meant. She knew my mother would never let that happen. She wanted me to hear it loud and clear: You're out.

Lisa turned on her heel before I could get in another word. And just like that, it was over. My heart sank. The floor dropped out from under me, and I couldn't tell if I was falling or floating. The hallway buzzed around me—shoes squeaking, doors slamming, voices echoing—but I couldn't move.

The world had swallowed me whole. My mother would never let me come to those visits. She wouldn't even let me back into her house. There was nothing left for me here. No home. No family. No one. Nowhere to go... except maybe one place, thirteen hundred miles from Dallas. The only place that didn't ask for anything but my grades. The place I'd applied to because my school counselor made me. The University of Miami.

Alana

♫ 3-5

A LITTLE OVER THREE YEARS LATER...

The ocean really did carry some kind of magic. At least, it did for me. I could get lost out here for hours on mornings like this. The cold sand soft beneath my feet, the tide creeping up to nip my ankles, a trail of broken shells and sand dollars scattered like forgotten promises. No one out here but me—and the occasional golden girl on her morning jog. The yawning Miami sun kissed my face, soft and warm. That was always the best part. In a moment like this, I could almost forget everything. Exams, grades, research papers. But never Macy.

Even after three and a half years, it still stung. The silence. The terse emails from Lisa. The occasional photo of Macy, carefully posed in stuffy dresses. And still, every week, I wrote back. Hoping that someday, Macy would know I never stopped trying. Now, with only one semester left before I graduate, summer break couldn't come soon enough. Between final exams and law school applications, my brain was fraying at the edges. But even with all that, I felt it—just a little closer to seeing my girl again.

9

Closer to a chance to prove myself, that I was good enough for her now. To being good enough to be around her. To no longer being labeled as the half-sister or the junkie's other daughter. But as someone respectable. And if the Estepps didn't see me that way I'd use my law degree to fight for myself until they changed their mind. For Macy and every other kid who fell through the cracks of the broken family court system.

"Can we go, please? I'm freezing," Jasmine groaned beside me.

Since move-in day freshman year, she'd never missed a chance to complain about something—though back then, I think her main concern was getting the side of the dorm with the best sunlight for selfies.

"Why do you have to be such a buzzkill, Jazz?" I muttered, eyes still closed, soaking in the sun's last soft caress.

"I am a good time girl, okay? Just not at five in the freaking morning."

I laughed. "Fine, come on." I opened my eyes and hooked my arm through hers as we turned away from the beach and headed to the parking lot.

Even when sleep-deprived, Jasmine was beautiful in the kind of way I envied. Her long, silky black hair was pulled back in a sleek braid, her skin sun-kissed and clear, her waist cinched tight enough to make gym sponsors weep. If she ever decided to become a fitness influencer, she'd have six brand deals by lunch.

"When's your shift?" I asked as we crossed the parking lot.

"Two to close. You?"

I shook my head. "Off."

"You bitch," she teased with a groan.

"I've been pulling doubles for two weeks straight." I grinned as I slid into the passenger seat of her sun-faded yellow Alfa Romeo Sprint. The velour itched like hell, but it had character.

"Any way I can sucker you into picking up a shift?" She pouted as she turned the engine over. "I hate being at the restaurant without you."

"Why— there's more annoyingly rich assholes to flirt with you when I'm not there?" I smirked.

"I am *a taken woman*, thank you very much." She queued up some Latin pop I didn't recognize, turning it up like a shield against the morning.

"That's right—what's the new guy's name again? Ben?"

"*Jaden*," she corrected, scandalized. "And I'll have you know, I feel *great* about him. You're just bitter because you've committed yourself to being a nun."

"I've dated," I said, narrowing my eyes.

"Yeah, your ex-boyfriend creeping back around and a handful of sad Tinder dates don't count." She pulled into our apartment complex, already victorious.

"I haven't seen him in over a year," I muttered. "And it's not my fault every guy in this city is a man-whore."

She threw the car in park, tossing up her hands. "All I'm saying, baby doll, is that maybe—*maybe*—it wouldn't kill you to let those beautiful Diana Ross curls down and do something that's not school, work, or taking care of your grown-ass mom. Preferably something in the shape of a man."

I rolled my eyes and climbed out of the car.

"Find me someone who's not an asshole and actually knows how to converse about something other than himself, and we'll talk." I said, as we made our way up the steps to our apartment.

"Challenge accepted," she called over her shoulder. "You weren't blessed with all this to hide it behind books." She waved a perfectly manicured hand over me before slipping inside.

I followed behind her, disappearing into my room—intent on scrolling away her nonsense. I wasn't a nun. I'd been in love before. I think. And the absolute devastation of watching it crash down because someone couldn't keep it in their pants? Yeah. That didn't exactly make the idea of dating again sound appealing. But still—I stayed too long. Entertained too many "I'm sorry" texts. Filled the gutting loneliness with his presence, because I had no one else when I first got here. I've learned since then. Grown. *I can date again.*

I pulled out my phone and opened my dating app. Swipe. No. Swipe. No. Swipe. Hell no. And then—*My ex*. Of course.

My phone rings, interrupting my descent into despair. *Mom.*

I sighed, hard and heavy. "Hello?"

A jumble of noise crackled in the background—plastic rustling, keys jangling—like she was busy doing something *other* than being more annoying than a picture of my ex.

"Hello," I said again, dragging the word out.

"Hey, sorry. I was getting in the car," she replied, like I was someone she casually called to chit-chat with.

"What's up, Mom?" My voice came out cold and exasperated.

"I need to borrow some money."

Of course. The *only* reason she ever calls.

"For what now?"

She snorted, like I didn't have the right to ask. "For Macy. Lisa's asking me for money to put her in some dance class. It's due today."

Go figure. She always used Macy to get to me. Always dangled her like bait, especially since she knew I couldn't verify a damn thing she said.

"How much?" I asked with a sigh.

"Four hundred," she said, like it was nothing and not more than I make in a week.

I let out a dry laugh. "In what world, Mother?"

More rustling. Then: "What am I supposed to do, Alana? You know I can't work right now. I'm doing my best. If you don't want to be a part of her life anymore, fine. I'm sorry I even asked."

And predictably, the gaslighting. Smooth as ever.

"I never said that." My jaw clenched. "I'll send you the money. Just—make sure you give her that doll I sent, okay? Lisa's last email said she's been trying to collect them, and they've been sold out since Christmas. I was lucky to find that one."

She let out dramatic breath, as if I'd asked her to move a mountain. "Yes, I will, Alana. Can you app me the money now?"

No *please*. No *thank you*. No *how's life*. Just do it because she said the magic word.

"Yeah, I will," I exhaled. "Alright, well, I gotta go. I'll call you in a few days when I see her."

The line clicked dead. I pressed my fingers to my eyes, trying to calm the pulse jumping at my temples. Then, with the kind of muscle memory that only years of guilt and emotional trauma can build, I sent off four hundred dollars. And stared at my bank app that all but laughed at me.

Balance: *fifty-two dollars and eighty-seven cents.*

No day off for me now.

I pushed off the bed and headed to Jazzy's room, where she was already deep into a full glam makeup tutorial for her socials—one she probably wouldn't finish before work, but would definitely try to edit until the second she clocked in.

"Looks like a few less entitled assholes for you tonight," I said, leaning against the doorframe. "I'm going in."

She beamed at me through the mirror. "Yes, chica. I love that for me. Why don't you do your makeup, and wear one of my skirts instead of those librarian pants you love so much?"

"I said I'm going to work, not fishing for a man, Jasmine. I can dress myself when I decide to do that," I called over my shoulder, already disappearing back down the hall.

Back in my room, my phone was lit up on the bed with a new email. I flopped down, thumbing it open.

From: *Lisa Estepp*

Subject: *Macy's Summer*

I skimmed it fast, but one line caught and stuck:

"We will be out of town for the next four months. Emails sent after today will not be read until then."

Heat crept up the back of my neck. Not because Lisa was boxing me out using one of the most archaic forms of communication known to man—but because how does a girl who's suppos-edly *traveling the country for four months* need money for a *dance class*? I didn't need to read it again. My fingers moved on their own, calling my mom. Straight to voicemail. Figures. I'd sooner get that money back betting on where it went than ever hearing the truth of it from her.

FINALS WEEK CAME like a freight train. My brain was a minefield of essay prompts, caffeine jitters, and a to-do list that never got shorter. The sun was already threatening to melt my scalp as Jasmine and I stepped out of her car and headed toward the restaurant—our fifth shift since my mom disappeared. We adjusted our uniforms as we walked, Jasmine twisting her hair into a braid while I tried to tame my ponytail into something resem-bling professional.

"I swear," Jasmine muttered, tugging her black shirt down over her hips, "if someone asks for gluten-free risotto again, I'm throwing myself into the fountain."

I snorted. "Pretty sure the fountain's out of order still."

"Even better. I'll just lay there. Let the algae take me."

I smiled, but it didn't quite reach. My brain was still fogged over from a week of exams, application decisions, and an increas-ingly alarming bank account. At least with this shift, I could stretch the grocery budget past boxed penne and butter.

We rounded the back of the hotel where the busboys were already on a smoke break, just as a matte black G-Wagon pulled into the lot. Clean. Quiet. Not a single speck of dirt on it, despite the chaos of Miami's streets. Jasmine slowed slightly, her curiosity seemingly piqued. I pulled out my phone to check it one last time.

"Alana," she hissed, grabbing my arm like she'd just spotted a celebrity. "I swear to God—he looks like the type of man who drinks whiskey that costs more than our rent. Sharkskin suit. Watch that's probably insured. Like he could kidnap you, but you'd like it."

I laughed under my breath and kept walking. "You've been watching too many flop rom-coms."

"Don't act like you don't want to look," she teased, bumping my shoulder.

My eyes found him the moment he stepped from the truck and toward the private access doors. He was handsomely tailored in that effortless, quietly expensive way. His suit bent to his will, not the other way around. He moved like he owned every room he entered. Like he had never second-guessed a thing in his life. He didn't look at anyone, just walked like he'd already mapped out exactly who—and what—he'd come for. Something in me leaned forward just slightly, before I forced it back.

"If I go missing and they find me tied up in that man's basement, please don't rescue me," Jasmine whispered.

I didn't say anything. Didn't stop walking until we reached the service door. But something in me went still. Just for a moment some weird sense of *deja vu* washing over me like I've been here before, maybe seen that man before. And then I looked away. Just a man. Just a weird stressed-brain moment. Just another long shift ahead.

Kais

-2-

🎵6

"KAIS, THIS IS THE BIG ONE, LAD. THE WHOLE WORLD has been waiting for you to step in the ring again." Montee's voice crackled through the phone, thick with excitement.

He was overstepping, knew I couldn't give a fuck about what *anyone* wanted but he also knew I respected his opinion more than anyone else's. The elevator chimed, signaling my floor.

"I get that, mate, but if the numbers don't make sense, I don't give a fuck," I said flatly.

Montee sighed. "Right, fuck off then. I'll see you in the morning."

I chuckled, stepping into the hallway. He'd spark me out in training, but I welcome it.

"Don't be that way, dear," I taunted. "It always goes my way, yeah?"

His curses were drowned out as I ended the call. The second I stepped inside the excessively luxe Miami hotel suite, the room shifted. Lawyers. Promoters. Suits who thought they had the upper hand sat in a row on the couch at the center of the room.

My side sat across from them—George, my agent, whose only job was to work out the details of whatever I agreed to, and Alanzo, head of my security and the only person I trusted to handle what I didn't have time for. The group was all pressed suits and forced smiles. They thought this was theirs to dictate. *It wasn't.*

A blonde woman sat beside the promoters, every detail of her appearance neatly polished. She smiled too eagerly as I settled into the armchair beside George.

"Mr. Reinhardt, I think we have something very close to a deal here," one of the promoters said.

I said nothing. George slid the contract toward me. I skimmed it, tuning out the noise as they started rattling off percentages, TV rights, and sponsorship clauses. *Always smoke and mirrors.*

They wanted my name. The ticket sales, the international pull, the marketing power that came with it. But they wanted it on their terms. They thought I'd jump for the right number. They didn't know me at all. I let them carry on. Gave nods where they expected them. Occasionally glanced up. Just enough to let them think I was considering it. People like this mistook silence for hesitation. They never realized it was simply patience. I leaned back, observing. Calculating their next move. The next angle they'd try to sell me on, the next attempt to make me believe I needed them. Then, when the moment was right, I spoke.

"Right. I'm not interested in this." I tossed the contract, which landed on the table with a dull thud.

The room tensed. One of the promoters—bald, desperate-looking—leaned forward, already trying to salvage it.

"We're offering you the biggest purse of your career. That alone should—"

I lifted a hand. He stopped. *Good.*

"Let's not pretend I don't bring more to this than just a title."

He shifted uncomfortably. A man in a terrible suit fidgeted, trying to find his next play.

"You're leveraging my image in your media campaigns. You're

already counting my numbers against your projections. You want my name on the ticket, it comes at my terms," I said with a dismissive shrug.

Lousy Suit cleared his throat. "It's a fair offer, Mr. Reinhardt. One hundred-fifty million. Prestige. Pay-per-view percentages—"

I tilted my head, unimpressed.

They needed me more than I needed them. And they fucking knew it. I needed no help bolstering my net worth, which had landed me on a very short list of billionaires under thirty. Nor did I need to add another fight to my undefeated boxing career that's been turned to a past time behind my business.

I let the silence stretch, let them feel it.

"Are we here to waste each other's time?" I said.

Their eyes darted between each other, none of them speaking.

Then the bald man straightened his tie, steadied his voice. "We can discuss additional incentives, but the base offer is solid."

I pushed up from my seat. Alanzo did the same. George already knew the drill.

"We have nothing more to discuss then. I believe you've forgotten—I don't need to fight at all."

I didn't have to look to know they were scrambling. I already knew what came next. The only man in the room who had said nothing finally leaned forward and spoke up. Older. A canny look about him. Not flashy like the others—just efficient. The one who made the real decisions.

"What do you want, Mr. Reinhardt?"

There it was. Now we were getting somewhere.

I held his gaze steadily. "Double the purse. Raise the equity in pay-per-view by three points. Full control over my sponsorships— no exclusivity clauses."

He blinked, absorbing it. "That's... aggressive."

I rolled my shoulders back, observing him, my expression unchanged. It wasn't aggression. It was certainty. The room thickened with tension, but I didn't need to press. This was already done. They just hadn't accepted it yet.

"Then I'm not your man," I replied.

The older man exhaled, rubbing his temple. He knew they had already lost the battle. "We'll draft the revised contract."

I moved toward the door, adjusting my watch as I nodded to George. "Brilliant. George will stay and refine the details."

No pleasantries. No goodbyes. They weren't people—they were business. And I never let business waste my time.

"Montee called. Everything's set for training at the gym near your place tomorrow at 4:30," Alanzo said from behind me in the elevator.

My mind was already moving to the next thing—the never-ending list of shit to sift. The meeting had been handled. The fight was in motion. Now, the rest of the pieces had to fall into place. The elevator doors slid open. I stepped into the lobby, my thoughts still on the negotiation. Numbers. Contracts. Logistics. A fight that would be my biggest yet.

Then I saw her.

This woman. With a presence that hit me harder than anything I'd walked into a ring for. She didn't just catch my eye—she pulled something in me taut. Like recognition. Like consequence.

She was standing near the staircase, phone pressed to her ear. Not just beautiful.

Fucking stunning.

The kind of beauty that wasn't curated, wasn't asking to be noticed—but demanded it all the same. Long dark brown hair, glossy curls gathered in a ponytail. Smooth, golden-brown skin that caught the low light. Big brown eyes, framed by thick lashes. Full, plush lips—soft, pink, unintentional perfection. And a body —*fuck.* Curved in a way that made a man's hands ache to touch, but with a posture that told you she wasn't for the taking.

I'm not the type to stare, but something held me there.

I walked forward, half-answering Alanzo, "Yeah, mate. Tomorrow's fine."

My gaze flicked back to her. She looked tired. Not in a way that could be fixed with sleep, but in the way that came from carrying too much for too long. I was about to step past her when I caught the shift in her voice.

"I can't keep doing this, Mom."

I stopped. I didn't mean to listen, but I did. She wasn't angry. Just exhausted. She shook her head like she was listening, squeezing her eyes closed like she was drowning out the noise of the lobby.

Then, quieter: "If I send you money again, I know where it's going. You promised you'd go back to rehab."

Bloody hell. Poor girl.

Her mother kept talking—pleading, maybe.

She exhaled, pinching the bridge of her nose before finally conceding. "Send me the details. I'll pay the bill myself."

Not if. Not I'll try. Just I'll handle it. She already knew this wouldn't be the last time. Never is in situations like that. And she was going to do it anyway.

It's none of my business what's going on in this woman's life. It wouldn't usually matter. Never has before. I've never been sidetracked by a pretty face—not like this. Never cared enough to wonder what story lived behind one. I let myself indulge now and then, sure, but it's always been simple. Easy. No questions. No aftermath. But this woman—There's something different about her. Something that doesn't ask for attention but holds it nonetheless. And I can't look away.

I turned to Alanzo. "Let me know when George sends over the contract. I'm grabbing supper."

He nodded, heading out. But food wasn't why I stayed. For some reason I needed to know who she was. Maybe to convince myself I'm losing my bloody mind by being this damn interested in a woman I know nothing about.

I busied myself checking emails, standing like an idiot in the middle of the lobby. I didn't give a shit. She lingered after she hung up, like she was trying to breathe through the frustration. Then, she squared her shoulders, tucked her phone into her apron, and walked inside the restaurant attached to the lobby.

I should leave. *Just go home.* Handle the list of things that require my time and signature to move forward. I couldn't. I have never believed in fate, but something like it kept my feet planted where they were.

She disappeared inside. I followed. Not after her, necessarily... just inside—for a drink.

"Weller full proof, neat." I ordered without looking at the bartender, my attention still fixed on the woman taking an order across the room.

I had no plan here. No reason to be standing in the middle of a hotel restaurant, watching a woman I didn't know. And yet—I wasn't ready to take my eyes off her.

The bartender slid my drink across the counter. I lifted it, took a slow sip, barely tasting it. My attention kept drifting—drawn back to her like a gravitational pull I had no interest in resisting.

She moved through the restaurant with light ease, as if the conversation she'd just had outside never happened. Her smile was somehow effortless and sweet. She lingered at tables longer than the other waitresses, listening intently, as if each customer was her best friend. Like she had time for everyone.

More than a handful of men tried to make a pass at her. They saw a beautiful woman. A prize. And to be fair—she is. But they didn't see her. They didn't clock the way she went still when they leaned in too close, or the tight flick of her smile when they spoke like they already owned her time. Arrogant, entitled yuppies in suits with wedding rings they conveniently forgot about. Red-faced from long lunches and used to getting what they want. She gave them nothing. Not even a reaction. And I admired the hell out of that.

Not a chance I was going to approach her the same way. Not that I've ever approached a woman, full stop. I never needed to.

They always just... found me. Something I could orbit for a night, fill a need, scratch at the quiet. Never anything I wanted to keep. Never anyone I wanted to be kept by. But with her, I could feel myself wanting something completely different. I just didn't know what.

There was something behind her eyes when she wasn't in a conversation with a customer. Something restrained. She was here, but not really. And yet—she wasn't cold. Wasn't detached. She was just somewhere else possessed by a stillness I recognized—too much weight carried too long. Then, she did something that pulled me in even deeper. The thing that made me sit up a little straighter. The thing that made me lean forward, just enough to get a better look.

A girl—petite, dark-haired—leaned against the counter near her, talking fast, complaining about something. Her shift? Maybe something more. I couldn't hear the words, but I could read the frustration on her face.

I grasped for anything I could make out, not realizing I'd moved forward until I found myself leaning closer. My chest tightened with something I didn't have a name for yet. Curiosity. Or hunger, maybe. More than anything: need. Not the usual kind. Not the kind I knew how to control. Just one need circled in my head, louder with every second:

What's her name? Fuck, I need her name.

She was listening to the other waitress. Really listening, as she had with everyone she'd been talking to tonight. Then—she pulled out a wad of bills and split her tips in half, pressing them into the girl's palm before she could argue. Just gave them away.

Bloody hell, why is this woman so kind?

The girl protested. She waved her off, smiling like it didn't matter. Like this kind of thing happened all the time and it cost her nothing to do. Though I'd just heard her say she couldn't do it on the phone a few hours ago. Yet here she was, doing it for someone else *again*. It was clear she took care of everyone over herself. Gave money she didn't have to give. Smiled even when she was shattered. Listened to people who saw her as nothing more than a vehicle for their own desires. She was different. Good, in a way that felt impossible. I'd met a lot of people and never come across someone like her. That fact settled into my chest like an immovable weight.

My gaze must have lingered too long, because suddenly—*she looked up.*

Shit.

She was going to think I was just as dodgy as every other sad bastard who had hit on her tonight. Her gaze flicked over me— quick, unassuming, but lingering a second too long to be an accident. Something flickered in her eyes. She didn't smile. She didn't look away too quickly, either. She just... saw me. And for a moment, I let her. I held my gaze steady. No smirk. No reaction. Just control. Even though my pulse had picked up slightly. *Just two strangers making eye contact.* I told myself. Not like I'd followed her in here like a fucking nutter.

Something ignited in that brief second that her eyes held mine. Then a voice from the kitchen called out to her, breaking the moment. She turned. I exhaled slowly, dragging a hand over my jaw.

A second later, a waitress appeared in front of me. The same one she had just given money to. "Hey, handsome." She leaned against the bar, smiling. "My name's Jazzy. Can I get you a menu? Another drink?"

Her flirtation was direct and practiced. She was attractive, clearly put together for someone's benefit, but it did nothing for me. Not now. Not after her. I drained my glass and pulled out my wallet. "How much did she give you?" I nodded to the kitchen.

She blinked. "What?"

"The woman who just handed you half her tips."

Her brows knit in confusion. She hesitated, then lowered her voice.

"Two hundred fifty dollars."

I pulled at least three times that from my wallet and pushed it toward her.

"Give it back."

Her mouth parted, eyes flicking between me and the money.

"You don't have to—"

I held up a hand, already standing. "Do it. And don't tell her why, yeah?"

She swallowed hard, nodding.

I turned toward the exit, catching another glimpse of her coming out of the kitchen—the woman who didn't even realize someone had just put her first for once. She wouldn't know it was me. That was fine. But now—I know who *she* is. That's enough for me. I glanced at my phone. A text from Alanzo flashed across the screen, confirming our flight back to London in two days. Maybe I'd push it back. Extend my meetings. Drag out negotiations. Another week in Miami wouldn't kill me. But leaving before I knew her name might.

I looked back one last time.

Then, finally, I stepped into the night.

I WALKED INTO THE RESTAURANT, scanning the room out of habit as I'd done the last three nights. I already knew she was here. I called ahead. Didn't ask for her name—just described her. It should've unsettled me, how easy that description came. How I knew exactly how to define her. How I knew the way her curls flowed over her shoulders when she wore her hair down, the way her uniform fit snug against the lines of her body, how her smile lingered for most customers, but never for the men who wanted something from her.

I wasn't sure what *I* wanted. I just knew I wasn't finished watching her. The first night, I left, walked out before I could start something I wasn't ready to finish.

The second night, I nearly missed her, walked in just as soon as her shift finished.

And now, tonight, she wasn't even working. She was sitting at the bar, off to the side, a bowl of salad and glass of wine in front of her. And she was singing, her voice soft and unbothered as it whispered through the air, something classic and warm.

I recognized the song immediately. Righteous Brothers. 'Unchained Melody'. My mum's favorite song, one I can remember her singing when I was a boy. The girl wasn't just singing. She was bringing something back to life. A song no one else in this place would've given a second thought. No one except me. Something about that particular song, about her singing it here like she didn't have a care in the world, felt like she'd been waiting for me to walk in.

I sat at my new favorite spot, a table in the corner with a full view of the place. Quietly observing her. She was beautiful like this. Unburdened, unobserved. Or at least, she thought she was. No one noticed her yet tonight, at least not the way I did.

She was still in her uniform, her apron folded over the stool beside her. She ate slowly, eyes on her phone, her nails tapping lightly against the glass of wine in front of her. At peace. Unaware of her power over me. I should've walked out again. Left before she became something I couldn't stay quiet about anymore. She hummed the last few notes, took a sip of wine, licked a stray drop off her bottom lip.

Christ.

I gripped my glass a little tighter. *Three nights.* I spent three shit nights pretending I wasn't coming back for her. *Fuck it.* I wasn't pretending anymore. I took a drink then slid out of my chair, moving toward her. Not too fast. Not desperate. But intentional. She didn't look up until I was close. And when she did—when those big brown eyes finally landed on mine—something ancient stirred in my chest. Not lust. Not possession. Something quieter. Hungrier. Like I'd been waiting for her gaze my whole life and didn't know it until it landed. I didn't move—but inside, *everything did*.

Alana

-3-

Jazzy: Hey, baby doll…

Me: Uh oh. What do you want?

Jazzy: Why do I have to want something?

Me: Because you only call me "baby doll" when you do, Jazz.

Jazzy: Fine, you caught me. Can you take your time coming back home? Jaden's here…

Me: That's all you had to say. I just got off—I'll hang out at the restaurant for a bit.

Jazzy: Ooo. Is that guy in again?

♫ 7

I SLID MY PHONE BACK INTO MY POCKET AND SCANNED the room, exhaling slowly. Jasmine had been trying to push me toward every man with a pulse lately, but I wasn't interested. It wasn't even about healing anymore. I just wasn't sure I had it in me to trust anyone again let alone love the way I had before. And if I couldn't love someone like that again... what was the point?

So here I am—sitting alone at the bar at work, that I can barely afford to eat in apart from my one free meal, with a half empty glass of wine, poking at a Caesar salad like it held all the answers. I knew exactly which guy she was referring to—the same one she'd practically drooled over a few days ago.

The one who never flirted with me but always left hundred-dollar tips. He was easily the most stunning man I'd ever seen, from afar at least... and yet, he showed no interest. Not that I had any in him. I just appreciated the unspoken truce—he was beautiful, quiet, and generous for no reason. Always ordered one whiskey that he picked up from the bar himself. Always read a book. I'd filled his water a few times but never lingered enough to get a good look at him up close, never even heard his voice.

The restaurant was unusually quiet for a Saturday night—just a few couples nestled in candlelit corners and the usual cluster of businessmen hunched over their third drinks at the bar. For once, I could actually hear the overhead music. My ears perked at one of my favorites—'Unchained Melody'—soft and hauntingly romantic. I hummed along absentmindedly, pushing a crouton around my plate, letting the music blur everything else out. Until a voice broke through the quiet.

"You like this song?" Low. Smooth. Slightly rough at the edges —like honey stirred with gravel.

There was an accent tucked into it too, but I couldn't place it, like it had traveled too many places to belong to just one. Enticing enough to make me forget how to breathe. I turned toward the sound, half-startled—only to find *him* standing beside the stool next to mine.

Him.

The mysterious and silent big tipper...all-consuming in his presence, unbelievably tall and built like a damn bronze statue.

Up close, he was devastating. Worse than I'd prepared for.

I shamelessly studied every detail. He was the kind of beautiful that didn't look real in this kind of lighting—like he'd been carved from shadows and sun, all sharp angles softened by just enough warmth to make him dangerous. He smelled like leather, whiskey, and cloves. His hair was longer than I remembered, dark and thick, swept back in careless waves that curled slightly at the ends, like he'd just run a hand through it. His skin was golden-brown, sun-kissed, but not beach-earned—something deeper, warmer, inherited like mine.

My stomach dipped. I forced myself to speak before the silence stretched too long.

"The real question is—do you?" My voice barely came out. I cleared my throat, tried again. "I've never met another person my age who actually knows who The Righteous Brothers are."

The depth of his eyes held mine captive—deep brown, nearly black, framed by lashes so long they made no sense on a man like him.

The most beautiful man I've ever seen.

His face was all strong cheekbones and a chiseled jaw dusted with stubble. His nose was slightly crooked, like it had been broken once – probably a story there. A faint scar cut through one brow. And his lips—*God*—thin but plush, naturally upturned, like they'd been built to smirk. There was a small beauty mark on his left cheek, barely visible unless you were this close. And I hadn't been—*this close*— Until now.

"I do." His mouth curved into a smile so lethal, my chest burned. It wasn't cocky—it was confident. Like he was used to people staring. Like he knew exactly the effect he had on them.

"May I join you?" he asked, gesturing toward the stool next to mine.

He studied me like I was something he'd already decided to want. Not in a sleazy way. Not like the others. It was quiet. Focused. *Very fucking dangerous.* Everything in me screamed *don't do it. Say no. Finish your salad. Go home.*

But I couldn't.

"Yeah, sure," I said, the words slipping out before I could catch them. I swallowed hard, trying not to seem flustered. *Failing* miserably.

He waved the bartender over with a lift of his hand, subtle but commanding.

The man responded instantly, posture straightening. "What can I get you, Mr. Reinhardt?"

Mr. Reinhardt? Okay, so he wasn't just a guy with good bone structure. He was *someone*.

"I'll take my drink over here, lad, if you don't mind." There it was again—that low, clipped accent. Between London and somewhere colder. *Swedish? Russian?*

"Of course, sir." The bartender nodded and cast me a quick, curious glance before walking off.

I turned back to him, pushing down the flurry in my chest.

"I'm Alana Cameron." I offered my hand.

He paused for a moment, something flickering behind his eyes —amusement, maybe curiosity—before a quiet chuckle rumbled low in his chest.

"Kais Reinhardt." His hand wrapped around mine—warm, solid, a little rough from whatever he did with his days. The kind of grip that made it hard to remember what my name was.

"Case?" I repeated, uncertain of the pronunciation. His smile curved slightly, understated but devastating.

"Kai-eez."

"Kai-eez," I echoed, letting it roll off my tongue.

He leaned in, just a fraction. "Uh-la-nuh, right?"

That sent a shiver right down my spine. The way he said my name made it sound expensive.

I laughed, soft and unguarded. "Yeah. Pretty much. Most people here pronounce it Bob, though."

That grin widened, white and perfect teeth catching the light.

I mean come on, no one should be allowed to look like this. Not in real life anyway.

"You're a cheeky little thing, aren't you?" he said.

"Maybe a little," I admitted, watching the corners of his lips twitch.

I've served plenty of wealthy men in this restaurant. Enough to know the name Patek on his watch meant it cost more than my entire education, and the faint LV logos stitched into the black suede of his jacket didn't exactly scream bargain hunter.

Normally, that alone would've been enough to make me steer clear, keep it surface-level. Just smile. Walk away. Life has taught me too many times that money doesn't always mean safety in a man —some at least use it for more evil than good. But something about him made me pause. Not in fear. Not in caution. Just... pause. Like whatever he was didn't quite fit that type.

"Where are you from?" he asked. Voice smooth as the twenty-year whiskey he drank, his posture easy but attentive.

I arched a brow. "Oh, we're getting deep already? You've barely sat down."

"Just curious," he shrugged, that faint smirk still playing at the edge of his lips. "You're American, obviously. But you don't sound or look like you're from around here."

I smiled into my wine. "Well, everyone in Miami is from somewhere else at this point. But I'm from Texas. Dallas specifically. My dad's from there, born and raised. My mom was born in Marrakech, Morocco."

His expression didn't change exactly, but something shifted. A stillness behind his eyes. Calculating. Like he was cataloging that information somewhere private.

"Your mother's from Marrakech?" he asked, slower this time. Leaning into me just slightly, like he's got all the time in the world.

"Yeah, immigrated to the U.S. when she was eight. With her mom and her sister."

He leaned back a little, resting an arm on the back of his stool, his bicep flexing against the sleeve of his jacket, studying me like I'd just said something that turned the world sideways.

"That's... interesting." His voice was thoughtful.

"Why?" I narrowed my eyes.

"Because my mum is, too."

I blinked.

That was the last thing I expected him to say. Though he had that whole tall, dark, and handsome thing down pretty damn well.

"Really?" I said wearily.

He nodded, lifting his glass to his lips. "She was born there. Father's German—Munich—but I spent most of my life in London."

"Huh." I tilted my head, smiling softly. "I guess we have more in common than I thought."

His brows lifted. "Like what?"

"Well, for one, you're also sitting alone at a nearly empty bar on a Saturday night." I motioned to his glass. "You like The Righteous Brothers. And apparently— we're ancestral neighbors."

A dry chuckle escaped him as he swirled his drink. "Fascinating."

He wasn't teasing. He meant it.

"So, tell me—why are you alone?" he asked, voice smooth, like it was meant to linger in the air between us.

Usually, I'd hate a question like that. But from him it sounded curious, like an opening rather than a line. I smiled faintly, eyes dropping to my glass for half a second before looking back at him.

"I haven't met anyone worth my time." It slipped out more honestly than I meant it to.

His brow arched, like that answer genuinely surprised him.

"Is that so?"

"It is."

This time, my smile stayed. I felt as if something in me was leaning forward again, exactly like the first time I saw him.

He shifted, his knee brushing mine again—no way it was an

accident, not with the way his gaze tracked every flicker of my reaction.

"You're intriguing, you know that?" he said, like it wasn't meant to charm, just to name what he saw. "Smart. Astute. A little guarded... but there's still light in you. You haven't hardened. Not yet anyway."

That last part caught something in me. I felt it behind my ribs, like he'd touched a bruise no one else could see. This wasn't flattery. It was observation. And somehow, that felt infinitely more dangerous than this already was.

I laughed quietly, trying to brush it off. "Are you always this observant?"

"Only when I care to be." His voice dipped lower. "And I care to be now."

I swallowed, pulse tapping lightly at my throat.

"Careful," I said softly. "You're starting to sound like someone who could actually be worth the time."

That grin turned lethal in a way that felt like a dare and a promise all at once.

"Guess you'll have to find out."

I inhaled briskly and took another sip of my wine, hoping it would ease the heat creeping up my chest. Or take the edge off of how tempting this man was. His eyes stayed on mine, intent, ruthlessly devastating. I swallowed and cleared my throat.

"So, tell me about you. What is it that you're always reading over there?" I asked, nudging the conversation somewhere softer.

He rubbed his jaw, the faintest flicker of embarrassment crossing his face. "Lately? English classics in Arabic. I've been trying to learn the language."

"Mmm, I love that," I hummed, genuinely impressed. "I've always wanted to visit Morocco."

His jaw flexed, something unreadable flickering behind his eyes before he smoothed it over with another drink of his bourbon, "I haven't been yet."

"Really?"

"Not yet," he said, voice steady, but not simple. Like there was more there—something heavy he wouldn't readily admit.

Before I could ask, he leaned in slightly, lowering his voice.

"Would you be interested in seeing a film with me?"

"A movie?"

"There's a black and white screening in Little Havana. *Casablanca.* I think you might like it."

I blinked, surprised by how right he was. *Casablanca* was exactly the kind of movie I'd choose myself—classic, timeless, the kind most people my age would probably find boring. But somehow he'd pegged me perfectly.

"Are you asking me out, Kai?" I teased his name, unable to hold back the flirtatious grin I felt pull at my lips. His smirk deepened—slow and confident, like he already knew the answer.

"I believe I am, Alana."

A soft laugh escaped me, small, reluctant, a little breathless. But real. My stomach was doing hurdles in time with my mind. I don't date. I study, I work, I take care of the people around me. Going out with this dangerously hot man who could probably talk me out of all my willpower is the last thing I should be doing but something deep in my gut is telling me to do it, pulling me to him like a magnet. So, I used the only external excuse I have.

"I'd love the opportunity to decipher whether you side with Rick or Victor. And maybe if I weren't in my work clothes," I said, suddenly self-conscious, "I'd say yes. Rain check?"

I began to gather my things to leave. My heart was hammering. *Jesus. I just gave him an opening. Rain check, that's basically yes.* And I hadn't said yes to anyone in a long time. Not since... well. Not since I learned what it felt like to lose yourself in someone and get nothing back but wreckage. And yet, here I was, grabbing my bag like I hadn't just walked straight off a cliff. He didn't flinch. Didn't press. Like he already knew I'd come back.

"I'd be heartbroken if you didn't," he said. Smooth as ever.

There was something knowing in his look, a confidence that I'd make good on my promise. He rose from his stool, then casually slid four hundred-dollar bills onto the bar. Far too much for a single drink. He didn't even glance at them, just stood there tall and confident despite the fact that we'd just casually agreed to change the entire trajectory of my nonexistent dating life.

Then he did something that caught me completely off guard. He reached for my hand. Not in a showy way. Just—offered it. Like it was the most natural thing in the world to help me out of my seat. I took it without another thought. And when his palm met mine, something fired off in my chest. His fingers curled around mine, and it was like my body remembered something it had no business knowing: safety, intensity, a quiet kind of desire.

Then he leaned in. Just enough that his voice brushed my ear, low and warm and ruinous in the best worst way.

"Meet me here tomorrow at seven," he said.

The way he said it left no room for argument. He spoke as though he'd already made space for me in whatever overly glamorous schedule he had. I'd usually roll my eyes at something like that. At least make a joke. I should've done something other than *feel this much*. But all I could do was nod like the universe ordered it to be so.

"See you then," I muttered, barely above a whisper.

And then I walked away—cheeks flushed, heart pounding, my hand clutched tight around my bag strap. My whole body buzzed. My thoughts a total mess. *What are you doing, Alana?* He's clearly trouble. Likely a playboy. Way too fucking rich for someone like me. But even as I told myself all the reasons to stay above water, I knew the truth. It didn't feel like meeting someone. It was different. It felt like surrendering to fate, though I don't know if I believe in that sort of thing. On the contrary, my heart—stupid, reckless thing—was already buying in.

Alana

-4-

♫ 10

Jasmine's voice rang through the bathroom, her head poked around the doorframe with a grin that said she was entirely too pleased with herself.

"There is a very gorgeous man waiting for you in the lobby. If you don't want him, I'll gladly take him off your hands."

I cut my eyes at her. "I'm coming, Jasmine. Throw some cold water on yourself, please."

She didn't budge—still grinning, still eyeing me like she couldn't believe what she was seeing.

"Damn, I've never seen you dressed up like this, girl. You look hot as hell."

I had never dressed up like this. Not for dates. Not for anyone. But tonight...tonight felt different. Like I wasn't just trying to impress someone. I was reclaiming a piece of myself I'd buried. The part that wanted. The part that hoped. That could have fun. The loose-fitting, backless baby-blue mini dress draped perfectly over my chest, the silky fabric hugging and skimming in all the right places. Strappy white heels, hair in soft waves, a dewy glow on my cheeks, and a smokey eye I had actually taken my time on. I looked how I felt: good. Also nervous. Excited. And more than a little out of my depth. But if I was going to try this whole dating thing again —this opening-my-heart-up-to-potential-devastation thing—it should at least be fun, right?

"Thanks," I said, handing her a bag with my work clothes. "Take this home with you?"

She nodded, still peeking past me like she couldn't help herself.

"If you don't climb this man like a tree, I swear to God—"

I rolled my eyes but didn't respond.

My heart had already leapt into my throat. I stepped past her toward the door, trying to keep my breathing steady despite this being the first real date I'd said yes to in a year. And there he was.

Kais Reinhardt stood waiting with that effortless quality, like the world bent around his stillness. His thick, dark hair was finger-combed back in that infuriatingly careless way, the ends curling slightly at his neck. A loose linen button-down hung open just enough to hint at the kind of abs sculpted by devotion. Matching linen pants draped over his long legs, brown leather loafers and square designer sunglasses finished the look like microgreens on a perfectly plated entrée. He looked like summer in human form, rich and relaxed and completely unattainable.

His eyes met mine, and something shifted. His lips parted slightly as he took me in—slowly, thoroughly—his gaze raking down the length of me like he could see through the thin layer of blue silk straight to my skin. My pulse pounded in my ears. For a second, I forgot how to stand still. Then he stepped forward. His hand was warm as it brushed my waist, steadying me like he already knew he'd unhinged something.

His lips grazed my cheek, his voice a low rasp in my ear. "You're well fit."

I barely held onto my composure.

"That means 'good-looking,' right?" I asked, but my voice had softened—thinned out under the weight of his attention.

He grinned, head tilting. "It does." And then, he pushed the door open, "Shall we?" His hand slid to the small of my back as he guided me outside. Normally such a casual touch on what felt so intimate of a place would make my skin crawl. Especially when overzealous customers flashing me tips would do it. Not with Kais. His touch wasn't demanding—but it was *confident, possessive* in a way that made my skin hum. I should've pulled away. I would usually pull away.

Then I saw the car. A Porsche. Sleek. Shamelessly parked in the fire lane with the confidence that money could fix any ticket. And the color—baby blue. The exact shade of my dress. **918 *Spyder*** gleamed across the back in silver lettering. I am way out of my fucking depths here. *What the actual hell does this man do for a living?* I don't even think I want to know. I think I'd much rather know who he is underneath all this. But something in my gut told me I wouldn't get that opportunity tonight.

Kais walked a step ahead of me and opened the passenger door. A single Casablanca lily rested on the seat. He picked it up without a word and handed it to me like it was nothing—like this kind of thing just happened in his world. Small gesture to him, sure, but I can't remember the last time *anyone* gave *me* anything.

"Thank you, Kai Kai," I teased, sliding into the seat. Playful. Light. Pretending like hell my hands weren't shaking. His lips twitched as he tried not to smile, but I saw it. Felt it. He liked that I called him that. Liked *me*, maybe. And for some reason, that did something dangerous to my heart.

Inside, the car was smaller than I expected. Sleek, low to the ground, and so refined it felt more like the cockpit of a jet than anything meant for the road. The leather seats were buttery-soft, the dash lit in subtle blue light. Every inch whispered money. *Old* money. The kind you don't brag about because you don't have to.

Not the ill-gotten kind I grew up around, sporadic, never enough and prone to being spent faster than it arrived.

Kais slid into the driver's seat with practiced ease, moving with that casual confidence I was already starting to recognize. The small space of the car made me acutely aware of just how big he was. Not just physically, but his presence.

Then, without a word, he reached across me. His arm grazed my chest as he leaned in, pulling the seat belt slowly across my lap. His cologne surrounded me with that clean, masculine scent that probably cost more than my rent. It wrapped around me, dizzying. His fingers brushed my ribs as he clicked the buckle into place.

There was something deliberate in the way he did it, gentle and sure, as if making me feel safe mattered to him. And I was lost. My breath stuttered but I stared straight ahead hoping that would help steady me. My heart had other plans; it was pounding like it wanted out. And I knew—*he knew*. The slight curve of his mouth said it all. That same little lift of his lips. Assured, like he'd already read the ending of a book I hadn't even opened yet.

I wanted to say something. To tease him. Push the moment away. But I couldn't. I just sat there like a frozen fool, pulse racing, as he shifted the car into gear.

The engine purred, then growled, low and powerful, vibrating through the seat and right up my spine. My fingers curled around the edge of the leather, trying to anchor myself as he pulled into traffic like he owned it. He didn't speak. And he didn't need to. The way he handled the wheel and moved was intoxicating enough.

We rolled to a stop at a red light, the engine humming beneath us like something barely leashed. A car pulled up beside us: some souped-up thing with too much chrome and not enough horsepower. Inside, a swarm of frat boys hollered through the open windows, all backward caps and beer breath, gesturing for Kais to race.

He didn't flinch. Just grinned and leaned the smallest bit toward me.

"Should I?" His eyes were lighter than I'd seen them, sun-warm and playful, making him feel familiar like someone I'd known all my life and not the twenty minutes we'd actually shared.

I glanced at the boys, then at the empty stretch of road ahead, then back at him. It was stupid. It was reckless. It was... kind of thrilling. A giddy smile stretched across my face as I nodded. "Do it," I whispered, pulse skipping like it knew something I didn't.

He nodded once, that playful look still in his eyes. Then the light turned green. The engine roared to life, and the Porsche launched forward like a bullet, pinning me back against the seat. I gasped, gripping the door instinctively as the wind tangled in my hair and the city lights blurred. My heart thundered in my chest, laughter tumbling out of me before I could catch it.

Kais glanced over, and something shifted in his face. That perfectly collected cool cracked just enough to let something else through: *joy*.

Pure, unguarded delight. And then—he laughed. Not a smug chuckle. Not a breathy exhale. A real, full-bodied laugh that made him look mortal, almost boyish. Free. Like I was seeing a version of him he didn't show often. God, he was even more beautiful like this.

He took the next turn smoothly, and we dipped into an underground parking garage beneath an unmarked building. My nerves sparked at the dim glow of the space until I saw the cars. Lamborghinis. Ferraris. Sleek hyper cars that probably cost more than the building itself. *What the hell kind of night was this turning into?*

Kais parked smoothly, cutting the engine and stepping out as if this underground garage full of supercars was his daily routine.

The second he opened my door, the sound hit me like a heartbeat. Deep drums, low guitar, the slow rise of timba vocals that echoed through the garage. Kais reached for my hand, helping me out with the same quiet confidence he wore like a tailored suit. His palm was warm against mine, steady, and when he slipped his arm around my waist like a missing puzzle piece, I didn't flinch. I couldn't because my body and my heart were still in a mutiny against my very logical pre-law mind.

"What is this place?" I asked, glancing around at the entrance. It was low-lit, unmarked, exclusive in a way that didn't need a name to prove it. He just smiled, leading me down a narrow hallway that opened into something straight out of a movie— glowing bar shelves, velvet drapes, a wide-open space pulsing with music. The band was in the center, not on a stage but part of the crowd itself, pulling people in with the rhythm.

A woman in a tight floral dress spun past us, hips rolling, eyes closed like the beat was a language she didn't have to think about. I stopped in my tracks, suddenly hyper-aware of every inch of my own body. My dress. My heels. The way I didn't know what to do with my hands. Kais didn't miss it.

He guided me out onto the floor, pushing past the thick crowd of moving bodies and trilling Spanish. Then he stopped. Right in the heart of it all. My throat tightened. I didn't move. Not because I didn't want to—but because I did. And that scared the hell out of me. I was a hair close to pulling back, to cracking a joke, to saying something snarky just to break this whole Practical Magic, meant-to-be moment he had me trapped in. Anything to put some space between us. I could feel the wall I'd spent the last few years rebuilding press hard against my ribs.

But Kais didn't let go. His hands slid steadily to my waist. Gentle but centering, like the first deep inhale after being under-water too long. He turned me with such ease I barely noticed until my back was flush against his chest, the warmth of him sinking straight through the exposed skin of my back.

His breath fanned the shell of my ear. "You have to get out of that pretty little head of yours," he coaxed. "Don't find an excuse to say no. Listen to the beat. Let your body respond."

The music pulsed around us. I could feel it in my ribs, in the soles of my feet, in the space where my body met his. I closed my eyes. Tried to breathe past the knot in my chest. Tried not to think about how good it felt to be touched like this. Held like this. *Wanted like this.* The rhythm finally caught me like a drawing tide. And then I let go.

His body moved, effortless and confident, like the rhythm lived in his bones. Like he'd been doing this his whole life. And maybe he had. Maybe this was second nature to him—commanding space without ever having to take it. Once I stopped thinking, *mine* followed. The rhythm wove itself through my spine, curled into my hips, pulled me out of my head and into something warmer. Wilder.

We moved in sync, like we'd done this before in some other life —like we'd always known how to find each other in a crowd. The sway of our hips, the heat between us, the slide of his palm along my side—*God*. Every touch was patient but precise. The slight pressure of his fingers as he guided me sent sparks through my bloodstream. Just this steady, burning certainty between us.

We danced. All night, *we danced*. Time blurred around the edges, the music bleeding into itself. Laughter tangled between songs, his mouth brushing the top of my shoulder, my hands curling tighter into his shirt without thinking. We didn't need the awkward first date dinner and monotonous conversation, no, we communicated so much more without even saying a word.

By the time we stumbled out of the club, my hair was wild, my skin slick with heat, my cheeks aching from smiling. No alcohol. No pretending. Just *him*. And a high I hadn't felt in my entire life.

He opened the car door for me again, then climbed in the driver's seat. Without a word, he reached for me and pulled my feet into his lap. Like after all that dancing, my body was his now. Something about that thought shot a thrill through me. His fingers found the buckles of my heels, unfastening them one by one with a kind of admiration that made it hard to breathe. Then his thumb skimmed along my ankle in slow, idle circles—each pass softer than the last, like he was memorizing me by touch alone.

The silence between us buzzed, humming thick with everything we weren't saying. His hand was warm, sure. But it was the *softness* that undid me. Like he was touching something precious. Something he didn't want to break. No one had ever really cared about breaking me before.

"Do you want to go home," he asked, his tone dangerous in the way good wine can be dangerous, "or do you want to come with me?"

My breath caught. That question could mean so many things, could take me in so many directions. But I didn't care. I didn't know if it was the adrenaline or just how alluring he was, but I still felt bold.

"I want to be with you." It came out as if every defense I had was subconsciously stripped away.

His eyes held mine. Dark, intense and nothing like the summery gaze he looked at me with earlier. Something shimmered behind them, and I wasn't sure if it terrified me or made me want to crawl into his lap and stay there.

"I like watching you want me," he said.

A shiver rippled through me. *Not fear anymore. Desire.* He's so forward. So sure of himself. It rattled me in a way I liked far too much. *How do you hold your own with a man like this?* How do you keep your balance when everything about him pulls you off center?

I cleared my throat, trying to ground myself. But the heat had already crept up my neck, flushing my skin.

"You sure you're not just seeing what you want to see?" I asked, aiming for levity, for composure but my voice betrayed me. It was steadier than I felt, but only just.

He didn't flinch. Didn't look away. Just kept tracing those slow, soothing circles on the sore spot of my ankle with the pad of his thumb. Never rushing. Like he had time to unravel me piece by piece and knew exactly how to do it.

His jaw flexed. The muscle ticked once. "Would it help you be honest if you knew I wanted you just as much?"

Something small and sudden cracked in my chest. Similar to the sound of splintering ice just before it gives. "Maybe," I whispered, clinging to my composure like it was the only thing keeping me from falling. He studied me for a moment, completely still. The air between us seemed to thicken. And then, without a word he backed out of the parking space and put the car back into drive.

THE RIDE WAS QUIET. Short. But *charged*. A kind of tension that crackled just beneath the surface, like we were both waiting to see what the other would do. A few turns and a light later, he pulled into the valet of an impossibly expensive building. He stepped out immediately, tossed the valet his keys and a hundred-dollar bill without blinking. Opened my door, extended his hand, and waited. The second I slipped my hand into his, those fingers curled around mine like a question he was afraid to ask. The first hesitancy I'd seen from him all evening. Dark eyes locked on me, more certain than the hand holding mine. He let out a soft breath. Barely audible. But I felt it anyway.

Then he led me down a sandy path, the warm grains soft beneath my bare feet. A small wooden sign came into view, the letters etched in an elegant script.

Private Beach.

The moon hung high above the ocean, casting silver ribbons across the waves as they broke in quiet succession. I loved the beach: the steady hush of the tide, the salt in the air, the softness of nightfall folding over the city. But tonight, none of it held my attention the way he did. We walked side by side, a silence stretching between us, not awkward but dense. Like we were both waiting for something to shift. He hadn't said much since we left the car, which I didn't know whether to read as comfort or calculation. Conversation had come easy with him between dances, light and familiar almost but now that we were alone—*really alone*—something in me buzzed. It felt like anticipation more than nerves. As if my heart was waiting to see if this was all too good to be true.

I watched him look out at the horizon with that same steely expression, like the ocean was an old friend and he belonged to the night that blanketed it. The way he wore mystery was unfair. And yet, I still wanted in. I wanted to know what he was thinking. What he wanted from me. What his angle was.

Before I could stop myself, the words slipped out.

"You're quiet."

The corner of his mouth lifted. Still, he didn't look at me.

"And you talk when you're nervous."

I huffed, nudging his arm with my shoulder.

"I'm not nervous."

He tilted his head, finally glancing my way. His voice was low, almost amused. "No? Then why do you keep stealing glances at me when you think I'm not looking?"

God, he's impossible.

I bit the inside of my cheek, fighting the pull of a smile that wanted to give too much away. He didn't need encouragement, he already knew what he was doing to me. So I turned back toward the sky. The moon hung low above the water, heavy and silver, its reflection stretched thin across the ocean like a secret too delicate to be told. I'd always found comfort in it—it's quiet, its distance, its mystery. But sitting here, beside him, even the moon felt dim. Like his presence cast a gravity all its own.

"It's beautiful tonight," I mumbled, almost to myself. He didn't respond right away.

But I felt it—the shift in the air. The pull of his gaze. The way silence took on shape and weight between us.

Then, soft as dusk: "You remind me of it."

I blinked, slowly turning toward him. "The ocean?"

His eyes didn't leave mine. "No." His voice softened. "The moon." He let the words settle before adding, "Still. Luminous. And never once asking the tide to chase her—though it always does."

Something fluttered inside me. Too quick to be logic, too tangible to be brushed off. The door I'd spent years bolting shut started to crack. He reached out, like he couldn't help himself, slowly brushing the pad of his thumb over my bottom lip. Barely there. But it lit every nerve in my body like Christmas lights. That single touch sent heat surging up my spine, igniting something I'd kept buried for too long. I leaned forward without thinking, without fear—drawn not just by desire, but by *him*. By the quiet promise in his stillness. By the pull of something I didn't understand but couldn't walk away from. And then he stopped.

His fingers stilling my chin as his lips hovered over mine, so close I could feel the warmth of his breath.

"Not yet, Ya Amar," he whispered, the words fragile with restraint, laced with devotion. "For you, I can do better than this."

I sucked in a small breath, my heart beat in my chest like a war drum.

God, I knew he felt this tension too, and yet he still wanted to be careful with me. Like he saw something I didn't see in myself. Maybe what he wanted was less fleeting than this fire burning between us. That fact scared me more than any meaningless hookup ever could. But in that aching, suspended moment, I knew I wouldn't survive this. Not the slow burn of him. Not the tenderness. Not the way he was already reaching every part of me I'd tried to hide.

Kais

I NEARLY LOST THE BLOODY PLOT.

Nearly forgot the entire reason I stayed in Miami was to see if this could be something that lasts past a single night. The whole point of pursuing her is that she's nothing like anyone I've ever been with. And yet I almost treated her as if she were just another conquest.

I had a plan when I walked into that restaurant. Took her to the club to get her out of her own head. I saw it from the moment we met. The tension in her shoulders. The way she guarded every laugh like it cost her too much. And then, slowly, she let go. Eased into it. Smiled more. Leaned into me like she didn't realize she was doing it. As if whatever force pulled me to her was pulling her right back. But the second I asked her out properly, she retreated. Reached for the first excuse she could find.

Not because she didn't want to say yes.

I've watched her turn down a dozen blokes without blinking during her shifts. But with me? She hesitated. Couldn't bring herself to say no. Only... rain check. That's when I knew. She was giving me something fragile. Trust. A chance. And I swore I wouldn't blow it.

But then she looked at me like that—in the car—and said *I want to be with you,* and suddenly I'm driving her to my flat as though every ounce of restraint I've got doesn't mean a bloody thing. She didn't even know how close she was to my bedroom. I don't think she cared. And that's half the problem. She *trusts* me. And the minute her hand slipped into mine at the valet, I remembered why I couldn't fuck this up.

Something in those big brown eyes of hers told me she was already in. That I wasn't ready to walk away from this. So, I did the only thing I could do. I walked. And tried like hell not to look at her in that fucking dress until I'd taken her home.

I hadn't thought about her all morning. Or at least, that's what I told myself until I stepped into the gym, threw my first punch, and heard Montee's knowing fucking chuckle.

"Off today," he muttered.

I exhaled through my nose, steadying my stance.

"Fuck off."

The bag barely swung when I hit it. Not because the punch wasn't clean, but because I had controlled the force behind it. Calculated. I'm always calculated, but I was struggling.

Montee circled me, arms folded over his chest, his thick Scottish brogue laced with amusement.

"Right. And I suppose the reason you keep checkin' that damn phone has nothin' to do with the girl you were with last night?"

I snapped a jab—quick, precise. It landed solid, but the way Montee smirked told me he still wasn't impressed.

"Not checkin' my phone," I muttered.

He grinned.

"Ah, I see. So, you're just watchin' the screen light up for the sport of it, then?"

I exhaled, rolling my shoulders back. The gloves felt snug against my hands, the weight familiar, recentering. I flexed my fingers, adjusting to the fit, but the irritation in my chest had nothing to do with the wraps.

Then I pictured her fingers curled around mine, warm and delicate, just before I pulled her onto the dance floor. I tried to shake the thought and threw another combination. Left hook, right cross, quick footwork around the bag. Precise and clean.

Montee was quiet for a moment. "You finally letting someone get in your head?"

I didn't pause, didn't miss a step.

"No."

Too quick. Too distracted. *Fucking hell.* I stepped back, circling the bag, resetting my stance, ignoring the flicker of memory pressing at the edges. Her swaying in my arms, wearing that tiny dress, laughter spilling from her lips, the way she rolled her hips into mine.

Montee let out a slow, knowing breath. "Happens to the best of us, lad."

I reset, shifting my weight. I ignored him, pivoting into a right hook harder than necessary. The bag snapped back. Montee braced it without blinking.

It wasn't a question of if she was in my head. *She was.* It was a question of how long I'd let her stay there. How long I needed to get my act together, so I didn't piss it all away. No one else had ever lingered like this. *No one.* Most women were gone before I even had the chance to think twice. None of them ever made it past the night, let alone into my morning or into the fucking training room.

And fuck me, I hadn't even kissed her yet. But I knew the second I kissed her I couldn't stop at just one. And that wasn't what this was going to be.

I stepped in with a body shot, hard enough that the heavy bag swung back. Montee braced it without blinking.

"Gonna tell me about her?" he pushed.

"Not a chance."

Montee chuckled, stepping back, studying me like I was a puzzle he'd already solved.

"So, when's the next one?"

I dodged the bait, feinting left, then stepping back, making him wait for my answer.

"When I say so."

Then I pictured her perfect lips, parted without hesitation, The look in her soft brown eyes.

I exhaled through my nose.

Enough of this.

I moved in fast, pivoting swiftly as I threw a clean uppercut into the bag, knocking it back hard enough to make Montee take half a step. His chuckle faded. *That's better.* I pulled back, shaking out my hands, heart pounding, sweat rolling down my back. Montee grunted, rubbing his jaw as if he was considering saying more, then finally shrugged.

"Fine, fine. I'll leave it alone—until you start fightin' like a man who actually slept last night."

I wiped the sweat from my face, ignoring the way my pulse spiked at the memory of the warmth of her back pressed against my chest, the salt air of the ocean mixing with whatever she'd put in her hair. The way she turned to face me, wide-eyed and open. Achingly beautiful in every breath she took.

Fuck.

I grabbed my water bottle, drinking deep, willing my heartbeat back to normal. Then, I could nearly hear her voice teasing, the way her smile made me want to do reckless, stupid things just to make her laugh. Like race a bunch of college pricks at a red light.

Montee clapped me on the back. "Be here at four. And don't let this be the skirt you lose focus for, yeah?"

I didn't answer. I just tossed my gloves into my bag and reached for my phone.

Countless unread messages. *None from her.* Good.

I wasn't reaching out. Not yet. A text felt insignificant. Too small for something like this. She wasn't a woman you messaged between meetings or the kind of woman you just shagged and walked away from. *She was the kind you kept.* I wasn't sending some meaningless line that barely scratches the surface of what she was already doing to me. When I spoke to her again, it was going to be intentional. Not some fucking text. She deserved better than that. And for some reason, I wanted to be the man who gave it to her.

Instead, I scrolled down, tapped a name, and brought the phone to my ear. Alanzo picked up on the second ring.

"Send them tomorrow."

He didn't ask what. He already knew.

I hung up and exhaled slowly, flexing my fingers. It wasn't just about when I'd see her again. That was inevitable. I already knew I wasn't walking away from this. It was just a matter of how long I was going to make myself wait. Alanzo called back almost immediately.

"Boss," His voice was measured, always was. "Your father called an emergency meeting. London. Tonight."

I stilled. My jaw flexed. Of course he did. The man's a proper cunt.

"London. Tonight?"

Montee muttered something under his breath about blood pressure, but I ignored him. My mind was already shifting, pulling away from the warmth of her memory and snapping back into the cold reality of what I'd be walking into. An emergency board meeting. Last minute. Overseas. That meant one thing. My father wasn't just pulling rank. He was trying to put me in check. The tension I'd spent the last hour working out of my system coiled right back in.

My father knew I had a fight coming up. He knew I was negotiating my terms. And now he wanted me back in London, sitting across from him, playing his fucking game. I rolled my shoulders back, exhaling the irritation away. *Fine.* I'll play. But he wouldn't like the way this ended.

Alanzo was already waiting by the exit when I stepped out of the gym.

"Jet's ready whenever you are," he said, his tone professional. But I caught the flicker of hesitation.

Alanzo was the one man who knew the workings of my life. He already knew where my head was. I wasn't done here. I wasn't ready to leave Miami. Not yet. But I also knew my father didn't call emergency meetings unless he was playing a move. And this was a move I had no choice but to answer.

♪ 20

The boardroom felt heavy. Too much glass, too much steel. Everything in this room had been designed to make men feel small. Not me. Not anymore. I had watched my father chain himself to this very room my entire life. Watched him choose the power of his title over my mum, over me. *Reinhardt Capital*, he named it, as if that name meant a shit to him. Becoming the majority shareholder was something I had quite literally fought for, never to carry on *his* legacy, but for my own.

I was late. On purpose.

My father Oskar Reinhardt sat at the head of the long oak table, fingers steepled, expression schooled into something neutral. A performance. His anger was hidden well but not well enough. The resemblance between us always strikes me. Same build. Same jawline. But where my skin was warm, his was pale, my eyes were dark, his were icy, calculating—like they were constantly assessing the value of everything in the room, including people.

This was a man who had never once doubted he was the smartest person in any given space, until now. I let the weight of my presence settle before moving toward my seat, unhurried. Every move a clear reminder that I didn't answer to anyone. They had been talking about me before I got here. I could tell by how none of them other than my father would meet my gaze.

I unbuttoned my suit jacket with unbothered precision.

"You've been busy." His first shot. His voice was controlled but I heard the edge.

I didn't reply. Didn't take the bait. Oskar clasped his hands together, smiling like he wasn't already orchestrating my downfall.

"I hear you're negotiating another fight. This company needs a leader, not a fighter."

A few of the board members nodded in quiet agreement. Predictable. I just watched him. Unmoved. Letting him feel the silence. His fingers tapped once against the table. A tell. He was expecting pushback. I didn't give him any. So, he kept talking.

"I've called this meeting because I'm concerned."

Concerned. Right. What he meant was:

You're slipping out of my control, and I don't like it.

Still, I let him go on.

"This hobby of yours is a distraction. There are decisions being made that you should be a part of, but instead, you're off training for—what? Are you so insecure that you feel you need another belt?" He scoffed. "Tell me, son, what exactly are you fighting for?"

I exhaled slowly. Adjusted my watch. Then, finally, I leaned forward, elbows resting on the table.

"I don't recall ever needing the approval of a non-voting board member with no fiduciary duties." I kept my voice more even than his.

The room shifted. A muscle ticked in his jaw. There. *That's what he didn't want them to see.*

"Listen to yourself," he snapped, that thin veneer of patience cracking.

"No respect for the man who laid the foundation. Do you

think this empire was built on a name alone? I built this company from nothing, and I'll die before I see you tear it down. This isn't just yours, it's the Reinhardt legacy."

His expression cooled. "You don't belong in a boardroom."

Maybe not, but I *do* own *it*. A few of the older men nodded. The predictable ones. But the room wasn't fully his. *Not yet.* He thought I was impulsive. Reckless. That I didn't have a plan. That was his mistake.

I let the moment stretch. Made them wait. Then, when the tension had settled enough to suffocate the room, I cut through it with ease.

"I've actually been waiting to call this meeting, but since we're all here—."

The reaction was instant. The room fell silent. My father stilled.

"As of today," I continued, "I'm initiating the second phase of my original acquisition plan."

The room shifted. Several heads turned. Some glanced at one another, scrambling to recall exactly what the fuck I was talking about. But he knew. The tips of his ears turned red in rage. I leaned forward, holding his gaze as I said it.

"Effective immediately, control of my shares will be handled by Lars Gustafson."

Silence. The name landed like a fucking bomb. His jaw clenched so tight I thought his teeth might crack. Lars Gustafson. Former CFO of Gold Venture Capital. A shark but also a man who had once been my father's right-hand—until he wasn't. Until he backed my buyout. A man my father *loathed*. I trust Lars as much as I can anyone in this fucked up business which isn't much, but he was the best man for the job and ultimately just another piece of my plan.

The boardroom came to life. Hushed whispers. Questions. A shift in power so tangible it was almost visible. My father's blue eyes burned. Cold fury. And then, just to twist the knife, I waved toward the door. The heavy oak swung open. Lars walked in. My father sat still. But I saw the way his fingers twitched against the table.

Lars greeted the room calmly, smoothly. Like he belonged here. Because now, he did. He nodded once in my direction. I leaned back, exhaling slowly. *Checkmate.* The boardroom buzzed louder —some looking toward my father for his reaction, others suddenly reconsidering their alignment.

Oskar pushed to his feet, slowly. *Controlled rage.* Exactly the kind of rage he'd passed to me. Except, his entire life had been built by letting emotions dictate his actions. He was the impulsive and reckless one, not me, and this made him weak. His palm pressed against the table. A predator making one final show of dominance as he shot up to his feet.

"You think you can just run off and come back to this?" His voice was quiet now, coiled with barely restrained fury. "The second you let go, I'll make sure there's nothing left for you."

Ah. There it was. The real threat.

I didn't rise to meet him. Didn't move an inch. I just let my gaze lock onto his. Let him feel it—how little power he actually had over me. Then, low and even, I murmured:

"That's the thing, Oskar—I don't need any of this. But you? You need me."

His expression cracked, just slightly. That was enough. I pushed to my feet, adjusting my watch like I had nothing but time. Then, without looking back, I nodded to Lars.

"Handle it."

And then I walked out to get back to the one person that actually deserved my attention.

Alana

-6-

♪ 9

"ARE YOU EVER GOING TO SPILL ABOUT YOUR DATE WITH my future husband?" Jasmine asked, her voice hushed but brimming with nosiness as I cleared the last table of the evening.

"Good luck finding him," I muttered.

"What was that?" She stared at me like I was a platypus exhibit at the zoo.

I sighed.

"You'll have to get the man to call you before you start picking out wedding colors, Jazzy." My tone was more disappointed than I wanted to let on.

She scoffed, dramatically tossing her dish towel over her shoulder. "He'll call, baby doll. It's only been, what? A day?"

I huffed, lifting the heavy tub of dishes onto my hip. "Two, actually."

How do you have a date like that—slow dancing in an underground Cuban nightclub, strolling barefoot on a private beach under the stars—and *not even kiss a girl*? Then, to top it off, not even call her? I pushed through the kitchen doors, setting the tub near the wash station before turning back toward the dining room—only to hear Jasmine say, "We're closed for the evening, sir. We open again at four tomorrow." My heart skipped. Maybe... maybe it was—.

Heart pounding, I looked over to the front door, just to find a short, stocky man with terrible sunburn and an unbuttoned Hawaiian shirt coming into view. I forced a measured breath. *One kissless date, Alana. Snap out of it.*

Jasmine's voice pulled me back.

"Alana," she said in a sing-song voice, grinning as she gestured toward the host stand. "These are for you."

My eyes widened as I stepped closer, taking in the massive bouquet of deep blue forget-me-nots. The petals looked almost luminescent under the dim restaurant lighting. My fingers trembled slightly as I pulled the small card from the silk tie, reading the message written in extravagantly elegant script:

—Kai Kai

That was it. The nickname I'd teased him with. He'd tucked it away and remembered. Maybe it meant nothing. But for a man who didn't waste words, it felt like more. I was blushing before I even realized it.

The next day, I checked my phone incessantly. Still no word from him. He didn't need to send me flowers (although they were a nice reassurance I wasn't imagining this whole thing between us). I was already thinking about him more than I wanted to without them. The way he smelled, the flex of his arms when he pulled me close at the club, the way his lips hovered over mine without touching... I needed to get a grip.

I returned from my pre-rush break, forcing myself to focus. I had a shift to finish, and Kais Reinhardt had no business taking up this much space in my head. "Alana, you have someone requesting you at table eleven." I hardly registered the hostess's words before rounding the corner—only to freeze in place.

There he was.

Kais Reinhardt. Dressed in all black, his suit tailored to perfection, the shirt unbuttoned just enough to tease the golden skin of his sculpted chest. Finger-combed black hair. A single gold chain glinted at his throat, rings adorned nearly every long, tapered finger, and a green-faced Rolex sat heavy on his wrist. *Does he always have to look like he's auditioning for Bond?*

I swallowed, gathering myself as I approached, though my gaze involuntarily snagged on the small cut on his left cheek. It was fresh. My stomach tightened at the thought of him being hurt but I pushed the thought aside.

It was one date. One kissless date.

"Good evening," I said in a professional voice, trying to sound composed in case my boss was around, "How can I serve you?"

Unbothered by my guarded tone, Kais leaned back in his chair, legs stretching out, shamelessly occupying the space around him. His dark eyes lingered on me a moment too long before he finally spoke.

"Did you like the flowers?" He said lazily.

I crossed my arms. "I did. Thank you. Blue is my favorite color actually." Though I wished he would have called or texted me too, seeing him now was nice.

He nodded, as if tucking that fact away for later. "Good."

Then, to my complete surprise, he stood, buttoning his jacket in one fluid motion before stepping close. *So damn close.*

Heat curled in my stomach as he loomed over me, his scent washing over me: spicy, warm, leathery. "I'm done here," he murmured. His impossibly deep eyes bored into me. "I just wanted to see you before I left."

I tilted my head, pulse picking up. "Well, now you have. What's next?"

A small chuckle rumbled from his chest, offering me a glimpse at his perfect smile. And that damn beauty mark on his cheek.

"I'll see you this weekend, Ya Amar." His lips brushed the top of my hair, featherlight, before he turned and walked away, leaving me frozen in his wake.

"This weekend," I echoed under my breath, confused, blinking myself back into reality.

Then I noticed it. On the table, neatly placed beside his untouched drink, was a sleek black box. A single forget-me-not lay across the top, its stem wrapped in cream silk ribbon. My breath ceased to exist. I scanned the room quickly before picking up the box and slipping away to the break room.

Before I could even sit, Jasmine rushed in behind me.

"Oh my God," she whisper-yelled. "I just saw Kais leave. Did he say anything to—" She stopped, her eyes immediately zeroing in on the box in my hands. "Wait. What is that? Is it from him?"

I nodded, still unsure if I should open it.

"Babe, open it before I do!"

I shot her a look before carefully pulling the ribbon loose, lifting the lid to reveal a small note card neatly set on cream tissue paper.

Eight o'clock, Friday. Figured I'd remove the excuse.

-Kai Kai

Setting the card aside, I peeled back the layers of delicate tissue, revealing a black corseted mini dress with a sweetheart neckline, the unmistakable Dolce & Gabbana tag stitched into the clasp. Beneath it, a pair of black suede bow heels—*Aquazzura*— not just luxury for the brand, but intentional, like he'd hand-picked something he thought I'd like. Everything in my exact size. Better than anything I could have picked for myself. The only time I'd ever worn anything this nice was when my mom needed me to help her pretend to be something she wasn't. But coming from him it felt ... good. Like I was wanted. Seen.

Jazzy let out a high-pitched noise, half gasp, half squeal. "I'm sorry, you go on one date with the man and he's already sending you flowers *and* designer clothes?!"

"I couldn't care less about that kind of stuff," I said, though I couldn't stop the slow, satisfied smile that spread across my face as I traced the fabric. "I just want to see him." I paused, fingertips brushing the bow on one heel. "But this *is* really pretty." We exchanged giddy looks, both of us grinning like idiots. As I carefully tucked the box away, my mind was already racing with thoughts of Kais Reinhardt.

There was no way I was getting him out of my head now.

Alana

♫ 8 & 40

A HEAVY KNOCK SOUNDED AT MY APARTMENT DOOR AT precisely seven-thirty that evening. I sighed, quickly tying the string of my robe around me as I rushed toward the door. "Jazzy, how can one person lose their keys so much?" I muttered, swinging it open. "I don't have time for—"

Only, it wasn't Jasmine. Standing before me was the same sunburned Italian man from the restaurant. Tonight, instead of his awful Hawaiian shirt, he was dressed in a crisp black suit. "Oh." I blinked, instinctively stepping back. "I'm sorry, I thought you were my roommate."

He smiled wide, revealing slightly gapped teeth which gave him an almost goofy warmth. "Good evening, Ms. Cameron. My name is Alanzo. I'll be your driver this evening." His thick Italian accent wrapped around each word in refined charm.

Driver? My brows knit together. "Wait... what?"

Alanzo tilted his head slightly. "You do still wish to see Mr. Reinhardt this evening, yes?" I blinked rapidly, processing.

"Uh—yeah. Is he here?" I asked, glancing over his shoulder. I pulled my robe tighter around me, the evening breeze reminding me that only a thin piece of silk stood between me and flashing a complete stranger.

Alanzo shook his head. "No, *signora*. He will be waiting for you there. Would you like a few more minutes to get dressed?"

I nodded stiffly. "Yes, please."

Then, as calmly as possible, I shut the door—before immediately bolting to the bathroom. My hair was still a mess of curls, and I didn't have time to straighten it. Flipping my head over, I quickly diffused it into a presentable, voluminous mane, then smoothed the edges of my rebellious baby hairs with gel. *Good enough.*

I rolled on a pair of black pantyhose, the delicate seam tracing up my legs like something out of an old Hollywood film. Then slipped into the corseted black mini dress and suede heels Kais had sent.

"This needs something else," I muttered, studying myself in the mirror.

Then, the idea struck. *A red lip.* The moment the deep crimson color slicked onto my lips, everything clicked. I fastened a pair of gold dangling earrings, gave myself one last once-over, and grabbed my clutch. *No way he doesn't kiss me tonight.*

When I opened the door, Alanzo's eyes widened—just for a second—before they quickly darted away, as if it was forbidden to look at me for too long. "Bellissima, signora," he said, his voice laced with approval as he offered his arm. "Shall we?" he asked. I slipped my hand into the crook of his elbow with a smile, my heartbeat quickening. *When did my life turn into The Princess Diaries?*

We walked past a group of raucous college boys playing beer pong in the breezeway.

"Damn, girl, where have you been my whole life?" one of them called out.

I ignored them, unable to properly retort, my eyes already fixed ahead—on the car parked at the curb. Or spaceship, rather. It was all black, sleek and low to the ground, with subtle chrome detailing and two interlocking R's on the wheels. At the front, a small silver angel-like figure poised on the hood. I froze. *Yet another way too expensive car.*

Alanzo opened the passenger door, revealing a sultry red leather interior—the same deep shade as my lipstick. *Interesting how that keeps happening.* The plush red carpet felt soft under my feet. The ceiling twinkled like stars. A single forget-me-not lay beside a chilled bottle of sparkling water on the center console. Even as my heart clenched at the gesture, something about it all felt... overwhelming. Like Kais had mistaken me for a girl who belonged in something this nice. Who was worth all this trouble.

I hesitated before speaking. "Hey, Alanzo?"

"Si, *signora*?" he responded sweetly, meeting my gaze in the rearview mirror.

I swallowed, trying to push down my nerves. "What kind of car is this?" I whispered like it was a secret.

Alanzo chuckled, eyes twinkling. "A Rolls Royce Ghost, *signora*."

My stomach twisted. My mother would have a field day if she knew about this. A thought which would have sent me running for the hills a few years back–the thought of dating someone who my mother would approve of. Someone that woman would shove me toward with both arms in pursuit of what they could provide, no matter what else it may cost.

I didn't hate money, I just hated what it *did* to people, how it controlled and changed them. But that didn't seem to be true for Kais, it just felt like a part of the world he lives in, and the unknown of that was even more terrifying.

The car hummed to life, pulling off smoothly. I sank into the seat, trying to settle the sudden knot in my chest. Then my phone vibrated. A new message lit up my screen:

Kai Kai: Can't wait to see you, Ya Amar.

My heart did that skip thing it's been doing since I met the man, but my attention was turned to that phrase he continues to call me like it's my name. Quickly, I tab over to the internet to search for the term "Ya Amar", I could never get the spelling of it down until now. The butterflies swarmed my stomach instantly as I read the definition:

"Ya Amar" (يا قمر) is an Arabic phrase that means "my moon".

Well shit, there goes my excuse to bolt. Now I don't care about this stupid car at all.

WE ARRIVED at the same luxurious high-rise Kais had brought me to the weekend before—only this time, we weren't heading toward the beach. Instead, Alanzo led me inside. The building's marble floors gleamed under the grand chandeliers, each step of my heels echoing softly in the vast lobby. Without a word, we entered a mirrored elevator.

Alanzo swiped a card, and with a soft *ding*, we began our ascent—all the way to the top. I mean, hell, the rent in this place must be insane. Probably more than the year's tuition I was quoted by Columbia. This man was going to see in a heartbeat that this parentless Texas girl didn't belong here. I started to feel like an imposter all over again.

As the doors slid open, I stepped into an entryway bathed in warm, golden light. I followed Alanzo toward the living area, an expansive space adorned by rich brown marble floors, toasted lime-washed walls, and antique landscape paintings. Beyond the open-concept room, two chefs dressed in crisp white uniforms worked with focused intensity in the kitchen, the scent of something deca-dent filling the air. *This place looks like a damn RH Warehouse showroom. I bet I can bolt before anyone notices the imposter entered.*

The knot in my chest tightened until I hear it— a soft, misty rendition of *Corcovado* floated from unseen speakers. The song had been on repeat on my record player since I found a mint Getz Gilberto record at the thrift store last year. The knot loosened, *a little.*

A row of large glass doors lined the far wall, already pushed open to reveal a breathtaking view of the ocean. An infinity pool stretched seamlessly into the horizon, but what caught my attention was the dining table resting in the center—atop a glass platform over the water, bathed in soft candlelight. My breath caught. *This isn't just rich-person nice. Every detail feels hand-picked, like he actually thought about what he wanted instead of hiring someone to make it look impressive.*

Suddenly, I was hyperaware that I was still wearing heels on this man's marble floors. Slipping them off, I quickly stashed them by the elevator door and padded back to the living room like nothing had happened.

My stomach twisted nervously. Still no Kais in sight. Needing a distraction from the *Beverly Hillbillies* act I was apparently cast in, I let the plush cream area rug tickle my feet as I wandered toward the endless collection of records displayed against the wall. *My dream collection.* I traced my fingers along the spines in awe, lost in the sheer magnitude of it. *This is the kind of luxury I'm talking about. Just leave me in the corner with the dusty records and I'll blend in just fine.*

"Would you two like to be alone?" Kais' warm voice teased from behind me.

I jerked my hand back as if I'd been caught stealing, turning to find him perched on the arm of the couch, watching me with a lazy, knowing smirk. The sight of him—cream dress shirt teasingly unbuttoned, gray slacks hanging just right at his hips, bare feet against the marble floor—made my pulse hammer in my ears. He raked a hand through his raven-black hair, his eyes devouring me. *Illegal. It should be illegal to look like that.*

"I was just admiring your impeccable taste in music," I said, stepping between the splay of his legs, feigning a confidence I did not possess.

His hands landed at my hips, warm and sure, his fingers flexing against the silky fabric of my dress. His brown eyes—framed by lashes any woman would envy—flickered up at me, sending fire through my belly. Someone should study what this man does to my brain.

My gaze softened when I noticed the small cut on his cheek, now bruised a light purple. Instinctively, I ran my thumb over the healing wound.

"What happened?" I asked gently.

He smirked. "Got beasted at the gym."

Right. That felt like a lie. But I didn't care to push when he was looking at me like that.

He leaned in slightly, his voice dropping lower. "Loving this dress on you, by the way."

I turned slightly, flashing my shoulder, pulling at the fabric on my thigh just enough to tease. "Thank you. Some guy left it at my table the other night," I joked, fluttering my lashes. Then I changed my tone to reflect my gratitude, "Thank you though. I love it. I left the shoes by the door—I didn't want to ruin the floor."

"Very thoughtful of you." His eyes darkened. "I, on the other hand, am going to have a bit of trouble not ruining that pretty red mouth of yours."

God, I wish you would.

Heat rushed to my cheeks. And he noticed. Of course he did. His gaze dipped briefly to my lips before flicking back to my eyes, that slow smile ghosting across his mouth. No apology. No shame. Just the quiet satisfaction of a man who knew exactly what he was doing. Without another word, he led me outside and guided me across the glass platform over the pool.

A beautifully arranged appetizer tray sat at the center of the candlelit table: fruit, cheese, caviar, and decadent sauces displayed like art. Kais pulled out my chair, waiting for me to settle before taking his seat across from me.

"This place is amazing," I said, popping a grape between my lips.

"Yeah?" he said, as if it were a question, though his tone was thoughtful. "I don't get to be here much."

He looked at me like I was the only thing he cared about right now. And damn, did that feel like a drug all of its own. I could've asked why he wasn't here more often. I could've asked what he did, how he could afford all this when he didn't look a day over thirty. Questions like: why are there always men in suits lingering around him? Why are his hands so calloused despite looking like he spends his days in boardrooms? Why did he buy me this expensive dress and court me like I'm someone worth all the trouble? But I didn't ask any of them.

As breathtaking as all of it was—the view, the wine, the absurd elegance—I didn't want facts. I wanted *him*. And as long as he kept looking at me like that, I didn't even care about the details. So I tried to see if I could chip through that marble composure of his and find the man inside.

"Where's your favorite place to be?"

He didn't answer right away. Just reached forward, graceful as always, and scooped a mound of black caviar onto the back of his hand. "At the moment—with you."

Then, without breaking eye contact, he lifted his hand and slowly licked the caviar clean. My thighs clenched at the sight of his mouth, heat pooling instantly between them.

The way he moved, smooth and lethal, like he wasn't just enjoying the taste, but my reaction to it. His lips curled into a knowing smirk, like he could feel the shift in my breath from across the table. And then, as if he'd planned this all along, he slid his chair closer. The proximity alone made my pulse spike.

He took another small dollop and placed it on the soft skin

between my thumb and forefinger. I stared down at the contrast of black against my skin, heart pounding. And then—his hand on mine, steady and sure—he brought it to his mouth. His warm tongue flicked against my skin, languid and intentional, as he licked the caviar away. My breath froze in my chest. The heat was unbearable. My skin was singing with electricity, and my pulse had relocated somewhere between my thighs.

Fuck this.

I grabbed his hand and pulled it toward me, scooped a dollop of caviar onto his skin, then brought it straight to my mouth. The moment my tongue touched his hand, his eyes widened with surprise. Then his lips curved, like that was exactly what he wanted me to do.

"Good girl," he chuckled, brushing his mouth over the same place mine had just been.

My stomach tightened. How this man folds me with next to no words should be a crime. *Do I like to be praised?* When it comes out of that mouth, absolutely. I'd never survive being in a bedroom with him if this is how I react to a dinner. I'd spent the last three years playing it safe—head in my books, eyes on law school, always trying to make myself into something worthy of the space I took up. But with Kais, it never felt like he was measuring me. It felt like what I saw as rust, he might see as something that could still shine.

A chef appeared with the first course, and the spell shattered just enough for me to catch my breath. I sat back in my chair, heart still thrumming, fingers pulling against the soft edge of my napkin.

Then, we talked. Well, *I* talked—while plates of intricately arranged dishes came and went, each one more beautiful than the last, though I barely registered them; I was too caught up in him, fascinated by his every expression, every flicker of thought behind those dark eyes.

Kais was a quiet man, but not distant. He listened with this focused kind of stillness, like he was soaking in every word, not just to respond but to *understand*. Like he wanted to *know* me.

I wasn't used to being looked at that way. My instincts were screaming to curl into myself—don't show him too much, don't give him reasons to leave. Maybe it wasn't too late to play this thing cool and pretend to be the girl everyone else preferred. The girl a man like him might prefer.

So, I gave him what I always gave people on dates. My dreams of becoming a family lawyer. Goofy stories. Embarrassing ones. All the light, safe pieces I'd practiced—refined over the years to make myself sound *normal*. Relatable. Like I hadn't lived a life that might scare someone off.

He sat through all of it without interrupting once. Then, after a quiet moment, he leaned back, eyes scanning my face like he was trying to solve a case I didn't realize I was presenting.

"You don't like talking about your childhood, do you?" He asked softly. But his eyes held mine like he could see straight through the polished version I'd just offered him.

"Um," I cleared my throat, sweeping my hair back over my shoulder, nerves suddenly prickling under my skin. "It's not my favorite subject," I said lightly. "I'd much rather talk about federal civil procedure, but..." I let out a deflective laugh and waited for him to move on.

But he didn't. He just stayed there quietly holding space like he *actually cared* to know. I set my fork down, my heart suddenly too loud in my chest.

"What do you want to know, Kai Kai?" I asked softly, the nickname slipping out like a shield and a tether all at once.

He didn't smile. Didn't tease. "I'll only take what you give me, *Ya Amar.*"

God. There it was again. Every time he calls me that, I unravel just a little more. Like Pavlov's bell—one *Ya Amar* and I'm toast.

I sat back in my chair, arms loosely crossed. "Let's go three for three. You ask me three questions, I'll ask you three. No cross-examination. Deal?" I stuck my hand out.

He took it without hesitation, brushing a soft kiss over the top before whispering, "Deal."

"Approach," I said with a quiet smile, nodding him on.

He chuckled lightly and crossed his arms, his biceps flexing just enough to derail my train of thought. "Tell me about your parents."

Of course. Go straight for the jugular. I gave him a practiced smile—nervous as hell, but I didn't let it crack all the way through.

"Ah, the classic," I teased, then went on before I could talk myself out of it. "My mom's name is Melanie Assad. My dad's David Cameron. They had me when they were sixteen. Stayed together for a few years—until my mom left him for my stepdad, who could, and I quote, 'provide us with a better life.'" I lifted my glass, took a slow sip.

"You know," I said, voice light, "the usual trade: safety for money and abuse. My dad lost interest in me after that. Started a new family, sent a card every few years around Christmas."

I waved a hand like it was nothing. Like I hadn't just unraveled one of the deepest knots inside me. Like I hadn't just summed up every day I'd spent wondering if I was too broken for someone good.

He nodded thoughtfully. His expression wasn't one I'd read as judgy. Then: "How's your relationship with your mom and stepdad?"

Fuck. This guy should be a lawyer. No small talk, just straight to the marrow. My chest tightened, but I cleared my throat and pressed on. *If I scare him off, at least it's good practice for the courtroom.*

"Not great," I said, trying to keep my voice even. "My stepdad—Victor—was pretty abusive. Physically, emotionally. The whole package." I paused, willing the memories clawing at the back of my mind to stay quiet. "But he had money. At least from my mom's perspective, that was enough. She stayed. Made a life with him. Didn't matter what it cost me—or my sister." I rubbed at the center of my chest, like I could smooth the ache away.

"My mom used to be really great," I added, softer now. "She was beautiful. Warm. She modeled for a while, back when I was little." I laughed under my breath. The kind that used to cover my bruises. "But he broke something in her. Everything looked picture-perfect on the outside. Suburban, successful. But it was a nightmare behind closed doors. When he started hitting her instead of me and cheating, she started using. Pills, mostly. That was when I was eleven. She hasn't been the same since."

Kais said nothing. His expression didn't falter but something in it had *settled*. I couldn't tell if he was regretting ever asking me out... or just seeing me clearly now.

"How about your sister. Where's she?"

That one hit harder than I expected. I rarely talked about her. Only Jasmine and my cousin Penelope knew the full story. "She's in Texas," I said quietly. "Her name's Macy. She's six now. Lives with Victor's parents—her grandparents. The same people who basically raised me when my mom would disappear, so... she's in good-ish hands." I hesitated, fingers tightening slightly around my fork. "Even though they won't let me see her, I get emails every few weeks. Usually photos or little updates, but that's it."

"Why?" Kais asked, his brows pinched.

"Because I still talk to my mom, I guess. Her grandmother says it's too dangerous." I tried to keep my tone casual, but my throat burned. "Which hurts a little," I admitted, "since I'm the one who raised her until she was three while my mom pretended to not be an addict. And the one who turned her in finally so they could get custody."

Kais' eyes narrowed. "Email? Not even a bloody phone call?"

I let out a soft laugh, trying to cut the ache before it settled too deep. "Not even a bloody phone call," I echoed, mocking his accent just enough to tease. "But that's technically five questions, so now it's my turn, Kai Kai."

He huffed a dry laugh, took a sip of his drink. "Go on, then."

I leaned forward, grinning. "What's your favorite ice cream?"

He blinked. "That's what you want to ask me?" I raised my brows. "I'm waiting."

"Alright," he said slowly, "I hate to disappoint you, but I've never had ice cream."

My eyes widened. "What? How have you *never* had ice cream?"

He shrugged, unfazed, "Too indulgent. Useless calories."

I stared at him like he'd just confessed to murder. He basically had, in my eyes.

"Next question," he added, unbothered.

I shook my head in mock horror. "That's criminal. Ice cream and movies are life's essentials."

His mouth twitched, but he didn't argue.

"Okay," I continued, leaning in a little, "why do you have so many records?"

His eyes lit with subtle amusement. Maybe even a flicker of affection.

"My mum. Layla Al-Rafi," he said, almost gently. "She had a massive collection. Some of my earliest memories are of her dusting them off and dancing with me while she sang." He raked a hand through his hair, gaze unfocused, like he was seeing something far away.

"She died when I was five. My father donated most of her things, but I kept a few of her records. She used to write poems on the sleeves—little notes, lyrics, whatever came to her. Now, whenever I travel, I stop in record shops. Just in case. I guess I hope I'll find one she loved. Something I can still remember her singing." His voice was steady. But the way he gripped his glass, the slight tension in his jaw—it said what his words didn't. That he didn't talk about this often. That it still hurt.

"God," I said softly, "that's a much better reason than I have for collecting them. I just love good music. Anything from before TV had color. And that crackle when the needle hits the vinyl."

"Me too," he said, his smile quiet, almost shy. He drained the rest of his drink, then leaned forward, gently lifting my leg across his lap. His hand stayed there—comfortable, warm—a feeling I could get used to. "Last question," he said softly, holding my gaze. I shifted in my seat, settling into the weight of his touch.

"What about your dad?" I felt the tension immediately. The warmth he'd had talking about his mom vanished like it had never been there.

"His name's Oskar Reinhardt," he said, draining the last of his bourbon. "We're... close enough. He kept his distance after my mum died—unless he needed someone to take his anger out on." He paused; eyes fixed somewhere over my shoulder. "Sent me to boarding school the second I was old enough. Came back for me later, once he realized I was better at his business than he ever was."

His tone was matter-of-fact. Like it didn't cost him anything to say it. But I felt the weight of every word. I had a million questions, but I didn't ask them. This felt like enough. And Kais seemed lighter. Like saying it out loud had chipped something away. Not everything, but enough to make space.

The chef returned and cleared the last of our dishes. We sat in comfortable silence, watching the moonlight ripple across the surface of the water. My legs rested in his lap, and his fingers moved absently along the fabric of my tights in slow, aimless shapes that made it hard to breathe. All the beauty around us—the view, the dinner, the luxury—suddenly felt like a cage. Like it wasn't built to dazzle, but to keep something locked in. *He needed out.* And I had just the idea.

"Can I take you somewhere?" I asked, turning to him. His brows lifted in surprise.

"Take *me* somewhere?"

I grinned. "Yes, *Kai-Kai*. Loosen up. We don't even have to drive."

I stood, offering my hand. For a moment, he just looked at me, his head tilted slightly, something unreadable passed through his eyes. Then, slowly, he smiled. Not a smirk, not his usual amused expression but a real, boyish, heartwarming smile. And judging by what he had just told me about his childhood, I didn't think he did that often. I would take pride in helping him do it more.

I led him to the elevator, stealing a glance over my shoulder as he slipped on a pair of loafers by the entryway. I sat on the bench to put on my heels, but before I could, he was already there. Without a word, Kais knelt in front of me, his fingers whispering over my ankle as he slid the first shoe on. Then, he pressed a slow, methodical kiss to the top of my foot.

Oh, God. If this man doesn't kiss me on my mouth tonight, I might actually turn feral.

He repeated the motion with the second shoe, his warm lips branding my skin before standing to his full towering height, draping a jacket over my shoulders. I swallowed hard. He's so intentional, everything he does feels deliberate, but because he cares rather than he expects something.

Fingers lacing through mine, he guided me into the elevator. He kept me snuggled into his side as we rode to the bottom, his scent all around me, his warmth, the intensity of his thick, muscular frame like the safest shelter. I was so drunk on his presence I barely noticed him pull out his phone, tilting it slightly to snap a candid picture of us in the mirrored ceiling.

"Saving memories, Kai Kai?" I teased.

"Every second that I can, love."

Something about him wanting a memory with me was intoxicating in a way I didn't care to admit to myself, for fear of how much it would suck when he woke up and realized I wasn't what he's looking for, but I pushed that feeling down for the time being.

The second the doors slid open, I grabbed his hand, dragging him into the street.

"Where are we going?" he grinned.

"Ice cream." I shot him a full smile as we entered the little shop across from his building.

He scanned the menu, looking utterly unimpressed. "I can't eat this."

I raised a brow. "Are you allergic?"

"No. It'll put me out of shape."

I rolled my eyes. "Kais, you're in no danger of being out of shape anytime soon." I shamelessly looked him up and down. He smirked, that damn beauty mark creasing in his cheek—his dark gaze tempting me to lose my composure all the more. I ignored the warmth creeping up my neck and tapped my finger against my chin, pretending to think. "Yep, you're a cookies and cream kind of guy."

His smile widened. "I'm not an anything type of lad. I don't eat ice cream, Alana."

I waved him off, turning to the cashier. "Two scoops of cookies and cream, please."

With ice cream in hand, we took a seat at the metal bistro tables outside, the late-night buzz of the city settling around us.

It took Kais less than five minutes to absolutely inhale his ice cream. I arched a brow, tossing my empty cup into the trash.

"So, I guess you're a cookies and cream kind of lad now."

He pressed a finger to his lips. "Shh. Keep that between me and you, yeah?"

We both laughed, the sound blending into the soft echo of a song playing from inside the shop. The warm, velvety melody drifted through the air, settling into the quiet between us.

"You wanna dance?" Kais asked suddenly, stretching a hand across the table.

"Here?" I wrinkled my nose.

He gave me a look that said, *'you can't be serious'*.

"What was it you said to me earlier? Loosen up?" he said, his boyish smirk in full force.

I narrowed my eyes at him.

"Take your own advice, love," he teased.

I exhaled a laugh, sliding my fingers into his. He pulled me up gently, drawing me against him as we swayed to the honeyed rhythm of the music.

"Is this 'Unchained Melody' *again*?" I laughed, looking up at him.

"I think so," he chuckled softly, his lips brushing against my forehead.

"I never hear this song in the wild... now it follows us everywhere." I laughed quietly, tilting my chin up to meet his gaze. His usual stoic, controlled demeanor had melted into something lighter.

"Let's call it ours, then," he said.

I smiled. "I like that idea."

For a moment, we just kept swaying, bodies pressed close, the world blurring around us. His eyes held mine, like there was nowhere else he'd rather be. My heart hammered against my ribs. I licked my lips, barely breathing when I whispered, "Will you kiss me already?"

A slow, knowing smile pulled at his mouth.

And then, he did.

He leaned in, teasing at first, catching my bottom lip between his teeth before finally, *finally* pulling me into him. The kiss was everything I had been waiting for. Firm but soft, needy yet patient, completely intoxicating. Every careful wall I'd built crumbled in the space between one heartbeat and the next. I felt weightless. Breathless. Falling, with no desire to stop.

Kais

-8-

♪ 11

"HOW HAVE YOU NEVER SEEN *FIFTY FIRST DATES*, KAI-Kai?" Alana asked in disbelief, staring at me from the couch in my living room as I grabbed water from the icebox.

No one in my entire life had ever called me anything other than Kais or Mr. Reinhardt, but this woman was insistent on referring to me in toddler-speak. If she were anyone else, I wouldn't allow it. But she was so fucking irresistible, she could call me a prick and I'd still be turned on.

"I don't watch trash American films, Alana. Directors have a real knack for rubbish over here."

She clutched her chest in exaggerated offense as I sat next to her, handing her a glass. "You know what, I'm not even going to be offended by that, Kai. I'll just consider you unenlightened to the magic of Adam Sandler."

She narrowed her eyes at me and hit play anyway. *Man, she's fucking adorable.*

"This is your one chance to enchant me. If this is as terrible as I suspect it to be, I'll never trust your taste in film again," I said, holding up a single finger.

Her lips stretched into a wide grin. "Alright, and if you *do* like it, I get to pick every movie we ever watch until you find one you don't like."

I could never dislike watching a film with this girl, no matter how shit it was. I was just going to be watching her anyway. She settled next to me, leaning her body into the open splay of my arm, her legs tucked at her side. She fitted against me so perfectly—something about this whole thing felt way more intimate than if we were just to shag. In fact, I had never felt more intimate with anyone in my life.

God, the way she giggled at nearly every scene, the way her eyes flicked up to me when something funny was coming and she wanted to watch my reaction. She was just *herself*, not pretending to be someone she thought I wanted her to be, and that unraveled me.

Her eyes met mine again. "I like this," she said softly. "Dinner and dancing was nice, but I like this just being with you part best —especially when it includes you rubbing circles into my thigh with your fingers."

I stilled my hand. I hadn't even realized I was doing that. She was too easy to touch. Too easy to *want*. And the way she let me? Fucking hell. It made it impossible to stop. I should have stopped. I should have pulled away before I made this worse. But then she exhaled, leaned into me like she didn't want me to go anywhere. And fuck, I couldn't.

My mouth was on hers all over again. She tasted too fucking good. Too soft. Too warm. Too much of everything I didn't let myself have. Her hand moved from my jaw to the back of my hair, and instinct took over—I pulled her into my lap. She didn't resist. Not even a little.

Shit.

She fitted against me too well. Like she was fucking made for this. For me. Her tongue hungrily met mine, her hands slipping under the fabric of my shirt, and when I pulled her hips closer, she rolled into me—making a tiny fucking noise in the back of her throat. And I was gone. *Fuck holding back. Fuck slow. I want her.*

But I can't. *Not yet. Not like this.*

So, I kissed her harder instead. Kissed her like I was trying to tell her all the things I couldn't say out loud. She responded so easily, so fucking sweetly, and it drove me insane. Like she was always meant to be here. In my arms. *Like she's mine.* I should stop before this gets dangerous, I thought. Before I do something I can't take back. I tried to pull away—but she rolls her hips into me again, and fuck, my vision goes white for a second.

I fist my hand in her hair, dragging her back from me, but I fucking *hate* that, so I catch her neck with my tongue. She moans again. And I know I could have her just like this. Right here, and she'd let me. But no matter how intense the attraction was between us, I'm not taking anything from her that didn't come with her heart too.

Our mouths meet again, and I've got a proper vlad at this point. I need to put space between us before I *ruin* this. If I don't, I'll keep fucking kissing her. *And if I keep kissing her—I'm not stopping at just that.* I want to do this right. And it's the thought of all of this going to shit that pulls me back.

I moved my hand from her arse, running both hands into her hair and tilting her face back, both of us catching a breath.

"Alana." Her name felt like a lifeline, keeping me from the cliff I was about to throw myself from.

"We're on the same page, Kai," she purred, leaning back to press a kiss to my palm before settling next to me once again—just as the credits of the movie we barely watched rolled.

We sat in silence for a moment. It was well past one in the morning. *She should probably go*, I thought. But I didn't want her to. Which was fucking *mad* to admit to myself, because I had never felt like that in my life. I was completely out of my weight class here.

I racked my brain for a reason to make her want to stay. Then she broke the silence.

"Should we do another? You laughed, so I feel like this counts, but we didn't really get to watch it all."

I smiled like a damn schoolboy. She wanted to stay too.

"Yeah, I suppose you deserve a fighting chance."

I played it off like I wasn't *internally begging* for her to stay.

She grinned.

"You just want me to stay, Kai-Kai," she said, rolling her eyes, smiling, tempting me to show her what that does to me all over again.

So, I did the only thing I could—I pulled back, laid my head in her lap, and forced myself *not* to. She let me. Without hesitation. Her body sank back into the cushions like this was relaxing for her.

"Go on, what's next?" I jested.

She began flicking through titles, landing on something called *The Goofy Movie*, which sounded fucking bleak. But then—she trailed her fingers through my hair. Slow. Absentminded. Like this was *normal* for us. And suddenly, the movie sounded bloody brilliant.

Everything about her completely disarmed me, made me feel like I didn't *need* to be on guard. Maybe that should have scared me. Maybe it did. Letting someone have power over me in a way that could make me everything I've spent my whole life trying not to be—reckless and impulsive.

But something in my chest knew that wasn't the case here. That I could trust her. And I'd move the fucking mountains to make sure she felt that way about me too. Her laughter pulled me back to the moment, making me join in—she had the most infectious laugh. But then she started slowly threading her fingers through my hair again, and my eyes were slipping closed before I could think too much more.

A HAND ON MY SHOULDER. A low voice. *Too fucking early.* I cracked one eye open.

Alanzo.

"Boss. It's four."

Right. *Training.* I exhaled slowly, about to sit up—

And then I saw her. Alana. Curled up on the couch, fast asleep, still in that bloody dress. *Shit.*

I felt like a right bastard. I should've prepared for this. I should have known she'd stay after that last film. Should have made sure she had something comfortable to sleep in. Instead, she was tangled up in that too-fucking-fancy dress I bought her, bare legs tucked under her, breathing slow and even. Looking too damn soft. Like she could care less. But fuck me—*I* cared.

I dragged a hand over my face, exhaling through my nose. I needed to get to training. But first, I grabbed a pillow from my bedroom and slid it beneath her head. She barely stirred, just burrowed deeper into the warmth. Then, I reached for the throw blanket over the chair and unfolded it, draping it over her body, making sure she was covered. Still, the sight of her in that dress made my jaw clench.

I turned to Alanzo, in a whisper.

"Let her sleep. But before she wakes up, grab something for her to change into and hang it in the bathroom. Something comfortable."

He gave a small nod. "Anything specific?"

I thought about it. Something simple. Nothing too formal. Something she won't overthink.

"Soft. Oversized. Something that won't make her feel like I went out of my way." My fingers flexed.

Christ, when did I start giving a fuck about details like this?

Alanzo didn't ask questions. Just nodded once, waiting for the next instruction. I glanced back at her one last time before stepping away, reached for my bag and moved toward the door.

"Let her sleep. When she wakes up, tell her to stay put and I'll be back."

THE MOMENT I stepped into the gym, Montee was already wrapping his hands, watching me wrap mine.

"Finally got some sleep?" he muttered, voice thick with amusement. I ignored him, stepping into the ring, rolling out my shoulders.

"What are you on about, you daft cunt?" I said, jerking my chin. "You gonna keep talking, or are we getting started?"

Montee grinned, pulling on his gloves.

"Feisty today, huh? Good. I was hopin' you'd show up mean."

I wasn't mean. I was unfocused. Two very different things. And very unlike me. He came in first, quick and clean. I dodged, pivoting out, returning with a jab, testing the distance.

"You're thinkin' about somethin'."

I threw a left hook.

"I'm always thinking about somethin'."

Montee dodged easily, stepping back.

"Yeah? This ain't numbers, lad."

She's in my head like she's supposed to be there. Like she's meant to be in every space I exist in. And maybe I want that. More than I'm willing to admit.

"This is different." Montee went on.

I didn't reply. Didn't need to. Because the second my silence stretched too long, Montee's grin widened. He was fucking *right*. I was thinking about something. I should be thinking about defense. About my left guard. About the next strike. Instead, I was thinking about how easy it would be to take her away from all of this fucking distraction.

I adjusted my stance.

"I might head out of town soon."

Montee's smirk faded slightly, replaced with something closer to consideration.

"When?"

I rolled my shoulders, breathing through the burn.

"Not sure yet."

He landed a quick shot to my ribs—nothing I couldn't shake off.

"You want me on standby?"

I didn't answer immediately. Just let the thought roll around in my head. Then—

"Yeah."

Montee grunted, "Heard."

We went another three rounds. I let myself focus. Let myself work. But the thought was still there. Building. I didn't even know where I'd take her yet. I just knew I didn't want to be here anymore. Not in this city. Not in this routine. Not in a place where she felt like she had to keep one foot out the door.

The sun was barely stretching its legs, the Miami heat at a low boil on my jog back home. Alanzo was waiting outside the elevator, already checking his watch when I stepped back into the lobby.

"She still asleep?" I asked. Alanzo nodded.

"Hasn't moved."

Good.

I rolled out my shoulders, dragging a hand over my jaw.

"Take her shopping today."

Alanzo flicked his gaze toward me. "Understood."

The elevator began to pull up. I unwrapped my hands, rolling the tape between my fingers. She'd fight me on this. I knew that already. But I also knew she didn't own a single thing that suited where we were going. And she couldn't buy it for herself—not if she can talk herself out of it. I watched her talk herself out of a dozen things she's wanted since the night we met.

"Webster. Shut it down for an hour. Tell them to pull whatever she touches in her size—no price tags, no receipts in the bags."

She doesn't know how to take things without feeling like she owes something in return. She'd offered to pay me back for the dress and shoes I bought her more than a handful of times last night, clearly uncomfortable with accepting them—like she'd never learned how to simply receive.

Alanzo nodded, already expecting this level of instruction.

"And if she tries to argue?"

"She will. Let her think she's choosing—but make sure she leaves with everything." I muttered, drumming my fingers against my thigh, watching the floors tick by. Thinking through every way I knew she'd try to wiggle out of it. "And make sure it's *her* style. If she thinks I went too far, she won't take any of it. Send me pictures, I'll double check it."

Alanzo let out a small, knowing breath. "Understood."

I checked my phone. A flood of things begging for my attention. Then—the screen lit up again.

Oskar Reinhardt.

Fucking perfect. I stared at it for half a second, jaw clenching. Then, finally, I answered.

"Father."

Alana

9

♫ 33

A COOL MORNING DRAFT NIPPED AT THE TIP OF MY NOSE, a stark contrast to the warmth of the sun flooding through the sheer curtains. I shifted against the plush couch, blinking awake, my body protesting against the corseted dress I had now been wearing for far too long. After the ice cream shop, we had come back to Kais', where I somehow convinced Kais to stay up way too late watching old movies. He had rolled his eyes, muttered something about British sensibilities and not watching "stuff like that," but I caught him laughing—real, belly-deep laughter—more than a handful of times.

A heavy black plush blanket had been draped over me, tucked neatly into the couch cushions. A silk pillow had been placed under my head. Not at all how I fell asleep.

A deep voice carried through the open balcony doors, speaking in German. I sat up carefully, stretching the stiffness from my spine, then peeked toward the glass wall of doors behind the couch. Kais stood outside, pacing, his shirtless frame silhouetted against the city skyline. The golden glow of morning stretched long shadows over the marble floor and painted him in soft light.

He was speaking into his phone, his words bitten off and clipped, his entire posture tense, his movements rigid. He looked nothing like the playful man who had laughed into my lap as I ran my fingers through his hair last night, eventually falling asleep to animated dogs.

Suddenly, I felt like I shouldn't be here—like I was seeing a part of him I wasn't meant to yet. I scanned the room for my purse and shoes, trying to move as quietly as possible. But just as I started to stand, a firm hand pressed gently against my shoulder, easing me back down. I turned, my breath catching as I met Kais' gaze.

His expression was softer now, affectionate even, his phone still pressed to his ear as someone spoke on the other end. Without a word, he leaned down, brushing a slow, lingering kiss against my lips before pulling back just enough to whisper,

"Wait."

I swallowed, covering his hand with mine and nodding. He pulled back his hand, rubbing it through his hair, nodding curtly as he responded to whoever was on the line.

"Tschüss." Then, he ended the call.

"You okay?" I asked as he circled the couch to sit beside me.

"Yeah, very well, thanks." He pulled my feet effortlessly into his lap like it was a habit now. His gaze flicked to me, dark and intent. "Where are you running off to?"

"School."

He raised a brow. "It's summer break. You have a party to get to this early?"

I blinked, thrown off by the assumption. "Uh... no. I don't party. I'm working all break. School isn't cheap."

Kais studied me for a moment, his gaze calculating. Then, he tilted his head.

"Come away with me, then."

I frowned.

"Come away with you?"

He nodded, brushing his thumb absently over my ankle.

"Yeah. On holiday. Just for a bit. Do you have a passport?"

I nodded, my brain scrambling to catch up.

"I do."

"Good." He tapped my thigh lightly. "Then the only thing stopping you is yourself, my love."

I hesitated. It *wouldn't* kill me to take a week off. I could pick up extra shifts when I got back. But this was reckless. And impulsive. And completely unlike me. I caught my bottom lip between my teeth, a nervous habit.

"Isn't that kind of crazy, Kai? We've only been on two dates."

He reached over, gently freeing my bottom lip from between my teeth with the pad of his thumb. Then, tilting my chin up, he held my gaze steady.

"Does it feel crazy to you, Ya Amar?"

God, he's dangerous.

I bit back a smile.

"I don't know, Kai Kai. You could convince me to do all types of crazy things when you call me that."

And there was that knowing smile again, I was starting to question if he could actually see inside my head. Leaning in, he kissed me, lazy and unhurried, his tongue teasing against mine before he sucked my bottom lip between his teeth and pulled away just slightly.

"It's sorted, then." His voice was smooth as silk, already shifting back into control.

"I'll arrange for us to leave tonight. Alanzo will take you to the shops so you can pick out some proper clothes." He pulled out his phone, working intently on something.

I exhaled a quiet laugh.

"If you *tell* me where we're going, I can pack my own clothes, Kai."

He glanced at me over his shoulder, smirking. "Do you trust me?"

I cocked my head. "I do."

Setting his phone back down, he turned back toward me, his heavy hand sliding over my hip, his fingers teasing at the silk of my dress.

"Then go down that hall," he pointed, eyes locked on mine. "Second door on the left. Shower. There's an outfit waiting for you. Alanzo will be downstairs when you're ready." He kissed the tip of my nose, then—just like that—stood, already answering another call as he walked away.

I sat there for a moment, still half-draped across the couch, the imprint of his kiss lingering at the tip of my nose.

What the hell just happened? Go away with him? Just like that?

The logical part of my brain was already scribbling a list: work shifts I'd need to cover, the reading I planned to do, my budget, my sanity. But none of it was loud enough to drown out the way he'd looked at me—like the world could wait, as long as I said yes.

Does it feel crazy to you, Ya Amar?

Maybe it was. But for once, I didn't feel scared of the crazy. I felt... pulled. Like some thread between us was already tied, tugging me forward no matter how much I tried to think my way out of it. I'd never had a man like this—not just because of the luxury or the control—but because of the way he listened. The way he saw through me. The way he asked me to come closer without pushing, like he already knew I wanted to.

I looked toward the hall he'd pointed to, heart still stuttering in my chest. With a quiet laugh to myself, I pushed off the couch and padded toward the bathroom. I wasn't sure what kind of outfit Kais Reinhardt considered appropriate for shopping... but I had a feeling it wasn't jeans and a t-shirt.

A PERFECT MIAMI NIGHT: balmy air, a warm breeze rustling through the palm trees, the sky fading into a deep indigo streaked with orange. As Alanzo pulled onto the tarmac, a sleek navy-blue private jet came into view, its polished exterior gleaming under the runway lights, Kais' baby blue Porsche parked next to it.

I'd spent the day shopping in stores I never imagined setting foot in—racks of designer gowns, delicate bikinis, and silk dresses slipping through my fingers. It felt too indulgent, entirely undeserved. I knew Kais wouldn't let me walk away with nothing, so I tried to find the cheapest version of everything that caught my eye. But there were no tags on anything, and every time I touched something, Alanzo nodded, and the women following me brought it in my size. I tried to pretend I didn't like any of it. Alanzo knew better. By the time we were done, about a dozen bags and a full luggage set were loaded into the car. I never stood a chance.

After a night spent in that corseted dress, then a day in the admittedly gorgeous halter sundress and kitten heels Kais had somehow procured for me (casual enough to move in but elegant enough that I didn't feel out of place in those high-end stores) I was long overdue for something that I could exhale in.

So, when it came time to dress for this mysterious flight, I reached for something comfortable. Something I bought myself from a store with tags and discounts. An electric blue hoodie, matching sweatpants, and a pair of cream sneakers. Emotional armor in the shape of cozy sweats. I would never get used to that level of pampering, showing up in something I could afford felt like a safer option.

The car rolled to a stop, but instead of Alanzo opening the door, Kais did. He stood there, tall and effortless—wearing the *exact same* outfit as me. All my jittery nerves went out the window immediately. I smiled a mile wide, barely containing my laugh before we both cracked up.

"Nice outfit," I teased, stepping out as he took my hand.

He ran a slow hand down his chest, eyes glinting with amusement. "Yeah, I quite like it. Had Alanzo send one over after he showed me a picture of yours."

I batted my lashes. "Did you also have him send you the bikinis?"

Kais grinned, completely unbothered.

"No, preferred the idea of seeing those on... or off of you." His voice was smooth as he guided me up the steps of the jet, his hand firm at the small of my back.

"Welcome aboard, Miss Cameron, Mr. Reinhardt." The stewardess nodded politely as we stepped inside.

The interior was stunning—dark wood-grain paneling, plush peanut-butter leather seats, and the kind of luxury that felt both effortless and impossible. Past the row of captain's chairs near the front, a softly lit cabin revealed a bed draped in a cashmere blanket, a bouquet of Casablanca lilies and forget-me-nots resting on the pillows.

I turned over my shoulder, eyes wide, mouthing, '*Wow*'. Kais shot me a small smile, handing off a carry-on bag before sliding into one of the captain's chairs. I settled beside him, shifting against the cloud-soft leather, trying to tamp down my excitement as the flight attendant secured everything for takeoff. Kais, meanwhile, was focused on his phone, his fingers moving deftly across the screen.

The plane began to taxi as a voice with a thick French accent crackled over the speaker.

"Good evening and welcome aboard. This is Captain Louis Dubois. Flight time to Marrakech Menara Airport is approximately nine hours. We're expecting clear skies and a smooth flight. Sit back, relax, and enjoy your journey."

My head snapped toward Kais.

"Morocco?" I whispered.

Kais slid his phone into his pocket, turning toward me as he took my hand, his fingers threading through mine.

"I wouldn't want to go with anyone but you, Ya Amar." His voice was soft, but his eyes—filled with something heavier than affection— held me in place.

My heart clenched. He studied me, searching my face as if making sure I understood what this meant to him. *And I did.* I lifted a hand, tracing my thumb over that perfect beauty mark before leaning in and pressing a slow kiss to his lips. The moment our mouths met, a fire sparked low in my belly, the urge to push it deeper nearly overtaking me. But I pulled back whispering, "Thank you for trusting me with this."

Kais smiled, slight and achingly sweet. As the plane lifted into the sky, he didn't need to say another word.

A few quiet hours into the flight, I tired of watching Kai work on spreadsheets and my eyelids grew heavy, my body sinking into the plush seat. Kais' fingers brushed against my knee.

"Let's go to bed, love."

Before I could protest, he scooped me up effortlessly, cradling me to his chest and carrying me into the back cabin. He laid me down gently, pulling off my socks and shoes with a careful touch. I yawned, tugging off my hoodie and sweatpants, ready to sleep in just my tank top and underwear without a second thought.

Kais sucked in a breath.

"Shit," he hissed.

I grinned sleepily, rolling onto my side. "What?"

He exhaled through his nose, his dark eyes dragging over my bare legs before flicking back up to meet mine.

"If you can't handle me in a tank top and underwear," I yawned, "how will you hold up against a bikini?"

"I should be asking what you can handle, Ya Amar."

"Well, Kai Kai, I guess we'll find out soon enough."

A smile played on his lips as he reached for the hem of his hoodie, pulling it over his head in one smooth motion.

Unfair.

That was the only word that came to mind. My breath stalled slightly as his impossibly built body came into view. Defined muscle, warm golden skin, every inch of him chiseled like he was carved from something divine. Catching my expression with obvious amusement, he slid into bed beside me and tucked me into his chest. *Must he always one up me?* My irritation at this cat and mouse we were playing was quelled in an instant by his touch. His body was warm, solid, his spiced scent blanketed me.

"Any chance you've got Casablanca on that fancy thing?" I gestured toward the sleek overhead projector.

Kais let out a soft laugh, tilting his head toward me.

"You were absolutely knackered a moment ago, and now you want a film?"

I dragged my fingers lazily across his chest, tracing languid circles. "Caught a second wind, I guess."

He reached for the remote, handing it to me before leaning over, rummaging in a small cabinet. A second later, he pulled out a pint of cookies and cream ice cream and two chilled spoons.

"Go on then," he said, tossing me a spoon.

I laughed, shaking my head. *This man.* Something inside me cracked open at that moment. Every logical voice in my head told me to slow down. To be careful. That I was on the fast track to the worst heartbreak of my life. But sitting here, wrapped in Kais' warmth, on a private jet bound for the one place we both had always dreamed of seeing, while he pulled out my favorite movie and a shared inside joke in the form of ice cream?

I knew. It was too late; I was already gone.

Alana

10

♪ 16

THE LAST THING I REMEMBERED WAS STEPPING OFF THE plane into the warm night air of Marrakech, thick with the scent of spice and jasmine. It was quiet but alive—runway lights flickering, the noise of the distant city echoed even at that late hour. Kais had barely let go of my hand as we were whisked through the airport, then into the waiting car that carried us through winding streets until we reached a hidden riad tucked behind an unassuming doorway. By the time my head hit the pillow, exhaustion won. The downy bedding enveloped me, Kais' warmth settled nearby, and sleep took me before I could even take in where I was.

Morning came, and the first thing I registered was warmth. The silk-soft blankets wrapped around me, the lingering traces of Kais' body heat and above all, the golden glow pressing against my eyelids. I opened them to sunlight streaming through intricately carved wooden screens, painting light and shadow in shifting patterns across the walls.

The distant commotion of the city filtered through the open balcony doors: faint voices, the occasional trill of laughter, the rhythmic clatter of carts rolling over cobblestone streets. The air was thick with the scent of fresh mint and oranges with undertones of something sweet and buttery. I stretched lazily, my fingers grazing the cool linen sheets, the soft texture whispering against my skin. The bed was too comfortable, the kind that made leaving feel like a crime.

Blinking awake, I pushed my hair from my face, taking in my surroundings. The riad was breathtaking—tall arched ceilings, terracotta-colored walls, hand-painted tiles in intricate Moroccan patterns. Lush greenery spilled from hanging planters, the leaves dancing gently in the warm morning breeze. A sheer canopy of fabric swayed above the bed, moving like water in the sunlight.

My gaze snagged on the open balcony, where the curtains billowed lazily. Beyond it, rooftops stretched toward the horizon, bathed in the soft pink hues of dawn. It felt like something out of a dream. A low clatter of dishes sounded from the other room, followed by a very distinct, very irritated mutter in German. My smile was immediate.

Kais.

Tossing the blankets aside, I padded barefoot across the cool tiled floor, pulling on a floor length yellow silk robe before following the scent of fresh bread and the unmistakable sound of a man who was clearly losing a battle with breakfast. He stood at the stove, barefoot, wearing nothing but a pair of loose linen pants, his broad back tense as he angrily scraped at a pan.

He was muttering curses in German, frustration lacing each syllable. The scene so unlike the cool and composed Kais I had come to know, that I bit my lip to keep from laughing.

Quietly, I slipped behind him, wrapping my arms around his waist and pressing soft kisses up his spine. His skin was smooth beneath my lips, muscles flexing under my touch.

"What exactly are you making, Kai?" I said, barely biting back a grin.

He turned to face me, dark curls an absolute mess, his usual stoicism softened by sleepy eyes and sheer frustration. "A real shit, sticky, burned mess of msemen," he grumbled, looking down at the pan as if it had personally offended him.

I smiled, peering over his shoulder at the charred, misshapen pieces of dough.

"Do you have a recipe, or are you just winging it?"

He exhaled heavily, grabbing his phone from the counter. When he unlocked it, a photo of me sleeping on his chest on the plane filled the screen. I held my breath, about to tease him, but something in the way he looked at that picture stopped me. Like he hadn't even realized it was there. Like it simply belonged to him.

Instead, I took the phone from his hands, scanning the recipe he had pulled up. Flour, butter, eggs. Simple enough. As a girl who grew up in an ingredients house, I knew my way around a kitchen. Not that this particular recipe was anything challenging. There wasn't much I couldn't figure out. And the furrow in Kais's brow told me maybe he'd never had to develop that survival skill. The effort was still endearing.

"I've got this, babe. Go sit down."

Kais arched a brow but didn't argue, stepping aside as I took over the stove.

"Is it alright if I just watch, then?" he asked, his voice smoother now, the edge of frustration melting away.

I grinned, tossing a glance over my shoulder. "Watch all you want, sir."

Then, just to be a menace, I wiggled my hips slightly as I reached for the flour.

Kais let out a breathy laugh, dragging a hand down his face as if to hide his flushed cheeks. "You are absolute trouble, *Ya Amar*."

AFTER A BREAKFAST OF HOT, butter-drizzled msemen and honey-sweetened fruit, we set off into the Medina. It was a labyrinth of narrow, winding streets teeming with color, scent, and sound. Sunlight filtered through the wooden latticework of awnings onto the terracotta walls of the souks.

The scent of freshly ground spices thickened the air—cumin, saffron, cinnamon—intertwined with sweet citrusy orange blossoms and the smoky char of sizzling lamb skewers from a nearby stall.

Kais moved through the marketplace with ease, haggling in a fluid mix of Arabic and French, his voice lilting with amusement each time he bantered with a vendor. He was charming, quick-witted, and utterly in his element, generously tipping the trinket sellers as we passed.

"*Ya Amar*, come here." His voice pulled me from the spice stall I'd been ogling.

The more he called me that, the more I forget that I had any other name. I turned to find him at a jewelry stand, kneeling in front of me, an unmistakable glint in his eye.

"Your foot," he instructed, patting his knee.

I arched a brow but slid off my far too expensive Hermès sandal, placing my foot lightly atop his leg. His fingers, warm and sure, clasped a delicate gold anklet with dangling crescent moons around my ankle, the fine metal glinting in the sunlight. I lifted the hem of my silk pants to admire it, unable to suppress my smile.

"You like it?" he asked, grinning.

I let out a breath and nodded rapidly.

"You're spoiling me entirely too much," I replied.

He stood, brushing off his pants before threading his fingers through mine. "You've seen nothing yet, my love."

The older woman behind the stall clasped my shoulder, her piercing blue eyes crinkling with warmth.

"This man, he loves you," she said through her thick accent. "You hold on tight, yes?"

I swallowed, forcing a small smile. "I'll try my best."

Kais said nothing, just gave my hand a soft squeeze as we walked away.

Don't fall in love. Don't fall in love. Don't fall in love.

Scooters buzzed past, stirring up the heat of the afternoon sun, but a breeze cut through it, carrying the tang of briny olives, the nutty warmth of roasted almonds, and the faintest wisp of sandalwood incense carrying from a hidden courtyard.

Behind thick wooden doors, riads occasionally allowed us glimpses of lush greenery and cool marble fountains—serene escapes from the dizzying pulse of the streets. A small boutique caught my eye, its display of intricately embroidered djellabas and gandouras swaying gently on a wooden rack. Nearby, a neat stack of deep-red fez hats and crisp white taqiyahs sat beside them.

I grabbed Kais' arm. "You have to try that on."

He turned, narrowing his eyes at me, "You're mad."

I tugged him toward the shop, "Come on, Kai Kai, live a little."

With an exaggerated sigh, he gave in, calling toward a gray-haired man in the back, who barely paused his phone conversation before waving him toward the garments. Kais pulled on a sky-blue gandoura, the fabric sliding effortlessly over his broad frame.

I grabbed a scarlet-red fez and held it out to him. "Here, put this on too."

He shot me a deadpan look, tilting his head in mock exhaustion, but obliged. Before he could adjust it properly, I was already snapping pictures. The second he caught on, he let out a rare, full-bodied laugh (a sound I immediately committed to memory). My heart fluttered. *New screensaver.*

The shopkeeper, noticing the moment, grinned and stepped closer, switching seamlessly from Arabic to French as he addressed Kais. Their exchange was lively, the older man's excitement clear, but Kais hesitated at whatever he was saying. Still, he nodded, indicating he wanted to buy the gandoura.

I followed as they moved toward the counter, watching as the shopkeeper gestured toward a poster displayed behind the register. A black-and-white action shot of a boxer mid-fight: muscles taut, poised in victory over a fallen opponent.

The name *"Kais Reinhardt"* was scrawled in elegant, simple script at the bottom. My stomach dropped. I turned slowly toward Kais, whose usual quick wit and easy charm had suddenly stilled. His jaw ticked. This wasn't just any fight poster. *It was his.* And judging by the recognition flickering through the shopkeeper's eyes, Kais was someone much bigger than I'd realized.

"Kais, Kais" the man repeated, gesturing to the poster smiling, as he pulled out his phone to ask for a picture.

Looking over at me for a moment, his expression like something had just shattered, Kais agreed to pose with the man. The shopkeeper thanked Kais repeatedly, gifting him the blue gandoura and the fez.

The walk from the shop was quiet. Kais' fingers were still knit with mine but that carefree quality he'd worn all day had dimmed slightly. He wasn't sulking, not quite, but something about the way his jaw remained tight, the way his free hand occasionally raked through his hair, told me he was trying to push something down. Still, I didn't press.

Instead, as we wound through the Medina, I followed my nose, pulling him toward a narrow alleyway where a modest, white-washed stairwell spiraled upward. A discreet wooden sign, painted in elegant Arabic script, hinted at something above. I nudged Kais toward it.

"Come on," I said, giving his hand a tug. "Trust me."

He let out a slow breath before finally following me up the steps.

The second we stepped onto the terrace, the city seemed to stretch out before us. The rooftop was open-air, strung with delicate, woven lanterns that cast golden halos against the walls, and an endless amount of lush green plants. Colorful cushions lined low-seated tables, where a handful of locals leaned in close over steaming plates of food. The scent of saffron, preserved lemon, and honeyed dates floated through the warm evening air. Kais exhaled through his nose, a quiet chuckle escaping him.

"You always seem to take me to the most unexpected places."

"I have good instincts." I replied, nudging him.

A waitress sat us at a cozy table nestled in a corner. The city stirred below, its golden lights flickering against the deep blue sky. From here, we could see the rooftops of the Medina, the distant calls of shopkeepers still lingering in the air. A faint drumbeat from a far-off square echoed against the walls, blending seamlessly with the sound of overlapping conversation. Thankfully, the menu had English descriptions next to everything. I'd felt lost all day next to Kais.

"I've got this." I said, pulling the menu from his hands. He twitched his head, studying me.

"Oh, yeah?" he let out a breathy laugh.

"Indeed, good sir." I teased with a fake and terrible British accent, waving over the waiter.

I covered my mouth speaking in a low murmur as I ordered. Kais watched in amusement as his tension faded by the minute.

In no time, the table was set with a feast of colors and scents, each dish arranged with artful precision on hand-painted ceramic plates. The glow of the lanterns flickered over polished brass serving trays. A tower of fluffy, sesame-studded khobz bread sat in a woven basket, flanked by small, earthenware bowls of silky argan oil and amber-hued honey, their rich fragrances rising from the table.

A tagine—its clay lid still steaming as it was lifted away—revealed slow-cooked lamb, its tender meat falling from the bone into a bed of spiced apricots and caramelized onions, the rich scent of saffron and ginger enveloping us. Beside it, a plate of crispy briouats (delicate, phyllo-wrapped pastries filled with fragrant spiced chicken and almonds) their edges dusted with powdered sugar and cinnamon.

A vibrant salad of oranges and black olives sat in a glazed clay dish, bright slivers of preserved lemon tucked between the glistening citrus. A silver teapot rested beside two delicate, etched glasses, where fresh mint tea steamed invitingly. Kais reached for a slender skewer of charred lamb kofta, its edges crisp from the fire, tearing a piece off with his teeth before nudging the plate toward me.

"Eat," he muttered, amusement finally sparking in those dark eyes again. "Before you get distracted again."

I held back my grin and dug in.

Once we were full to our hearts' content, the air between us turned light and easy. A comfortable silence stretched between us, the kind that was becoming familiar with him. I traced my finger over the rim of my tea glass, watching the way Kais leaned back slightly, the tension in his jaw finally softening. He looked peaceful compared to before dinner. I hesitated, not wanting to ruin it. But I couldn't ignore the poster in the shop any longer. Couldn't unsee the way the shopkeeper looked at him like he was some kind of legend. I took a breath, savoring the quiet once more before breaking it.

"So... how long were you a fighter?" I asked gently. "Or... are you still?"

His eyes flicked to mine as he set down his cup. He studied me for a second too long before he spoke.

"I am still," he drawled.

I nodded, waiting.

"I started as a kid. Mostly to quiet the anger. To stop scrapping with the blokes at school who thought picking on the only brown kid was a good time." He wiped his mouth with his napkin, gaze drifting out toward the street.

"Then in secondary school I dabbled with the whole underground thing and met my trainer Montee, won my first title when I was twenty. Been at it ever since."

His voice was calm, but something about the way his fingers

tapped slightly against the table told me this wasn't just a career. It was something deeper. Something he was destined to become. I let his words settle, watching him. *I needed to know more.*

"Is that... what got you here?" I asked softly. "The fighting?" I regretted the question a little as it left my lips.

He looked at me—*really* looked at me—like he wasn't sure what he expected, but it wasn't that. He didn't waver.

"It's what started it," he said finally. "Don't get me wrong, fighting pays well. But I only do it maybe once a year now."

His fingers tapped lightly against his glass.

"I took over my dad's investment firm a few years ago. He left me the name. I built the rest."

I nodded, sipping my now cold tea. Suddenly, his cut-up physique and the quiet bruises made sense. His effortless control. The way his body always seemed ready, coiled energy beneath calm control. I watched him carefully, searching his face. He didn't look ashamed nor arrogant. If anything, he looked almost relieved. Like saying it out loud to me was somehow easier than he thought it would be. I swallowed. Then, before I could overthink it—

"Can I watch you sometime?"

He let out a low laugh, but it wasn't his usual easy, confident chuckle. This one was quieter, almost thoughtful. He studied me, searching my face like he was trying to figure out if I was serious.

"Watch me what? *Fight?*"

I nodded, "Yeah."

He exhaled through his nose, shaking his head slightly, but there was something else in his expression.

"You continue to surprise me, *Ya Amar.*" His voice was softer now, as if he was rolling the thought around in his head. Then, a slow, devastating smile spread across his lips.

"I was certain you'd nail me for not telling you sooner."

I shook my head, threading my fingers through his. "I knew you did something grand, obviously, but I honestly didn't care to know what. I just wanted to know you, for you, not what you do."

Something warmed in his eyes. Then, just as quickly, he smiled softly and brushed his thumb over the back of my hand.

"Though I was pretty certain you were in some sort of British mafia," I teased.

An amused breath escaped him. He shook his head before leaning in slightly, voice a whisper against my skin— *"Ya Amar"* — as he planted a tender kiss.

11

Lars: Oskar's pressing hard. He's got half the board convinced.

Me: That didn't take long.

Lars: Not with the way he's selling it. "Once-in-a-lifetime opportunity."

Me: That's what he said about the last one. How much exposure are we looking at?

Lars: Too much. If it tanks, it'll sink the smaller portfolios tied to it. You already know his angle: high risk, high reward. But this one? It's all risk.

Me: Hold position. No further capital movement until I'm back.

Lars: Understood. But you should know he's pushing for a vote next week.

Me: Of course he is.

> Lars: You sure you want to hold out? The buyout talks are crawling. If Oskar moves first…

> Me: He won't. He's desperate, not strategic. Let him overplay his hand.

> Lars: Your call. Just don't take too long, mate. Oskar doesn't like to lose.

> Me: Neither do I.

🎵 13

THE SKY WAS STILL BRUISED WITH THE LAST SHADES OF night when I stepped through the doors of the riad, the air cool from the lingering morning. Alana was usually still tangled in the sheets when I got back from training. Bare-cheeked, fast asleep, the picture of temptation I'd been stubbornly keeping my hands off.

But this morning, the scent of something savory and spiced wafted through the courtyard, pulling me in like a fucking spell. The bedroom doors were wide open. Empty. A musical hum drifted from the kitchen, sweet and unbothered. I followed the sound, stepping into the courtyard. And there she was.

Barefoot, singing softly, her hips shifting slightly as she prepared breakfast. Sunlight filtered through the carved lattice-work, catching the curve of her neck, the loose curls slipping from her bun, the soft press of her mouth as she tasted something off the spoon.

She was fucking beautiful like this. Carefree. A little messy. Completely unaware of the way she was undoing me. I could stand here and watch her all morning. Or I could do what I really want —press her against the counter, pull that robe from her shoulders, and finally let my hands go where they've been itching to. *Not yet.*

Instead, I stepped behind her, palm sliding over the dip of her waist as I leaned in, letting my lips brush against her neck. A small, pleased noise escaped her. A breathy little sigh. Her body shifted, molding into mine without thinking. *When she's ready, I'll be the only man her body ever answers like this.*

"Mmm," She exhaled, turning toward me with a spoon in hand, half-lidded eyes flicking up lazily. "Something about you all hot and sweaty post-gym does it for me."

That makes two of us.

"Try this, Shakshuka," she said, lifting the spoon to my lips. She eased it into my mouth, and—fuck. It was perfect. I hummed in approval, reaching for the spoon to go for another bite, but she swatted my hand.

"Let me make you a bowl, Kai." Her laugh was soft, teasing as she turned back to the counter, moving easily in the kitchen like she owned the space entirely.

The sight of her here, so naturally woven into my morning routine, hit me harder than any punch I'd taken in the ring. I'd built my life around keeping people at arm's length. But everything about her made me want to pull her closer, and I wasn't sure I knew how to do that without breaking something. Even so, keeping my hands off her was becoming nearly impossible. I rubbed a hand over my jaw, exhaling slowly.

"I should shower first," I said, still watching her. "Did you decide if you wanted to go camel riding or not?"

She turned, a slow, suspicious smile spreading across her lips. There was something playful in her expression, something that told me she already had an answer.

"Actually," she mused, setting the table, "I was thinking we could ride quads in the Agafay."

My brow lifted. That caught me off guard. I studied her, trying to work out if this is for me or if she actually wanted it. This was the kind of thing I'd drag her into like I had with the dancing, the race at the stoplight, this trip. But her? She hesitates. Holds back. Never asks for anything. Just quietly enjoys the ride. And now—

"You want to ride quad bikes in the desert?"

Even though my voice was skeptical, she just laughed as she set down a plate.

"With you, I do, Kai-Kai." Then she kissed my cheek like it was easy. Like she didn't feel the way I went tense every time she got this close. "Go shower, please," she said, settling into her chair. "We've got a car coming to get us in an hour."

I lingered for half a second enjoying the moment. She was excited—genuinely excited. And given how rare it was for her to say what she actually wanted, I'd call that a victory. An easy smile tugged at my lips as I turned for the shower. She had no idea what she just signed up for.

HEAT SLAMMED into us the second we stepped out of the car. Thick and stifling. The kind that clung to your skin relentlessly. Sand stretched endlessly in every direction, rolling dunes bleeding into the sky, a sun-bleached haze swallowing the horizon.

Alana exhaled roughly, her eyes wide as she took it in, "Okay, this is... insane."

I grinned at her. She didn't react like this often. Didn't let herself just feel without weighing it first. But here, she did. I handed her a helmet.

"Scared yet?"

She glared, pulling the helmet over her head, "Not even a little."

Liar.

I swung my leg over my quad and turned over the engine, petrol fumes immediate as it vibrated beneath me. Alana did the same, rolling her shoulders like she was trying to steady herself, but I didn't miss the way her breath wobbled just slightly. She was thinking too much.

I gunned the throttle a bit, rolling up beside her, raising my voice just enough to make her really hear me over the engine.

"You waiting for an invitation, my love?"

Her nose wrinkled as she looked at me like she was trying to find an excuse not to do it.

"No, I'm just figuring it out."

She wants to gun it. Every inch of her body is bracing for it. But she's waiting—for permission, for reassurance.

And that's what gets in her way. Every. Fucking. Time.

Because Alana always second-guessed, talking herself out of things before she even gave herself the chance to try. It fucking killed me. Someone did this to her. Someone made her believe she can't trust herself. That she had to hold herself back. For fuck's sake, that she couldn't just enjoy herself without earning it first. I'd work that out of her. Every damn chance I got.

I exhaled, watching her.

"Yeah?" I mumble. "Figuring it out, or talking yourself out of it?"

Her grip tightened around the handlebars. She stared out at the open stretch of sand ahead, at all that space to be completely fucking free, and still, she hesitated. I leaned in slightly.

"Oi, babe—stop thinking about it. Let your body respond."

She snapped her eyes to mine, something flickering behind them. A challenge. I winked. And then I took off. She didn't even hesitate this time. A giddy smile split across her face before she twisted her wrist on the throttle, surging after me.

Good fucking girl.

She pulled ahead of me, fast, reckless in a way that made me want to completely devour her. She bounced over the dunes, her movements shifting from tense to fluid as she found her rhythm. No more overthinking. Just pure instinct and motion. Exactly what I'd hoped for.

She taunted me, standing as she cleared a dip, throwing me a look over her shoulder like she was daring me to chase her. I let her pull ahead—partly because her arse looked fucking phenomenal in those utility trousers, but mostly because I loved seeing her like this. A little reckless. Unrestrained. She'd never been more beautiful to me than in this exact moment. I let her think she won, gunning the engine just enough to push her, but holding back enough to make her feel like she earned it. I'd never tell her.

A few hours later, the sun beat down on us, dragging sweat down our backs, our bodies coated in dust. We pulled off onto a lookout point, the world stretching open beneath us, sand bleeding into the horizon like an endless golden sea. She yanked her helmet off, breathless, laughter spilling from her lips. Fucking hell, she was stunning. She pulled her hair up into a bun, taking a swig from a water bottle before handing it to me.

"See? Told you I wasn't scared."

I wiped the sweat from my jaw, taking a slow sip, eyes locked on hers.

"No, Ya Amar. You weren't. You just needed a little push."

She smiled softly, turning to the open landscape.

"This place is so damn beautiful. I'll never forget this."

Something shifted in my chest. Warms. I wouldn't forget this either. Being with her was the most alive I felt in years. But the thought that followed it was fucking suffocating. We had to go back eventually. Back to life before this. And for the first time since I could remember, the thought of leaving somewhere didn't feel like freedom. It felt like being buried alive.

I tucked the feeling away, turning my attention back to her. She'd been quiet for a few minutes now, turning something over in her head. I could see it.

"You know, Kais," she started, biting her lip slightly. "I kind of know my roots to this place. My grandfather is the only one left here, and the man's a raging alcoholic." She winced at the admission, like it made her less than the fucking blue diamond that she was. I didn't push. Just let her say what she wanted.

She exhaled. Then, she turned to me fully. "I have no interest in seeing that man, but you..." she paused, considering her words. "You have a lot unanswered for you here. Maybe you should try to find your mom's family."

It was the first time she'd said something I hadn't already been thinking about myself. I'd wondered about it before, what it would be like to meet even one person who could tell me about her. My father never did. Once she was gone, he erased her completely. Wiped her out of existence like she never fucking mattered. Then he shipped me off to the UK like he was just clearing a mess. I didn't see how finding my mother's family could be worse than that.

I held Alana's gaze as I pulled out my phone. Her brows furrowed slightly in confusion as I dialed.

"Boss?" Alanzo answered on the second ring.

"I need you to find me some information on my mum's family," I said, voice steady. "Where they are. If any of them are still alive. Whatever you can."

There was a small pause. Then— "Got it. I'll get back to you."

I hung up and found Alana watching me, her bright, fucking gorgeous smile creeping across her dimpled cheeks. Something about that look in her eyes did something to me. Without hesitating, I snapped a picture of her. My dust-covered, sun-kissed girl, smiling at me like she saw something good there.

"Hungry?" I asked, tucking my phone away.

"Starving. And I've got just the place for us."

She stretched, standing, brushing sand from her legs. Knowing her, it was probably junk food I had no business eating. But fuck it. I watched her ride back ahead of me, no helmet, her hair wild in the wind, completely unbothered. Completely her.

But that thought from earlier wouldn't leave me alone.

What happens when this is over? What happens when we leave? What happens when I don't see her every day?

And the idea of that—of waking up without her, of returning to life before her—made my chest fucking cave in.

🎵 14

The drive back to the riad was long and hot, my mind still reeling from watching Alana come alive out there. Window down, she took the landscape in, wind tangling her hair, dust streaking her cheeks, completely unbothered by the mess. She didn't think to fix it, just let me see her exactly as she was. It wasn't until we pulled up to the riad that she looked at me, a lazy, satisfied grin curling at the edges of her lips. And fuck me I'd never felt such raw need for someone.

"This is going to be a bitch to wash out," she sighed, pulling at a strand of sand-coated hair.

I huffed a laugh, pulling open my door.

"You're the one who wanted to go flying over dunes, love."

She rolled her eyes but doesn't argue. Just wiped her hands against her thighs as I opened her door.

"Well, let's clean up quickly. All the magic begins at sundown." She grinned, disappearing inside.

We emerged a short while later, mostly sand-free. Alana was wearing a short cream sundress with a slit up the thigh that did wicked things to my composure. But I tucked that away and led her back to the car.

The second we hit the crowded streets of Jemaa el-Fnaa, the shift was instant, the opposite of our day excursions. From quiet desert vastness to absolute fucking chaos. A thousand conversations happening at once, that scent of spices, roasting lamb, and fresh citrus curling through the air. Alana inhaled deeply, eyes flicking toward the marketplace with barely restrained excitement.

"You look like you're scheming, my love," I muttered, eyeing her suspiciously as she scrolled through her phone, pulling up some kind of hit list for street food.

She snorted, "Please, you're acting like I'm going to make you eat deep-fried ice cream or something."

I arched a brow.

"Are you?"

She grinned, tucking her phone away. "Guess you'll have to find out."

We moved through an ungodly amount of food stalls. She tried everything on her dodgy internet list, handing me bites of things my nutritionist would have my head for, her easy laughter made it impossible to complain. I kept her tucked at my hip to keep the vendors from harassing her. Well, that was my excuse anyway—truth was, I just liked having her there. She leaned into me just as naturally, tightening her grip on my hand as she dragged me toward another stall.

"That looks fun," she beamed, eyeing a ring toss game surrounded by giggling children and tourists.

Bloody hell. She's going to make me play this.

"Go on then, let's see what you're made of," I couldn't fight my smile as I tugged her toward it.

I looped all three rings in one go, while hers pinged off the sides. She shrugged, completely unbothered.

"Hey, well at least I mopped the floor with you on those quads." She walked back toward me, clearly proud of her afternoon victory.

I nodded toward the game.

"Try again, Ya Amar."

She hesitated for half a second—then went for it again. The first two bounced off, and she full-on belly-laughed.

Not just any laugh. Not the polite, pretty one she gives when she's being charming. Not the soft, reserved ones she gives when she's thinking too much.

A real laugh. Uninhibited. Absolutely hers. And fuck, I love it.

Seeing her *this* free, *this* unguarded, made something click in my chest. I didn't want to go back to life before this. Before her. *What the fuck am I supposed to do when we leave?* Going back to how anything was before wasn't an option.

She tossed her last ring and it landed. She turned to me like she just won the World Cup, that fucking *brilliant* smile lighting up her whole face. And I swear to God— I could feel it. The moment *it happened. When it clicked.* When something inside me shifted— locked into place, permanent and undeniable. *She doesn't even fucking know.* I smiled at her, but my mind was suddenly five steps ahead, *ten years ahead*, some fucked-up montage of waking up beside her, seeing her like this, *always like this.*

I didn't want to go back to life before this. Before her. And if the big, idiotic fucking grin on my face wasn't enough to tell me what's happening, the pounding in my fucking chest is. And there it was. The moment I realized I was in love with this girl. And worse? I didn't even panic. Because some part of me—some deep, quiet, unshakable part of me—knew from the very start it was going to be her.

"I'm going to end on a high note, I'll never be able to compete with those kids." She laughed, walking back to me.

She doesn't even know. Doesn't even fucking know.

"To be fair, those kids have a height advantage," I managed, grabbing her hand as we walk away.

She giggled, still riding the high, then suddenly lit up. "Ooo, hey—I wanna stop at this booth before we head back. One sec."

She was off in an instant, disappearing into the crowd. I lingered near a nearby stand where an older woman, wrapped in deep indigo fabric, was sitting behind a wooden stall stacked high with scarves. Most were too gaudy, too bright, but one—one was perfect. Royal blue. Deep, endless, the exact shade of the ocean before it breaks into foam. The blue she'd told me was her favorite. Forget-me-nots were stitched in delicate threads along the border.

I reached for it, brushing my fingers over the embroidery. The fabric was soft, lightweight enough to drape easily but woven strong enough to last. The woman behind the stall smiled knowingly, her eyes flicking past me toward Alana, still completely unaware of what I was doing.

"For your wife?" she asked in Arabic.

As I traced the embroidery, my chest tightened. *Wife.* I could correct her. I could shake my head, let the word pass without catching. But the thing was—it didn't feel like a mistake. It didn't feel wrong. It felt... like something I could hold onto.

Instead, I nodded, slipping a few folded bills into her waiting palm. No haggling. Alana turned, scanning the crowd for me, and I was already tucking the scarf into my bag. I knew exactly when she would need it; I wouldn't show her before she did.

When she finally caught my gaze, she grinned—*too wide*—crossing the crowd with something tucked under her arm.

"You bought something," I said suspiciously, eyeing the glossy paper roll.

"I did," she grinned, unrolling it painstakingly slow like she was savoring the moment.

"That better not be what I think it is." My voice was flat, but she was already *beaming*. I already knew before I saw it. And sure enough—

My own face stared back at me. Sweaty. Glowering. Mid-fight, fists raised, the overhead lights cutting shadows against my jaw. A fucking fight poster. *Of me.*

"What? You don't think my living room was missing *true art*?" she teased, rolling it back up before I could snatch it. "Jazzy will absolutely love it."

"You're mad," I muttered, rubbing a hand down my face. "Truly, certifiably mad."

She tilted her head, all fake consideration.

"Should I get it framed or just pin it *straight to the ceiling above my bed*? Decisions, decisions."

She twirled away from me and into the car before I could grab it. *Brilliant. I'm in love with an absolute menace.*

WE RODE SLEEPILY BACK to the riad. The teasing from earlier was still hanging between us, but a heavier mood had settled in, too. She was tucked into my side, scrolling through her camera roll, occasionally flashing me glimpses of our day. A blurred shot of me at the food stalls. The two of us in the desert. A photo she snuck while I was distracted. Every time she leaned in just a little, I felt it. The warmth of her skin. The press of her thigh against mine. I tapped my fingers against my knee, resisting the urge to touch her, not trusting that I wouldn't completely black out and tear her out of that goddamn dress.

We pulled up to the riad, and Alana stretched, yawning softly.

"I need a cold shower," she muttered, pulling at the front of her dress like it was clinging to her skin.

Yeah. That makes two of us.

We stepped into the cool, quiet courtyard, and the contrast from the bustling market was instant. No shouting vendors. No ringing laughter. Just running water from the stone fountain in the center, the scent of orange blossoms drifting through the warm air.

She sighed, rolling her shoulders back, her muscles still loose from the adrenaline of earlier. I watched her as she walked toward the fountain, dipping her hands into the water and pressing them to the sides of her throat, as if her pulse were still racing beneath her fingertips. *Or maybe it's my pulse that's fucking racing.*

"You alright, my love?" I managed, my mouth suddenly dry.

She turned slightly, her eyes shining in the dim light.

"Yeah," she breathed, "just... today was perfect." She tilted her head back, letting the water drip down her collarbones, and I had to physically bite down on the inside of my cheek to keep myself from reacting.

I should walk away. I should tell her to shower, to rest, to keep this easy.

But then she smiled—like she knew exactly what she was doing, like she felt this *too*—and I was gone. I closed the distance between us in a few short strides, fingers finding her waist, pinning her gently against the stone edge of the fountain. She sucked in a breath but didn't pull away. She never fucking pulled away.

"*Kai—*"

I cut her off with my mouth. It was slow at first: deep, careful, a question instead of a demand. But when she gripped my hip, angling herself to press deeper, something inside me fucking snapped. I scooped her into my arms, her legs wrapped around my waist, my hands slid beneath the hem of her dress. *Soft. Warm. So fucking perfect.*

She gasped into my mouth, and my grip tightened. I walked until her back met the wall. *I can't stop. I don't want to stop.* But then she shifted, unbuttoning my shirt and pushing it down my arms, pressing into me so fucking sweetly, and something about it was so open, so trusting, that I suddenly needed her to *say it*. To say she *knew* what this was. To say she *wanted* it. Because *I knew*. I knew exactly what this meant for me.

I slowed the kiss, breaking away just enough to rest my forehead against hers, our breathing heavy, tangled. Her arms tightened around my neck. I dragged my thumb over her bottom lip, searching her eyes.

"Why?" I asked quietly.

Her brow furrowed slightly, her breath catching. I watched the way her throat bobbed, the way her body leaned into mine, like she was answering me without words. But then she whispered—

"Don't you want to?"

And fuck me, I hated it. Because the way she said it: it was like she was asking if this was what she was *supposed* to do. Not what she *wanted*. Like some part of her still thought she had to earn this. Like some part of her still didn't fucking know she already belonged to me.

I exhaled slowly, tightening my hold on her for just a second before I pulled back. Not much. Just enough to make her look at me, really look at me. Her eyes were wide, lips parted, cheeks flushed, and fuck, *I wanted her*. I wanted her so fucking badly. But not like this. *Not until she knows exactly what she's asking for.* I brushed my nose against hers, easing her feet back to the ground.

"Not like this," I rasped.

She stiffened slightly; her expression dropped like she did something wrong, like she couldn't see I was holding on by a fucking thread.

"I'm not stopping because I don't want you, *Ya Amar*. I'm stopping because when this happens, I want you to be fucking sure," I paused, letting it sink in, "like you can't fucking breathe without me."

Her breath was shaky, but she didn't argue. Just pressed her forehead to my shoulder, exhaling slowly, as if she were trying to pull herself together. I brushed a kiss to her temple, lingering for a second longer than I should.

"Come on, my love," I rasped, my voice tight with restraint. "Let's get you inside."

Her fingers lingered on my wrist for a second—like she was trying to hold onto the moment, like she was debating whether she wanted to push me further. But then, finally, she nodded. I laced my fingers through hers, leading her back into the riad. And fuck — *I'm the one who needs the cold shower.*

Alana

-12-

♫ 15

I'd never wanted a man the way I wanted Kais. Never burned like this before. The man had done nothing more than kiss me, and still my body contorted toward him like it was under some kind of spell. And he knew it. I could see it in his eyes every time I so much as twitched.

So tonight, when he had me pinned to the wall—when I could feel the steady throb of him between my legs, pressing into me like his body needed mine to live—I thought we'd finally give in. But he didn't. Instead, he muttered the most impossibly ruinous words anyone's ever said to me in a moment like that: *"I want you to be sure... like you can't breathe without me."*

Shit.

How the hell was I supposed to respond to that? He didn't even give me a chance before ushering me off to the shower like I was being sent to time-out. So now here I am. In bed. Wet hair, silk teddy, and a face glazed in skincare, pouting while he showers... without me. Should be a crime, really. I mean, the man whisked me halfway across the world. I kind of expected there'd be some hot sex involved. I was prepared for it: waxed, trimmed. *A waste.*

The shower water pattered on like rain, and I needed something—anything—to distract me from the throbbing between my thighs. So, for the first time since we got here, I connected my phone to the WiFi. I'd actually loved the peace of not having an international SIM. The radio silence. No constant buzzing, no pressure to check in. I'd only been using my phone as a camera, soaking up every second with him.

Even when he was glued to his laptop or phone (conquering whatever rival hedge fund overlord he was currently outmaneuvering) I still wasn't tempted. I could watch him for hours. I could live off the quiet thrill of him just brushing past me. But I needed the distraction tonight. So, I tapped in my passcode, and my notifications rolled in like a tsunami.

A few emails from law schools—Stanford, Yale, and Berkeley pushing for enrollment decisions, Oxford keeping me posted on their waitlist status. All dream schools I only applied to so I could prove a point. To my mom. To myself. To everyone who looked at me like I was an idiot for saying I wanted to be a lawyer. I got in. But getting in didn't mean I could go. They were all too fucking expensive. And while my grades held up, working as much as I had didn't leave much time for the kind of résumé scholarships looked for.

I swiped the messages away with a sigh and refreshed my inbox, hoping for an update from Macy. Nothing. So, I sent a quick email to Jasmine and Penelope instead, attaching some pictures to let them know I was alive. Judging by the look on my face in every single one, I looked really freaking happy. So did Kais.

One picture stopped me cold. It was from the dunes. Me leaning into him, sand dusted across our skin, both of us grinning like idiots. His smile wasn't his usual smirk. It was crooked in the corner, unguarded, the kind you can't fake even if you try.

The kind that sneaks up on you when you're perfectly happy and don't realize the camera's out.

The shower turned off just as I hit send. I powered my phone down and tucked it away just after that soft little *whoosh* of confirmation. Kais stepped out of the bathroom like a sin I was about to commit. His body was a study in control: ripped, towering, glistening with leftover steam. Moving across the room, towel hanging low on his hips, water tracking the carved ridges of his chest, down to the deep cut of his abs. He raked a hand through his damp hair, leaving it messy and unfairly hot. I bit my bottom lip just to keep from moaning.

He moved with unbothered ease to the dresser drawer, entirely aware I was watching him like prey. My eyes dragged lower, locked on the towel and silently begging it to slip. He must've felt it—felt how desperate I was—because he glanced over his shoulder, caught me staring, and smirked like he'd just won a bet.

"What are you doing?" He sounded wickedly amused.

"Just enjoying the show." I didn't even try to sound innocent.

He dropped the towel with a devious smirk. And holy hell. Taking his sweet time, he stepped into his boxers like he was putting on a show, enjoying every second of my obvious staring as he gave me a perfect, maddening view of the sculpted lines of his ass. Turns out, I was absolutely the kind of girl who got turned on by a man's ass.

He climbed into bed beside me, the mattress dipping under his weight as he wrapped one arm around my waist, resting his head on the flat of my belly.

"I like this," he rasped, his fingers toying with the lace hem of my teddy.

"You should," I said, combing my fingers through his damp hair. "You bought it."

A grin tugged at my lips.

"Though I don't know what you're going to do with it once

I'm done borrowing it. No way it's fitting over those massive shoulders."

A deep chuckle rumbled in his chest, the sound vibrating straight through his body and into mine—settling low in my belly, lighting up every nerve along the way. His mouth was dangerously close to where I ached the most, and every breath he took felt like a threat I desperately wanted him to make good on.

His hand slid down my inner thigh, long fingers splaying against my skin, warm and steady. Goosebumps flared up my legs, a shiver crawling beneath my ribs as he gripped me just hard enough to remind me how much he was holding back.

"*Ya Amar*," he murmured, his lips grazing the curve of my hip.

"Yes, *Kai-Kai*?" I breathed, not trusting myself with anything more.

"I'll never give you anything I don't want you to keep."

That simple promise stopped me cold. My whole body stilled, breath caught somewhere between a sigh and a sob.

His words cracked something inside me, something I'd kept buried beneath layers of learned caution. Because I'd never been given anything without a cost before. Every gift from my stepfather came with an invisible price tag. Every sweet moment with my mom came tied to a lie or a secret I had to carry. Every 'I love you' from my ex? A manipulation. A way to keep me close while he pulled away.

There were always strings. Always conditions. But Kais... Kais made it feel like maybe I didn't have to earn love just by surviving it. Like maybe being me— *just me*—was enough. And that did something to me. But more than I wanted to sit with that, more than I wanted to unpack what it might mean, I needed answers. I needed him to say something that made this ache make sense.

"Is that why you don't want to touch me?" I asked, the words slipping out on instinct. "Because you don't want me to keep you?"

He sat up fully facing me. His expression shifted, like I'd just punched the breath out of him.

"Alana," he said, almost stunned. "I told you I don't pull away because I don't want you. I pull away because I want *everything*. And I'm not going to take a single fucking thing from you until you do too."

I huffed a humorless laugh.

"Kai, come on," I said, pushing myself up by my palms to sit up fully.

"What the hell do I have to offer you? I come from nothing. I quite literally have *nothing*. I'm a waitress, who barely scraped by to get into law school because I have to work every waking second I have so my mother— who just in case you forgot is an *addict* — doesn't end up on the streets. What is there to gain from that? I'm not the one you keep *Kai*, I'm the one you take a pretty picture with and toss back."

The words tasted bitter and insecure as they left my mouth, but no less true.

For a moment, Kais didn't speak. Didn't move. Just sat there, jaw tight, those deep brown eyes boring into me like I'd said something unforgivable. Then, without a word, his gaze flicked between my mouth and my eyes. And in the next breath, he pulled me into his lap. I barely had time to gasp before his mouth crashed into mine, stealing my breath completely.

He kissed me like he could devour every last insecure word I'd just spewed. Like erasing them from my lips would somehow erase them from my memory too. His large hands cradled the sides of my face with impossible gentleness—hands built for destruction choosing tenderness instead. I moaned into his mouth as his tongue tangled with mine, my whole body aching like it had been parched for years and only he could quench it.

My thighs tightened around his waist. I rocked against him, desperate for friction, grinding into the hard, growing heat of him only covered by the thin cotton of his underwear beneath me.

I could feel him—thick and swelling—and I pressed closer, shameless and pulsing against him. A groan rumbled up from his chest. He caught my bottom lip between his teeth, then let it go with a soft snap, dragging his mouth down my jawline until it found the curve of my neck.

"*Ya Amar*," he whispered, the words kissing my skin. Then something new—words I didn't know but felt in my bones. "*Mein Herz.*" He kissed the hollow of my collarbone as he said it.

I closed my eyes, baring my throat, drinking in every brush of his lips like it was scripture. He dragged his teeth softly up the centerline of my throat. Then he curled his fingers in my hair and tugged my head to the side, exposing more skin to his mouth. He nipped me, just enough to make me gasp. Then he went deadly still, his words coming out like a threat.

"Don't *ever* say that shit again."

The protectiveness in his voice sent a chill down my spine. And a pulse straight between my thighs.

"*Kai*"

I started to argue, but he cut me off, his mouth sealing mine, harder this time. When he pulled back, it was only far enough to make me look at him. His eyes were dark, steely. There wasn't a flicker of doubt in them.

"You think I'd cross oceans for you," he rasped, "change the fucking shape of my life for you... if you were temporary?"

I didn't answer.

Because I didn't know how. Because deep down I *knew* he wouldn't. Knew he wasn't a man who wasted time or breath. That he dedicated himself fully to the things he deemed important in his life. Knew the way he made space for me in the quiet, how he laid everything down without ever calling attention to it —*for me.*

Whether it was to ride around the desert or just sit and have tea with me. But the kind of doubt I've carried since childhood has teeth. And even when it doesn't make sense, it still sinks in.

So instead of saying what I wanted, what I *knew*, I said what that old voice inside me still believed:

"I have no fucking clue, Kais. You won't even touch me."

He blinked once, then without breaking eye contact, he slid his hand from my ass under the hem of my nightgown and between my thighs. Hovered his fingers just over the lace of my panties.

"You want me to touch you, *Ya Amar*?"

I couldn't lie. I rocked against his hand, grinding him against the ache he wasn't yet soothing.

"I need you to, Kai," I breathed.

Still moving. Still desperate. The friction was delicious and teasing, but not nearly enough. His head dropped, a low, broken groan slipping from him. I couldn't tell if it was German or just heat and restraint tangled into something primal.

"Fuck, you make me want to lose every bit of my resolve."

My heart thrashed as I pulled myself flush against his chest, arms looping around his neck. I whispered into his ear. "If I'm what you say I am... lose it. For me. Just a little."

He sucked in a breath. Then he moved.

There was no warning. No tease. Just a sudden, brutal shift, my panties tugged aside in one smooth motion before two fingers thrust deep and harsh inside me. I cried out, my body clenching tight around him, hips jolting as the burning sensation slammed into me all at once.

"Oh god," I gasped, the word breaking apart on a shudder.

It wasn't soft, wasn't gentle. But god if it wasn't everything I hoped I'd get from him. His thumb found me, dragging slow, torturous circles over my swollen flesh. My hips moved on instinct, grinding into him, chasing more. His name caught in my throat. I couldn't breathe, couldn't *think*, not with the way he worked me, like he already knew how to unravel every last part of me. He pulled his mouth to my ear, his voice ragged and close to breaking.

"*Fuck*, I want to be inside you," he growled, each word seething with need.

"Then take it, Kai," I moaned, locking eyes with him, daring him.

He froze for a heartbeat, fighting every instinct in his body, before crushing his mouth to mine. His thumb didn't stop. If anything, it moved faster, tighter, dragging me toward the edge with ruthless precision. He added another finger, the sensation stealing my breath. Aching, full and insanely euphoric.

"I'll take every fucking piece of you, Alana," he gritted against my lips, "but only when you're ready to *keep* me." God. That voice. That *command*. That offer wrapped in demand. I was already gone.

"Kai, I—"

The rest of the sentence shattered in my throat as my body broke apart violently over his hand. I cried out, sobbed his name, clutching at his back as pleasure tore through me, leaving me trembling and breathless.

He stayed with me through it all, his fingers steady, his mouth soft against my neck like he was mooring me through a storm. My body slackened, every muscle heavy, spent like I'd run until there was nothing left. Kais kissed my shoulder, then my jaw, his touch shifting from punishing to devout as he laid me on my back.

Then, without a word, he rose and disappeared into the bathroom. When he returned, he sat beside me, quiet and composed, a warm washcloth in his hand. He peeled my panties down again with care, parted my legs, and wiped me clean with slow, steady strokes over skin still sensitive and tingling. I flinched softly, his other hand soothing over my thigh, reading my hesitation and answering it with patience.

"You weren't meant to be kept by anyone else. Only me," he said quietly, pulling the nightgown back down over my hips.

My chest tightened with something dangerously close to hope. I'd never wanted anything to be more true. But saying that out loud felt like I might jinx it.

He tossed the cloth into the hamper, then climbed into bed

behind me, gathering me against him like I belonged there. Like I always had. One arm slid beneath my pillow, the other stretched across my waist, his hand settling between my thighs.

"Now go to sleep," he muttered against my hair. "Before I decide I'm never letting you out of this bed again."

I wanted to take him up on that. But also, to tell him everything my heart was ready to spill, how deeply he'd already been kept. But his body was too perfect against mine, too warm, too steady. And my eyes were too heavy. Sleep stole me before I could say a word.

♫ 22

"KAIS, IT'S BEEN TWO WEEKS. WILL I EVER GET A morning where I wake up with you undressed and still in bed with me?" I groaned, blinking awake to find him standing beside the bed, fully dressed, of course.

He chuckled. "You'll have to stop sleeping in to experience that, my love."

I grabbed a pillow and muffled a dramatic protest into it.

His warm fingers found the edge of my robe, tugging it open just enough for his lips to press slow, soft kisses along my collarbone.

I whimpered. "Kai, unless you're planning on getting in this bed and *finally* putting me out of my misery, I suggest you stop."

His breath caught slightly before a quiet laugh escaped him.

"I'd take you up on that if we didn't need to leave, *Ya Amar*."

I sighed, flipping onto my stomach to escape his teasing. "Give me five minutes and a cold shower." My voice was muffled against the pillow.

I've thrown myself at this man in every way I know how and he still won't budge, even though it's clear he wants to and even more clear that I'm nearly begging for it.

A shower and a few minutes later, I found Kais at the front door in his blue gandoura from the souks, white pants, and red suede loafers. His hair was pushed back with some band that disappeared into the dark strands. Unfairly handsome. The kind that made my simple sea-foam maxi dress pale in comparison.

"Stunner," he muttered, ushering me out the door by the small of my back.

The compliment sounded nice rolling off of his tongue. The man talked to me like I personally hung the stars. And it did all kinds of crazy things to my confidence. I don't know what he wants from me to get him to take his pants off but I'll do just about anything at this point. Including getting in a car with the sketchiest looking man I've ever seen.

A small off-white car idled outside the riad, its aged exterior dusted with the desert's golden residue. The man in question is our driver, toothless and grinning wildly at us as we approached, nodding in greeting.

Kais spoke to him in Arabic, then opened the back door, gesturing for me to slide inside. He took the front passenger seat— not that he had much of a choice. There was no way his long legs would fit comfortably in the back of this tiny car with me.

I muttered a little prayer to myself before the car jerked forward violently, weaving into traffic with a kind of reckless ease that had my stomach lurching. Like I said, sketchy as hell, like might not survive the ride sketchy. Kais' jaw ticked, his fingers tapping his knee before he muttered something low to the driver in Arabic.

Whatever he said must have worked. The driver let out a good-natured chuckle before adjusting his grip on the wheel, easing into a steadier pace. I sighed in relief to myself. The quiet power of this man turned me on more and more every day. Though that doesn't matter much at the moment. He's not touching me again until I can't breathe without him. Whatever that means. Cruel little riddle.

A few minutes into the ride, Kais glanced back at me like he was weighing something before reaching into his bag.

"Here, my love," his voice softened as he reached back, passing me a royal blue scarf. The fabric intricately embroidered with tiny stems that looked like forget-me-nots.

It was a complete joke for me to think I could come on this trip and not fall in love with him. He never stops taking care of me. I turned it over in my hands, brushing my fingers over the delicate stitching.

"This is beautiful, Kai. What do you want me to do with it?"

He twisted slightly in his seat, his gaze locking onto mine. "You may need it later to block the sun, but for now, I want you to cover your hair. The part of town we're going to doesn't usually see tourists, and for today..." his grin deepened. "You're my wife. Yeah?"

A thrill shot up my spine at the way he said it with no effort. Almost as if he likes the sound of it.

I swallowed, nodding. "Got it."

My agreement came mostly because he seemed so serious about it, but honestly, pretending to be Mrs. Reinhardt didn't sound half bad.

The ride was bumpy but beautiful. The bustling city faded into the distance, giving way to a quieter stretch of low-rise, sunbaked buildings. We passed an electric blue villa hidden in lush greenery, then a sleek, oasis-like resort with palm-lined courtyards. Kais didn't react to any of it. Even though places like that were usually his scene, his gaze remained distant, locked on the shifting landscape outside the window.

The further we drove, the more sparse the buildings became. The wide roads were now bordered by groves of towering date palms and open stretches of desert-dusted land. The occasional donkey-pulled cart passed by, children kicking up dust as they played soccer on the roadside.

Kais' fingers drummed against his knee, his jaw tight. He wasn't his usual, assured self. For the first time since I'd met him, uncertainty flickered beneath his carefully composed surface. Not that I expected him to always be composed, but the thought of him being upset or hurt physically made me nauseous. I reached up, placing my hand on his shoulder, giving it a gentle squeeze, my thumb tracing slow lines. He let out a quiet breath through his nose, then—without looking at me—pressed his cheek to my hand, his lips grazing my fingers in a fleeting kiss.

It was little things like these that were the most dangerous to my heart. Despite his words last night, however beautiful, that annoying voice still creeps into my head and tells me I'm not enough to be loved by someone like him, that nothing real could ever feel this good. But then he does something gentle that quiets it again.

The taxi slowed in front of a large, terracotta-colored apartment complex, its warm, earthy walls blending into the landscape. Wooden shutters framed an arched entryway, leading up a short flight of sun-worn stairs. Kais exchanged a few words with the driver, handed him a few dirhams, then stepped out, opening my door. The taxi pulled off, leaving only silence and the settling dust behind. His shoulders were tense and his expression still in a way that made it all feel heavy and not at all like the fun filled excursions we'd been spending our days doing.

I followed Kais' gaze up the length of the building.

"What is this place?" I asked softly.

He shielded his eyes from the sun, studying the top-floor apartments.

"The gaff my mum's sister lives in," he replied.

Shit. Suddenly everything made sense. This was huge for him and the fact that he brought me along means a whole lot more than I can analyze at this moment. I just know I need to be here for him however this plays out. I gathered my thoughts and tried to speak in a calm tone.

"Do you know which one?"

He let out an unsteady breath, then nodded toward a blue-painted door at the top of the stairs. "That one, I think."

I hesitated. He was clearly nervous, which wasn't like him at all (that was more my thing). *How can I channel Kais in this situation, unmovable, steady, safe?* The way he always makes me feel protected. I could certainly swallow my fear and help him.

"Do you want me to knock? She might feel weird answering the door for a man she doesn't know," I offered quietly.

Kais' brows pulled together slightly—like he hadn't considered that. After a pause, he nodded.

"Yeah, you knock. But I'm going with you."

Good. Right, I've got this, I can be his Kais for once. We climbed the stairs, his palm warm and steady against the small of my back. We stood for a moment in front of the door secured by a single iron latch. I raised my fist to knock, glancing at him first.

"Ready?"

He swallowed. Then, a single pointed nod. I knocked. Once. Then again.

Nothing.

Kais' mouth twisted slightly, worry creasing his brow. Watching him struggle was killing me a little bit every second, especially since I'd been the one to push for this visit. Just as I raised my hand for a third knock, a neighboring door creaked open.

An elderly man with deep-set wrinkles and a neatly trimmed beard stepped out, his eyes flicking between us before saying something in a blend of French and Arabic. Kais spoke back, his voice softer than usual. I only caught one word: Fatima.

The man shook his head. Kais stilled. His jaw clenched, his Adam's apple shifting slightly as he swallowed. I could tell by the light dimming in his eyes whatever it was wasn't great. They spoke back and forth for a few moments before the man gestured for us to follow him inside. Kais' reached for my hand, his grip was tight like he needed me to steady *him*.

The apartment's interior was simple and dimly lit, with cushions arranged on the floor and a lone window filtering in the warm afternoon light. A prayer mat rested near the corner, its fabric well-worn from years of devotion. The old man and Kais continued their quiet conversation. I couldn't read Kais' expression, but something in his posture made my stomach tighten.

The man motioned for me to sit. I happily obliged. If I was going to be here the best thing I could do was not be in the way. A small gray kitten rubbed against my ankle bracelet, its soft fur tickling my skin. I smiled, scratching behind its ears as Kais disappeared into another room with the man. He returned only a minute later, a small cardboard box in his hands. The man spoke gently now, gesturing toward the box, his voice edged with something—*sympathy? Regret?* Kais, however, was silent. My pulse picked up as I watched him.

He lowered himself onto the cushion beside me, flipping open the box. Inside were a few pieces of clothing, some jewelry, a worn leather journal, and a thick photo album. As Kais lifted the album, the old man poured two cups of tea, settling onto a cushion beside us. I watched as Kais carefully opened the book, his thumb grazing the edge of the pages.

The man leaned in, pointing at different photos as he spoke softly to Kais, offering small explanations that I couldn't understand. Kais listened, his lips parting slightly in surprise at one photo, his jaw setting at another. Suddenly, he froze.

A photo of a woman filled the page: his eyes, his beauty mark, his features staring back at him, her arm wrapped around a small boy, his head resting against her shoulder. He stared at it for a long time, his breathing deep and uneven despite his obvious attempt at composure. Slowly, he removed the picture from the sleeve, flipping it over. There, in neat, elegant script, was a message in French. At the bottom, one part stood out.

Kais, 4.

A tear dropped onto his cheek. He swiped it away before it could fully fall. Tears instantly pricked mine at the sight of him, this safe house of a man forcing down that kind of hurt. I didn't say anything, just swallowed the dry lump in my throat and tried really, really hard to distract myself by petting the kitten. *What could I say? 'I'm sorry'?*

I just let him have his moment rubbing my hand on his back for just a second to let him know I was here. He handed the picture to me without a word, just quietly watched me as I studied it, memorized it. Kais' long untamed black wavy hair, his chubby dimpled smile, how beautiful his mom was, the familiar warmth in her eyes that's been passed down to Kais. My heart ached for him. He needed answers needed to feel like he belonged, like he had family. All he got was a dusty box and a single forgotten picture. Such a beautiful little boy with a mountain of pain in front of him.

I handed it back with trembling fingers, wiping a tear before it could fall. Then quietly returned my focus to the kitten, like I wasn't falling apart inside.

The old man, now quiet, reached forward, pouring more tea into Kais' untouched cup. He muttered something to Kais, then looked at me, speaking again. I shook my head politely, confused. Kais finally exhaled, the tension in his jaw relaxing slightly.

"He's asking if you'd like to keep the cat," he muttered. "Says it's a stray."

I huffed a quiet laugh, blinking away my tears, looking down at the kitten now purring against my leg.

"I can't do that," I whispered, "even if I kind of want to."

Kais' eyes raked over mine as if he noted their glassiness, he smiled warmly, his gaze softened more than it had been all afternoon.

"I know. Just nod and thank him anyway."

I did as he asked. Kais said a final goodbye, clasping the man's hand before leading me toward the door. As we stepped out into the cooling afternoon air, he exhaled deeply. His fingers laced with mine, but his grip was looser. Not at peace. But lighter. I squeezed his hand. He squeezed back. The realization that I'd do anything for this man made a home in my mind at that moment and it terrified me.

The sun hung low in the sky, casting a warm hue over the rippling orange sand. We made our way down the steps where a doorless white Jeep idled at the curb. Kais held my hand firmly until I hopped into the backseat. The driver, a young man dressed cleanly in dark frames and linen, nodded in acknowledgment before shifting the vehicle into gear. Kais handed me the cardboard box the man had given him; he seemed distant. His fingers gripped the handle above the door, his gaze fixed out at the open road.

The breeze whipped my scarf loose as the mud brick buildings and swaying palm groves blurred past. The driver barely slowed, careening through the desert roads like we were being chased by the wind itself. I clutched onto the seat for balance. Kais, of course, looked entirely unfazed. One arm resting against the open frame, hair tousled by the wind like he was in some damn cologne ad. Even when he was sad, *he was breathtaking.*

A resort entrance unfolded before us. A decadent retreat hidden within the dunes. The jeep came to a stop just in front of carved wooden arches that framed an endless path lined with palm trees and glowing jewel-colored lanterns.

As we stepped out of the car, the low trickle of a fountain and the scent of orange blossoms and sweet, spiced wood smoke greeted us. Kais' hand found mine as we walked, passing through lush gardens and private villas before finally reaching the edge of the desert.

"Do I need to put this back on?" I asked, holding up my scarf.

He shook his head, "No, *Ya Amar.* I wasn't sure what we'd walk into back there, I wanted to be respectful and keep you safe."

There was something sacred about him saying that out loud—like even after everything, he still thought about me first. Every fiber in me wanted to know what happened back there, to somehow make it better for him, let him know he isn't alone. But I wanted him to tell me on his own, not like how things had been in my past, pushing my way into people's lives. He needed to let me in.

Ahead of us, a line of richly woven Berber rugs stretched across the sand, leading to a secluded candlelit cabana. A low wooden table sat at its center, colorful cushions tucked beneath it, the desert stretching endlessly around us, the sky deepening into a wash of indigo and lavender. Even knowing the day he had ahead of him somehow, he did this.

God, the woman that gets to marry this man is so damn lucky. But for now, I get to be here and I tell myself that's enough.

I squeezed Kais' hand. "Did you plan this?"

His lips tilted in a small smile, though his eyes were still shadowed.

"Consider it payback for last night," he replied, releasing my hand with a kiss.

I took my seat, sinking into the cushions, and let the night fold around us. An indulgent spread of food appeared before us in a matter of minutes, including tagines, fresh-baked bread, and golden honey, but Kais barely touched his plate. He was quiet. Not in a closed-off way, but in a gathering-his-thoughts way. I didn't push. I simply sipped my tea and let the weight of the moment breathe between us, stealing glances at him as much as I could because I was still aware of the fact that the end of all this was coming sooner than later. And I wanted to remember every second of what it felt like to be with him, to be seen by him.

After a while, he moved closer, resting his head in my lap like he had every night. His dark eyes met mine, searching, hesitant. I was completely wrecked by him every time he touches me but when he looked at me like this, I wished I could freeze us in time. I ran my fingers through his hair. I could sense he wanted to say something, so I waited.

"Thank you for being there for me today." His voice was soft.

I smiled, leaning down to press a slow, lingering kiss between his brows, smoothing the tension that had lived there all day.

"I'm grateful that you let me."

He exhaled deeply, then he opened up.

"Apparently, Fatima died a few years back. That man was her neighbor for twenty years."

His voice was even, but I felt the ache beneath it. I continued stroking his hair, steadying him. He leaned into it like it did just as much for him as it did for me.

"He told me a lot about my mum's sister, but... there was that picture of my mum and me that I've never seen." He swallowed hard, his Adam's apple bobbing.

"She must've sent it to her just before she passed. Her sister seemed really into poetry like my mum. She wrote a ton of poems in that journal. My mum wrote *Clair de Lune* on the back of that picture."

His eyes flickered, searching mine, as if waiting to see if I knew it. I didn't. But I could tell it meant something to him. He sighed, his eyes still flicking between mine like there was more he needed to say but couldn't. Then he reached for the nape of my neck, his fingers pressing there, drawing me down into a slow, achingly tender kiss. There was a weight to it, something I couldn't put into words, something I couldn't quite explain. It sent chills all over my body and set an ache into my heart. He pulled back.

"Can we get out of here?" His voice was soft against my lips, but there was something wanting beneath it.

I pulled back slightly, searching his face.

"Yeah... are you tired?"

He shook his head, his fingers tracing lazy circles at the nape of my neck.

"No." He breathed, "I mean... out of Morocco."

My heart stopped.

"Right... yeah," I drawled. "I guess we've been here a while."

I knew this was coming, the return to normal life, but everything before him seemed colorless now. I wanted to tell him that, but saying it would make losing him hurt even more.

His lashes flickered slightly before he looked at me again, his gaze unguarded. "Somewhere else. Just for us. No distractions of the past."

And just like that, the air shifted.

The ache in my chest unraveled into something warm, almost dizzying. He wasn't pulling away. He was pulling me closer. The way he said it—like he needed more time just as much as I did—made something in me break loose. I smiled softly, threading my fingers into his hair.

"Whatever you want, Kai Kai."

And for the first time all day, he really smiled. "Mallorca," he said firmly, and in no time we were in the navy-blue jet again.

Alana

-14-

♫ 17

THE PLANE TOUCHED DOWN SMOOTHLY, SKIMMING across the tarmac as the morning sun stretched glittering ripples over the vibrant blue waters of Mallorca. Smooth notes of Ella Fitzgerald and Louis Armstrong flitted through my headphones, the perfect soundtrack for a picturesque landing, but it did nothing for the familiar ache in my chest.

A similar ache had taken up residence in me once, years ago for a guy who wasn't a single percent of who Kais is. Only this feels bigger, enormous. Like I might actually understand what Kais meant when he said *I want you to be sure... like you can't breathe without me.* Now... I think I get it.

That terrifying, bottomless kind of wanting. I've tried to push it away, but it resurfaces every time he speaks, every time I catch his eyes, every time I watch him sleep. I ache for him like I'm yearning to go home but he's the door.

A light tap on my knee pulled me from my trance. I turned to find Kais watching me, his square tortoiseshell shades slipping slightly down his nose. How is he so gorgeous every waking minute? I pulled out an earbud.

"Time to put on one of those bikinis, my love."

I scoffed softly but couldn't fight the smile tugging at my lips. He'd spent most of the flight working, brow furrowed in quiet focus, but now he seemed effortlessly relaxed. His hair pushed back in a ball cap, cream crochet shirt hanging completely unbuttoned over his sun-kissed skin, deep blue swim shorts resting low on his hips, white sneakers completing the look. A living, breathing vacation ad.

"I guess it is," I yawned, stretching before heading to the bathroom to change. Trying to shake away the thoughts wreaking havoc in my mind.

I slipped into a bright orange bikini, the color popping perfectly against my fresh Morocco tan, then layered it with a colorful crochet maxi dress. Its cowl neckline draped just right, shimmering with delicate threads of silver. I completed the look with white leather sandals I'd picked up in Marrakech. There was no way this outfit wouldn't at least score me a farewell make-out.

When I stepped off the plane, the first thing I saw was Kais leaning against a candy-red Porsche convertible. Golden skin, devil-may-care grin, wind already teasing at his unbuttoned shirt. His lips quirked into a ruinous smile as his gaze roved over me.

Why I put myself in danger of such impending heartbreak, I'd never know. For now I chose to savor the moment I had with him, drinking in every last bit of it before he went back to his life and I went back to mine.

"Buckle up, beautiful," he said as I slid into the passenger seat.

In an instant, we were off. The warm wind moved through my hair as Mallorca stretched wide and endless before us. Kais whipped through the scenic, winding roads with his usual control and ease, his expert hands shifting gears as we climbed higher along the cliffs. His playful smile hadn't faded since we landed. Just the look I love most on him. I lifted my phone and snapped a picture in the way he does to me, capturing him in that exact way. *At least I'd have this.*

"Saving memories again?" he shouted over the wind.

To which I replied teasingly, "Any chance I get, my love."

The Porsche coasted to a smooth stop at a small marina, the scent of salt and sun-warmed teak drifting through the air.

Yachts of every shape and size bobbed gently along the docks, their white hulls gleaming under the mid-morning light. But Kais bypassed them all, leading me toward a sleek mahogany boat, its rich wood polished to a honey-like shine, chrome detailing flashing in the sun. Buttery cream leather seats curved around a small built-in bar, with a navy canvas canopy tucked behind the cockpit.

I dragged my fingers over the glossy wood, admiring the crafts-manship. "This is yours?"

"One of," Kais said, smirking as he adjusted his sunglasses and tossed his bag onto the seat.

I narrowed my eyes, but before I could press further, I stopped myself. He'd brought us to Mallorca to get away from everything complicated, to just be together without distractions. The clock was already ticking on our time together. I wasn't going to spend what might be our last perfect day picking apart the mechanics of his world.

He stepped aside, offering me a hand onto the boat. "Shall we?"

I let him guide me aboard and settled onto one of the cush-ioned seats. A wicker picnic basket caught my eye, tucked into the side compartment with a bottle of chilled rosé in a small ice bucket beside it.

I glanced at Kais. "Is that lunch?"

He slid behind the wheel, hand already finding the throttle. "I figured we'd make a day of it," he said, flashing me a sideways glance. "Unless you'd rather rush back to land?"

I shook my head, stretching my legs out lazily. "No rush at all."

Little did he know I'd go full Gilligan for him.

He exhaled through his nose, pleased, before turning his full attention to the controls. The engine vibrated beneath us. We idled past the no-wake zone, slipping through the marina's outer edge until the last buoy bounced in our wake. Then Kais shot me a dangerous grin.

"Hold on tight, love."

With a flick of his wrist, he pushed the throttle forward. The sudden burst of speed threw me back against the seat as we sliced through the crystal-clear waves. Salt air rushed through my hair, mingling with Kais' thrilled chuckle and my squeal of delight. I held on for dear life, that roller coaster thrill tickling my belly as we crashed over the waves. My mind was finally clear for the first time since Morocco. I was just present with him. The rest didn't matter.

After he satisfied his inner daredevil, we settled into a leisurely cruise along the coast. Sade's music wove through the air, the perfect soundtrack for taking in the cliffside villages and crystal blue waters with Kais beside me. He maneuvered past a cluster of anchored yachts and sailboats, where music and laughter echoed, people dancing on decks and diving into the sea. But he floated past them, easing us toward a more secluded cove where the water turned to liquid sapphire, so clear I could see the boat's shadow rippling against the seafloor.

Kais lowered the anchor. Instinctively, I reached for the basket, unpacking cheese, fruit, olives, and cured meats, arranging them on a wooden board over the flat cushions at the back of the deck. He turned up the music, popping open the rosé, and the jazzy saxophone of *Smooth Operator* wrapped around us as we laughed and ate.

He was carefree and extremely fucking hot. I needed a distraction before I embarrassed myself by jumping him again, so I stood up.

"What are you doing?" Kais laughed over a bite.

I licked a bit of honey from my finger, flashing him a teasing glance over my shoulder.

"Getting in."

His eyes roved over me as I slipped my cover-up off slowly, intentionally trying to tempt him. The fabric dropped to my feet, revealing the cheeky orange bikini beneath. Kais dramatically tipped his sunglasses down the bridge of his nose, his dark eyes burning through me.

"Why must you be so cruel to me, *Ya Amar*?" He placed a hand to his chest, shaking his head in mock devastation.

The irony of that statement.

"Get in the water, Kai." I whispered before diving in.

A splash followed moments after I surfaced.

"God, it's bloody freezing!" he cursed.

I smooth my hair out of my face, rolling my eyes. "Oh, come on, Kai Kai. This can't be worse than those ice baths you submerge yourself in after the gym."

He slicked his hair back, laughing. "You know nothing."

Grinning, I swam toward a nearby rock formation, where a questionable-looking rope ladder dangled.

"Should I do it?" I yelled.

Kais' head snapped up. "Are you mad? That thing is dodgy!" He swam after me, clearly intending to stop me, but I was already halfway up and fully committed to my promise to seize the day.

At the top, the rock was warm beneath my feet, the jagged edges biting against my skin. Below, Kais treaded water, his expression stormy. I've never done anything like this in my life but something about staring down the barrel of this summer love affair made me feel especially bold.

"Alana, listen to me. Jump out as far as you can, yeah? And don't bloody kill yourself!"

He was very cute and very British when he was angry.

"I'll remember you well!" I teased before plunging into the water.

The moment I surfaced, I whooped in victory—until I realized

Kais was no longer in the water. My stomach flipped. *He's on the damn cliff.*

"Kais, you can't do that! What if you get hurt and can't fight?"

From above, his deep laugh rolled across the cove.

"Now look who's concerned. What was it you said? 'I'll remember you well'?"

I shielded my eyes from the sun, glaring up at him. "That's not funny when you say it, Kai."

And then he jumped. A perfect, unhesitating dive. I held my breath, wading, waiting until suddenly, my legs were yanked under the water. My breath caught as I was dragged down, my heart hammering as our eyes met beneath the water, his puffed cheeks vibrating with silent laughter. When we finally surfaced, gasping, eyes burning, and breathless, I splashed him.

"You think you're so funny."

His boyish chuckle vibrated through the water as he smoothed his hair back.

"No, but you do."

Before I could retort, he closed the space between us, pulling my legs around his waist, his arms locking me against him. My heart beat out of my chest. That homesick feeling washed over me all over again.

I can't take another moment of *almost*s and unspoken truths. Time stilled. His gaze softened, fingertips tucking loose strands of hair behind my ear. I wrapped my arms around his neck, searching his brown eyes.

My heart screamed that this was probably my last chance to put it all out there. If I told him the truth about how I feel, at least I'd have no regrets. Warmth, nerves, maybe even fear, unfurled in my stomach as something inevitable began blooming between us. Without thinking, I whispered —

"I love you."

Kais froze. His eyes widened slightly, head tilting back, blinking as that slow, knowing smile stretched across his face.

Shit.

Shit. Shit. Shit.

My chest went hot.

What the hell did I just say?

His grip on me tightened slightly, his voice teasing and too knowing.

"What did you just say?"

My eyes went wide. *No.* I shook my head, biting my lip, *mortified*. I've completely ruined all of this now. You don't tell someone you love them this soon. Not even just someone, but *him*, I've completely lost my fucking mind.

Kais pulled me closer, "Say it again."

"No." I shook my head harder, trying to suppress the nervous laugh creeping up my throat.

He didn't let up. His cheek brushed mine, lips grazing my ear. "Say it again, *Ya Amar.*"

His whisper sent chills down my spine. My heart pounded. Pulse thundered. *It's true so I have nothing left to lose.* I exhaled.

"I love you," I whispered shakily.

The second confession was like the final nail in the coffin of everything I've tried to hold back and protect. His eyes searched mine, revealing a vulnerability so deep it left him looking undone. Then, his thumb stroked along my cheek, his fingers steady at the nape of my neck.

"I love you too." The words came out steady, but his breathing wasn't.

That was it, the key to the door I'd been clawing at for weeks. And then his mouth was on mine. The kiss was unleashed, nothing held back. His muscles flexed against me, his fingers gripping my hair tighter as our bodies fit seamlessly together. His tongue swept against mine, the rhythm intoxicating, pulling a soft whimper from my throat as my chest pressed against his, my hips instinctively rolling into him. I pulled back, gasping.

"Kai, please."

His teeth scraped gently along my jawline, lips teasing along my neck before his grip tightened in my hair, pulling my head back slightly.

"Please what, *Ya Amar*?"

My mind raced, every nerve in my body on fire.

"*Fuck*," I groaned, fisting my hands against his chest. "Anything, everything, just please don't stop again."

His chest shook with a low, breathy laugh.

"As much as I'd love to hear that pretty mouth plead and moan my name again…"

His lips brushed the center of my throat, "I can't do that here. Not with an audience."

I froze. My head snapped over my shoulder. A yacht we'd passed earlier had drifted closer, its passengers clearly enjoying the show. A dark-haired woman with deep tan lines dangled her legs over the bow, raising a wine glass in salute.

"Don't stop on my account!" she called out, smirking. "You guys are very fuckin' hot."

My cheeks burned. Kais and I locked eyes—then broke into laughter.

"Shall we go somewhere more private then?" he asked, his lips still curved in amusement. I tilted my head, feigning nonchalance. "I thought you didn't want me to plead here."

His smirk deepened. "Let's go then."

Smoothly, he untangled from me and swam back toward the boat.

Alana

♫ 18

NEITHER OF US SPOKE AS WE LEFT THE COVE, BUT THE air between us said everything. I had no clue where Kais was taking us, and I didn't care. The only thing that mattered was getting there. Judging by the intensity of his driving, he felt the same. I leaned back against the seat, tilting my head toward the sun, letting the warm sea breeze dry my hair.

My head was still trying to rationalize it: *this man just told me he loves me too.* Every so often, I could feel his gaze flick toward me, but I refused to look at him. Not when he was sitting there, shirt-less, one hand gripping the wheel, that damn backwards cap making him look like some devastating combination of boyish and irresistible.

The boat slowed. The sudden absence of wind made me lift my head. We weren't heading back to shore. We were tying up to something massive.

A towering yacht, sleek and intimidating, its smoke-gray and rich black hull gleaming under the midday sun.

My stomach lurched. Kais turned his head slightly, watching

145

me over the rim of his sunglasses, amusement flickering at the edges of his lips.

"Kai." I sat up straighter, swallowing.

"Yeah?"

"That is not a boat."

He smiled, tapping the wheel under his hands. "No, my love. *This* is a boat."

The understatement of the century.

I barely registered the small crew waiting at the stern, dressed in matching black uniforms, their expressions professional but expectant. My eyes drank in everything else; the expansive teak decks, the infinity pool glistening in the sunlight, the softly lit staircase winding up to the top deck. A floating palace.

I exhaled slowly, squinting up at it. "So... how many rival gangs did you take out to afford this?"

Kais let out a quiet laugh. The kind I loved most from him, that only made me feel for him more.

"I'll never confess."

I tilted my head. "I have ways of making you."

His eyes darkened with interest. "We'll see about that."

I opened my mouth. Closed it. My words gone from me completely.

The truth is really, *he* had ways of making *me* do things, like whatever spell he possessed me with to make me say *'I love you'* first.

Kais reached for my hand, his grip steady as he helped me onto the swimming platform, then up the wide, honey-colored steps leading to the main deck.

The boat was breathtaking: a hot tub overlooking the endless blue horizon, a sprawling, cloud-soft sectional wrapping in front of a sleek glass wall. The glass doors were slightly open, revealing a glimpse inside with white and gold marble floors, a table being set for something magical...which Kais was seemingly scrapping the idea of now.

The crew stood at attention as we stepped forward, but before the head steward could even speak, Kais raised a hand.

"We'll be back for dinner service. Until then, no interruptions."

The crew nodded and swiftly disappeared. *Damn. He's hot when he controls a room like that.*

His grip tightened as he led me through the glass doors, past a plush living area dominated by a massive projector screen, the décor a perfect reflection of him: modern, moody, shades of black and gray, small hints of red tucked in places where they'd hit just right.

We moved down a narrow hall, passing several bedrooms before stopping at the last door. The *owner's* suite.

Kais didn't pause.

He pushed the door open, leading me straight through the bedroom with its massive king bed and floor-to-ceiling windows, before stopping at the entrance of a bathroom. Top-to-bottom gray marble, brass accents gleaming under soft lighting.

He reached past me, pushing open a set of glass doors leading into the most ridiculous shower I'd ever seen. A rainfall shower head. Half a dozen jets lining the walls. Big enough for... *several people.*

Kais turned the dials and a low hiss filled the space as water tumbled from the shower heads, steam rolling up in slow, lazy waves. The nervous flutter in my stomach hadn't stopped since we left the cove; my mind, heart, and body were still trying to catch up with each other.

He leaned back against the counter, effortlessly composed yet unmistakably commanding.

"Take that off," he commanded, watching me with unwavering focus.

I bit back a grin, loving the way that steely voice of his could control my body without a single touch and I didn't want to do shit but listen. There was something deeply erotic about pleasing a man who treated me the way he did.

I worked my fingers to untie the strings of my bikini, top first, then the bottom, tossing the fabric aside. A smoldering look ignited in his eyes, his pupils dilating as his gaze swept over me, gluttonous and unashamed. His tongue flicked across his bottom lip as if savoring the sight.

I cocked my head, amused by his sudden lack of restraint. "Your turn now, Kai Kai." I gestured towards his shorts.

A cruel smile played on his lips.

"No," he breathed, shaking his head. "You don't get to rush this, *Ya Amar.*"

He closed the distance; the heat of his bare chest sent a jolt of electricity between my thighs. His fingers, strong and possessive, tangled in my hair, tilting my head back, forcing my gaze to meet the storm brewing in his eyes.

"Do you have any idea how torturous it's been restraining myself around you?" His voice was rough, each word dragging fire down my spine.

I swallowed hard, holding his gaze half-lidded.

"No," I whispered.

His smirk turned wicked. His free hand slid to my hip, pulling me flush against him, pressing into me so I could feel exactly how torturous it had been, all the way down my thigh.

Fuck. I had never been more desperate to be touched.

His mouth found mine, placing slow bites on my bottom lip before sucking it between his teeth, leaving me craving more.

"Get in," he commanded, ticking his chin toward the steaming shower.

I didn't need to be told twice.

The hot water stung my back, adding to the heat already coursing through me. He followed, discarding his trunks with casual ease. All those weeks of wanting this, of him pulling back at the last moment. And now it was as if he'd been waiting for me to catch up.

Seeing him completely bare, all that raw masculinity on display, awakened some lustful version of myself I couldn't recognize. Kais Reinhardt is a big man, imposingly so. Six-foot-five according to his boxing stats and two-hundred-something pounds of muscle. Even that is a laughable indicator of just how hung the man is.

"God," I whispered, mostly to myself, but the look in his eyes told me he caught it.

I reached for him, determined to undo him the way he'd undone me in Morocco, to end this unbearable want between us. My fingers barely grazed his skin before he caught my wrists, holding me just out of reach.

His lips brushed my ear. "Do I need to teach you restraint?"

A shudder ran through me, a shiver that had nothing to do with the water.

I tilted my head to meet his gaze. "Teach me whatever you want, Kai."

His eyes darkened at my words before his hands spun me effortlessly, pressing my chest into the cool marble, his body a wall behind me. His grip on my arms was firm, his muscles taut with barely contained restraint.

He wasn't kissing me. He wasn't touching me. He was holding something back. A bit of the brutality from Morocco, maybe? *Fuck, do I want every bit that he could give me.* His jaw flexed hard against my temple, as if it physically pained him not to devour me.

Merging both my hands into one of his, he secured them at the small of my back, then pressed his hips into mine. I gasped. Every inch of him was rigid against me—thick, pulsing, overwhelmingly immense—so fucking close to where I needed him, but not close enough.

My body bucked instinctively into him, taunting him, letting him feel the slickness between my thighs, a quiet admission of how desperately I burned for him. Needed to be claimed by him.

"Fuck, Alana," he groaned, raking a hand through his wet hair.

The sound of him slipping from control was pure agony and ecstasy. I hummed a breathless impatient moan as his grip tightened to bruising.

He pumped soap into his free palm, the scent of jasmine rising between us. His touch was achingly slow. Those calloused hands that had seen so much violence moved across my skin with impossible tenderness. How could someone so powerful touch me like I was made of glass?

I couldn't see him, but the thought of his hands rubbing me this way was enough to tip me over the edge, and he hadn't even passed my hips. He moved lower, his touch rewiring every nerve as he caressed my chest, my stomach, my thighs—a gasp tore from my lips, swallowed by the steam as his fingers split me open.

"Kai, please," I moaned, rolling my hips into him, *fucking begging.*

He stilled for half a breath. His mouth found my ear. "You think I don't want to bury myself in you right now?" he growled, every word a promise. "But I'm going to take my fucking time, Alana. You asked to be taught, didn't you?" His hand curled tighter around my wrists.

I gasped, nodding, "Yes."

He kissed my shoulder softly, his breath igniting my every nerve. "Good. Now let me teach you who you belong to, *Ya Amar.*" He removed his hand from my legs just long enough to rinse away the soap.

Then that same hand—one that had destroyed men without hesitation—finally found its true purpose, sliding effortlessly to the swollen throb between my legs again. With expert precision, he began rolling, teasing, and moving in a dance of torment and pleasure, perfectly in rhythm with my chasing hips.

Just when I thought I might shatter from the pressure, he spun me back around, smooth and fast, kneeling before me in the steam. His palms slid up my thighs, then he hooked one of my legs over his shoulder. He looked up, eyes locked on mine, drinking in my ragged breath and trembling limbs like they were the only proof he needed.

"You'd come for me right now if I told you to, wouldn't you my love?"

"Yes, sir," I breathed, my voice frayed with want.

His lips curved, pleased. "Your body already knows where it belongs," he said. "Let's see if we can get that pretty mouth of yours to catch up."

Then his mouth was on me, hot and consuming. A low, strangled cry escaped my lips. Some sadistic part of me forced my eyes to watch, like I didn't already know how fucking beautiful he was. But the sight of him down there—*criminal* wouldn't even cover it. He looked like lust incarnate with my leg draped over his shoulder, his mouth devouring me like he'd been starving for this. I clung to his hair, desperate for an anchor as his tongue mimicked his fingers' brutal dance, rolling, sucking, lapping, claiming.

"Fuck—Kai," I whimpered, my hands fisted in his hair as the world narrowed to his mouth, the tension winding tighter inside me.

He didn't let up. His tongue rolled and dragged and sucked until I was shaking, sobbing, and my climax ripped through me like a hurricane. My legs went weightless in his grip, my entire body trembling as I broke apart for him. With one hand he held me up, the other coaxing me through every last pulse of pleasure.

When I started to come down, my fingers were still tangled in his hair, desperate to hold on to just one more second of it. My legs trembled. My lungs forgot how to work. I looked down at Kais through heavy lids, a soft smile on his lips like a man who'd just claimed something he'd been waiting his whole damn life to touch.

I didn't even clock his hand moving to cut the water off. The sudden silence was a jolt after the storm he'd dragged from me. My skin was hot, my body still twitching from the aftermath of his mouth.

Then, without warning, he scooped me up, carrying me toward the bed like he was claiming his prize. He laid me down gently and stood over me, his gaze a physical weight, consuming me with his eyes.

"Look at you, shaking for me," he said, the words rough. "You're perfect, Alana. So *fucking* perfect."

A feral grin split my lips. I pushed up, a desperate need to claim him, to match the havoc he'd wreaked on me. To prove myself worthy of him. But he knew better. He caught my chin, kissing me deeply, his tongue reigniting every nerve ending like I hadn't just come for him moments ago. *Greedy for him.*

He pulled back, his lips hovering over mine.

"Believe me," he breathed, his voice ragged, "I will ruin that gorgeous mouth and that delicate fucking throat... but not yet."

He stepped back, opening a cabinet and fiddling with something, the smooth click of the cabinet door a metallic counterpoint to the slow, sensual opening notes of *No Ordinary Love* that began drifting through the overhead speakers. Resuming the same album from the boat. *Of course he is.* A pleased smirk tugged at his lips.

"For privacy." He winked.

I didn't even try to hide my smile. Of course, Kais Reinhardt, in all his impossible, ruinous perfection, would be so *damn intentional* about everything—even this.

He climbed onto the bed, stretched out beside me, reaching into a nearby drawer. A soft rip cut through the air as he tore open a box, pulling out a small gold wrapper. Before he could go any further, I pushed his hand away.

"I'm covered."

He smirked slightly, running a thumb along my jaw before he

gritted out, "You're a fast learner," voice rough with approval. "Good. I want to feel every bit of this mess you've made."

His hand slid down my thigh, possessive and unhurried. He clearly likes it when I'm blunt, so I decided to be just that.

Quickly, I mounted him, wrapping my thighs around his hips, gripping him with the palm of my hand, and guiding the heavy head of him through my slickness. I dragged him slowly over my slit, teasing, unable to stop my trembling.

A deep growl rumbled from his throat that took my last shred of patience.

"Fuck, please teach me Kai," I whispered, grinding my hips against him.

"Good fucking girl," he ground out.

His hand gripped my hip, steadying me, and in one slow pull, he seated me onto him. Inch by aching inch. I let out a ragged breath as my body adjusted, trying to find the space to fit him.

"Fuck, you're tight. Fucking soaked for me," he growled.

The stretch burned and bloomed at once. My breath caught, eyes stinging, body trembling as he filled me completely. I let out a ragged gasp. The sensation was overwhelming: a perfect, agonizing press that blurred the line between pain and pleasure until it was only need. The muscle in his jaw fluttered rapidly.

A hiss broke through his teeth. "You fit me so perfectly, my love."

He gathered me to his chest, his arms a cage of strength and possession around my back. His mouth covered mine again, kissing me just as deep as he filled me. Our bodies fell into rhythm, hips grinding, slow and aching, like a dance we'd already known in another life. Like the full embodiment of how we danced in that club but fucking intoxicating. God, the feel of him was more euphoric than I could ever imagine. As if my body found a missing piece.

"I think—I think I was made for you Kai." I breathed against his lips, the words barely stuttering out of me.

His tongue brushed mine before he kissed me again, gripping my hair to angle my head as he trailed his lips to my jaw.

"You were, baby," he rasped against my neck, "and I'm not letting you fucking go."

He hooked his hands on my shoulder, his grip tight as he drove deeper into me, grinding against a spot in my stomach that made stars dance behind my eyes.

"God. Please don't," I gasped, clutching at his back, nails dragging down the ridges of muscle, desperate to stay grounded in the wreckage of him.

Then his mouth found mine again. A hungry claim, devouring every breath, like he needed to taste the plea I'd just made. Our bodies kept moving together with the fluid grace of a dance, the rhythm as familiar as our own heartbeats. Like my body spoke a language only he could understand. Like my damn soul was bound to his.

My eyes pricked with heat, my heart wanting to spill tears from the sheer ecstasy of the overwhelm of loving him this much, of feeling this much pleasure.

"I've died a thousand deaths waiting for you Alana," he breathed against my lips, pushing deeper, slower, rougher now.

A whimper tore from my belly. Goddamn, the feel of him inside me was already too much to bear, but if he kept talking to me like this I might actually implode.

"So have I, Kai," I whispered, kissing him deeper.

The song bloomed louder overhead, the slow, aching rhythm matching the way he moved inside me. Like worship. Like ruin. Like being reborn into something else entirely. His thrusts turned precise, building the tension until it was a taut, screaming wire, ready to snap.

He pulled back, his eyes narrowing on me as he swept the hair from my face.

"You're going to cry for me again, aren't you?" he hissed, his voice a venomous whisper against my ear.

A desperate, choked, "Yes, Kai" escaped my lips.

He raked his fingers through my hair, gripping it at the nape of my neck as he tilted my head back to meet his gaze.

"Remember what you said earlier?"

I'd said so much, felt so much, but I knew exactly what he wanted to hear. The words lived on my tongue but the screaming tension boiling in me wouldn't allow me to say it.

Only another breathless "Yeah" tore from me.

"Say it, Ya Amar. Say it like you need it."

His movements slowed, each touch a deliberate torture, drawing out the last vestiges of my self-control. They were right there on my tongue. I just couldn't reach them. He felt too good, my heart felt too much, I could only beg.

"Please, Kais," I whimpered, the words desperate, a wild wave of something greater than need crashing over me.

"You're mine, and I'm fucking yours, Alana. Every part of me. You're safe, let go for me."

He tipped my head back, his teeth sinking into my shoulder, a searing bite that sent a jolt of agonizing pleasure surging through me. Followed by the hot drag of his lips on my neck, a prelude to oblivion.

"I fucking need it, please baby," he groaned.

Please? Did he just fucking plead?

Something inside me broke wide open. Not just from the way he touched me. But from the way he meant every word. That this man—this chaos and calm and impossible depth—was mine. That he actually wanted me. For everything I am. Needed *me*.

The feeling was too big. Too much. I couldn't hold it in. I grabbed the back of his neck with both of my hands, holding his gaze steady on mine as the words tore out of me, raw and unbidden.

"I love you," I cried in repetition, bathing him in the words as my body clenched around him, the pressure crashing down in a blinding wave.

I shattered once more as his mouth devoured the words, nails digging into his back, every nerve ending lit like fire. A harsh curse ripped from him, his body rigid with the force of his own release, his voice a broken whisper, a sweet hushed confession against my lips—*"I love you too."*

Alana

-16-

♫ 19

I LAY TANGLED AGAINST HIM, MY CHEEK RESTING OVER his heartbeat, the warmth of his skin lulling me closer to peace than I'd ever been. His fingers traced lazy patterns along my spine, neither of us speaking, simply existing in the moment we had created.

Eventually, Kais pushed himself up from the bed, stretching lazily before reaching for a pair of black gym shorts. He pulled them on, the waistband resting low on his hips, then ran a hand through his tousled hair. I moved to stand, but his hand caught my wrist, stopping me.

"Don't," he said, eyes flicking over me with quiet appreciation. "Stay just like this."

I arched a brow, "Like what?"

His lips tilted in that easy, devastating smirk. "Like mine. With nothing touching you but me or my sheets."

A now-familiar heat stirred in my belly, but I rolled my eyes to hide it.

"You just don't want me putting clothes on."

"Of course not," he said simply, taking my hand and pulling me toward the deck. "Why would I?"

Three words never sounded so sweet, well, other than his *I love you*. I giggled, padding behind him through the hall barefoot. The cool evening air wrapped around us as we stepped onto the back deck, I shivered into the sheet wrapped around me, trying to preserve some of the warmth we'd created.

The afternoon sun had long since slipped beneath the horizon, leaving behind a sky so thick with stars it looked like it could shatter. The sea stretched dark and infinite beyond the glow of the yacht's lights, the hush of waves a quiet lull beneath us.

Kais muttered something in French to one of the servers waiting nearby. A moment later, he guided me toward a wide, low-slung bed of cushions facing the open water, the glow of a modern fire pit flickering in the center of the deck.

He sat first, pulling me into his side, wrapping his arms lazily around my waist as I settled against his chest, slinging my legs across his lap. Soft piano music floated from the speakers through the ocean breeze. I rested my head on his chest. *The beat of his heart and warmth of his skin are my heaven*, I think. *I could live in this feeling for the rest of my life*. He kissed the crown of my head as we sat quietly, looking out at the dark moon-soaked ocean ahead of us.

Not long after, a server arrived, setting down a tray of small glass dishes, each filled with a mouthful of ice cream in different flavors. A grin split Kais' lips.

"At this rate, you are indeed going to be put out of shape, Kai Kai." I laughed softly, shaking my head.

"With you in my bed, I don't see how that's possible, love."

How does he always say things like that with a straight face? I swatted his chest playfully, but the heat crawling up my neck betrayed me. He kissed my bare shoulder before holding a spoon to my lips. I took a bite, then watched as he took the rest for himself, nodding in mock contemplation.

"Definitely not as good as biscuits and cream," he muttered.

I laughed, "Cookies Kai, cookies and cream."

He hummed, lips brushing my shoulder again. "Mmm, I like when you correct me."

I nudged him, smiling softly. We worked through the tray slowly before requesting real food, eating it there, wrapped up in each other beneath the stars.

Everything about the moment felt easy, unrushed. After Kais mangled his way through ordering chimichangas, he made a joke about the server clearly despising his pronunciation, and I nearly choked on my wine laughing at his attempt to redeem himself. I called him dramatic. He called me heartless.

Eventually, the laughter softened, the food forgotten. Kais shifted, pulling me closer again, my head resting against his chest, rising and falling with his breath. He traced absent patterns over my shoulder, his touch warm and more like home than I'd ever felt before. Music kept whispering in the background, a soft, familiar, piano piece.

"I've always thought this song was really pretty, But I can never remember the name of it." I whispered.

"Clair de Lune," Kais said simply.

"Oh yeah! Like the poem on your mom's picture?" I asked, gently tracing circles on his chest.

"Yeah," he whispered, brushing a kiss into my hair.

I let my eyes close for a moment, letting myself just exist, wrapped in him. No expectations. No past, no future. Just now. My life has always been so chaotic, full of hurt, and just trying to survive the next day. I never thought I'd have this—this kind of peace. I didn't realize how much I'd needed it until now, how much I'd needed *him*.

Because when I'm with him, it feels like the entire world could go quiet. I don't worry about tomorrow. I'm not running from yesterday. Not holding my breath, waiting for something to go wrong. I'm just *here*. And God, I want to stay. To hold onto this forever, to him. I took a deep breath, grateful to have a love like this even if it doesn't last forever.

Kais' fingers stilled on my shoulder. Then, quietly—like it had been sitting on the tip of his tongue all night—he said it.

"Marry me."

My eyes shot open as I let out a breathy laugh, "Okay, Casanova, you've officially had too much wine."

I lifted my head over his shoulder, peeking over at his nearly untouched wine glass. My eyes darted back to his. He didn't laugh. Didn't smirk. Didn't take it back.

"I'm serious," he said.

I held his gaze, studying him, finding his expression so damn certain it made my chest ache. I sat up straight, fully facing him.

"Kais, we can't do that. We've only known each other for what —a month? Can you imagine what people would say?"

His brows lifted slightly, shaking his head. "I don't give a shit what anyone else thinks." His hand settled firm and steady on my thigh. "I'm in love with you, Alana. Desperately. Entirely."

My heart slammed against my ribs. I swallowed. "Kai—"

"I know how it looks to someone other than us. But I also know what I feel isn't temporary." His voice was sure, unwavering. "I'm not the kind of man who makes promises I can't keep. I don't waste words."

His thumb brushed slow circles over the skin on my thigh. "And I sure as hell don't love lightly."

My chest feels like it's going to explode.

He exhaled, running a hand through his hair, as if letting himself say this was harder than anything else. His voice was softer now, almost shy.

"I don't know how to explain it, Alana. It's like I already knew you before I met you. Like... I've carried you with me somehow." His throat bobbed. He reached for my hand, his fingers tightening over mine. "And now, I don't know how to exist without you anymore."

The world tipped beneath me. How could his thoughts and feelings be exactly the same as mine? How was it possible that we had both spent the past few weeks falling off the same cliff—only he had the nerve to say it out loud? I told myself this feeling was too big, too fast. That I needed to be careful. That I couldn't let myself need him. I've never been allowed to need anyone. Always used and discarded when I've served my purpose.

But looking at him now... God, he wasn't afraid, didn't need anything from me, just wanted me. I don't know how to be wanted like that, loved like that. My breath stilled. It felt like the universe had played a cruel joke, giving me everything I never dared to ask for all at once. I pressed my hand to his chest, steadying myself.

"I want a life with you," he continued. "I want your voice to be the last thing I hear before I sleep, and the first thing when I wake up. I want your hand in mine when we're eighty and wrinkled and giving each other hell."

I laughed softly, my eyes stinging and watery.

He let out a rough exhale, his eyes never leaving mine.

"I don't care if the whole damn world thinks it's mad. I don't care if you need *time*. But don't tell me to wait because of what anyone else might say."

My words tangled in my throat. I knew I loved him—I had known for a while. Maybe even longer. As crazy as it sounds, maybe since the beginning.

When I met him, something just clicked. Like the moment our eyes met, my soul woke up and said this is it, *this is him.* But to say yes to this? To marriage? That scared the shit out of me. It would feel like stepping into open air, like reaching for something I wasn't sure I was worthy of holding. No matter how many times he's told me otherwise. Marriage felt like something I could break too easily with my own seemingly unshakeable brokenness.

"Kai, it's just been an amazing whirlwind of a day. You're love-drunk. Let's just sleep on it. You'll feel differently tomorrow," I said, trying to convince us both we're out of our minds.

His expression didn't shift. Not an inch. He leaned in and kissed me. Slow. Deep. A kiss that held everything he wouldn't put into words.

Then, pulling back just enough to whisper against my lips—

"Sleep all you want, Ya Amar. It won't change a thing."

-17-

EVEN BEFORE SUNRISE, MONACO WAS MOVING: DRIVERS, handlers, cameras. The circus never really slept. We'd sailed in from Mallorca overnight, docked just before dawn. No fanfare. No one watching. Just the way I liked it.

Monaco might've still been sleeping, but my pulse was wired. I rolled my neck as I stepped out of the gym, shirt clinging to my back, breath still even after twelve rounds on the bag. My knuckles ached just enough to remind me I was still in form.

James Del Toro followed a few steps behind, stretching like he'd done more than jog a mile and sip a protein shake he'd barely touched. Ritual over necessity, claimed it calmed his nerves. I figured it just made him harder to kill. The man had lights out in a few hours and was still grinning like it was a goddamn holiday. I'd known the bastard since we were thirteen—grinning meant trouble.

"I'd hate to be the poor fuck in the ring with you this year," James said, clapping a hand on my shoulder.

We both looked out over a city which was still shadows and glow, like it was holding its breath.

"Yeah, well," I muttered, tugging my cap lower. "I'm not exactly lining up for a lap on your track either."

He grinned, all polished menace and sponsor money.

"That's because you can't fucking fit in the car, Reinhardt," he said smugly.

"Piss off," I shot back, giving him a shove that barely rocked him.

"Oi! Mates!" Ollie Bisset's voice rang out across the lot.

He jogged over, gym bag swinging, red-faced and already winded like the light cardio of a jog had personally betrayed him. He slapped my back in greeting, and James stretched his arms wide like he expected a hug.

"Fuck off, Del Toro," Ollie panted, pointing at him. "You smug bastard." His face turned a deeper shade of red.

"Oh, come on," James drawled, laughing. "Not my fault you spun out and fucked your car in qualifiers. You just can't fucking drive, you twat."

They started half-swinging at each other like children, and I just stood there, amused, still high off the night before. Alana. Her mouth, her laugh, her I love you's. And...the ring I'd slipped onto her finger while she slept wearing nothing but sheets. Bold move on my part, no doubt. But I knew the answer, just needed to wait and watch her catch up like I have since we met.

"Oi, Reinhardt! Nice fucking pictures, mate. That girl is *mad* fit," Ollie said, turning to me with a grin.

James chimed in amused, "Ah, yes. The mysterious Mallorca goddess. Hell of a headline."

They looked at each other, too fucking excited.

"What the hell are you twats on about?" I frowned, pulling out my phone and scrolling my media alerts until a headline lit up the screen:

WORLD CHAMP PLAYBOY KAIS REINHARDT SPOTTED MID-SHAG WITH MYSTERY WOMAN IN MALLORCA—AND IT'S STEAMY! PICS INSIDE.

Fucking charming. The photo was grainy, but obvious: my mouth at her neck, her lips parted like she was moaning, both of us half-submerged in the ocean. Probably taken by the boat that floated past. We hadn't noticed a camera. I should've. About ten more followed. All commenting on her like a bloody calendar girl.

"Them the pictures then?" Ollie leaned in over my shoulder, James right behind him.

I turned the screen off. "Oi. Anyone ever teach you lot about manners?"

That wasn't a tabloid shot. That was *ours.* And the way they were looking at her—like she was for the world to see—set something hot and ugly crawling up my spine.

"It's just a shag session, Reinhardt," Ollie said, still grinning. "Happens to the best of us."

I didn't blink. "It's not a shag session, you twat. She's my fiancée." That shut them up for a breath.

"Christ," Ollie muttered, eyes wide. "That's two twats in one morning. He *is* in love."

James shook his head, smirking. "So that's the mystery woman, yeah? And here I thought you'd go your whole life without settling down," he said.

"Right, well—doesn't matter what I said before. Just keep your eyes to yourself, yeah?"

Ollie raised his brows. "You're dangerous when you're in love."

I shot him a fuck off look.

"James was just hoping you'd bring her to the race later," Ollie added. "Said she's prettier than the grid girls were."

James shoved him. "Come on, don't get me fucking punched," He muttered. "I've gotta focus on staying out front today. I'm on pole, remember? I've got to carry your shit so we don't lose constructors, *cunt.*" He added.

"We'll be there," I said, silencing the alarm buzzing on my phone. "Just keep your comments to yourself, wanker."

Meeting in ten.

"Good lad," James called. "Don't kill anyone before noon, yeah?"

I grunted in reply, waving them off as I rounded the corner.

♪ 20

I got to the café first. By design. Never walk into a conversation like this second. The place was glass and chrome, tucked into the terrace level of a luxury hotel, with a panoramic view of the harbor and just enough seclusion to keep out prying eyes. I picked the table facing the entrance.

The sun just high enough to catch the water in gold flashes. Monaco doing its best impression of heaven. Didn't matter. I wasn't here for the view. A hostess tried to flirt while setting down an espresso I didn't order. I didn't flirt back. By the time Lars arrived (crisp suit and humorless as ever) I'd already skimmed the headlines. More noise about Mallorca. No real damage. Yet. But it would come.

"Morning," he said, pulling out a chair.

"Barely," I replied, eyes still on the harbor. "Sebastian?"

"Two minutes out," Lars said. "He's bringing a junior partner. Don't worry, he won't talk."

I arched a brow, "They never do. Until they do."

He smirked slightly, rare for him. "You're in a cheery mood?"

I didn't answer. I didn't need to, I don't mix my personal shit with business.

A polished figure in designer linen strolled toward the table, cigar already lit between his fingers like he'd been holding court elsewhere. Sebastian Voss. I clocked the cigar before I clocked the man. Of course he was smoking before nine a.m. Of course he showed up dressed like he'd just rolled off his yacht (I assumed he had, just like everyone else during GP weekend).

Casual power. He didn't need announcing. He looked like a man who already owned half the world and was just here to see if the other half was for sale. Voss wasn't trying to impress anyone. He was here to make sure I wanted to impress *him*.

Didn't work. I didn't stand. Just offered the barest nod as he approached, letting him come to *me*. Let him wonder if that meant anything. Let him wonder if I'd already made up my mind on whether I'd give him the key to the empire I built. I shifted slightly in my chair, elbow hooking over the backrest, one ankle resting over my opposite knee.

The coffee in front of me was still half full, cold by now, untouched. I wasn't here to sip lattes and chat synergy. I was here to get what I came for. The kid behind him looked like he was about to choke on the air, like he'd been born in a Hugo Boss suit: nervous, overdressed, and already sweating through his collar. Too many nerves, not enough blood sugar. I give him ten minutes before he excuses himself to throw up behind a palm tree.

"Kais Reinhardt. Monaco suits you." Sebastian extended a hand.

"Appreciate that," I said, reaching to shake his hand. Firm grip, just long enough to be polite. "I'm here on other business this time."

Sebastian grinned, flicking his cigar as he gestured to the view. "And what better backdrop for a conversation about empire?"

Sunlit opulence, gilded excess. The kind of city that made men like Sebastian feel invincible. Like gold-plated yachts and women in diamond swimsuits were proof of conquest. I gave the faintest smile.

I knew his type—the kind of man who only gets hard in the presence of marble floors and market domination. Hell, I was raised to be like him, but life shaped me differently. I can play the game, dress the part, but I will never be a man like him.

Lars, thankfully, cut in. Blunt, efficient, already pulling out the numbers. It's the reason I hired the man.

"Sebastian's team wrapped their due diligence last week. They're aligned with our valuation." He slid his tablet onto the table, the screen already lit.

"A well-oiled machine you've got going. I'm surprised you want to sell, Reinhardt," Sebastian said, then took a long drag of his cigar.

His gaze narrowed slightly, reading me through one eye like I was a number he hadn't quite reconciled yet. He was circling something.

"And yet you're already reaching for a 'but.'" I said flatly.

He chuckled in amusement, ash building near the tip of his cigar.

"You know how we are. We like a clear line of succession. No ghost captains floating around after the handover."

His hands opened in a casual shrug, then flicked more ash from his cigar like punctuation.

"I'd like you to stay on, advisory or operational. We'd pay well for the continuity. Your name carries weight."

There it was. The real ask.

I leaned back in my chair, stretching one arm across the backrest. "You want clean, you'll get clean. But I'm not interested in inheriting my own grave."

Sebastian laughed like I'd said something clever instead of something final.

"Fair. But you built a beast, Reinhardt. Hard to walk away from something you bled for."

"I bled to clean up what came before. Now I get to choose what comes after," I calmly retorted.

Lars remained cool, but I caught his eyes flick to me. Measuring. Tracking the pivot. Sebastian went quiet for a moment. Took a slow sip of coffee, thumb dragging across the rim of the cup like he was polishing a thought. Or weighing whether I was still worth the number he had in mind.

"We saw the headlines," he said at last, head ticking slightly to the side. "Mystery woman, eh?" He let the words hang like bait. "Big moves tend to bring distractions. I assume you've accounted for yours?"

Ah yes, a man who has a new woman half his age taking his name every year knows all about distraction.

"I account for everything," I replied without blinking. "Especially the things I value most."

That landed. He nodded, clearly satisfied, even if part of him still didn't know where to file me.

"You've got a clean setup here, Reinhardt," he said, taking another drag. "But your father still has a seat at the table. That going to be a problem?"

I didn't hesitate.

"He won't be quiet forever. But he doesn't get a vote. Not really."

Sebastian's brows lifted, then dipped again, squinting slightly like he was watching for hairline fractures. "And if he tries to get one?"

Oskar could posture all he wanted. Stir up noise. Try to make the board flinch. It wouldn't change a bloody thing. The company is mine and he's merely a relic at this point. But Sebastian cared about optics. About marble floors and domination. So, I gave him something better. I gave him blood.

"Then he gets to learn what it feels like to be irrelevant in public," I said with a shrug.

He took a breath, a dry chuckle rumbling low in his chest.

"Well, I must say, Kais—may I call you that? We're good friends now, I'd like to think."

I gave a short nod, unbothered. Let him have his familiarity. It cost me nothing.

"I'm ready to bring the bride home for consummation," he went on, grinning like he fancied himself poetic.

The metaphor landed like rot. I didn't blink.

"If you want the deal, here's how it plays out," I said steadily. "We announce quietly. You roll out your rebrand after Q3. My name stays on the product for eighteen months max. No advisory, no transition. My people stay paid."

He nodded slowly, puffing the last drag of his cigar like he was sealing something sacred.

"And your father?"

"Irrelevant."

That earned a bark of laughter from him.

"Well, damn," he said, pushing back in his chair slightly. "I do love a man who knows exactly what he wants."

He extended his hand across the table. I met it with a firm grip and a silent nod.

"Excuse me, gorgeous!" Sebastian called out to a waitress as she passed. "Could you please bring us a bottle of Dom? I believe we'll want to seal this moment with a toast." He grinned, all charm and ego.

"Absolutely, Mr. Voss," she said quickly, pivoting away with a polite smile.

Sebastian's gaze lingered a second too long. He stamped out his cigar. "She was quite pretty. You think I can land myself a bit of distraction while I'm here?"

Of course he did. Of course, he thought every woman in Monaco might be up for auction. Including mine. The thought grates.

Lars chuckled, cutting in, "I'll have one of those too."

He looked to me like he expected a laugh. He didn't get one.

I stood, collected but bloody finished with the whole dance.

"Right, well. Gentlemen—as much as I love champagne to break my fast, I've got another engagement." I extended a hand. Sebastian took it, shaking firmly.

"Right, our man is a boxer, his celebrity is needed elsewhere" he said with a grin. "You'll get me seats to your next match, won't you, mate? I just love those girls in the small metallic shorts."

I nodded once.

"Of course. 'Til next time, gentlemen. Lars brief me later."

Lars nodded, tablet already tucked under his arm. I didn't look back. Just stepped into the sun and made my way off to the yacht intent on washing the filth of that conversation off my skin.

Alana

-18-

♫ 25

THE SWEET SCENT OF CINNAMON AND BAKED BREAD filled the air, warm spice and vanilla bending through my lungs, coaxing me from the deepest sleep of my life. I stretched lazily against the impossibly soft sheets, my body still heavy with sleep as my eyes swept over the suite. *I was alone.* The only sounds were the gentle rock of water against the yacht and the faint vibration of music drifting in from outside. My gaze landed on the pillow beside me—Kais' pillow—where a folded cream note card rested,

Ya Amar

—written in elegant, delicate script across the front. A small giddy smile tugged at my lips as I reached for it. Then I froze. A glint of light flickered at the edge of my vision, drawing my attention downward to my left hand. The air left my lungs. *A ring.*

My fingers stretched instinctively, turning my hand slightly as I lifted it into the morning light. The weight on my left ring finger was undeniable now.

A halo of brilliant diamonds surrounded a large oval stone, its subtle blue hue catching the sun in glimmering flashes. The setting sat low, the heavy stone nestled perfectly against my skin, not spinning or begging to fall off, as if it had always belonged there. The realization slammed into me, a quiet, breathtaking force. My pulse fluttered wildly as I flexed my fingers, as if testing whether this was real. *How did I not notice?* I had slept with it on, curled into the sheets, completely unaware that my life had shifted in a way I couldn't yet wrap my mind around.

My heart pounded, thoughts tumbling over each other in frantic succession. *Did he do this while I was sleeping? Did I say yes? Did I dream it?* But no—this wasn't a dream. The weight on my hand was too real. And God help me, so was the way my chest tightened, how something deep in me whispered that this was exactly where I was always meant to be. I swallowed hard, exhaling through my nose as I forced myself to move, to breathe. *The note.* Quickly, I snatched the note card from the pillow. It read:

Ya Amar,

If you're reading this, it means you've found the ring. And before your beautiful mind starts to spiral—no, I didn't just pick it up yesterday. I had it sent ahead while we were still in Morocco. After that night in the Jemaa el-Fnaa, actually. I knew then. And watching you hold that photo like it meant something to you—like you felt the weight of it too—I knew I didn't want to wait another minute. There's something about moonlight that makes everything feel quieter. Truer. I read that poem a thousand times growing up and never really understood it. Not until you. The way you look at me. The quiet that settles in every time you touch me. The way it feels like home when you're near. I see now why my mother wrote it down. Why my aunt kept that photo. And how I knew—without question—that I wanted this with you. All of it.

When you wake, I imagine your fingers will find it first. You'll turn it over a few times. Wonder if I mean it. I do. If I rushed it. I didn't. If I'll ask you again. I won't. Because I already know. This isn't a question, Alana. It's a promise. I had it made for you. Blue stone—your favorite. That dress you wore on our first date. That ridiculous sweat suit. The ocean when you're in it. You'll probably say the ring doesn't matter. But it does. To me. Simple band. The kind of quiet, undeniable beauty that reminds me of you. I knew what it meant when I had it made. I know what it means now. And I'll know what it means tomorrow. I know it's bold. Mad, even. You'll probably call me a romantic. You wouldn't be wrong. Though I've never been accused of that before. I don't care what anyone else thinks. Let them call it fast, call it reckless. Let them wonder. What we have isn't ordinary. It's rare. Beautiful. And it's completely undone everything I thought I was before it.

I love you into every depth of me. The ring on your finger isn't a maybe. It's a vow. One I *made long before I even realized it. You said we should sleep on it. I tried. Got maybe twenty minutes. Then I watched the moon move across the water and decided I wasn't going to pretend this is anything less than what it is. It's real. It's yours. It's mine. Ours. Take the time you need. But I won't take the ring back. And I'll never belong to anyone else.*

Yours without condition,

Kai Kai

P.S. I've gone ashore to train. Have a slow morning. Eat something. Let the sun warm your shoulders. And when you're done pretending to be unsure... come find me.

By the time I reached the end, my breath was coming too fast. My fingers tightened around the note like I could hold onto him through the ink alone. My cheeks wet with tears as I exhaled, long and slow, my eyes drifting toward the empty space beside me in the bed, my fingers brushing against the ring on my hand. How could he be so damn sure of me? How could he see every broken piece and still...I pressed my lips together, closing my eyes for a second too long. I wasn't ready to answer that yet.

WITH MY HAIR still wrapped in a towel, wearing nothing but the plush, spa-like robe I'd found after my shower and a pair of oversized black sunglasses, I followed the enticing smell of pastries drifting down the hall. A woman waited near the end of the corridor, her crisp black uniform immaculate.

"Good morning, ma'am,"she greeted warmly, her British accent thick and elegant. "Breakfast is waiting for you on the top deck. Would you prefer coffee or tea?"

I smiled brightly, holding out my hand. "I'm Alana."

She hesitated briefly before shaking it. "Margret," she replied politely.

"Margret, it's nice to meet you. But please, never call me 'ma'am' again."

She let out a posh laugh, relaxing visibly. "Of course."

I paused thoughtfully. "Do you happen to have mint tea?"

After Morocco, coffee could never compete with a good cup of mint tea.

"We do," she said with a knowing smirk. "I believe Mr. Reinhardt specifically requested we use the mint he brought from Morocco." We shared a conspiratorial smile.

"Perfect, thank you."

She nodded gracefully.

"Is there anything else I can help you with, ma—" She stopped herself, eyes sparkling playfully. "Alana."

I grinned.

"Actually, could you replace this awful spa music with Astrid Gilberto or Chet Baker?" I pointed to the speakers.

"Right away." Her smile widened knowingly, walking off.

Moments later, smooth notes of bossa nova filled the yacht, following me onto the upper deck. I wasn't used to this. Any of this. Personal staff. Imported tea leaves. A yacht with a top deck. But the strangest part? It wasn't hard to sink into today. The plush robe, the indulgence of pastries waiting somewhere above me, the way Margret smirked like we were sharing an inside joke. It felt... *easy*. Natural in a way it absolutely *shouldn't* be.

And yet part of me still resisted it. Like one of those annoying girls in movies who refuse the really pretty shoes because—*pride*.

Because they *shouldn't* like it, even though they obviously do. This wasn't my life. It was his. I was just existing inside it for now. A guest. An interloper playing dress-up in something that wasn't meant for me.

But then again, I woke up wearing his ring. And that letter, *god*. That thought alone sent something tight through my chest. I swallowed it down, adjusting my sunglasses as I followed the scent of warm bread toward the deck.

I would love Kais if he lived in a one-bedroom apartment and ate instant ramen. But he doesn't. Maybe it would be easier for me to feel worthy if he did. And this? This was simply part of him. Something I had to reckon with. And maybe, for once, I could let myself enjoy it.

Just a little.

Outside, the cool morning greeted me gently, the soft sea breeze teasing through my robe, mingling faintly with the aroma of coffee and warm pastries already waiting at the breakfast table. I stilled, blinking against the early sunlight.

We'd moved? I hadn't even noticed. How had I slept through that?

A harbor stretched wide in the distance, lined with yachts that made even this one seem modest. The air was thick with something electric: excitement, anticipation. My gaze swept across the skyline, recognition tugging at the edges of my memory. I knew this place. Not firsthand, but from somewhere. Maybe an episode of *I Love Lucy*, maybe even in a few movies. The pastel buildings, the rocky hillsides, the way everything shimmered beneath the Mediterranean sun felt nostalgic and welcoming, though I couldn't quite place them.

Shrugging it off, I settled onto one of the soft cushions arranged around a polished table, pouring a cup of tea from a pot a server had just placed, easing back to watch the lively scene unfolding in the distance.

The quiet from the morning slowly gave way to the distant

sounds of engines roaring, and drifting club music. I took a slow sip, letting the warmth of the tea settle me. The morning still felt indulgent, unreal in a way that should have made me uneasy but instead, it just felt... nice. A little too nice. Just as I cozied up to the feeling, the sound of footsteps pulled my focus.

Kais walked up the deck stairs like he'd done it a million times before. He belonged here in a way I never could. He could make a yacht feel like the most natural thing in the world, like waking up somewhere new wasn't anything worth questioning. And maybe, to him, it wasn't.

I pushed off my glasses to get a better look at him. He looked light and easy, dressed in a way that made casual still look expensive: black joggers, a crisp white tee, sunglasses perched high on his nose, and a dark ball cap shading his eyes.

"Morning, my love," he said, eyes gleaming with quiet amusement as he leaned down to place a lingering kiss on the top of my head.

His gaze drifted briefly to my hand, noting the ring before meeting my eyes with a gentle smile. That look. A look like he'd known it would still be there, like it belonged there, like he'd known what my answer would be all along. The weight of it suddenly felt even heavier, more real and less fantastical.

"How was your morning?" he asked, with a grin.

"Perfect," I replied, unable to keep my smile at bay. And it was. Unreal, but perfect. "Where are we?" I nodded toward the noisy harbor, still trying to wrap my head around the fact that we were somewhere new—*again.*

"Monaco," he said, settling beside me.

Monaco... I thought for a moment before a scene of Lucille Ball gambling her life away came into my head. *Monte Carlo.* The words sat rich on my tongue, too luxurious to belong to me. Grace Kelly's Monte Carlo. James Bond's Monte Carlo. The kind of place that existed in movies, in old Hollywood fantasies, not in my morning reality.

"Like Grace Kelly's Monte Carlo? With St. Nicholas Cathedral?" I said, wincing against the sunlight.

"I suppose so." He snickered, "It's the last day of the Grand Prix, thought we'd catch the end of it. I've got a mate driving today, he invited us along."

Of course he did. The world seemed to be constantly offering Kais invitations to places people could only dream of. And just like that, he made me a part of it. He took a sip of my tea, relaxed, waiting patiently for my reaction. Like this was any other morning. Like waking up in Monte Carlo was just as normal as waking up in Dallas.

"Sounds fancy," I teased gently, trying to match his ease.

He chuckled. "You'll handle it beautifully. As you do everything else."

I arched a brow at the innuendo, leaning back slightly.

"Can you be ready in thirty?" he asked, standing once more.

"Depends," I mused, twisting the ring between my fingers. "Is this another 'pretend we're married' kind of day?"

I expected another teasing remark, another grin, but instead he leaned in close. "No pretending necessary, *Ya Amar*."

He took my hand in his, brushing his thumb over the ring in slow admiration. "Suits you," he said, smiling softly.

I grinned, twisting it between my fingers. "Alana Reinhardt does have a nice ring to it."

His smile deepened, but he didn't say anything else. Just brought my hand to his lips and kissed the spot just beneath the band.

Alana

♪ 38

A SMALL, ELEGANT WATER TAXI IDLED BESIDE THE yacht's platform. Despite the vacation setting, Kais was focused on his phone, though he still managed to look effortlessly handsome in his navy button-up and backwards Red Energy cap.

I'd chosen a linen halter top and matching skirt, trying to channel confidence in the designer clothes Kais had bought me. Cat-eye sunglasses and gold jewelry. Understated enough to blend in...*hopefully*.

He extended a steady hand, helping me down gently. The driver, a young man with bright eyes and an eager smile, nodded politely. Kais exchanged a few quiet words with him before turning back to me.

"Comfortable?" he asked, sliding his fingers through mine.

"Yeah," I nodded, trying to mirror his ease, though a small flutter of nerves had started in my gut.

Then the driver glanced back, hesitant yet eager. "Hey, mate, would you mind terribly if we took a quick snap once we dock?"

Kais grinned, unbothered. "Of course, mate."

The realization struck like a slow-building wave. This wasn't just another private getaway. Kais wasn't anonymous here. People knew him. They were excited to see him. To capture a piece of him. Which meant they would see me, too.

The thought sent a quiet jolt through me. Suddenly, I was hyper-aware of my hand in his, of the way he moved so easily through all of this. And more painfully, the way I awkwardly stumbled through it. Because it wasn't mine and I reeked of the stench of an imposter. Kais squeezed my hand gently, as if he could sense the shift. I let out a slow breath, steadying myself.

The boat glided toward the docks of Monte Carlo. Extravagant yachts stretched endlessly before us, draped in racing banners. The distant growl of engines sent a shiver up my spine. Salt and fuel mixed in the heat. You'd think by now I'd expect the contrast between the world Kais had pulled me from and the one he lived in, but it still hit me full force.

Everywhere, women moved like polished diamonds in designer cocktail dresses and sky-high heels. Men stood in tailored linen, their watches glinting in the sun. My outfit looked polished, thoughtful, but suddenly felt insufficient. Like I'd shown up to the wrong party.

Kais took a quick photo with the driver and gave casual nods to people shouting his name as we stepped onto a floating glass-and-steel structure. Paparazzi were snapping away without a second thought. He barely acknowledged them, tugging the brim of his red cap over his eyes as he draped an easy arm around my shoulders. I, on the other hand, felt entirely aware of every step, resisting the urge to shrink under the weight of so many eyes.

We walked into the floating building. Sunlight filtered through the towering floor-to-ceiling windows, bouncing off polished hardwoods and the steel Red Energy logos plastered everywhere.

The atmosphere was elegant but not rigid, almost comfortable. Kais walked like he'd been here a hundred times before, his hand steady at the small of my back, guiding me toward an open-air balcony, a tight curve of the race circuit just off in the distance. The view was breathtaking. The asphalt wound between packed grandstands, engines growling like distant thunder. People leaned against glass railings with drinks in hand, eyes already scanning the empty road like they were watching the final act of a show I didn't know the plot of.

"Kais!" A cheerful voice rose above the chatter.

A tall, athletic-looking blonde man approached, his Red Energy team polo shirt bright against his sun-reddened skin. Kais smiled warmly, his typically reserved demeanor giving way to genuine affection. He greeted the man, exchanging a firm hand-shake that quickly shifted into a brotherly embrace.

"You act as if I didn't see you this morning, twat," he said, clapping the guy on the back.

"Wasn't sure you'd actually show, but I guess James draws a crowd, yeah?" his friend grinned, turning toward me with curious eyes. "I'm Oliver but call me Ollie. Kais doesn't share much, but when he mentioned bringing someone special, I had to see it myself."

I smiled warmly, extending my hand. "Alana. Nice to meet you." Ollie took it enthusiastically. "Pleasure's mine. My wife Emilia is over here, come join us."

We followed behind him. Emilia, a striking woman with a golden blowout cascading loosely over her shoulders, turned as we approached, offering a gracious smile.

"So glad you could join us," she said, leaning in to kiss both of my cheeks. "Make yourselves comfortable. It'll be quite the race, even if Ollie's little mishap during quali benched him for the week-end. James is still the weapon on the grid."

Ollie shook his head good-naturedly. "You don't have to remind everyone," he laughed.

Kais chuckled softly, squeezing Ollie's shoulder. "Cheer up, mate. We're here for moral support and champagne, even if you didn't win it."

"Yeah, well, I've got a few PR bits later and a debrief after the race," Ollie sighed, already sipping from his glass. "But I'm off-duty till lap fifty. Figured I'd enjoy being treated like a VIP while it lasts."

The setting was stunning, sure. Sunlight glinting off the harbor, the echo of distant engines drifting up from the track, but my pulse had little to do with the view.

It was seeing Kais this way, relaxed, at ease among old friends. It was an unexpected but entirely welcome glimpse into his life. Though I grew increasingly more unsure how exactly I fit into it the longer I sat there. Kais and Ollie slipped into their own world, trading stories and inside jokes that I had no context for.

My focus drifted, taking in the space before catching on a group of women lingering nearby. All of them dressed in tiny dresses and towering heels, their eyes flicking toward Kais like he was something to be won. Of course, they knew him. Of course, they were watching. Can't say I blame them. The man looks like a piece of artwork. But, unlike me, they actually looked like they belonged next to him. The jealous thought was ridiculous, fleeting even but it still settled uncomfortably somewhere deep in my chest.

"When's your next fight, man?" Ollie said, nudging Kais playfully.

"Hasn't been announced yet, but Autumn. Wembley." Kais rested his hand on my thigh.

"Brilliant. I'll be there. James tell you what happened last night after quali's..." Ollie launched into a story, their easy laughter threading through the conversation. I let my gaze wander again, my attention drawn back to the group of women. Emilia coaxed me gently into a conversation.

"Are you just loving Monaco?" she asked warmly.

Her breezy blouse and tailored linen shorts were an inviting change from the typical glamour around us. I straightened myself out and tried to remember how to be a social person. I had served people like this in the restaurant; I could hold a conversation now too. I think.

"I haven't seen much, we just got in this morning," I replied with a soft smile.

"Oh, you guys must come out with us tonight, then! Consider me your guide to a good time," she said enthusiastically, immediately reclaiming Kais and Ollie's attention. "We're hitting the casino, and there's an after-party black tie, but it'll be great fun."

My gaze flicked to Kais, searching for his reaction, but before I could fully read him, Emilia caught my hand in hers, eyes widening dramatically.

"Oh. My. God. *You guys are engaged?*"

I stilled.

Her eyes shot to Kais. "How did we not know you were getting serious with someone?"

He gave an easy grin, but Ollie quickly chimed in, laughing.

"When does he tell anyone but James anything, Emilia? The man is an island."

I let out a small breath, laughing along, but my mind was spinning. *Engaged.* God I'd nearly forgot about the ring, I was so damn distracted by my annoying insecurities.

Now, hearing it out loud, in someone else's voice, made it sound more real than when Kais asked me last night. More real than when I'd woken up with the weight of the ring pressing into my skin. More real than when I'd *chosen* to leave it on. I could have taken it off. Slipped it quietly into a pocket when we got here, saved myself the questions, the looks, the imposter syndrome. But I hadn't.

Because I think I want this. Despite every instinct screaming that this couldn't be real, that things like this didn't happen for people like me—I still want *him*. And somehow, impossibly, I think he really does want me too.

Emilia turned my hand gently, inspecting the ring closely.

"I mean, my god, it's a blue diamond. What is that, eight

carats? I'm downright jealous!" she finally said, releasing my hand with an affectionate squeeze.

I let out another small nervous laugh, shaking off the tension.

Blue diamond? I hadn't considered the significance of that until now. I just saw *him* when I looked at it. But the way Emilia looked at it, like it was something rare and valuable, made it hit me all at once. This wasn't just thoughtful. It was... significant.

"I think Kais just wanted an excuse to show off his taste," I teased lightly, slipping back into the rhythm of the conversation.

She hummed into her champagne flute, eyes twinkling. "He certainly did. That stone's rarer than some royal titles."

I swallowed hard, twisting the ring instinctively. I hadn't even thought to ask. Not what it cost, not what it meant. I just knew that it was beautiful. And loved that it was his.

"So, when's the big day, mate?" Ollie nudged Kais with a grin.

Kais' grip tightened just a bit on my thigh, protectively, almost reassuringly.

"We're still deciding," I offered quickly, clearing my throat to ease the sudden tension. "But it'll probably be something small and intimate. Maybe Saint Nicholas Cathedral. I'm a big Grace Kelly fan," I teased, my voice steadying us both. Kais glanced at me, his lips quirking into an appreciative smile as the tension loosened slightly.

Emilia clapped her hands together. "Oh, I love you two together! You have to come. It wouldn't be the same without you."

I hesitated, shifting slightly as Kais' fingers traced an absent-minded pattern against my thigh. The invitation was tempting, the energy of Monaco was electric, but the idea of being underdressed in a sea of beautiful desperate women made my stomach ache.

"I don't have anything black-tie with me," I shrugged, glancing at Kais as if that settled it. His lips curved, something knowing flickering behind his gaze.

"I can fix that." His easy words sent a quiet thrill down my spine.

Of course, he could. Kais never saw obstacles, only solutions. One word from me and my problem wouldn't just be solved, obliterated. And yet, that was the part that unsettled me the most. No one had ever made things this easy for me. No one had ever wanted to.

I'd spent my life adjusting, making do, figuring things out on my own. But Kais? He never let me struggle, not even for a second.

Ollie laughed into his drink, "That's Kais for you. One phone call and *poof*—problem solved."

Kais lifted a brow at me, waiting. I exhaled, letting the last of my hesitation melt into the warmth of his certainty. Maybe it was okay to let someone take care of me for once. Not just anyone, but him.

"Okay," I muttered, finally giving in. "Let's go out."

Kais

-20-

♪ 24

THE MOMENT ALANA AGREED TO GO OUT, EMILIA WAS already scheming.

"I've got a friend—Margaux. Met her when we first moved here. Amazing designer in the most darling private boutique in town. She'll get us in, no problem," she said, fingers already flying over her phone. "Might have to sweet-talk her into a rush fitting, but for you, gorgeous? Worth it."

She gave Alana's knee a squeeze. Subtle. Thoughtful. But I saw the way Alana stiffened. Barely noticeable, but enough. Any act of kindness feels like it comes with strings for her. And honestly, it usually does. But Emilia? She's one of the few people I trust not to be full of shit. If I thought for a second she had an angle, I wouldn't bring Alana anywhere near her. Hell, seeing that Ollie's the only mate I've got who's taken the leap, I count myself lucky he married someone I'd trust with my own wife.

Doesn't hurt that the woman is a PR pitbull who's already sorting the tabloid shit from this morning for me. I imagine that fact might make Alana shift a bit more, but when I told her about the pictures this morning she said she'd rather not know. Can't say I blame her.

Alana exhaled a quiet laugh, nodding. "Alright, if you think it's not too much trouble."

"Trust me." Emilia winked, stepping away to make the call.

The second she was out of earshot, Alana turned those big, accusing eyes on me. The *what the fuck have you gotten me into* look.

I just grinned because, for once, I didn't have to be anywhere else. Didn't have a fight to train for, yet. A board meeting to sit through. A deadline to meet. All I had was her, all I'll ever need. The race roared on, but my focus never strayed from Alana. She looked completely at ease, eyes locked on the track, excitedly waiting for someone else to crash on that shit corner.

Which, to be fair, was the only thing worth watching, overtaking was nearly impossible on these tight fucking roads. I should have been watching, too. James is the closest thing I have to a brother. Four-time champion, and he's about to win Monaco for the first time. All I wanted to do was sit here and watch her wearing my ring, caught between wanting to believe this is real and being terrified that it is. She doesn't have to say anything yet. I already know. The look in her eyes says it all.

But then, I noticed it. Her expression shifted as her gaze flicked toward the corner, tracking something—*someone*—and a look I didn't quite recognize crept across her face. Not annoyance. Not jealousy. Something quieter. Something that made my fucking chest tighten. Before I could piece it together—

"Um, excuse me."

A woman's voice cut through the noise, followed by a light tap on my shoulder.

I turned to find a tall woman with long blonde hair and a fucking see-through dress standing beside me, two equally overdressed, giggling girls behind her. "You're Kais Reinhardt and Oliver Bisset, right?" She smiled, batting her lashes.

Ollie—who was supposed to be watching the race, not entertaining a damn fan club—turned his attention from the track, grinning.

"Yes, we are. How are you ladies?"

The man's still a fucking slag. My gaze flicked toward Alana. She was staring at the race on the projector now, pretending not to hear any of it. But I wasn't stupid. Her fingers twisted at the ring on her hand, her shoulders locked tight with a tension I knew all too well at this point. And that look in her eyes. The one that fucking wrecks me.

"Could we get a picture with you guys?" The woman asked, shifting between me and Ollie. *Fuck no.*

"Sure, sure! Kais?"

Ollie perked up, tapping my shoulder like he expected me to actually stand for this shit. I shot him a look. *Absolutely not.* But I stood anyway, not for the picture, but to get the fuck out of dodge. Because I knew exactly where Alana's mind was going, and I hated it. I leaned into her ear.

"Come with me."

Her head cocked slightly in confusion, but she didn't argue. Just slipped her hand into mine: warm skin against cold metal, my ring still sitting pretty on her finger. That did something to me. I turned to Ollie, clapping him on the shoulder.

"Have at it, you slag. Tell Emilia we'll be back in a bit."

And then, without another glance at the woman in the see-through dress, or the bullshit lingering in Alana's mind, I walked away, taking her with me.

"Where are we going, Kais?" She said cautiously.

Not Kai. Not Kai-Kai. *Fucking Kais.* I don't know why that bothers me now, but it fucking does. I gave her hand a squeeze, leading her down the hall, slipping into a bathroom and locking the door behind us. It was one of those over-the-top, private, marble-and-gold affairs, but honestly, I wouldn't have given a shit if it wasn't. I'd have made a show of it in front of everyone if that's what it took to pull her out of her head. She blinked up at me, arms folding.

"Really?" A half-laugh, half-scoff, like she wasn't sure if this was a joke.

I didn't answer. Just closed the space between us, tilting her chin up, backing her into the wall. Her eyes flicked up to mine, big, dark, and impossible to resist.

"Tell me what you were thinking out there," I asked.

She inhaled, slow. Rolled her eyes like she wasn't about to fucking lie to me.

"I was just watching the race. Your friend James is really fast. I wasn't thinking about anything."

Bullshit.

I leaned in, brushing my mouth just above hers. Close enough for her to feel me, far enough to keep her wanting.

"You're a real shit liar."

Her breath caught, but before she could reach for me, I pulled back, forcing space between us, arms crossed. One touch, and I'd forget where we were. I'd end up fucking her in the toilet like some desperate, lovesick idiot and I wouldn't even be sorry. And that isn't the kind of press I want for either of us right now, but Christ, she was making it hard to remember that. She huffed, looking at me for a long moment before tipping her head back to stare at the ceiling. Like she could blink the thought away.

"I don't belong here, Kais," She whispered in frustration. Then, with hesitation, "You belong with girls like that. Not me."

She waved a hand over herself like she was less than rare, less than fucking exquisite, like she wasn't the single most dangerous thing that had ever happened to me.

That. Fucking. Does it.

I dragged a hand down my face, exhaling slowly. I didn't want to lose my temper over this, but fuck.

"You think I give a fuck about girls like that, Alana?" I grit.

Her arms wrapped around herself, like she was actively fighting whatever fucked-up scenario was playing in her head. I wasn't having it. I closed the space again, pulling her hand to my chest, tapping my fingers against the ring on hers.

"You belong with me."

She started to say something—some other rubbish I don't want to fucking hear—so I cut her off, catching her mouth with mine. She gasped into me, soft, perfect, and then she was gone. Hands in my hair, body pressing into mine like she already knew where this is going. I lost it. My grip tightened, hauling her against me, her legs wrapping around my waist, exactly where she was made to be.

I carried her to the counter, my grip tightening against the heat of her skin as I slide my hands up her thighs— Then I froze. No fucking panties. A guttural sound rips from my throat as I break away just enough to look at her.

"Where are your panties, Alana?"

She giggled, wicked, like it's some cruel joke. "I'm not wearing any, Kai. Didn't want lines in this skirt that you're currently wrinkling up."

Bloody fucking hell.

How can she not see? How can she possibly think I'd want anyone but her? She doesn't let me take a breath, tilting her face up, pressing slow, delicate kisses down my jaw, tracing the shell of my ear, catching my earlobe between her teeth. My vision whites out for half a second. And then she swirls her tongue down my throat and I nearly fucking snap. It takes every ounce of restraint I have to stop her. Because I don't have a slow, patient shag in me right now. I'm too close to the kind of feeling I only get in the ring. Violence. Frenzy. The need to claim.

I steel myself, gripping the counter like it might stop me. "Do we need to leave?" I say, voice wrecked.

She shook her head, lips curling. "No," she whispers like a confession, "I can be quiet."

Liar.

A slow, knowing smile creeps onto her face because she already knows she can't. I drag a rough hand down my face, trying—fucking trying—to think clearly.

"Alana, you don't know what you're asking for." My voice is raw, barely restrained. "I'm not in my right mind for this."

She doesn't hesitate. Just slowly moves her hands under my shirt before reaching lower, fingers working at my belt, undoing my jeans. Then she presses her mouth to my throat, one small, devastating kiss, gripping me in her soft palm before whispering, "I belong with you, Kai."

And that's it. That's fucking it. For a second, all I can do is stare at her—this woman who just wrecked me with five words. Who has no idea what she just invited. The next breath I've got one hand to her throat, the other burying myself home—deep, unforgiving—as she arches for me, her head snapping back against the mirror.

"Fuck, yes" she groaned, softly.

Taking every bit of me beautifully, hungrily as she moans my name like a prayer she doesn't know she's saying.

"You feel that?" I hissed, driving deeper. "I'm yours. You're mine. I'm not fucking sharing."

Her whole body tightens. Nails rake down my back.

"God, I love you Kai," she whimpered.

Her breath shuttering with every thrust, wrecked and crying but still begging for more, gripping me with every desperate clench like her body knew no one else would ever be enough.

And fuck , *I love it that way.* Her voice. Her sweet perfume. The way she opens for me, fits me, made *for only me.*

"That's it, Ya Amar," I growled, pressing deeper, both hands gripping her like she might disappear. "You wear my ring on your hand and my fucking heart in your body—now you'll take my name."

She wrapped her arms around me, pressing her chest to mine, greedily riding every thrust like she couldn't get close enough. Her mouth crashed into mine hungrily before she pulled back, breath hot against my lips.

"Yes, sir," she whispered, soft and obedient, like she'd finally stopped fighting fate. Then she tipped her head back, baring her throat like a fucking offering. I don't know where I ended and she began. And I didn't fucking care. I fucked her until I lived in her bones and she buried herself deeper into mine.

"How bad was that? Do you think anyone heard?" Alana whispered, her reflection watching me through the mirror as she adjusted an earring.

"Brilliant. You're whispering. And here I thought you didn't know how."

She huffed, then threw my shirt at my chest.

"Oi, don't start. You asked for it. Now I'm the one needing to sneak us out like criminals," I laughed.

She grinned, barely biting it back, and fucking hell I almost scrapped the idea of leaving. My phone rattled against the counter.

"How much do you want to wager it's Ollie complaining about the noise?"

She flashed me that dimpled smile, flipping her hair over one shoulder. "I'd take that bet."

I looked at the screen.

Lars Gustafson.

I exhaled slowly, dragging a hand over my jaw before answering.

"Go ahead, Lars."

"We have a situation," he said abruptly.

I yanked my belt through the loops, arching a brow.

"Since when do you lead with dramatics?"

Across the mirror, Alana's smirk faded. She stilled slightly, one hand still resting on her earring, watching me now instead of her reflection.

"Since your father just played his hand in front of the entire industry."

That got my attention. I straightened, fixing my watch, jaw ticking once.

"Go on."

"He announced a merger proposal with an independent valuation that was 'privately conducted'—he's spinning it like a nobrainer, like it's already in motion. The board's eating it up."

Of course they are. Flashy numbers. Clean narrative. All surface. "And our valuation?" I asked calmly, reaching for my cap, dragging it through my fingers.

"Locked under internal review at your request." Lars paused. "Which means Oskar's numbers are the only ones on the table."

I caught Alana's reflection again, still watching, but trying not to look like she was. Her arms had dropped to her sides, tension crawling back into her posture. I gave her a slow smirk in the mirror. Reassuring her. She needed to think this was nothing. Then I turned away, grounding my palm on the counter as the full scope of the situation became clear.

"And let me guess," I muttered, "He made it public?"

"Front page. *Financial Times*. This morning." Lars' voice lowered. "Accompanied by a photo of you nearly shagging that girl in Mallorca."

I braced both hands against the counter now. Heat pressed behind my ribs.

"Oskar commented," he added.

Of course, he fucking did.

"Want me to read it?"

I rubbed my jaw, "Go ahead."

Lars read, "When I handed my son the reins of this company, I did so believing he had the discipline and foresight I once lacked. I was his age when I let a pretty face derail me, one that cost me far more than she was worth. But I had the sense to cut my losses and build something that lasts. I can only hope he learns to do the same before it's too late."

A coldness moved through me with a single thought: *always did have a habit of burying your mistakes, didn't you, old cunt?*

I tightened the strap of my watch, probably more than necessary. My hands were steady. My thoughts were not.

"And what's the reception?" I asked, calm again.

"Promising. Investors are listening… he's positioning it as a 'natural evolution' of the firm." Lars' tone was clipped. "If you block it now, you'll look like the one holding us back."

He's boxed me in. That was the move. Not the merger. The narrative. I glanced at Alana again, she was staring down at her hands now, lips slightly parted. *She doesn't interrupt, just watches. Clever girl. Always keeping up.*

I took a breath. "Good."

There was a pause. "What?" Lars asked, incredulous.

"Let him pitch it." I rolled my shoulders back and picked up my shirt, smoothing it over my arms.

"Come again?"

I smiled tightly. "Let him take the stage. Let him believe he's won."

"Kais, if he gets board traction—"

I stopped him, "He won't."

He scoffed, "You're betting on timing."

"No," I said coolly. "I'm betting on facts. And when I drop the real numbers, he'll have built his whole comeback on a lie."

Lars exhaled. A hard breath. "This will bury him."

I looked at Alana one last time. Her gaze was on me now. Fully. Like she was trying to figure out how deep in I was. I gave her nothing but a small lift of my brow, like I was weighing nothing more than whether we should have tea or champagne.

"It's time, Lars," I said. "Pull the trigger. Line up the vote."

He let out a breathe, half-laugh, half-sigh. "It's going to be messy."

I grinned. "I fucking hope so."

I hung up, slipping my phone into my pocket, and turn back to Alana. She was quiet. Not uneasy. Not questioning. Just *watching*. Then, before I could say anything, she stepped in close and presses her mouth to mine. Slow. Deep. Hungry even. I feel her sigh against me, like she's settling into something. Like this is her answer to a question she doesn't even know how to ask.

I let her take her time, let her kiss me the way she wants to, meeting her there as my hands found her hips, gripping just enough to feel her shiver. And when she finally pulled back, her lashes were low, her lips just barely curved. *Fucking hell is she turned on?*

A grin smirk tugged at my lips. "Did that *do* something for you, my love?"

She rolls her eyes, smoothing down her skirt like she wasn't just melting against me.

"Shut up."

I chuckle, brushing a thumb over her lips. She wet them with her tongue still tasting me.

"We should go. You've got a dress to pick out." She let me change the subject. But we *both* know what just happened. Neither of us will forget it.

Alana

-21-

"You know, we could just stay right here," Kais growled against my neck, clicking the clasp of my necklace into place. "And you could stay just like that."

I grinned, even as a shiver curled down my spine. His tuxedo brushed my bare back as he leaned in to press a kiss just below my nape, his lips a soft compliment to the heat rolling off him.

"If we don't go," I murmured, "when will I ever get to wear this amazing dress?"

The mirror caught our reflection: his tall broad frame looming behind mine, the contrast between us stark and sinful. My gown shimmered like liquid silver, beading catching every flicker of light like it was begging to be undone. The straps were delicate. The back dipped indecently low, its crisscross of crystals hanging like constellations across my spine. The sheer skirt floated around me like mist. A dress built for indulgence. For fantasy. It wasn't something I should be allowed to wear. And yet... it fit. It started to feel like I did, too.

He didn't speak for a moment just watched me in the mirror with something unreadable, his gaze skating over my reflection like a slow drag of silk.

"Why are you staring at me like that?" I asked softly, adjusting the knot of his bowtie.

"I can't help it. You've gone and done all this." He gestured vaguely, like I was something untouchable.

I turned back toward the mirror, smoothing my hair. The woman looking back at me didn't look invisible anymore. And with him I never felt it. I wasn't overlooked or used up or trying to hold everyone else together. Here, I was his. And giving myself to him (knowing he'd never take it for granted) felt like the most powerful thing I could do.

The adrenaline from earlier still pulsed under my skin, not from the roar of engines, but from *him*. From the bathroom. From the way he'd looked at me like it hurt him for me to doubt him. Then lost every ounce of his self-control to show me why I shouldn't. I couldn't stop thinking about the way his grip bruised with tenderness, the way he spoke like possession wasn't just a choice but something inevitable. I loved it, needed it. Maybe I'd been searching for it my whole life. To belong to someone, to him.

When he snapped back into something cool and lethal on that call with Lars. His authoritative tone still echoed in my ears. It wasn't for business or for strategy. But *for me*. Like he was protecting me from something. I could tell. I caught the shift in him.

I'd seen it before, briefly, in Miami the day we left for Morocco. But now it was louder. Clearer. Kais doesn't lose control. Doesn't waver. Doesn't give his words freely. Unless it's for me. And God, I want that again. Want *all* of him: the fire, the frenzy, the hard grip of his hands, the snap of his restraint, the way he'd taken me like it was the only thing keeping him on the ground. Like I could heal something in him he hadn't let be seen. And maybe I was.

That kind of need, reckless, feral, terrifying in its certainty, it should've scared me. But it didn't. It lit something in me. Because when Kais unravels, he doesn't come undone. He *gives*. All of himself. I want to be the place he can let the storm that rages in him blow until it settles into calm.

I reached for my red lipstick. *The* red lipstick. The very shade I wore on our second date, the first time he bought me a dress this pretty. An offer to him, a little wicked, a little soft. Something that would pull him out of his head and keep him present with me.

"Fuck," he muttered behind me, dragging a hand over his face.

I caught his eyes in the mirror as I popped the cap, the scent of crushed rose petals blooming between us. My hands were steady. My heart wasn't.

"Ready?" I asked, popping my lips.

He stepped forward, arm coiling around my waist, pulling me flush against the hard wall of his body. "What did I tell you the last time you put that on?"

I turned in his arms slowly, my mouth hovering just above his. Close enough to feel the tension in his breath. Close enough to tempt. "That you'd do exactly what I want you to," I whispered. "*Ruin it.*"

His whole body tensed like the word *ruin* had pulled a trigger in him. His eyes darkened. I kissed him once. Light. Barely there. And then I slipped out the door, a wicked smile on my lips and a laugh bubbling in my throat.

"Very fucking unfair, Ya Amar," he muttered behind me. But I could hear the grin in it. Could feel the storm brewing just beneath his control. And that was exactly the point.

🎵 28

A water taxi and short car ride later, we stepped onto a narrow stone street that felt older than the rest of Monaco, just as the sun began its descent behind the rooftops. The neighborhood was older, quieter than the glittering marina or the pulse of the race circuit. Here, the air smelled like sun-warmed stone and sea breeze, and the streets curved in narrow, winding ribbons that made the city feel ancient and intimate.

Alanzo waited at the curb in his usual crisp black suit, backed by a row of shiny sports cars more extravagant than any I'd ever seen. His goofy smile stretched wide as we walked up, and Kais clapped a hand to his shoulder in greeting.

"How was your vacation?" Kais asked warmly.

"Very good, sir. Thank you." Alanzo nodded. "Yours as well, yes?"

Kais smiled, just a little. "Yes."

Alanzo's gaze flicked between us with the faintest twitch of amusement, as if he could see something neither of us was saying, before he straightened and gestured to one of the cars behind him.

"This way."

The car he motioned to looked more like something out of a sci-fi movie rather than something meant for actual roads. Its body was all sleek metal and smooth curves, sculpted from pure shadow. Glossy black paint that devoured the light, broken only by the sheen of carbon fiber slashing across the hood. Massive wheels with gold-trimmed spokes so thin and elegant they looked almost fragile.

"Nice to see James didn't bang it up too much," Kais said, rounding the car with a grin.

Alanzo huffed a laugh, "No, man was born for that track. Good to see him finally take the crown here."

I walked to the passenger side. There wasn't even a handle. Just a seamless frame, until Kais pressed something and the doors lifted toward the sky like wings. Of course they did. He winked at me, sliding into the driver's seat like he was James Bond and this was just another Sunday off duty.

Alanzo helped me down into the impossibly low passenger seat, smiling politely before closing the door behind me, and walking off. The second it shut the car seemed to exhale. A screen lit up on the dash in clean silver text: *Valkyrie*. A small emblem—a pair of outstretched wings—appeared and then disappeared just as quickly. I smoothed my dress over my lap, careful not to catch the beading. My gown shimmered even in the dim light. Then I noticed the harness.

"Okay, but how exactly am I supposed to buckle in with a floor-length dress?" I raised an eyebrow at him.

His smirk was slow, taunting.

"You're not."

He leaned across the console, a slow invasion of space. His fingers brushed my thigh, far higher than necessary as he reached for the buckle. Heat flared instantly between my legs, blooming outward like wildfire.

"This is my job," he growled. "Open your legs."

My knees parted before my mind even told them to, like my body didn't belong to me anymore. The smile he gave me was lethal. Every movement was intentional. His hands moved with infuriating patience, skimming the inside of my thighs as he worked the harness into place. His knuckles dragged against my bare skin, featherlight, like he was mapping me, committing every contour to memory.

Then he slid his hand over the lace of my thong, his rough palm pressing against me with devastating purpose. I swallowed hard, holding my breath, pulse hammering. He stayed there just long enough to feel the throb of want beneath his hand before clipping the buckles into place. Then came the tug. He tightened the harness slowly until the pressure was pointed and unavoidable, until I could feel the strap bite through silk and lace and every last shred of composure.

"Can't have you squirming too much."

I exhaled, a quiet gasp slipping out before I could catch it. My fingers curled against the seat. He chuckled, low and dark, then dragged his thumb—once, just once—up the soft, sensitive line of my inner thigh. The touch was fleeting. A warning and a promise all at once.

Then, like nothing had happened, he shifted into gear.

"Now sit there," he said, smiling as the engine rumbled to life. "Be a good girl and try not to make a mess of that pretty dress."

My lips parted. Every nerve in my body buzzed. Heat pooled between my legs. I glanced over at him, trying to bite back the smile that curved without my permission. He knew. He always knew. That lipstick hadn't just lit a fire. It had *summoned a storm*.

"Shall we go around the track once before the casino?" he asked casually, like his hands hadn't just *branded me*.

"Absolutely," I said, somehow managing to sound composed. Even though I was *definitely not*.

As the car prowled forward, the city shifted around us, narrow streets widening just enough to reveal Saint Nicholas Cathedral. The only place in Monaco I recognized without a Google search. It stood bright against the dusky sky, all clean lines and white stone like something Cary Grant would lean against in a black and white film, cigarette in hand and trouble in his eyes. Though Kais would look a lot more handsome than any golden age actor. I tilted my head toward it, a smile tugging at my lips.

"I'd marry you right now if we could do it there," I teased dreamily.

My focus shifted to the way the engine whined as we left the stillness behind and rejoined the city's pulse—that distinctive *stututu* that made my heart race almost as much as the man driving. Lights flickered across the windshield. Music drifted from open terraces. Monaco after dark somehow pulsed with more energy than it did during the day. Even the lights looked like diamonds against the velvet darkness above. Kais handled every turn like the car was an extension of him, his jaw set, completely in control, one hand resting loose on the wheel, one on my thigh. It felt like flying. Like falling. Like both at once.

The casino waited ahead, paparazzi clustered around its gilded doorways like moths to flame. He slowed, pulling up to the steps as flashes of camera light sparked like static outside the windows. Kais raised one finger as the valet approached.

"Ready?" he asked, reaching over to unbuckle the harness with quiet precision.

I exhaled, smoothing my dress over my lap. "If you are."

Kais slipped out, saying something in French to the valet before coming around to my door. Offering me a hand and privacy as I stepped out, adjusting my dress. About a thousand pictures snapped the second he kissed me on my temple, before lacing his fingers with mine and walking me in.

The casino was breathtaking, less a building, more a cathedral to indulgence. Gold gleamed from every corner, chandeliers dripping crystals from vaulted ceilings, their soft light catching the marble floors below. Music drifted through the air, elegant and distant. Somewhere, a woman laughed. Glasses clinked. Fortunes were won and lost in the span of seconds. It was the kind of place people dreamed of stepping into.

And yet, I barely saw it. Because Kais was magnetic in any world. Not just because of his name or the way people turned as we passed, whispering like they already knew who he was. It was something quieter, something rooted in the way he carried himself. That confidence. That effortless grace. Like no one could shake him, and he knew it. He didn't need to command the room. He *was* the room.

My hand stayed tucked in the crook of his arm, my heels clicking softly across the marble, but my heart was still somewhere back in the car, fluttering like it couldn't decide if it should be afraid or in awe. Because being here... with him... it felt impossible and inevitable all at once.

Even in a place built on power and performance, he was kind.

Controlled, yes—but never cold. Never malicious. There was a thread of warmth under everything, even when he shifted into that king-of-his-empire mode. His quiet steadiness never wavered. Like he was built from something stronger than whatever held the walls of this casino up.

If I was the moon for him, he was the damn sun for me: blinding, inescapable. Something I couldn't help but orbit, no matter how dark the sky got. And God help me, I'd learn to breathe this rarefied air if it meant I got him at the end of the night. *Just him. Always him.*

"God, you're a vision!" Emilia beamed as she walked up, arm in arm with Ollie, both of them looking like they'd just stepped out of a high-fashion ad for Monaco.

"Thank you," I said with a soft smile. "Your friend is extremely talented."

Behind them stood a man just barely shorter than Kais: lean, tan, and unfairly handsome, with the kind of face that looked more at home on a billboard than in real life.

"Reinhardt," he said, wrapping his arms around Kais.

"Cheers. Happy to see you finally won it." Kais replied, hugging him back.

The man turned to me, a dimpled smile lighting up his face as if we'd known each other our whole lives.

"This is her?" he asked, gesturing toward me.

Kais rested his hand on the small of my back and gave a nod. The man pulled me into a hug without hesitation.

"I'm James Del Toro. Kais' best mate, though he probably wouldn't admit that out loud. Too sentimental for him."

I laughed as he pulled back, catching my hand to study the ring.

His brows shot up. "Well, damn. Looks like you might've changed his tune a bit." He glanced at Kais and mouthed a slow, dramatic *Wow Congratulations*, he said sincerely, eyes still gleaming with curiosity and something like quiet approval.

I glanced at Kais, and the proud look in his eyes brought a helpless smile to my face.

"Thank you," I replied. "I couldn't be happier."

"Can we get some more drinks going, mates? I need to forget how fuckin' behind I am in points," Ollie groaned.

"Such a fuckin' baby," James muttered, giving him a shove.

Emilia laughed, moving to my side. "Let's get you away from the testosterone before they start wrestling in front of the black-jack tables." She turned to the boys. "James, am I to suffer through Francesca's company tonight, or can I finally set you up with someone decent?"

James tilted his head, unconcerned. "It's been a year, Em. If you've got someone worth the trouble, be my guest."

Pleased, she turned her attention to Kais, who was already halfway into his phone.

"Kais, I'm stealing your fiancée for a bit. Keep these two out of trouble."

His hand tensed slightly at the small of my back before he looked up, eyes bouncing between us.

"Fine. But the second some prick so much as breathes in her direction, I'm handing Ollie back to you, three sheets to the wind."

Emilia saluted him mockingly.

Kais pulled me closer, his breath brushing my ear. "Stay where I can see you, *Ya Amar.*" He pressed a kiss to my temple, then raised a hand—summoning a man in a neat black suit from the shadows. He muttered something in German before adding in English, "She doesn't carry cash. See to it." Then he was back to his phone, into whatever silent war he was waging in the background.

James let out a low whistle, nudging Ollie.

"Fucking hell, mate. Do your women even breathe without clearance?" Ollie laughed into his whiskey.

"It's not clearance. It's concierge-level obsession," James added.

Emilia rolled her eyes. "You're all insufferable."

I turned back to Kais, smoothing my hand over the front of his jacket. "Don't let them corrupt you while I'm gone."

His eyes drifted to my ring, then to mine. "Not possible."

I smiled, then let Emilia pull me toward the tables, already missing him before I'd even stepped away. It was too easy to want this. Too easy to love him.

The hours blurred, but I hardly noticed. I kept finding him. Across the room. Across the table. Across a dozen conversations I didn't care about. I was endlessly and obsessively drawn to him, my eyes constantly finding his even as Emilia was introducing me to everybody worth knowing in Monaco.

Kais leaned back in his chair at the blackjack table, long fingers tapping lazily against his stack of chips. The overhead lights caught the edge of his jaw, casting shadows that only made him look more untouchably gorgeous. There was a quiet focus to him. Like he was calculating. The dealer flipped another card. The others at the table shifted, glancing, bluffing, second-guessing. But not Kais. He didn't flinch. He didn't blink. He just waited. Watched. Always so damn controlled.

I let myself wonder what he'd looked like before all this. Before the power. Before the suits and the strategies. The boy beneath the man. But even in that imagining, the core of him was the same.

The realization hit me all at once: We were always going to end up here. Maybe not Monaco. Maybe not this exact version of us. But *together*. That was always going to be the through line. I didn't know how I knew that, only that I did. Unseen as gravity. Vital as breath. An inherent, bone-deep knowing I couldn't shake, even if I wanted to.

His eyes flicked over, catching me watching. As they had all night —like he felt me before he saw me. This time when our eyes met, his expression softened. His lips curled into a knowing smirk and in that single look, I felt it all over again: that I was his, and he was mine.

I turned my attention back to the baccarat game Emilia was

playing. Trying not to be a love drunk fool. But heat rolled down my spine before I could even try. That awareness only we seem to share told me he was there. He leaned in close, the warmth of him addictive and calming.

"Stay with Emilia, I need to make a call" he rasped, brushing a kiss to my temple, "I won't bc long."

I nodded, watching him disappear into the crowd. I let Emilia pull me toward a roulette table, the swirl of the wheel and the sound of chips stacking blending into the casino's buzz. The music thrummed low, decadent, like it knew everyone here had something to prove. I didn't. Not tonight. I wasn't alone for long.

"Who would leave a pretty little thing like you all alone?"

The voice was too confident. Some guy: tan, designer suit, expensive-smelling. His cologne turned my nose before his charm did. He slid into the seat beside me like he was already certain of his chances. Typical.

I didn't even flinch. Just held up my hand, the blue diamond catching the light like it knew it had a job to do. "Not alone. And not interested."

His grin faltered just a twitch, but I caught it. His eyes cut to Emilia, probably hoping for a signal, some hint that I was bluffing. She didn't even glance up from her drink.

"Kais Reinhardt." She sipped her drink, not sparing him a glance, "But go on—by all means, humiliate yourself further."

That was all she said. It was all she needed to say. The guy blinked once, muttered something in French that probably wasn't complimentary, and disappeared into the crowd. And damn, it felt good. Emilia raised a brow, grinning into her glass.

"That was the thirstiest man I've seen all week and I've been to Saint-Tropez."

I snorted, "Do guys actually think that works?"

She rolled her eyes.

"Only on the girls who think a spray tan and daddy's Amex make them irresistible." She tilted her glass toward me, "They take one look at you and go feral because you don't have to try to be beautiful. You just are." Then just sipped her drink, like it wasn't the kindest thing any woman in her tax bracket has said to me.

I just smiled faintly, because I'd surprised myself. Not for knowing how to shut him down, but for how certain I'd felt. There was no twinge of doubt in me.

Because I wasn't just wearing his ring. I was his.

Before long Kais was at my side again, slipping behind me, whispering into my ear.

"Did you mean it?"

I turned, blinking up at him with a confused smile, "Mean what?"

His eyes held mine. "What you said earlier. About getting married at the cathedral."

I let out a nervous laugh, unsure whether to brush it off or double down.

"What?" I raised my brows.

"It's ready," he said, voice soft. "You just have to say it."

My heart skipped a dozen beats. Not because I was surprised but because deep down, I'd known he would do something like this. Knew, in the way you know when the sky turns that shade of gold before a storm, that something was coming. Something inevitable. I could say no. Tell him we were being reckless. That the world would eat us alive for moving this fast. But the truth? None of that mattered to me anymore. Because this—*him*—he had become the thing I trusted most.

I nodded. Once. Clear and unshakably certain. Kais inhaled like he'd been holding that breath all night—like he'd been waiting for me to catch up. He took my hand.

And then we left.

Kais

-22-

🎵 26

THE CATHEDRAL WAS QUIET, FOOTSTEPS HUSHED BY polished stone, the stillness stretched taut like even the room knew what was coming. Saint Nicholas looked exactly how I imagined it would: vaulted ceilings, tall arched windows spilling amber light over marble floors, everything glowing under a thousand flickering candles. It was the kind of place made for kings. Or, maybe, just for her.

I stood alone at the altar, my hands steady, my stance relaxed, but something inside me was coiled tight. It wasn't nerves. I've fought in front of tens of thousands. Taken hits that split skin and broke bone. I don't shake. But this? This had me holding my breath. Not because I wasn't sure. Because I knew, down to the fucking atom, what this was. Because for the first time, I wasn't walking into a fight. I was walking into peace, into forever. And I was doing it with *her*.

I'd called in every favor I had. Paid whatever it took. No spectacle. No crowd. Just this place. This place I'd been waiting my entire life to step into without even knowing it.

The pianist touched the keys gently, warming up. I recognized the first few notes instantly, 'Unchained Melody'. My request. Because somehow my mother's favorite record fit the love of my life as perfectly as her hand fit my palm.

I exhaled slowly, tightening the cufflink on my left wrist. A ripple of sound moved through the cathedral. Then silence. Alanzo gave me a nod. Everything was ready. The music shifted. Louder now. My heart pounded in my chest. The doors opened.

And there she was.

Lit by candlelight like some celestial fucking vision. Her gown shimmered, silver and soft, hugging her body like it had been sewn to her bones. Crystal strands traced patterns across her skin that made her every movement glitter. Her hair was swept up. Shoulders bare. Lips red. Eyes only for me. She looked like a miracle. And she was mine.

My lungs forgot how to work. Every part of me just... locked into place. Like the world had been lopsided until this exact second. I didn't breathe again until she was close enough to reach. And even then, it was only because she did.

Her scent hit me first. That perfume I'd never forget. A smell I'd come to crave. It wrapped around me, recentered me. Like her. Like she always does. She smiled at me then—slow, trembling slightly, like she wasn't sure whether to laugh or cry. And God help me... I nearly broke. Not because I deserve her. But because I fully understood how much I had to lose if I ever forgot that I don't.

I'd imagined this a dozen different ways. But nothing came close to how it felt to have her in front of me, her fingers tangled in mine, eyes bright, not from the light, not from the tears, but from that fire she carried. The same one that refused to go out, even when the world tried its hardest to snuff it out.

She looked at me like she knew. Knew I wasn't perfect. Knew I'd always carry the darker parts of everything that made me. Knew I'd still burn the world if it meant keeping her safe. And she chose me anyway.

The priest said my name. I nodded. Reached for the wedding band I'd kept in my pocket for what felt like a lifetime. Slipping it onto her finger didn't feel like a finish line, it felt like *permission*.

Permission to finally stop holding my breath. To believe this was real. To let her be mine, fully. She looked down at her hand then back to me like I was her whole fucking world. And then she smiled. Just for me.

When it was her turn, her fingers trembled. Just long enough for me to feel it. I didn't flinch. I bent my head toward hers so only she would hear me. My words just for her. Always just for her.

"I'm not going anywhere, Ya Amar."

She smiled like she believed me. Because she does. My wedding band felt heavy, foreign. Like the weight of a crown I didn't deserve until her.

Until she walked into my life and showed me what it felt like to be really seen. Loved by someone without condition or motive. To be loved by her. The priest's voice lifted again, saying something final, something binding. But I didn't need his words to make this true. I already knew what I was standing in. I already knew what I'd chosen.

My moon.

Alana

-23-

♫ 27

WE SCAMPERED FROM THE CAR, HEARTS RACING, breathless laughter tumbling from our lips as we stumbled onto the lamp-lit midnight streets of Monaco. The notes of 'Unchained Melody' were still echoing in my head. The song Kais had quietly requested I walk down the aisle to. *Ridiculously perfect, just like him.*

His tuxedo jacket was draped loosely over my shoulders, carrying his warmth and scent, his arm wrapped securely around my waist as if he was afraid I might disappear into the night. *Though I'm so stupidly in love with the man, I don't know how he could believe I'd go anywhere.*

Our mouths had barely left each other for more than a second since we said 'I do'. I didn't even bother to look where we were going until my heel slipped against the wet cobblestones, causing a small gasp to escape me. He caught my hand instantly, lowering himself smoothly onto one knee.

My heart fluttered wildly with deja vu as his fingers gently fixed the strap around my ankle, his lips brushed softly against the anklet he'd given me in Morocco. Then slowly, he kissed my ring finger, where the cool metal of my new wedding band accompanied my engagement ring. Finally, he stood, cupping my face in his hands, his eyes dark and impossibly soft before his mouth captured mine again: a kiss filled with certainty, possessiveness, and something that felt terrifyingly close to worship.

"Come on," he whispered against my lips, pulling back just enough to let me breathe. His smirk returned, warm and reckless, as he tugged me toward the glittering steps of the Hôtel de Paris. "The evening's just beginning, my love," he chuckled like a damn boy. And God, my heart exploded all over again.

We burst into the grand lobby of the hotel, tangled up in laughter and kisses, utterly oblivious to the elegant surroundings. Kais kept me pulled tightly to his side, his mouth brushing warmly against mine as we finally slowed our pace.

"Mr. Reinhardt," a familiar voice called softly, bringing us back to reality.

Alanzo stood waiting in the center of the lobby, poised and patient, holding out a polished keycard with a gentle smile. "Everything is ready, just as you requested." His eyes flickered warmly toward me. "Congratulations, Mr. and Mrs. Reinhardt."

My breath caught at the sound of those words: *Mrs. Reinhardt.* It felt surreal, beautifully impossible.

Kais took the keycard with an appreciative nod. "Thank you, Alanzo."

Then, without another word, he lifted me off my feet, ignoring my startled laughter as he slung me over his shoulder and strode proudly toward the elevator tucked discreetly to the side hall.

"Kais!" I squealed.

He tapped my butt lightly, chuckling. "It's not time to start pleading yet, Mrs. Reinhardt."

I laughed, helplessly dangling at his back, heat flooding my cheeks as the elevator doors slid closed behind us, sealing us away from the world.

HE CARRIED me the whole way. The door to our room clicked shut behind us, and he lowered me carefully to my feet. The suite surrounded us in quiet opulence: rich fabrics, low lighting, the city twinkling like a spilled jewelry box just beyond the windows. But none of it mattered. Not when he looked at me like this.

He stepped closer, crowding me gently backward until I was pressed against the wall. His hands found my hips, strong and sure, pinning me against the cool marble.

Trailing his fingers down my spine, Kais pressed in close, his breath warm against my ear. "You were such a good girl tonight," he rasped, "flashing that sad bastard your ring like you knew exactly who you belong to, *Ya Amar.*"

I stilled, just for a second. He *saw* that? Heat surged through me, embarrassment quickly giving way to something darker. The memory of that man's smug voice, his stench, the way he looked at me like I was an easy win.

"I nearly ripped you out of this dress right on that fucking roulette table," Kais growled, and this time, when his grip tightened at my hips, I gasped—soft, helpless, and turned on out of my mind.

I swallowed hard, "I didn't know you were watching."

"I'm always watching you, my love," His voice was pure danger now, a promise of everything to come. A slow, wicked smile curled his lips as he leaned in close, his mouth brushing mine like he couldn't decide whether to kiss me or devour me.

"What do you say, Mrs. Reinhardt—" he breathed, "Shall we let all of Monaco hear exactly whose fucking name you wear?"

My hands curled in his shirt, heat flooding every part of me. "Yes," I whispered huskily. Then I met his steady, blazing eyes. "But first, Mr. Reinhardt, I'd like to personally show you exactly whose name I wear."

My restless hands found the buttons of his dress shirt. A gleam of amusement sparkled in his eyes as he shed his perfectly tailored tux. I stepped back toward the bed, drinking in his calculated, seductive movements. With each discarded piece of clothing, the air grew thicker with anticipation. My own dress fell away with a silken sigh, leaving behind only the whisper of my scarlet thong and the points of my heels.

Our lips met again, a collision of ravenous need. I pulled back, leaving a crimson smear—a map of my desire—down his jaw, his neck, across his chest. Then, kneeling, I traced the path of my kisses across his stomach, pausing just short of the hard line below his belly button, his anticipation was a delicious torment.

He let out a forced breath, every muscle rigid with want. I love that I can do that, have him begging *for me*. My eyes drifted upward holding his.

"Kai," I purred.

"You've been so patient, gentle, restrained..." I sealed my words with a featherlight kiss, "but you promised me ruin," I whispered, threading his wedding band through my fingers and pulling his hand to my hair in permission. My eyes locked with his. A devilish grin stretched across my lips. "So take me apart, Kais. Every single inch—until even my breath tastes like you, belongs to you—until even my ruin bears your name."

His grip on my hair tightened, just enough to make me shiver. His gaze dragged over my face, jaw ticking as he muttered something clipped and German that sounded more like a warning than an answer. Just like that, I felt it—the shift. This wasn't careful anymore. This was the cage door swinging open, no more restraint to protect me from the depth of him. He was going to claim me, show me the primal side that had always been there. And every part of me craved it.

He bent, his fingers twisting my hair around his hand, tugging my mouth to his. "Open it," he commanded.

I obeyed with a fervent eagerness, claiming him hungrily with my mouth. Moving my tongue in slow, teasing strokes. My hands twisted gently in tandem, his fist still knotted in my hair, guided my pace. Every intake of breath from him was rough and intoxicating. My hips rocked forward in sync with my rhythm, chasing friction, but needing *him*.

"Fuck," he rasped. "This soft fucking mouth... I've waited for this." The guttural sound he made reverberated through my bones.

"My fucking wife. You bend for no one but me," he growled, pulling me back just enough to meet my gaze.

"No one but you, Kai," I panted. Breathless and needing his command.

His smirk deepened. "So eager. So pretty when you're patient for me."

The heat coiling in my stomach ignited into a raging inferno. He bent down, his hand moved in swift precision beneath my underwear, finding their mark. Stealing my breath in a gasp as he thrust two fingers inside me. A shiver, splintering and electric, snaked up my spine. His eyes gleamed in amusement as I writhed, helpless to the rhythm he knew so well.

"Seems you've made a mess again, my love."

Then his mouth claimed mine. Hard. Deep. His tongue explored like it was trying to burn away every breath I had left.

"You want ruin?" His voice barely more than a snarl now.

I nodded, a single word escaping my lips. "Please."

His jaw clenched. "Show me where."

An untamed smirk split my lips as I traced the path his fingers had taken, dragging mine from my lips, to my tongue, and down to the pulsing ache between my thighs. A groan rumbled in his chest, nostrils flaring, His body coiled like a predator just given permission to pounce.

"You're going to take this like the fucking princess that you are. Hold your breath, baby." His voice low and intense as his thumb grazed my lips.

I inhaled deeply, filling my lungs with the promise of what was to come. Then, he was mine again. Eagerly I took him back into my mouth, sloppily wetting him and drinking him in through hollow cheeks as I ran my hands in a pepper-grinding twist up and down his length, letting him hit the back of my throat in repetition.

Our rings clinked together as my fingers intertwined with his, pulling him in, begging him for more. Tears burned down my cheeks. It still wasn't enough. I chased him: every thrust, every groan, leaving my throat raw and voice fractured.

His release was explosive, a violent shudder, his body pulsing in rigid waves, sending his ecstasy down my throat. I swallowed it all, soft licks and sucks, soothing what I'd just destroyed as he cursed my name. My name on his lips like that was a spell. I could've unraveled from that alone. The sounds he made lit something wild in my blood, made me starved for him.

He trembled above me. But it was fleeting. That look returned. That flash of something darker. Hungrier. The kind of hunger that dared me to ask for more. His gaze snagged on my hand, still restless between my legs. His jaw tightened, eyes flint-hard.

"You've forgotten your restraint, Mrs. Reinhardt."

A breathy, "Yes," rasped from my lips, a desperate plea. I was so close just another second and I—

In a heartbeat, he pinned me to the bed, my belly pressed flat against the cool linen, both my hands trapped in his. The void left behind was fucking unbearable.

"Kai, I need you," I whimpered, the words like a cry mixed with desperation for him, a white-hot agony.

"Christ, babe," His voice frayed at the edges, like it barely survived the war inside him. "You can't say that. Not like that."

In the next second, he released my hands and lifted my hips, tearing the thong from my body like it had *dared* to keep him from me.

His mouth descended between my thighs, a searing kiss, then hot suction on the throbbing center of me. His hands gripped the backs of my thighs, thumbs digging into the crease where flesh met hip, spreading me wider as his breath hitched against my skin.

I couldn't see him, only feel him. The slow drag of his tongue, the growl vibrating from his chest into the base of my spine. His mouth moved with merciless rhythm, all heat and pressure, coaxing my nerve endings into chaos.

Between strokes, I felt the warm pulse of his breath against soaked skin—ragged, uneven, like he was just as wrecked as I was. Each flick, each pull, sent shockwaves tearing through me, until my pulse lost all rhythm.

My fingers clawed at the sheets as my hips jerked back and my body snapped tight in a violent arch. A cry ripped from my sore throat as pleasure took hold in brutal, unrelenting waves.

Kais moved again, quickly. With tremors still wracking me, he filled me in one punishing thrust: deep, ruthless. Every nerve in my body screamed. My breath stuttered as I released a strangled moan. Even open to him, the sensation was overwhelmingly filling.

Still, I pushed back into him, needing more, until he hit a place so deep my vision blurred. I struggled for breath, hands clawing for anything—his arm, the sheets, the goddamn air—as he drove in even deeper, until I had nothing left to give.

He didn't move. Not right away. Just held me there, stretched and gasping, with a low growl building at the base of his throat like he was savoring it. Savoring me. Letting his heavy calloused hands caress every curve of me before connecting an approving smack to my ass that vibrated through my bones. I bit down a whimper that made my body open up even more to him.

"Christ. It's like your body was carved out to fuckin' worship mine."

I turned my head over my shoulders, meeting his eyes, then

clenched around him as I bounced my hips, desperate to feel the brutality of his power behind me.

"Fuckin' greedy for it," he muttered, watching me. "Keep bouncing, baby."

Then, without hesitation or apology, he thrust punishingly inside me. His hands, brutal and tender at once, gripped my hips, driving me against him in agonizing, breath-stealing thrusts I felt behind my eyes. Our bodies collided in thunderous crashes as I chased his rhythm.

"Oh my god, Kai," I begged, a broken cry.

Each plunge tightened the screaming wire of tension, stretched taut beyond endurance.

"Yeah, that's it, baby. Louder. Who the fuck do you belong to?"

My breath came ragged with a bubbling, pleading whimper as electricity danced in my nerves, begging for release. His arm locked around my waist, shifting his hips just slightly and hit something so devastating I came undone all over again. I shattered, calling his name with a crying whine that drowned out even the revelry of Monte Carlo. And still he held me through it, his own breath breaking down, low curses ghosting against my skin.

He released my hips, my pulsing body collapsing under the weight of his chest. My body trembled and jerked. Thighs burning, muscles weak as my core pulsed around him, sensitive and tingling with static.

"Easy," he breathed against my temple, "I've got you, baby."

His left hand closed over mine, our rings clicking together one last time before he unleashed himself again in a deep plunge. One final thrust. One final groan, in a final, heavenly wave as he spilled into me.

"It's so pretty here," I muttered, staring at the twinkling skyline from the oversized bathtub.

The city lights flickered across the water's surface, casting a soft blue hue over the room.

"I only see you, Ya Amar," Kais replied, as his hands moved slowly over my back, lathering soap down my skin. I leaned back into him, letting his arms settle around me, tilting my chin up to kiss him.

"I love you," I whispered, holding his gaze.

His lips pressed into my wet hair, firm and certain, "I love you too."

A comfortable silence stretched between us, the warmth of the water and the steady rhythm of his breathing wrapping around me like a cocoon. Tired and sore as hell but so goddamn happy.

"So what happens now?" I asked softly, absentmindedly playing with his wedding band. "Like... when do we go back to Miami?"

Kais cocked his head, watching me carefully. "What do you want to happen?"

I shrugged.

"Honestly? I didn't even think about it. I just knew I wanted to be with you. Everything else was a distant second."

He smiled, resting his head back against the edge of the tub. "I meant what I said in that cathedral, Alana." His tone was unwavering. "Wherever you are, that's where I'll be. If you want me in Miami, fine. If you want to move with me to London, just say the word."

I sighed, my fingers tracing slow circles over his wedding band. How was I supposed to decide that? His whole life was in London. Asking him to move to Miami just so I could finish school felt selfish. But I *did* want to finish. I changed the subject.

"Your dad's in London, right?"

Kais smoothed my damp hair back. "Right."

I hesitated before clearing my throat, "Should I... maybe meet him?"

He groaned, tilting his head back against the tub. "The man's a cunt, Alana."

I nodded, "I get that. But you work with him. I just don't know how great of an idea it is for me to move to London if you don't even want me around him."

His grip on me tightened slightly before he caught my chin, turning me to face him. His eyes were dark and unwavering.

"Alana Elaine Reinhardt, don't ever say that shit again." His voice was quiet, but there was an edge to it. "I don't give a fuck about you meeting that man. The only thing that matters is that *he* doesn't deserve to meet *you*. And if he so much as breathes the wrong way in your direction, I don't know how the hell I'll control myself."

A slow smile curled my lips. "Should I teach you restraint then?" I teased. Kais chuckled darkly before catching my mouth in his, claiming me once more.

Alana

-24-

"Wow, this whole husband thing really suits you, Kai-Kai," I said, wrapping my arms around the back of my half-naked husband as he made tea in the kitchen, wearing nothing but a towel. He turned to me with a lazy smile, his damp, unruly curls flopping into his face.

"You too," he said, and without missing a beat, tugged on the tie of my robe, revealing my own bareness beneath.

I yelped, clutching the fabric closed and quickly retying it before snatching the towel at his waist in retaliation. He didn't bother to fix it. He just turned back to the counter, completely unbothered, cheeks perfectly toned and unapologetically on display as he stirred honey into our tea.

"Kais," I hissed through a laugh, "put your towel back on. Alanzo could be here any minute."

He turned to face me, still utterly nude and entirely unbothered, like a Greek statue come to life. Handing me a warm cup of mint tea, he grinned.

"As I recall," he said, pulling me close by the hip, "you were begging me for something completely different a moment ago." His voice dropped an octave, brushing warm against my ear.

222

"Are you saying you're already sick of seeing me naked, after just two weeks of marriage, *Ya Amar*?"

I scoffed, "I think you know better than that."

The elevator dinged. Perfect timing. I snatched the towel off the counter, a wicked grin tugging at my lips.

"In fact," I said, draping the towel slowly around his waist, "now feels like the perfect time to see you naked, Mr. Reinhardt."

Footsteps echoed in the foyer. I stepped in closer, pressing my back to his chest as I clutched the towel at his waist, shielding him from view.

"Just not in front of an audience."

He chuckled low behind me as I adjusted the towel with a practiced tuck. I know he fights half naked in front of thousands but I'm not the sharing type. Not even with charming, short, and entirely-too-hairy Alanzo.

"Boss," Alanzo said, clearing his throat from the other side of the counter.

Kais gave him a nod.

"Everything's set for London. The pilot just needs to know what time you want to be wheels up."

He looked down to me then, voice softer. "You sure you want to do this? We can still stay here."

That's when I saw it—that flicker of hesitation he tried to bury. I leaned into him closer, lowering my voice to match his.

"Yeah, I'm sure. And no, we can't stay here. I'd much rather be where you are than have you flying back and forth every week." I smiled, trying to ease the tension I could feel tightening his shoulders. "We'll get enough of that in the fall."

His jaw ticked—barely, but I caught it. Even if he understood why, even if he'd fly across the world every day just to see me, I knew he hated the idea of us being apart. Not because he doubted us, just because he didn't want to miss a second more than he had to. Neither did I. *But when I'm so close to the end of this thing I put everything into, I have no choice. God, he's looking at me like he's already bracing to miss me.* My chest tightened. I wasn't ready to sit in that feeling yet, so I smiled again and nudged him gently.

"Don't be like that," I muttered. "You've got me for the rest of the summer. And after that? The rest of our lives. Fingers crossed this fancy new name you've given me helps get me off Oxford's waitlist. Then you really won't be able to get rid of me."

He leaned in, his mouth brushing my ear. "You're already mine for the rest of our lives, *Ya Amar.* Where you go to university doesn't bloody change that."

The words landed somewhere low and certain. Not just romantic—undoubtable. A vow we'd already made, sealed in something quieter than ceremony.

He kissed my temple, then turned to Alanzo. "Looks like we're still going, mate. I'm good to fly out anytime this afternoon." Then, back to me. "What about you, love? When do I need to grab your things from your old place?"

My mug clicked against the marble as I set it down.

"I've got it. I haven't turned my phone back on yet, so I'm not sure exactly when I'm heading over. But I want to see Jazzy before I do. Can we take off in the morning?"

I don't even know what's waiting for me on that phone, I thought. *But I know what's not: my sister.*

"Of course," he said without missing a beat. Alanzo nodded once.

"I'll get it sorted." Then he turned and disappeared back toward the foyer.

I stepped away, freeing Kais from my cloak of discretion and facing him again. He studied me for a moment, that steady gaze of his narrowing with concern.

"Why haven't you powered your cell back on?" he asked, his voice calm, but curious.

I hesitated, rolling the question around in my chest before I answered.

"Honestly? I don't want whatever flood is waiting behind it

from my mom. I already know there's nothing from my sister. I've still got a few weeks in email jail. And aside from school stuff and Jasmine probably losing her mind and maybe a message from my cousin Penelope—I just... I wasn't ready to deal with my mom. Not on a jet-lagged brain. Not when we just got back."

He nodded slowly, then set his mug down and stepped towards me. His arms wrapped around my waist, warm and sure. I melted into them with ease.

"Ya Amar." His voice was low. Still. "There's no one on this planet you need to fear. I'll burn the whole fucking thing down and place it at your feet before I let anyone hurt you again."

I laughed but then I looked up at him. And there wasn't even a flicker of humor in his eyes. He meant every word. Something lodged in my throat. A crack in the armor I didn't realize I was still wearing. All those years of standing on my own, holding my ground with no one behind me and now here he was. Offering fire. Offering war. Offering *me* a place to rest.

I nodded. "Okay. I'll turn it on. But maybe... after I get showered." I leaned up to kiss him, just a brush of my lips over his. It said *thank you* and *I see you* and *you scare the hell out of me in the best way*—all at once.

His smirk slid in like muscle memory, "Is that an invitation?"

"No, it is not." I giggled, swatting his chest.

"I've got a doctor's appointment later anyway," I added. "Birth control renewal since *someone* wanted to detour through Ibiza and made me miss it once already."

His hands tightened slightly around my waist, his thumb tracing a circle over my spine. "Do you want to go to that?"

I arched a brow. "Do *you* not want me to?"

He shrugged, but it was the kind of shrug that carried weight. "You can do what you want, love. It won't change how I feel. Just don't feel like you *have* to."

God. This man. I shook my head, smiling in awe of him.

"You really don't do anything halfway, do you?"

He grinned. "You wanna go to the shower and be reminded?"

I opened my mouth to tease him back but then something shifted. Just for a second. Something completely uninvited whispered in the back of my mind.

What if I didn't go? What if I let it happen? The thought flickered like a breeze that shouldn't have made it through the door. A maybe. A not-yet. A terrifying, impossible dream I'd never let myself want out loud. But now... I was married. I was loved. I was safe. And for the first time, the idea of a baby—*his* baby—didn't feel like something I had to run from. I blinked it away. Too much. Too fast. Still, something lingered. I leaned in, heart fluttering in my chest.

"Absolutely."

Alana

-25-

"WHERE THE FUCK HAVE YOU BEEN?" JASMINE STOOD IN the doorway, slack-jawed, one hand gripping the frame like she needed support to process the sight of me.

"Wow. Is that any way to greet your best friend?" I smirked, stepping inside. She sucked her teeth.

"Bitch, don't try that cute shit with me." Then she grabbed my wrist and yanked me toward the couch like I owed her rent. "Sit your ass down."

I gave her a look, partially amused. "I'm sitting because I missed you, not because you barked at me like I'm a damn dog."

She pounced next to me the second I hit the cushion, all heat and indignation wrapped in tight yoga pants.

"Well, fucking spill. You disappear for a month and come back married?" She slapped my arm.

I'm glad to see she hadn't lost her fire while I was gone.

"Aren't you the one who said if that man kidnaps you, don't rescue you? Do I not get the same courtesy?"

She scoffed.

"I didn't mean for you to take that shit literally. What's the story here? Does he need a green card or something?"

I laughed, a sound caught between nerves and wonder. I hadn't said it out loud yet. "The man needs nothing from me, Jazz." I shrugged, the words quiet but certain. "I just... fell in love."

She blinked. Once. Twice. Her already huge eyes somehow got even wider. "Oh, you're fucking serious." Before I could react, she snatched my hand. "This ring is huge, Alana!"

Her fingers turned my hand like I was under a damn forensic light. I pulled it back gently.

For a second, I didn't say anything. It was still surreal, even now, even after the wedding, the vows, the mornings waking up in his arms. Saying it out loud made it feel more real... but also more fragile.

"Well, I know you saw the headlines," I said, stretching out on the couch. "Considering you sent me every single one of them. Thank you for that, by the way. Really loved seeing my bikini pics immortalized on the internet. I was trying to avoid those, you know."

She sucked her teeth.

"Girl, please. You looked snatched to the heavens in every single one. Consider it a public service."

She crossed the room into the kitchen, her hair bouncing as she disappeared behind the fridge. The familiar hiss of cans being cracked made me smile. Then she reappeared, passing me a hard cider and settling back in beside me.

"But seriously," she added, shaking her head, "no one told your boujee ass to go off and marry a whole—*world champion*—boxer. What did you think was gonna happen?"

I took a sip, the cool fizz of the drink settling me for a second. "I didn't know," I admitted, my voice quieter than hers. "Not at first. And by the time I did, I was already in way too deep."

She squinted at me over the rim of her can like she was trying to scan my soul. "Mhm. I still can't believe we didn't fucking Google him."

I snorted a laugh. She had a point. But back then, I hadn't

wanted to know. Because knowing meant deciding. And I wasn't ready to walk away from him.

'I'm in fuckin' shock, I think," she muttered.

Of course, she was still in shock, I could tell. Jasmine cursed like a sailor when she was overwhelmed. She blamed it on being Colombian, but I knew it was just her way of staying upright when the world spun too fast.

"So, what now?" she asked, her voice dipping into something softer.

I hesitated for half a second, then said it like I was still getting used to the words. "I'm going to London with him for the rest of the summer... then I'll come back in the fall to finish my last semester."

She blinked, trying to catch up. I could already see the wheels turning in her head, trying to map out what that meant for us, for our apartment, for everything. So, I put her mind at ease.

"Oh—and he paid the rent here through next year." I gave my hand a little twirl like I was unveiling a magic trick.

Her jaw dropped.

"Shut. Up." Then a wild grin crept on her lips. "Can we make this a sister wife situation?"

I cut my eyes at her.

"Kidding! Kidding," she said throwing her hands up, laughing. Her expression shifted, more serious now. "So, you're still gonna live here while he's in London?"

I drained the last of my cider, letting the fizz coat whatever this strange ache in my chest was.

"I'll be back and forth. But he has a place south of fifth. I'll probably stay there when I'm in town or here with you, I don't know."

She sat back like I'd just knocked the wind out of her. "Wow. I really thought we were gonna be Blanche and Rose 'til the end."

My smile wilted just a bit. "Me too."

And I had. There was a version of my life where it was just us:

me and Jasmine against the world, eating cheap noodles on the floor and yelling at her telenovelas. But then Kais happened. And now everything was different.

"To be honest... it's been a whirlwind." I met her eyes. "But I really do love him. So much it— fucking hurts."

Her gaze settled on mine, heavier now.

"And it doesn't feel the way it looks on the outside, you know?" I added.

That one sentence cracked something open in me. Because it was true. All of this—the photos, the headlines, the ring that felt like it had its own gravity—none of it could explain how soft our kind of love actually was underneath it all. How quiet. How real. She reached for me, arms pulling me into a hug so fast it nearly knocked the wind out of me.

"I'm happy for you," she whispered, voice a little rough. "Like, truly. If anyone deserves a big, ridiculous kind of love—it's you." I swallowed against the lump in my throat.

"I'm gonna miss you," I said, hugging her tighter. "Like... a lot. You got me through some really hard shit."

She pulled back, wiping under her eye with the sleeve of her hoodie. "I know, Mama." Her grin came back, wide and wobbly. "I deserve a commission for all the training sessions I dragged you through. I personally sculpted the ass that caught a billionaire, don't play."

I laughed, shaking my head. "Delusional."

But before I could clap back, she snapped her fingers like she had just remembered something.

"Mmm, I forgot to tell you. Your mom showed up here a few weeks ago."

"What?" I snapped. "For what?"

She shrugged like it was nothing, but I could already feel my chest bracing.

"No idea. She didn't say anything specific. I just told her you weren't here."

Of course she didn't. My mother never said what she wanted outright—she just showed up like a storm, expecting the doors to open and the lights to stay on. I shook my head, already tired.

"Probably just needed money. I got a few messages when I finally turned my phone on, but she didn't pick up. And Macy's still off on her great American tour with her grandparents." The words came out flat, but my stomach was tightening. Because I knew what was underneath that silence. If she wasn't answering, it wasn't good.

Jasmine's whole body changed, shoulders going rigid, her lips tightening. Her fire faded into that quiet empathy she gives me when she's going to say something I don't want to hear. "She didn't look good, Alana." I looked up at her. She wasn't teasing anymore. "On the nod," she said softly. "Like, for real. Super skinny. Eyes barely open. Just... not all there."

The breath left my lungs jagged and shaky. Yeah. That sounds about right. That familiar ache opened up in my chest again. That helpless, nauseating space where hope used to be.

"I don't know what else to do anymore," I said quietly, my voice not much stronger than a whisper. "It's like watching someone walk toward a cliff and being told not to scream."

She scooted a little closer, her tone gentling even as her words hit hard.

"That's why I almost didn't tell your ass. You always think you have to do something. Like you're responsible for fixing it."

I didn't say anything, but she wasn't wrong. I didn't know how not to try.

"She has to want help, Alana. You giving her money, answering her every call, carrying the weight of every fucking thing she refuses to, It's just enabling her."

She looked at me like she needed me to believe it. Like someone had needed to say it a long time ago.

"I saw that shit with my Tío. Had to lose everything—his job, his house, almost his leg—before he cleaned up. It wasn't about love. It was about reality. And your mom? She's not ready for it. Not yet."

I blinked slowly, the words settling like pebbles in my chest. Not heavy, exactly. Just there. Truths I didn't want but recognized.

"Take some time. Take some space. Let her live with her choices, and you go live yours with that fine ass husband of yours, preferably on a yacht while wearing silk."

That earned a weak laugh from me, but it didn't shake the weight of what she had said. Maybe she was right. Maybe I didn't have to keep bleeding for someone who didn't even notice I was cut open. Maybe trying to save her was just another way I'd kept myself from saving me.

"Yeah," I said, quieter now. "You're right." I nodded.

"About which part?" she teased, nudging me with her foot.

"Both. You dirty ass girl." I tossed a throw pillow at her. She cackled, catching it mid-air.

"Hey, just teach me your ways so I can get one of him in my size," she said, eyes gleaming, "and I'll officially squash all the plans I had to murder your ass for ghosting me."

I grinned, rolling my eyes. "You would never."

"Oh, I already did," she said sweetly, holding up her cider like a toast. "Poisoned your drink. I'll look stunning in black, comforting your husband at your funeral. Tragic, but glamorous."

I barked out a laugh so loud I startled myself. It felt good— God, it felt good—to just be in this moment, held by the kind of friendship that didn't ask for perfection or explanations.

"Fuck you, Jazz."

"Love you too, bitch," she said, leaning her shoulder against mine.

Alana

I'M CONVINCED I NEED TO PUT A BELL ON MY HUSBAND. The man is always moving, as if some force inside him refuses stillness. Which, to be fair, isn't a surprise. I figured out pretty quick that being with Kais Reinhardt meant splitting my time with an endless rotation of meetings, phone calls, emails, and dawn workouts that made me question whether he was part machine.

The man is disciplined to his bones. Unshakeable. But since we got back to London, that intensity has dialed up even higher. He's building something, carrying something, closing chapters I haven't asked about yet. I just know I miss him. The kind of missing that shows up in my body first: empty arms, cold sheets, muscles tensed like they're waiting to exhale. I think I'd give up a limb just to wake up with him still in bed beside me.

So, after a quiet workout and a long, hot shower, I decide to do something about it. Not the limb sacrifice—just a soft ambush. Hair still wet, skin still warm, I pad barefoot through Kais' apartment (our apartment, I guess) on a mission to find Alanzo. Kais has a Rolodex of people orbiting him, all somehow essential to the machine he's built. But Alanzo's the guy who makes things happen. Usually, he shadows Kais. Lately, I have a feeling he's been reassigned. To me. And if I want to pull this off without Kais rearranging his whole day, I'm going to have to get a little sneaky.

"Morning, Alanzo," I said, toweling off my hair as I stepped into the kitchen.

"Morning, Signora," he replied, his voice warm, his smile easy, already settled into the cadence of his day. He stood at the counter, sipping tea like he'd lived in this kitchen his whole life.

This place is nothing like Miami. Here, everything felt older, quieter, more lived-in. Dark wood, exposed brick, worn leather. Masculine in that unintentional, effortless way like Kais hadn't tried to make it look like him, it just did. Photographs lined the walls, framed jerseys and gloves and fading championship posters tucked among sleek furniture. His belts—titles he never bragged about—hung like relics in glass, watching over the room. A full gym sat just off the living space, visible through steel-framed windows, proof that Kais built his temple in sweat and silence.

I moved toward the kettle, pouring myself a cup of tea as I let my gaze drift out the towering windows. Rain traced rivulets down the glass—the sky was in no rush to clear. London felt like it always kept a secret. Kais did too.

"Is he training today or at the office?" I asked, voice light, casual. Not pressing. Just enough curiosity to sound offhand.

Alanzo glanced down at his phone.

I knew better than to ask Kais directly. If he even sensed that I wanted him home, he'd be here before I could blink. And I didn't want to pull him away. I just wanted to see him. Steal a moment. Be near him without asking the world to pause for it.

"Office today," Alanzo said finally. "Meetings until three."

I nodded, sipping my tea, letting the steam warm the tip of my nose.

"Are you making plans?" he added, not looking up. "I can add it to his schedule if you'd like, Mrs. Reinhardt."

I smiled into my cup. I still wasn't used to hearing that, Mrs.

Reinhardt. Still startled a part of me, that low, quiet part that spent most of its life in survival mode.

"No, I was just curious," I said, setting my cup down. "I think I'm going to step out for a bit. Grab lunch. Walk." "Where would you like to go? I'll pull the car around."

I grinned.

"No, thanks, Alanzo. I'd like to be a civilian today."

He huffed a soft laugh, something fond in it.

"I'll be back in a little," I called, turning toward the bedroom. "No need to send up the bat signal or anything."

Alanzo's footsteps followed after mine, soft but determined. "You'll need this then, Signora," he said, handing me a key fob from his pocket like it was nothing.

Only it wasn't nothing. I paused, staring down at the familiar horse and shield logo gleaming from the fob: one of Kais' cars. The Panamera I think. It's the only one I've seen him drive since we got to London. Though there's at least six in the garage. My fingers curled around it, part of my daily reality check to make sure I was still me and not Eliza Dolittle.

"I have your spare," Alanzo added casually. "I'll pull it around for you."

My brain hiccuped. "Wait... did you say my spare?"

Alanzo just laughed, like the question itself was absurd. "Yes, Signora. This one is yours."

My mouth parted, something like protest catching on my tongue, but I swallowed it. I could argue. Could insist it was too much. That I didn't need it. That it wasn't mine.

But according to every marriage forum and book I've read lately, that would be ungrateful. And worse, it would go directly against everything Kais was trying to show me. His love wasn't measured in what was "needed." It was measured in intention. In provision. In the quiet insistence that what was his was already mine. Gift-giving was his love language. I was finally starting to learn how to receive. A little.

I forced my lips into a smile, the warmth creeping there slower than usual but sincere all the same. "I guess I'll see you downstairs then. Thanks, Alanzo."

He nodded, already halfway to the elevator.

"YOU HAVE ARRIVED," the British voice from the GPS announced, far too calm for what felt like the longest five miles of my life.

I exhaled, tension still knotted between my shoulder blades as I rolled to a stop outside the mirrored glass facade of Reinhardt Capital. Wrong side of the road. High-strung horsepower under my feet. Every turn felt like steering a spaceship in stilettos. And still... the drive had been worth it. I'd always been more of a city bus and borrowed ride kind of girl. But I had to admit, heated seats and controlling the radio without static were luxuries I could get used to. Even if the street signs and roundabouts still made my palms sweat.

I reached over and grabbed the box of cookies from the bakery near the apartment, flaky and buttery, dusted with sugar and still warm through the cardboard. My small offering, a silly, soft reason to see him.

Umbrella in one hand, I pushed the door open and dashed through the rain, narrowly avoiding a puddle that threatened to swallow my rain boots whole. The scent of stone and city and wet concrete hit me in waves as I stepped inside the lobby, shaking off water like a stray dog. Then I saw it.

Reinhardt Capital.

His last name, etched into glass and brushed steel behind the front desk. My name now. It stopped me cold, not because it looked unfamiliar, but because, somehow, it didn't. It felt right.

More mine than Cameron ever had. Like I'd stepped into a skin I hadn't realized was waiting for me.

"Good morning, can I help you?" the receptionist asked, her tone polite but brisk.

"Uh, yeah—one second." I set the cookie box on the desk, juggling the umbrella with a bit more awkwardness than I wanted to admit. Raindrops still clung to my hair, my sleeves, my eyelashes. The city had soaked into me like it wasn't quite ready to let go. "I'm here to see my husband," I said, trying to sound casual. "But I'd rather not alert him I'm here just yet."

That earned me a curious glance. A flicker of suspicion, the kind reserved for people claiming a last-minute reservation at a restaurant or dropping a name they shouldn't know.

"Uh, sure... let me get you a security pass. Can I have your driving license?"

I nodded, digging through my purse, fingertips brushing over receipts, lip gloss, pens, and finally the cool edges of the two cards that have become vital these days. I handed her my BRP first, then the shiny new Florida ID with a name that still made my breath catch. *Alana Reinhardt.*

She took them with a smile. But the moment her eyes landed on the name her expression changed like she'd touched something electric.

"Oh—Mrs. Reinhardt. I'm so sorry." Her voice shifted.

She shoved the cards back toward me like she'd committed some kind of offense. Her cheeks colored as she opened a drawer beneath her desk, sliding an unlabeled black key card across the counter.

"You don't have to check in with me," she said quickly. "That should get you anywhere in the building."

It took me a second to respond. I was used to watching people react this way around Kais. That quiet, deferential awe he inspired by just existing. But being on the receiving end of it? Being the

Mrs. Reinhardt someone apologized to? Yeah. That was new. And awkward.

I smiled anyway, needing to cut the weirdness. I flipped open the cookie box and offered it to her.

"Biscuit?" Cookie, but people around here don't seem to use that word.

Her eyes widened a little before a soft laugh slipped out. "Yes. Thank you."

"Consider it a peace offering," I said with a wink, closing the lid again. "What floor is he on?" I asked, gesturing vaguely upward.

She held up a finger as she chewed, typing something into her computer with her other hand. "Looks like he's in a meeting on nine for another three minutes, but his office is on twelve."

"Perfect."

I thanked her and turned toward the elevators, keycard in hand. My heart thudded as the doors slid open, the excitement of sneaking into Kais' world thrumming through me. Only I wasn't an outsider anymore, or even a visitor. The elevator was cool and silent as it ascended, that little black card warm in my hand. Tangible proof that I was his.

"Good morning, who are you looking for?" another receptionist called from behind the desk as I stepped off the elevator and into the quiet hum of the executive floor. I barely had time to glance in her direction before I heard his voice.

"Alana?"

I turned slowly, caught mid-step like a kid sneaking cookies instead of bringing them.

"Him," I muttered under my breath, scrunching my nose as I pivoted on my heel, a sheepish grin blooming on my face.

He was already walking toward me, navy suit practically painted on and brows drawn with that slight crease he got when something caught him off guard. But his eyes were warm. A little amused.

"Good morning," he said, stopping in front of me, and before

I could answer, his fingers flipped open the lid of the bakery box in my hands to peek inside. "Biscuits?"

"For your office," I said, gesturing toward the space behind him. I hadn't expected it to be so... still. Painfully sterile. Glass and steel and silence. It was nothing but function and lifeless decor. It didn't look like it belonged to a man who kisses my forehead when I'm asleep and warms his hands against the curve of my spine in the morning.

The woman stood from behind the desk. "I can take those for you, dear," she offered kindly.

I handed her the box, giving her a polite smile just as Kais turned slightly toward her. "Alana, this is my assistant Farrah," he said. Then, with that same effortless calm that always knocks the air from my lungs—

"Farrah, my wife, Alana."

We'd been married over a month and it still made me giddy every time he introduced me to someone.

She nodded with a warm smile. "I recognize her now from the photo on your desk, sir."

My head tilted, the comment catching me completely off guard. I looked up at him.

"You have a picture of me on your desk? Can I see it?" I whispered, a grin pulling at my lips.

He didn't answer with words. Just leaned in, brushing a kiss against my forehead, then moved his hand to the small of my back, guiding me gently. "You don't even have to ask," he said with a smile. "Come on."

"Farrah, I'm on lunch," he called over his shoulder as we walked.

I didn't look back. I didn't want to. All I could feel was his warm and steady hand on me like he always knew exactly where I fit.

"You don't make yourself at home here, do you?" I said, shrugging off my jacket as I stepped inside.

Kais' office looked like the kind of space that belonged in a glossy magazine: glass walls, fine lines, expensive furniture placed with the kind of intention that said everything in here served a purpose.

Everything except the one personal thing on his desk. A single black-and-white photo in a silver frame. Me. Bathed in candlelight, mascara half-ruined, holding it together by a thread, looking up at him like the whole world lived in his eyes. It was from our wedding night. The moment I said yes. I drifted toward it, brushing my thumb lightly over the glass.

"Not possible to make myself at home anywhere you aren't, Ya Amar," he muttered behind me.

The simplest words sounded like poetry when they came from his mouth. I turned, and he was already there, stepping towards me like it was second nature. His arms wrapped around my waist, firm and unhurried, like he had all the time in the world for me. I tilted my face up and kissed him—soft and grateful. If there'd been even an ounce more privacy, I'd have kissed him longer. Harder. Maybe found a better purpose for his desk. But I behaved.

"Did you pick up a dress for tonight?" he asked, voice a little rougher now, as he rested his forehead against mine.

I nodded.

"Sure did. It's hanging in my new car," I teased, arching a brow.

That crooked smile tugged at his lips.

"Figured I'd have it waiting for when you inevitably decided to ditch Alanzo."

I laughed under my breath, pressing a quick kiss to the corner of his mouth.

"Great instincts."

He kissed me back, then let me go gently, though his hands lingered like he wasn't quite ready. Neither was I.

"I won't stay," I said, brushing a hand down the front of his shirt. "I just wanted to see you. It's weird being at your place without you."

His brow knit, just a little. "*My place*?" he repeated. "Not ours?"

"I didn't mean it like that, Kai," I said quickly, reaching up to smooth the tension from his forehead. "My home is with you. That's the truth. But it's hard to feel at home when you're not there. Your things are everywhere... but you aren't."

He leaned back against his desk, guiding me with him until I stood between the splay of his legs. One of his hands rested on my hip, the other brushing a loose curl behind my ear.

"It'll get better once I'm done with this buy out," he said softly. His tone shifted lower, more certain. "But until then, let's find a place you'll call yours too."

I shook my head, brushing my fingers against the side of his thigh. "I'm perfectly fine with your apartment, Kai. We can think about something like that when I come back after graduation."

Without another word, he pulled his phone from his pocket and tapped a few times. Then handed it to me.

"Look at these first," he said. "Then tell me if you still want to wait."

It was his Notes app—lined with house listings, each one linked with a URL and typed-out commentary beneath. Meticulous. So him. Every entry was beautiful—classic Georgian townhomes, ivy-clad redbrick estates, cottages that looked like they belonged in fairytales. But it wasn't just the homes that stunned me. It was the care in the margins. *"Nice garden." "En suite nursery." "Close to the road. Dangerous for kids?"*

My throat tightened. I looked up at him, blinking. "You've put a lot of thought into this."

"Of course I have," he said simply.

"I don't think I even want to know what houses like this cost..." I muttered, scrolling past a picture of a three-story manor that seemed to have its own gravitational pull. He shook his head.

"Doesn't matter. Everything that was mine is yours. You've got every right to know, but I'd rather you didn't make your decision based on that." His thumb brushed lightly across my cheek like he was memorizing me again. "Just pick the one that feels like we could raise our family in."

Family. He said it so easily. Like it wasn't terrifying. Like it wasn't something I'd been gripping too tightly to hope for. I swallowed.

"I do hate the idea of moving around," I said quietly. "I've always dreamt of being in one house forever. The kind people come home to for holidays. The kind that hears first steps and terrible arguments and laughter so loud it spills into the street. The kind that grows up with you."

He smiled, then scrolled to the bottom of the list. "How about this one?"

It was... unreal. A historic brick house built in the 1700s, wrapped in walled gardens and climbing roses. A glass greenhouse tucked to the side. It looked like it had been plucked out of the kind of novel I used to sneak-read under the covers as a kid. The kind with heroines who got happy endings.

"God," I whispered, scrolling through the images. "This looks like something out of a Regency Romance fever dream."

The kitchen alone was enough to make me gasp: a cavernous, light-filled space with honey wood floors and curling cornices, piped like icing along the ceiling. There were endless fireplaces. Even one in the bathroom. And the way the afternoon light poured through the windows, it didn't feel like a house. It felt like a life. My chest tightened. My heart ached. Because it felt like maybe I *was* allowed to want something this good.

"Let's go see it," he said casually, like it wasn't the biggest offer anyone had ever made me.

"Kai, no," I gave him a protesting laugh, staring at the listing like it might leap off the screen and call me a fraud. "This place is insane. Your notes say it's only been in three families since it was built. It has a name. This place is for dukes or something."

He huffed a quiet laugh, tucking the phone into his pocket with the kind of certainty that didn't need convincing. "Dukes don't live in Hampstead, Ya Amar."

Then he kissed me quick and affectionate. Like this wasn't up for debate. "Come on. It's not far. I'll go home with you after and we can get ready for the charity ball."

A different version of me would've fought him on this. Would've insisted he stay at work. Would've shrunk myself down, worried I was asking for too much or taking up too much room in a life that already had its structure.

But that version of me? She's quieter now. Not gone, but quieter. Because Kais has proven—over and over—that our life matters to him. That I matter to him. And judging by the two full pages of notes he took on this house, this isn't just about me falling in love with a dream. He wants to fall in love with it too. With us in it. I breathed out a smile, feeling it tug at the edges of my doubt.

"Alright, Kai Kai," I said, grabbing my jacket. "But you're driving. I'm not trying to kill us on the wrong side of the road."

Alana

-27-

♪ 12

Kais drove us through Hampstead, past winding rows of charming shops and quaint cafés, the kind with chalkboard menus and windows white with steam. We rolled past cobbled streets lined with gnarled trees that looked like they'd stood watch through both world wars. His hand was wrapped in mine, steady and warm, his thumb rubbing lazy circles over the bands on my finger like it grounded him. Like I did.

"That's James' place," he said, nodding at a tall brick building just ahead.

"Building, or he like... lives there?"

"Both." He smirked. "He's only there half the year when he's not in Monaco. He rents out the other units."

I turned to him, one brow arched. "So, what I'm hearing is... you want to live near your bestie, Kai Kai."

He shot me a look. Affectionate. But slightly pained. I grinned, satisfied with myself.

The houses shifted as we climbed. Each one more distinctive than the last. Ivy-covered facades, copper gutters, rose vines

244

twisting over weathered brick like lace. We turned up a private drive hidden behind wrought iron gates and tree cover so thick it felt enchanted. Then it appeared.

Calico Hill.

It didn't look like a house. It looked like a secret kept by generations. The kind of place where time didn't pass so much as settle in layers. It was large, yes—but not loud about it. All warm brick, symmetrical windows, and ancient chimneys. Like something out of a period drama where someone falls madly in love under the wrong circumstances and a full moon. The gardens were lush and manicured, but in a way that felt cherished, not showy. Like someone had loved this house for a very long time.

A tall redhead in heels and a camel-colored pantsuit waved at us from the stone steps, clipboard in hand and confidence in her stride.

"She's spunky," I muttered, unbuckling. "Must be a hefty commission."

Kais said nothing just opened his door, then mine, like he always does. Like it's reflex now.

"Hi, I'm Julia," she said in a husky voice, her handshake firm and polished.

"Nice to meet you," I said.

"Good to see you again, Mr. Reinhardt. Shall we go in?" she added with a bright, knowing smile. I leaned in toward Kais as we followed her up the steps.

"Again?" I whispered.

"Once," he murmured back, knitting his fingers with mine. "Wanted to make sure it was worth showing you."

My heart tugged hard. That's the thing about Kais, he does things without ever making a show of them. Caring for me seems to come as naturally to him as breathing. I've never felt more safe or loved in my life.

'Calico Hill' was etched into the stone beside the front entrance, ivy and yellow roses growing around it like a frame. I looked at the house again. I mean *really* looked. I let myself imagine what it would feel like to call something like this ours. Pictures didn't do this place justice. Not even close. Every room we passed told a different story—some rich and dramatic, others quiet and sun-soaked—but they all came together like chapters of the same novel. Cohesive without being obvious. Timeless without trying.

"Second-oldest home in Hampstead," Julia announced as she started up the staircase, her heels echoing softly against the worn wood. "Six beds, four baths. Freehold."

My hand brushed the barley twist spindles as we climbed— slick beneath my fingers, polished by decades of touch. The kind of wood that held memory.

She pointed to a hallway that broke off to the right. "Guest rooms are that way." Then she turned toward a larger door, her voice light but measured. "Master's is this way."

I followed.

The master bedroom opened like a sigh: high ceilings, wavy-glass windows catching the low sun just right, a carved marble fireplace set into the far wall. The floors creaked beneath our feet, not in protest, but in greeting. Like the house was acknowledging us. Like it knew.

"You've got this little room adjoining it," Julia said, pushing open a smaller door beside the bed. Sunlight poured in, buttery and soft. A narrow room with deep windows, a cozy shape to the walls, and a quiet hush that made something in my chest ache in the best way.

"Could be an office," Julia continued. "But I think it would be really amazing as a nursery."

I let go of Kais' hand and stepped inside. Ran my fingers over the deep windowsill, the kind you could curl up in with a book— or a baby. The light touched everything like a blessing. I could see it all, clear as day. Little socks left by the window. A rocking chair creaking on quiet mornings. Sleepy laughter down the hall.

Dinners loud with joy. The smell of cookies and bread wafting from the kitchen. Holidays. Footsteps. Firelight. Time. My gaze landed on the marble-and-iron fireplace in the corner, and my throat went tight with something that felt a lot like wonder and a little like surrender.

"We should probably add 'fireplace in the nursery' to that list of yours, Kai," I said softly.

He didn't answer right away. When I turned, I found him standing just outside the doorway, not looking at the fireplace or the view or even the sun-drenched walls. Just me. Watching me like the only thing that mattered in this entire house was whether or not I could see a future inside it.

A slow smile pulled at his lips. He crossed the threshold, and I reached for him without thinking, tucking my arm under his and leaning into the solid warmth of him. He brushed a kiss into my hair, muttered so close I felt it in every nerve in my body, "Absolutely not an office."

I smiled up at him, "My thoughts exactly." I pressed a kiss to his chest, just over his heart, before letting myself look around the room one last time.

I didn't want to leave it yet but I also didn't want to lose momentum. It's awe inspiring how our kind of love makes me greedy for every next thing.

"Can we see the kitchen?" I asked, turning back toward Julia.

"Of course. This way," she chirped, already halfway down the stairs.

As we followed, my eye caught on a room just off the main hallway. Smaller, moodier, set into the corner of the house like a secret. I paused. Pushed the door open. Chocolate brown wood lined the walls from floor to ceiling, the grain catching the afternoon light like honey poured over whiskey. Coffered ceilings, heavy trim. A single, arched window with a sill deep enough to sleep in. It was the kind of room where you didn't just think—you brooded.

"See? This is what I imagined your office would look like, Kai," I said, stepping inside. "All brooding and mysterious. Possibly haunted."

He followed me in, slower this time, his fingers brushing the doorframe. He actually looked at the space now, like he could see it, too. His future here. His life folding around something soft.

"I mean," I continued, stretching my hand out dramatically to the back wall, "can't you just see your boy band posters right here?"

Kais snorted.

"Or maybe this is where you sit and get all offended when someone comes to you on the day your daughter is to be married." I dropped into the desk chair with a teasing grin, spinning it half a turn.

Kais leaned back against the windowsill, arms crossed, watching me in amusement. "Are you going to give me a daughter to be offended about, *Ya Amar?*" he asked, eyes glinting.

"I suppose we'll have to have a few dozen to fill this house," I said, standing again and brushing past him.

He laughed—a real one, hushed and warm in his chest—as he followed me out of the room. And maybe it was silly, maybe it was light, but there was something grounding in his laugh. Like he was already picturing it, too. Our house. Our family. Us growing old. Not running from anything, chasing anything, just being at home.

If I wasn't already dreaming of living here, this kitchen sealed it. The ceilings soared above us, crisscrossed with thick old beams that looked like they'd been plucked from a fairy tale cottage. Skylights welcomed rain-soaked light across the floor, catching in the glint of brass hardware that sparkled like heirloom jewelry.

The cabinets practically sung with history. The boldly veined marble countertops looked like something ripped from a magazine. And at the far end, past a generous island and a jewel-like brass sink tap, a glass solarium opened out onto the garden. A riot of roses.

Stone paths half-swallowed by ivy. It was all so alive. Truly the perfect blend of Kais' clean, moody aesthetic and my soft spot for anything that looked like it could've come from a Victorian estate sale.

"I'd have to call my cousin Penelope about that garden," I said, leaning close to the cool windowpane as I took it all in.

Kais didn't answer. He was behind me, but I could feel him watching me again—his quiet version of admiration. I walked over to the LaCanche—deep burgundy, absolutely enormous, regal in the way only French appliances can be, flanked by two extra ovens tucked into the cabinets.

"Is the current owner a chef or something?" I asked, running my fingers along the brass knobs.

Julia sighed, adjusting her blazer. "Surprisingly, no. They're rarely home. Say it's too much upkeep."

I blinked at her, scandalized.

"That's criminal. This is a stove that begs for feasts." My voice softened as I traced the lines of it, already picturing every dish I'd learned in Morocco. Every late-night Kais had practically begged me for seconds. "I could fit at least a dozen tagines in this," I whispered.

"Good for pastilla, too?" Kais said behind me, a lazy grin in his voice.

I looked over my shoulder, amused. "I think this is the only oven that can handle the amount of pastilla and basbousa you've consumed since Marrakesh."

He didn't deny it, just smiled wider.

"I'll leave you two to explore," Julia said, clearly sensing a moment. "I'll be just outside if you have questions." The swing door rocked shut behind her, and silence settled over the space.

I turned around to find Kais fiddling with the tap, looking far too domestic for a man who made opponents bleed for a living. Something about him there—sleeves pushed up, expression soft— felt like a punch to the chest.

"Do you like this place, Kai?" I asked, quieter this time. "Or are we here because you think I will?"

He glanced up from the sink, the weight of his gaze landing squarely on me and said, "Both."

Just one word. Simple, sure, but it pressed into me—into that part of my chest where things still lived on edge. That word made space. Put down roots. I let out a long breath, pressing my palms on the counter behind me, steadying myself against the cool marble.

"It's insanely perfect," I admitted. "Like... I can see it. Us here. The future. It's all laid out in my head like I've already lived it." My voice dropped, the truth tugging out slowly. "But—"

Kais rounded the island, standing across from me, mirroring me like we were two sides of the same thought. He waited patiently, his presence filling the space between us without pressure. "But what?" he asked.

I swallowed, the words thick.

"It just feels like a lot, Kai. Like I'm rearranging your whole life by even thinking about this place. You've got your apartment right next to where you train and your firm. Your whole world is already built." I paused, heart in my throat. "And I'm supposed to be at Oxford frying my brain next year. You'll probably be onto your next fight by then."

His eyes didn't flinch, didn't look away. So, I kept going, voice thinner now.

"This place... it's not just a house. It's a home. The kind people grow into. The kind people stay in. It deserves people who are ready."

He crossed his arms, leaned into the counter like he was settling himself in more ways than one. His voice when he spoke was steady but it cracked something open.

"What do you want, Alana?"

I blinked. Huffed a soft, helpless sound. "Our life shouldn't be based on what I want."

He stared at me like he could see something in me I hadn't said yet.

"Pretend for a second that it is," he said, low and calm. "Pretend that for once, you get to choose. Not based on fear. Not based on survival. Just what you want."

Damn him. Damn how deeply he knows me.

Or maybe just how plainly I wear it around him now. I looked down for a second, then back up into his eyes, letting the words come.

"If I'm dreaming..." I exhaled slowly. "I'm anywhere with you. That's enough for me."

He didn't blink. Didn't smile. Just held it.

"But if I'm pretending to write the rest of my life—" My voice caught. I shook my head, laughed a little. "It would be doing soft things. Baking pastilla and chocolate chip cookies. A kitchen that always smells like something good. A handful of kids with your face running around like chaos incarnate."

He laughed quietly, the corners of his mouth tugging into something devout. He stepped closer, a breath between us now, and rested a hand on my hip.

"And probably not balancing that with law school and trying to keep up with your schedule. I'd want to do something... different. Something that doesn't tear me in two to matter."

His smile faded into something softer like he was considering my every word.

"I'd want to start something of our own," I said, resting my palm on his chest.

"A Reinhardt foundation or whatever we'd call it—something that reaches the communities I wanted to become a lawyer for. But in a way that's more meaningful than pushing paper in a courtroom. I'd want that."

I didn't realize how hard I was gripping the edge of the counter until his hand covered mine—bringing me back to earth. His thumb swept once, lazy and tender.

"Then let's do that," he whispered.

He pulled me into him, strong and sure, his arms folding around me in that way that felt more like home than even this house. I melted against his chest, letting my cheek settle over the steady thrum of his heart as he held me close.

"It just sounds like you changed what you thought *your* life would be into what you want *our* life to be," he said gently. "I have too. Plans change—and that's okay. But if you trust me..."

He pressed a kiss into my hair. "Then stop holding back that part of your heart and just let me have it."

I closed my eyes as that low, quiet part of me stirred—where all my insecurity and trepidation still lived. "I'm trying," I whispered. "I just don't know how."

He didn't rush to fix it. Just held me tighter, his breath warm against the top of my head.

"You don't have to know how. Not yet." He pulled back just enough to meet my eyes. "But if you like this house... if you see that life here—the one you're dreaming of—then let me do this for us."

I tilted my chin, my gaze locking with his. And for once, the fear didn't surge. I didn't run from the feeling. I leaned into it.

"Only if it's your dream too, Kai."

He smiled, soft and crooked and filled with something that wrapped all the way around me. "Only if you add in a handful of kids with your face too," he replied.

And just like that, the future didn't feel so cloudy.

Kais

28

♫ 29

THE CAR WAS QUIET, EXCEPT FOR THE RAIN SLIDING
down the windows and the sound of her laughter.

"What's your level of commitment to this dress?" I asked, eyes
on the road but only barely.

Alana giggled. "Kai, don't start."

We were fifteen minutes out from some gala I couldn't be
bothered to care about: charity sponsors, cameras, free drinks. All
a bunch of noise for the fight. It didn't feel like progress. Just
distraction. Delay. Another thing between me and the life I actually wanted.

What wasn't noise? The woman in my passenger seat wearing a
dress that looked like it was sculpted out of bronze and lust. She
was still talking—teasing me about something—but all I could
focus on was the way the fabric moved like water over her skin.

Slit high enough to make my knuckles itch, low enough at the
sides to flash curves that made my pulse go tight. She didn't usually
dress like this. Not unless she wanted me to lose my entire fucking
mind. Which meant—she knew exactly what she was doing.

"I'm just saying," I muttered, barely restraining the grin tugging at my mouth, "we can skip the shag-in-the-toilet tradition and head home. I'll give that dress the attention it deserves."

She bit her lip like she was actually considering it. And that was nearly enough for me to flip the car around. Until—

"You can do whatever you want to me—or this dress—when we get home," she said, a teasing pause curling at the edge of her voice. "But we should really go to this. I think it's incredible what you're doing... giving kids who've got nothing a chance to find themselves in something that saved you."

She meant that.

I could hear it in her tone, see it in her expression. She thought this was my version of what law school was to her. Something noble. Something healing. But it wasn't. Not really. It was a photo op for suits who needed a tax write-off and a reason to clap for themselves. If I wasn't contractually obligated, I wouldn't set foot in the bloody building.

"We'd help more of those kids if we handed them the money ourselves," I muttered, flicking the wipers up a notch. "Half of what's raised tonight is covering the venue bill."

She turned to face me, entirely unbothered by my cynicism as usual.

"Have you ever thought about opening your own gym?" she asked. "A place a younger version of you could've escaped to, instead of getting sucked into underground fighting?"

Her question landed harder than I expected. I kept my eyes on the rain-blurred red light ahead, watching it bleed across the windshield. I used to want that. When I met Montee, owning a gym felt like the future. Then I got older, made bigger plans. Built an empire. Bought silence. Negotiated power. And somewhere in the middle of all that winning, I forgot why I ever gave a shit.

Alana made me remember. She brought it back without even trying—what matters. What was worth building, worth keeping. I could make all the right moves in the boardroom and the ring, but if I was only doing it to prove something to my father or myself… it would never be enough. The light turned green. I eased us forward.

"I haven't in a long while," I said, quieter now. "But it could be nice. One day."

She rested her hand on my thigh, softly tracing a line with her thumb.

"If you decide to," she said, "I want to do it with you. Add it to the whole Reinhardt foundation dream. Could be your way of investing in people who actually deserve it."

Reinhardt. Our name wasn't just known—it carried weight. In boardrooms. In locker rooms. In places that took more than they ever gave. It's a name that commands the room, sure. But she said it like it could shape something good. Like it could mean purpose. Like she saw a version of me I never thought I could be and still wants to build a future around it.

Watching her sign that name on every form that was handed to her during the last few weeks made me look at it differently. Like having her name attached to it could change it into something good, worthy of its gravitas.

"Careful, Ya Amar…" I drawled, as the rain tapped against the glass. "Keep talking like that, and you'll be carrying our name sooner than you can paint that nursery."

She went still beside me. Quiet. Like something in her had paused to take that in. Her gaze dropped to the window, lashes lowered, lips just barely parted.

"You keep joking like that, Kai." Her voice was velvet-soft, but her brow lifted just enough to challenge me. "Now, what happens if I take you seriously?"

I knew that look. The one she wore when she was trying not to want too much too soon. Not because she didn't feel it but because wanting, for her, had never ended well. And yet, she was still asking. Still hoping I'd say something that didn't scare her deeper into that guarded little shell of hers. She wanted to believe me. And I'd never wanted anything more than to be someone she could believe.

I didn't rush my answer. I never did with her. My hand found hers again, fingers threading together. I brought it to my mouth and kissed the inside of her wrist, slow and unhurried. Her pulse fluttered beneath my lips.

"You take me seriously," I murmured quietly into her skin, "and I'll spend the rest of my life proving you were right to."

That made her breath stutter slightly. But she covered it with a dry little laugh and leaned back into her seat, legs crossing tight.

"You really know how to strip a girl of her last shred of self-control, huh?"

I smiled, letting my thumb stroke slow circles over the inside of her wrist.

"Could say the same to you, Ya Amar. The way you're looking at me right now? Could ruin a man's whole sense of discipline."

She rolled her eyes, but her smile betrayed her. And when she didn't pull her hand away, I knew she was dreaming the same dream I was. If she let go fully, I'd give her everything she didn't even know how to ask for yet.

The rain picked up as I threaded my fingers through hers and rested them in my lap. Her skin was warm, soft, more familiar than my own. Her phone lit up in her lap. She tapped the notification without thinking, still holding my hand. Her eyes widened, grip tightening just slightly around my fingers like she needed the touch. A quick breath left her lips.

"It's Lisa," she said, already bracing. "I guess she's breaking her no-email rule because... apparently my mom hasn't called Macy in two weeks."

Of course she bloody hadn't. My jaw set, the muscle twitching hard enough to ache. That woman hadn't been a mother since Alana was old enough to stand on her own and from what I'd pieced together, she barely managed even then. Every story I'd heard—every quiet admission Alana had let slip—

made my skin crawl. Stranded for days. Left without food. Alone with men who should've had their bones broken just for looking at her, let alone the things she's hinted at. And still my wife shows up.

She stretched herself thin trying to be something solid for a woman who didn't deserve her name on her daughter's tongue. She worried for a sister who'd been placed so far out of reach it might as well be exile, all while pretending like it didn't rip her open every time. Like she wasn't the one who kept that little girl alive when no one else fucking would. The worst of it is that I couldn't protect her from any of this. Not the way I wanted to. Couldn't put my fists through it. Couldn't fix it.

Because she wouldn't let go. She still believed she has to carry it all herself—that it was her responsibility. Her cross to bear. And I saw it. Every time news like this landed. That flicker in her eyes like she was already bracing to do it alone. Again.

She didn't flinch when she read it. Not properly. But I saw the way her shoulders tucked in, like she could fold herself smaller. The way her breath turned shallow, quiet. Like she was preparing to bleed without making a sound. It never got easier for her. No matter how often it happened. *And that's what fucking ruins me. That she still hopes. Still aches for something better from a woman who's never lifted a finger to earn it.*

"Do you want me to have someone look into it?" I asked. "I can send Alanzo to Dallas. He'll be discreet."

She hesitated. Shrugged.

That shrug—*Christ*—it cut me more than a scream ever could. Like if she didn't put weight on it, it wouldn't matter. Like if she stayed casual, it wouldn't crack something in her. She still doesn't get it. That none of this makes her a burden. That loving someone who let her down didn't make her foolish, it made her fucking remarkable.

"I can just go out there myself. You don't have to—"

"No," I cut in quickly. In no way was I going to be passive

about her doing shit like this alone. "Alana. Whatever burdens you is mine to carry, yeah?"

Her eyes flicked toward me, surprised. I kept mine on the road. "The shit with your mum doesn't scare me. It pisses me off. I don't particularly like her—but I don't have to. You care about her. And that's enough. I'll get Alanzo on it tonight."

She didn't retreat. Not the way she used to. She folded into the seat like she was trying to absorb the blow, but she kept holding my hand. That part? That was new. Since Monaco I'd watched my wife slowly give me more and more pieces of herself, exhale like she trusted what I'd do with them.

The valet line moved ahead and I eased into it, jaw still tight. She should never have to carry this kind of disappointment alone. Not anymore. Not when she's spent her whole damn life doing just that. Her fingers squeezed mine again, this time not from fear, but something softer.

"Thank you," she whispered, those big brown eyes on me, wide and open and shining in the low light.

Fuck, she wrecks me.

"No thank-you necessary, Mrs. Reinhardt," I said, cutting the engine. "But if you're feeling generous later, I'd gladly accept payment in the form of fucking you out of that dress back home."

A sly smile curved her lips. "That's a dangerous threat to make."

I leaned in, brushing my nose against her temple, voice low at her ear. "That's not a threat, love. That's a promise." Then I stepped out into the rain, handed the valet my keys, and circled around to open her door. Everyone in that room would see the polished version of me. But this—her fingers in mine, her trust, her quiet thank you—this was the truth. I'd destroy the rest of it and never look back, if she asked me to. I didn't feel like a fighter or a name or a brand anymore. Just hers. And that felt like the most dangerous thing I'd ever become.

Alana

♪ 29

THE POUNDING RAIN OUTSIDE SAVED US FROM THE swarm of cameras camped beneath the awning, though tonight, I wouldn't have minded as much—not when I was fully dressed. Or at least, dressed enough to entertain the fantasy of Kais abandoning the evening entirely.

He hadn't taken his eyes off me since we walked in. Even from thirty feet across the ballroom, surrounded by tuxedos, camera flashes and the thrum of polite applause, I could feel his gaze like a physical touch. Like he was still weighing whether to drag me right back out the door.

The ballroom was beautiful in the way old money always is, vaulted ceilings, gilded edges, crystal chandeliers strung like galaxies. But my standards for beauty have been permanently altered since our wedding. Nothing in this room could touch that. I'd whispered something about the chandeliers when we arrived— half in awe, half in jest—and Kais had murmured, "Yes, how generous of them to turn the Dorchester ballroom into a photo op for the sake of disadvantaged youth." He hadn't smiled when he said it.

Something about this event rubbed him the wrong way. Maybe it was the gloss. The curated spectacle of good intentions dressed up in tax breaks and press coverage. Normally, he'd play the game—smile, shake hands, let the cameras catch a glimpse of the legend off-duty. But tonight, I could feel it. This space didn't sit right. And I knew better than anyone that when Kais Reinhardt's skin itches in a room, there's usually a reason.

I wove through the crowd looking for our table while he handled the press. He always looked absurdly good in a tux— unfair, really. The clean lines, neat bow tie, the sleeves tailored just enough to flash the glint of his watch. I could barely concentrate. My own thoughts drifted recklessly toward dragging him out of here myself.

Maybe it was the not so distant memory of our wedding night still living in my blood. Although even that felt like a lifetime ago. Or maybe it was the way we'd settled into each other since we'd got to London—like we'd been stitched together in the quiet moments no one else saw. It felt impossible now that, only a few months ago, we were orbiting separate lives. Separate continents. Separate plans. And yet somehow, we'd crashed into each other and screamed at the universe to make room for us. It did.

And now, I don't know how I'm supposed to go back to Miami in the fall without him. We both have commitments—old ones, signed before we ever knew we'd end up here. This gala was one of them. The obligations don't care that we've built something worth staying for. They don't care that this love is the only thing that feels like it's moving in the right direction. But I do. And I think he does too.

By the time I reached our seats (dead center, of course) I caught sight of a crisp black filigree card nestled into the place setting.

Mrs. Alana Reinhardt.

My stomach fluttered. How was I ever called anything else? I'd barely settled in when a deep, Scottish-accented voice rumbled behind me.

"Mrs. Reinhardt."

I blinked, still acclimating to anyone besides Kais calling me that. He'd conditioned me too well—it always landed like a whisper between my thighs. The man slid into the seat beside me before I could fully turn.

He looked to be in his early forties, handsome in the used-to-break-hearts-and-might-still-do-it kind of way. Umber skin, broad shoulders pushing the seams of his suit. A low salt-and-pepper buzzcut framed a face marked with smile lines and deep dimples that probably got him out of trouble more times than he deserved.

I turned to him with a smile because I knew exactly who he was.

"Montee Aitken, correct?" I said, holding out my hand.

He took it with both of his—big, warm palms—and planted a smacking kiss to the top like we were at a garden party in the Scottish countryside.

"That I am. Pleasure to finally meet you, *hen*."

Kais had painted him like the devil in headgear: his ruthless trainer, the man who turned him into a weapon. But this Montee was exuding favorite-uncle energy. The kind of man you sneak off to talk to when the rest of the family's driving you crazy.

"Honestly, you're the one person I've been nervous to meet," I admitted. "Kais talks about you like family."

He chuckled, the sound deep and easy.

"The lad's gone soft on me, huh?"

His eyes flicked toward Kais on the far side of the ballroom.

"He's like one of my own sons. But don't go tellin' him that. Need him to hate me in the training room, yeah?"

"No, can't have him getting soft," I laughed.

Then he tilted his head, studying me—not the intimidating kind of look. More like someone quietly measuring your soul.

"You've got that look about you," he said. "The one that settles a man down without him even noticing."

I blinked. Caught off guard.

"Is that a good thing or a bad thing?" I asked, trying to keep my voice light.

"It's rare," he said simply. "And important." He lifted his glass in a quiet toast. "Glad he found you."

I clinked mine to his, smiling. "I'd like to think I'm punching above my weight class—wait, is that how you say it?"

Montee's laugh rumbled through his chest.

"That's the one. But I wouldn't say that. You're a bonnie lass." He gave me a wink, then added more seriously, "But more than that, you slowed him down. That's no small thing."

He paused, glancing toward Kais again.

"He's been running most of his life... but I haven't seen that look in his eye since he was a boy. Like he's not chasing anything anymore. Just—standing still. You did that."

I followed his gaze. Kais was watching us. That soft, crooked smile on his face. The one he only ever gave me. Something in my chest went warm and wobbly. It was one thing to feel like I gave him the peace he gave me. It was another to hear it spoken by someone who'd seen every version of him.

I don't know if it was the soft gaze of my husband or Montee's whole favorite uncle vibe, but it was enough for me to be unexpectedly vulnerable for just a moment.

"Yet, I have no idea how to help him with everything coming at him," I said softly.

It wasn't really meant to be out loud. More like a quiet confession that slipped through the cracks. Montee caught it anyway. He shook his head slowly, then laid a calloused hand over mine—not heavy, just solid. Steady. It felt like something a father might do, and even though I've never had that, this felt close enough.

"You don't need to," he said, voice gentle but sure. "Just love him."

My throat tightened.

"Kais Reinhardt's a hard man. But he was built to love hard too. You give him a reason to come home, and he'll bring the whole world back with him."

His words sat like a warm hug around everything I knew in my soul about Kais. That under all that steel and stone he showed the world was an ocean of love. Dedication too deep for most to hold. Way too good for me. I looked back at Montee, smiling softly because it was nice to talk to someone who saw the same man I saw. Not the version the press sees. Not the one etched into highlight reels or company bios.

No, this Kais. The one who made mint tea because he's missing a memory we made. Who wraps me in a towel after a shower like I'm something to be cherished. Who kisses my temple when I fall quiet, like he can hear the thoughts I'm not saying. The one who made me believe—for the first time in my life—that home wasn't just something other people got to have.

Before I could say anything else, I felt him. That shift in the air. The warmth that always seemed to follow him into a room like gravity bending to make space. My heart stuttered in recognition before I even saw him.

"Careful, Montee," Kais said with amusement.

"Keep talking like that and she'll start thinking you're the soft one."

I turned just as he eased into the seat beside me, one hand slipping instinctively to the inside of my thigh like it belonged there—which, to be fair, it did. My body leaned toward him without permission, as always.

God, he is beautiful. It didn't matter how many times I'd seen him like this—handsome tux, the thick soft waves of his hair swept back effortlessly, the clean line of his jaw so unfairly designed to undo me. I still couldn't look away.

Those dark eyes always finding me in a room. The way they softened every time they landed on me, like I was his north star and he'd just found home again. The quiet curve of his mouth, the smile he never shared with anyone else. That beauty mark beneath his cheekbone still made my knees weak, just as much as it did when I was a waitress instead of his wife. He looked at me like *I* was the only thing that mattered in a room full of cameras and kings of empire.

Montee grinned, unfazed. "Aye, well. You've already made a liar out of me. I've told everyone you were heartless. Then you show up with her for a wife."

Kais smirked, but his eyes never left me. A soft warmth in them—that quiet kind of peace we'd found in each other.

"Everything alright?" he asked, just for me to hear.

I nodded. "More than alright."

He brushed a kiss to my temple—just a whisper of contact, but it lingered in the way only he could make it last. My body always seemed to settle just a little deeper when he touched me. Montee gave us both a look like he already knew. Like he'd been waiting to see it for himself.

"Enjoy your night, you two," he said, lifting his glass. "There's a whole room of people here that think they know who you are, Kais. Make sure they leave wondering."

Kais nodded. "Always do."

The rest of the evening passed in a blur of handshakes, speeches, clinking glasses, and slow rotations around the ballroom beneath the chandeliers that probably cost more than my undergrad degree. Kais drifted through the room like he was born to command it: shoulders back, expression measured, gaze cutting through the crowd with quiet observation. People watched him the way you watch a storm forming on the horizon. Something in his stillness made them nervous, like they couldn't decide if they wanted to run or stay rooted to the spot.

No matter how far he moved, his presence never left me. His hand found the small of my back every time he returned, his knuckles brushed my thigh under the table, his fingers skimmed my hip as we passed through clusters of donors and dignitaries.

I ducked away halfway through dessert, muttering something about needing a moment. Kais gave my hand a light squeeze beneath the table, his thumb tracing a line over the top of my hand before letting go. The air outside the ballroom was cooler, quieter. The velvet hush of thick carpeting and low-lit sconces was a welcome contrast to the champagne buzz behind me.

I just needed a breath. A second to myself to think. Something about all the flashing lights and polite questions had started to itch under my skin. And if I was honest, my mind was starting to drift back to that email. To Macy. To my mom. To what might be waiting once the music faded and life started knocking again. I turned down the corridor, aiming for the restroom.

"Ah. Mrs. Reinhardt."

The voice stopped me cold.

A tall man stood in the center of the hall. Extraordinarily handsome. Thick black hair, slicked neatly into place. If Don Draper had a few more inches and an even darker soul, he'd look like this.

"Yes, hi." I blinked, trying to remember if he was someone new or just one of the dozens I'd been introduced to tonight. Though he was so stunning I'd think I would remember. And then I caught his eyes. Eyes like ones I'd stared into a million times before. The shape of his mouth like one I'd memorized like my own heartbeat.

My stomach turned.

"Aren't you a vision?" he said, his gaze crawling over me, unashamed and uninvited.

Whatever confidence I'd felt about this dress earlier evaporated under the weight of it. So much for my innocent *this will drive your husband crazy* scheme. This man's gaze made me feel like I'd had nothing on at all. Like he was seeing me in a way I only ever meant for Kais.

I tried to shake the ick creeping across my skin and forced a smile, steadying my voice.

"I'm going to take a shot in the dark here and say you're Oskar Reinhardt."

He grinned—of course his teeth were perfect. Dazzling white and familiar as hell. That smile that was devastating on Kais. On Oskar, it felt like a weapon.

"Smart too. Interesting. My son has always liked them pretty, but never clever."

Great. So, he was going to be that kind of asshole. He stepped closer. Way too fucking close. A chill crept up my spine, instinct to fight my way out of this bullshit tightening in my gut.

Then he leaned in, voice slick and oily, "Tell me—what kind of tricks do you do that would make the boy ruin his life?"

My chest flared with heat. I might not know the politics of this world yet, but I knew men like him. Men who only felt powerful when they were trying to make someone else feel small. Who looked at your body like it's something they were entitled to. Something to use against you. He wouldn't be the first and I'd be damned if he was the one to see me shake. I didn't flinch. Didn't back up.

I tilted my chin, letting my words cut clean.

"Well, Oskar, my knee is dangerously close to your dick right now. So, if you'd like, I can show you one," I said, not hiding a bit of the condescension.

His smug grin twitched, then curved into something darker as he muttered something in German. I didn't understand it, but I caught the meaning well enough.

"Feisty too," he said. "Let's see if we can't work that out of you, hmm?"

Then he straightened his shoulders, smug and satisfied, like he was about to prove something. The door to the ballroom clinked open behind me. I didn't turn. I kept my eyes fixed on him knowing better than to turn my back.

"Right, well then. We'll have to sort that later. I'm certain we'll see each other again," Oskar said smoothly, brushing a hand down his lapel. "Hopefully before the divorce, yes?"

And just like that, he stepped away, brushing past me. I turned, ready to throw something at him—words, if not a heel—but I stopped short. Kais was already there.

He'd just come through the same door Oskar passed, eyes locked on his father, his entire body thrumming with tension. Oskar met him halfway, and the air between them thickened like static. They didn't touch, but they may as well have. The exchange was tense: German, low and clipped. I couldn't make out the words, but I didn't need to. Kais' voice was iron; Oskar's was oil slicked with disdain.

I stood frozen as their conversation ended in a stare-down that felt like it could crack glass. Then Oskar turned, walking off down the hall with his shoulders squared like he hadn't just been cracked open and put back together with nothing but Oskar's oversized ego. Kais didn't move for a second. His jaw clenched, breath shallow, the muscle at his temple ticking like a warning light.

Then he turned to me. Coming to my side in three long steps.

"What did he say to you?" His voice was low but rough, like he was still trying to force the venom down. He looked wrecked, fuming and unreadable in that way he got when he was holding back.

"Nothing I couldn't handle." I forced a small shrug. "He was only here for a second." I added, hoping it would make his anger settle.

His eyes searched mine in a way that told me he saw through my lie, but he didn't press. He kissed my forehead, lips soft but frustration in his breath, his arm slipping around my waist like he needed the contact to stay steady. I felt the tension radiating off him—held tight behind the way his fingers curled just a little too firmly into my hip.

"If he ever gets that close to you again, I'll break his fucking jaw and won't lose a second of sleep over it."

The words were calm. But they vibrated with something dangerous and deep. I didn't argue. I didn't tell him to calm down. I just let my hand settle over his heart, mooring him to now. To me.

"You don't need to," I said quietly. "He's not worth it."

His reply was instant. "But you are."

The fury was still there but now edged with that look. The one that slipped when his careful control finally gave way—that need to feel something better than rage. His hand shifted, dragging lightly along the fabric at my hip.

"I think I'm in need of ripping that dress off you sooner than I thought."

A flicker of heat rose in my cheeks, just enough to ease the chill Oskar had left behind. I tilted my head, voice soft but sure.

"Well then... we should probably go." I slipped my hand into his and let him take us home.

30

Ya Amar: Would nudes convince you to come back to bed?

> Me: Just when I thought I'd taught you so well...

Ya Amar: I'm practicing restraint. I asked first. That's progress.

> Me: Playing with fire, I see. You'll owe me something for this torture.

Ya Amar: I like the sound of that. Name the cost, Reinhardt?

> Me: As many of those shaking whimpers as you can give me.

Ya Amar: Just when I thought you'd play fair...

> Me: Not when the stakes are you, my love.

♫ 20

SHE SENT THE BLOODY PICTURE ANYWAY.

My very beautiful, very fucking naked wife was glowing on my phone screen when I stepped out of the car. Still tangled in our sheets, the curve of her body framed like art—just enough shown to make my blood rush, just enough hidden to make me crazy. I hadn't even let myself touch her last night. Didn't trust myself. Not after how my father looked at her. Not when I knew I'd come back from this meeting feral. She'd get exactly what she was asking for then and she'd take it beautifully, recklessly, like it would save us both.

The woman thrived on pulling every carnal desire out of me and making it something redemptive. Making *me* someone redemptive. Making even the worst parts of me feel worthy. Her body was my church. And I'd worship on my knees at its altar every chance I get.

I mean fuck, the way she looked at me. The way she opened up for me, let go for me. The way she cries my name like a prayer of her own—it rewired my blood. Made me feel less like a man walking into war, and more like one being beckoned back to something soft. Something warm. *Home.*

Oskar's days were already numbered. But after last night? I was done fucking counting. The chrome lettering of Reinhardt Capital blurred past me, Alana's voice followed me through the lobby, quiet but echoing in my head like a punch to the ribs: "*Nothing I can't handle.*"

My jaw tightened at the memory. I knew that wasn't true. I saw it in the way her shoulders pulled high. The way she gave me that soft little lie—like a balm, meant to settle me. But she was trying to protect me. Even then. And I'd rather bite through my own tongue than make her feel like she owed me the whole ugly truth of that moment. Still, I'd never said a word to my wife that I didn't mean.

So here I am. Flame in hand. Ready to ignite the whole fucking thing like I promised.

Lars was waiting outside the boardroom, jaw tight, expression calm but I could tell he was ready. Inside, Oskar was already five cunt grins deep into his pitch. I caught him through the glass, standing beneath a glowing presentation slide that read: MERGER: A VISION FOR GLOBAL EXPANSION.

Full performance mode. Charming, commanding—every bit the shark he's always been, wrapped in bespoke tailoring like it made him legitimate.

Fucking wanker.

"Do you have everything we need?" I asked, voice cool.

"I do," Lars replied, steady as ever.

I nodded once, pushed open the door, and walked in. I didn't say a word, just moved to the seat at the head of the table like it was mine. Because it fucking was.

The air shifted the second I sat. Everyone looked up, stiffening like they hadn't expected me to show. As if the man who'd turned this firm from a niche London operation into the only British venture capital name that could compete with the States didn't have the right to weigh in. Let them look. I've never gave a fuck about approval from any of them.

Oskar didn't even glance at me. Just kept on with his performance—clicking through slides like he hadn't just tried to fuck my wife with his eyes the night before.

"The numbers speak for themselves," he droned, gesturing to the screen. "With projected growth exceeding twenty-eight percent, year-over-year, this merger would position us at the forefront of the market into the top ten globally. We have the opportunity to outpace our competitors by a margin that is, quite frankly, unprecedented."

A few of the older board members nodded, eyes squinting at the slide like it had been written in gold. But the rest of the room? They were waiting. Holding their breath.

Wondering if I'd nod. If I'd give the green light. If I'd fucking fold. I didn't. I let him keep going.

"The valuation was verified by Langford & Price," he added, tone smug. "An independent firm. Sterling reputation. Their analysis supports this deal. Strongly."

He clicked the remote. A graph bloomed on the screen.

I gave a subtle nod to my assistant Farah. She crossed the room without a word and dropped a thick black folder onto the table in front of him.

Then another.

And another. One for every seat at the table. Every way he'd just fucked up, printed in black and white. Every head snapped to me. Oskar didn't move. Didn't reach for the one in front of him. He already fucking knew exactly what I'd done.

Lars cleared his throat softly, almost amused. The thud of the folders hitting the table snapped a few heads up. A few more leaned forward, flipping them open. Pages rustled. Eyebrows lifted.

I didn't say a word until the room settled.

"I commissioned my own valuation." I broke the silence. Leaning forward just so he could hear my every word. My eyes swept over each board member. "Two weeks ago. Didn't trust Langford & Price. Conflict of interest." My eyes locked on Oskar. "Their founder's your old university roommate, isn't he?"

His jaw tightened, pupils blowing out in a way I'd seen in the ring more times than I could count. That last flash of fight before the lights go out.

"We're not in the business of wishful thinking. We're in the business of facts. And the facts—real ones—don't support this merger."

One of the more senior members— a stiff, old-money bastard who usually spoke only to criticize—narrowed his eyes behind his gold-framed glasses as he turned a page.

"These numbers... don't align."

Another muttered, "That can't be right," while a third shook his head slowly, flipping back to the executive summary as if it might change under different lighting.

Oskar's voice cut through it, flat and dismissive. "It's a misunderstanding. I'm sure whatever this is—" he gestured vaguely toward the documents. "It can be clarified."

His breath picked up, rage swelling in his chest in a way I had feared as a boy. I couldn't give a fuck about it now.

"No," I said, finally. "It can't."

Every head turned to me like they'd just remembered whose name was on the glass outside. I leaned forward slightly. "Grey & Cooper performed a blind valuation. No bias. No stake. And they found inflated revenue projections, inconsistent growth claims, and misrepresented client contracts."

Lars stepped forward without needing a cue, steady and emotionless. "Page six," he said. "The projected EBITDA margin is off by nearly eleven percent. That's not a mistake. That's fraud."

A ripple passed through the room. A few board members turned pages quickly, brows pulling tighter as they scanned the numbers. Others froze, exchanging glances—concern tightening their expressions like they'd just realized they'd been standing on a cracked foundation. Oskar didn't even blink. But I watched him unravel anyway.

I added a bit more fuel.

"You were nearly sold a lie," I said, letting the words hang for a second. "Packaged in graphs and buzzwords. All it would've taken was one vote in the wrong direction, and this company would've been gutted from the inside out."

Silence gripped the room. No one dared shift. A few jaws were tight. One man palmed his forehead like he was already calculating the fallout. And Oskar—he just stood there. Frozen. Drowning in the stillness.

It was time for the fucking matches.

"It ends today. I'm moving to terminate Oskar Reinhardt's

consulting contract effective immediately, and I'm requesting the board vote to remove him from all active advisory roles."

Oskar's head snapped toward me.

"You don't have a vote to support that," he snapped, voice rising in a last-ditch scramble. His eyes darted around the table looking for an ally, for backup.

He found none.

"I do," I said calmly, not bothering to look away from him.

A moment passed. Then another. One board member gave a slight nod in my direction. Then two more. The dam cracked. Oskar saw it—his leverage crumbling beneath him.

I pressed forward. "You've coasted too long on what you built before I ever stepped in. But your time's up. You're a liability. And I won't let your pride bleed this company dry."

The silence around the table was no longer uncertain—it was decisive. Even the ones who feared him before weren't moving to stop me now.

I stood, gesturing to Lars.

"And since we're cleaning house, I'll be initiating a full buyout of remaining board-held shares. You'll all walk away wealthier than you walked in. The legal team is prepared to begin transition discussions immediately."

Oskar slammed the projector remote down. The sound cracked against the table like a gunshot. He stormed toward the door, muttering something under his breath—then stopped just short of the exit. Turned. His eyes locked on mine.

"If only your mother had taken you to that grave with her," he said in German.

A poison-tipped blade to the gut. I didn't flinch. Just closed the distance between us in three calm steps, my voice quiet and cold enough to frost glass.

"When I'm done with you," I said evenly, in English for anyone to hear, "you'll wish you'd put me there yourself."

His jaw twitched. But he said nothing. Couldn't. Then he turned—shoulders stiff, pace clipped—and walked out the door.

No one followed him.

The boardroom sat in stunned silence for a beat too long before Lars finally moved to my side.

"You want me to start digging through the expense accounts next?"

He didn't even need to ask.

"There's more rot. I can feel it." I kept my eyes on the door Oskar had vanished through. "I want every cent tracked. If he so much as signs a vending machine receipt, I want to know about it."

Lars gave a nod. "And the office?"

"Lock it down," I said flatly. "Nothing leaves until the audit is complete. Not even a fucking pen." He walked off to set it in motion, and I let out the breath I'd been holding since last night. The rage in me had finally gone quiet, replaced by the aching desire for an altar call—the kind only she could summon.

Kais

♫ 31

WE LAY IN BED QUIETLY. JUST THE SOUND OF OUR catching breaths and the soft patter of rain against the windows of our flat, still home for now, while Calico Hill waited for inspections and permits.

Her body sheeted in candlelight, her thigh draped over my waist, exactly where she belonged. My arm cradled her head to my chest, her breasts warm against my ribs. The. Fucking. Altar. I smoothed my palm over the sea of her dark curls, watching her in quiet awe. How her lips pouted pillow-soft. How her ring caught the light against my chest. How the candlelight bathed the deep gold of her skin—so soft I still didn't know how to touch it without complete admiration. I want nothing but this. Her. Us. I don't remember life before her anymore. We came together so fast... and somehow still too slow. I waited my whole life for her without even realizing it.

"Kai?" she whispered, her voice like silk against my chest. Thunder rumbled harder outside.

"Yes, *Ya Amar.*"

She didn't move, but I felt the faint tightening of her body, a breath held in her spine.

"I'm really... really going to miss you."

I pressed a kiss into her hair, breathing her in. She still smelled like the candlelight—vanilla and warmth and something sweeter I hadn't named yet. That scent that lived in my blood now.

"Me too, love. I'd like to say I wish I never took this bloody fight," I said quietly, "so we wouldn't have to be apart... but then I'd have never met you."

She shifted, lifting her head just enough to look at me, brows gently furrowed. "What's your fight got to do with meeting me?"

I reached down, tucking a curl behind her ear, letting my fingers linger along the edge of it.

"The first time I saw you was in the hotel above your restaurant. I'd taken a meeting with the promoters for my fight. Was supposed to fly out the next day."

Her laugh was quiet, caught between amusement and disbelief.

"Wait—what? I thought you just liked hanging out there. Like, you bumped into me by chance."

I shook my head.

"No chance about it. I stayed. Kept coming back. Waiting for you."

"But you didn't say anything," she said, eyeing me like I'd kept some kind of secret.

"You didn't notice me." I shrugged.

She rolled her eyes, a smile pulling at her lips.

"Oh, yeah right. I definitely noticed. I saw you go into the hotel once... then again. And again. You just never said anything. Until you finally did."

Her head found its way back to my chest, her fingertips gliding slowly over my ribs like she was drawing the shape of me.

"I feel like I knew even then," she said, barely above a whisper, "that this was something bigger than I could imagine. Like my soul had been molded with the shape of yours, and it was just waiting to find its way back."

I smiled, heat rising behind my ribs. The rain pattered harder against the windows.

"Those brilliant instincts of yours." I tilted my head against the pillow, brushing her bare shoulder with my knuckles.

"What was I doing when you saw me? Refilling drinks?" she laughed, light and curious.

My chest went heavy at the memory and what saying it aloud might stir in her. But I only ever wanted to be honest with her. Only ever wanted truth and trust.

"No," I said quietly. "You were by the stairs. Near the elevator. Talking on the phone." I paused, chewing on the thought for a moment. "It was your mum, I believe." I exhaled through my nose. "Didn't mean to overhear, but... you weren't exactly quiet."

She flushed faintly, like she knew exactly which call I meant. I went on before she could retreat into herself.

"You were leaning against the wall like your whole body was trying not to fall apart. Your voice was steady but only just. You were talking about a bill. Offering to cover something she couldn't. There was this edge to you—like you were exhausted, but you were still showing up anyway."

Her breath stalled.

"I watched you hang up the phone, plaster on a smile, and walk into work like nothing had happened." I let out a soft breath, letting the memory settle.

"You looked... devastating. And kind. And so beautiful I forgot why I was standing there in the first place."

She shifted, a smile catching the corner of her lips. "You didn't stay just because you thought I was beautiful?"

"No," I said, brushing her hair back again to catch her gaze. A flash of lightning brightened her face. "I stayed because I saw a woman with everything on her shoulders and still more light in her than anyone I'd ever known."

She lifted her head then, gaze wide and vulnerable, like she wasn't sure she'd heard me right.

"I couldn't leave after that," I said softly. "I think some part of me already knew too."

Her brow pinched, and I watched the recognition slowly build behind her eyes. "You came in that night, didn't you?" she said slowly. "The bar... I saw you."

I stayed quiet. Let her memory do the rest.

She blinked.

"Wait—wait. Jazz told me some guy tipped her a stupid amount of money that night. Said she didn't need to borrow it from me anymore." Her mouth parted as it hit her. "Oh my God. That was you."

I exhaled through a smile. "Nice to know she follows instructions as well as you do."

"She said you were just some rich guy who felt bad for her. She never told me it was you." Her fingers toyed absently with the sheet draped across my stomach, but her voice edged with something else. "You did that because you heard me on the phone, didn't you?" She narrowed her eyes, waiting for my answer.

I ran a hand through my hair. "Honestly, I didn't think about it. Just saw you—saw what it was doing to you—and something kicked up in me. I knew I couldn't walk away having done nothing."

She stared at me, quiet. Her gaze was distant now, back in time, maybe, seeing that night from a completely different angle.

"Wow," she whispered, almost to herself. "What a first impression."

I felt something flare low in my chest. The way she said it—it was that old reflex again. The one where she shrinks herself even after everything. I hated it. I shifted, brushing my thumb along her jaw until she looked at me again.

"What I saw was the most beautiful woman I'd seen in my life. Who loved people past reason. Who gave even when she had

279

nothing left. Who still had the grace to smile after all of it." My voice dipped. "So yes. What a fucking first impression."

She opened her mouth as if to argue, then closed it without a word. She just looked at me like she couldn't quite believe she was still allowed to be seen like this: whole, cherished. And then she stilled again. I held her chin gently until her gaze met mine. Her eyes were wide, glassy, searching, like they were carrying more than just this moment. They always did.

"*Ya amar*," I said, brushing my thumb across her cheek. "I love you exactly as you are. As you've been. And as you will be. I'll remind you as many times as it takes."

Her breath held but she nodded. Then she leaned in, her lips barely touching mine as she whispered, "I love you too, Kai. Like... earth-shattering, bury me with you if I ever lost you love."

Something cracked open in my chest. Quiet but deep. The kind of feeling that lingers in your bones. I brushed her cheek with the back of my fingers.

"*Ti'burni, omri*. If I ever lost you, there'd be nothing left worth walking through the world for."

"*Ti'burni?*" she whispered, trying to shape the words. "What's that one mean?"

"Same thing you just said to me, babe. Apparently, my grandmother was Lebanese—learned that one from my aunt's journal," I murmured against her lips. She smiled against me like I'd just given her a treasure.

Then I kissed her like I meant it because I always fucking do. The storm raging outside a stark contrast to the peace she brings to the one that rages in me.

Just as her words settled into the space between us, my phone vibrated on the nightstand. I didn't care but she pulled back, glanced at it, then back to me.

"You should get that."

I didn't want to. Not when she was still wrapped around me

like that. Not when I could still feel the echo of her words on my skin.

"Fine," I mumbled, brushing a kiss to her forehead. "But stay. Just like this."

She didn't move, just nodded, her hand splayed warm across my chest like she was tying me to her. I sat up just enough to reach for the phone.

Alanzo.

The name alone tightened something in my spine. I knew what the call would be before I even answered. It only took a minute. When I hung up, the room was still dim, still quiet, but I felt the shift in her. She was watching me. Waiting. I let out a slow breath and ran a hand down my face.

"Alanzo found your mum," I said softly.

She sat up, instantly alert. "Where?"

"Some run-down flat outside Fort Worth. She was strung out. In bad shape. He's with her now. Said he's getting her somewhere safe."

I hated being the one to say it but I needed her to hear it from me. Because I'm the one who will love her through the worst of it. The air thickened around us. She didn't speak at first, just laid back down slowly, curling into my chest like she was trying to steady herself with the rhythm of my breathing.

"Thank you... for doing that," she whispered.

I wrapped both arms around her, one hand smoothing over the crown of her head. "You don't owe me a thank you, *Ya Amar*. You just tell me what you want to do and I'll make it happen."

She nodded against me. I felt her tears before I heard them, and the quiet breath that followed.

"I want to send her somewhere real. Somewhere that might actually work this time." She said, voice trembling. "If she'll go.'" Her voice cracked just slightly at the end.

I kissed the top of her head, my hand already reaching for the phone. "Then that's what we'll do."

I texted Alanzo the green light. He'd handle it before the sun came up. She wasn't asking me to fix it. But I would. Quietly. Completely. Every time.

She kissed my chest, once, then let her lips trail higher, settling at the hollow of my throat. Her hand slid slowly over my ribs, thumb brushing back and forth the way she does when she needs the comfort. I held her tighter. She didn't say another word. She didn't want to. I could feel that she wanted to be closer, needed it even.

Then her mouth found mine. It was slow at first, as if she was taking a breath. But then she shifted beneath me, fingers curling around my wrist, her other hand pressing at my hip like she needed me to close every inch of space between us. She pulled at me with quiet urgency, a breathless, aching kind of need.

Her legs parted around me like she was opening a door she'd kept locked her whole life, and I stepped through because I never belonged anywhere else. I didn't tease her. Didn't wait. I was right there, where she needed me.

Deep and unhurried. One hand in her hair, the other cradling her thigh, hinging her open beneath me. She arched into me with a gasp. The sound was soft, barely a whisper, but it wrecked me. I felt it everywhere: in the hollow of my chest, in the curl of my fingers around her thigh, in the back of my throat where her name lived like a vow.

I bit back a curse, because fuck if this didn't feel like something more than physical. It felt like the world pulling us inward. Like the moment something shifts permanently and neither of you realize it until it's already done.

"I love you Kai," she whimpered against my lips, her big brown eyes holding mine. "I'll do whatever you want, be whatever you want. Just please don't ever let me go," she pleaded as I sank myself deeper into her.

"Never," I rasped, holding her gaze as I stilled inside her. "You are every breath I take, Alana. I suffocate the second you're gone.

I'm already dying at the thought of you going back to Miami." My voice broke, but I didn't stop. Couldn't. "I never want to know a world where you don't exist. Not in this life, not in the next. And if heaven's not you, I'll find you there, too."

A tear slipped across her cheek. I wiped it away with my thumb, kissed the trail, then claimed her mouth again. She breathed me in as I began to move in her, giving her every bit of me in every way I could. Every move a punctuation to just how much I meant what I said. Every brush of her skin against mine felt familiar and new all at once. As if we'd done this a thousand times in a thousand lives.

We moved together in that quiet, rain and lightning-lit room like there was no place else. No one else. Because there fucking isn't. Just the breath between our mouths and the sound of her whispering my name like it was the only word that had ever mattered. And maybe it was. Because when I'm with her—like this, in the dark, in the quiet—I don't just feel like a man who's been forgiven. I feel like one who's been chosen.

Alana

-32-

Four months later...

Mom: My flight leaves at 5. Can we meet for lunch or coffee before?

Me: Yeah, that would be great. Do you want me to send Alanzo to get you?

Mom: Nope. Keep your mean Italian henchman away from me lol. Roast house at 2?

Me: Alanzo wouldn't hurt a fly.

Mom: I wouldn't suggest you buzz at him to find out.

♫ 23

"Maybe you should reconsider my sister-wives offer," Jasmine said, sitting on the toilet lid, lazily filing her nails like she wasn't trying to ignite my nerves at nine a.m.

I paused mid-mascara, glaring at her through the mirror. "Don't start this again, Jazz."

"Not for me—for you," she said, placing a hand over her chest like I'd insulted her.

"You're always here. And I know it's not because you can't live without the aesthetic of this decaying '90s landlord special."

I let out a soft huff, pulling my hair free from a tie and fluffing out the curls.

"It's lonely in that big place with just Alanzo. I'd rather be here if Kais isn't there."

I wouldn't dare say how I still slept on his side of the bed or how I left the lights on when he wasn't home.

She hummed, standing to join me at the mirror. "Guess it is nicer to look at me than a penthouse."

"You know," I muttered, "I pray your level of self-confidence will rub off on me someday."

She plopped herself onto the counter, swiping a lip gloss from my makeup bag. "Please. Don't act like Mrs. Humble—you know you're hot. You just like to pretend you're not."

I turned sideways, eyeing my reflection critically.

"This is not hot," I said, gesturing to my stomach. "I'm constantly bloated. And you've seen how hard I've been pushing it in the gym."

She nodded. "Facts."

"I think I've developed some kind of gluten intolerance or something."

She groaned, throwing up her hands. "God. Please don't turn into one of those rich bitches who ask for gluten-free air."

I laughed. "I'm not. I'm just saying I don't feel hot. I think I'm overstressed."

Midterms. My mom. Even more silence from Macy since my mom's been in rehab. Kais being oceans away with a fight in a month. It all stacked up until even my body felt like it was holding its breath. Or maybe I was dying slowly from suppressed emotions and gluten. Either way, I didn't feel like myself.

Jasmine hopped down from the counter, grabbing her phone from her back pocket. "We all get like that before our period. You're hot one week, and the next you've gained ten pounds and cry on the Stairmaster. It's science."

"True," I muttered, still brushing my hand over the fabric of my tennis dress.

She glanced at her screen and her eyes widened. "Shit, we gotta go." She grabbed her bag and moved toward the door. "You can ask about your bread belly at the appointment, but I'll be damned if I spend all day in the student health center because you made us miss our last free coochie check."

Though Miami was starting to feel too heavy, Jasmine was the one thing light enough to carry me through it. Even when she was yelling about vaginal checkups.

"*Coochie* is a disgusting word, Jazz."

She rolled her eyes. "Whatever, bitch. Just hurry yours up."

THE STICKY HEAT followed us into the clinic, clinging to my skin like a blanket of regret. I'd spent the summer convincing myself that England's overcast skies and crisp air had reset my internal thermostat—clearly, Florida didn't get the memo. Late September and it still felt like walking through soup.

Inside, the waiting room was the usual mix of frat boys scratching themselves like they had no shame, and girls trying to squeeze in their free annual checkup before graduation.

"See," Jasmine muttered, glaring at one guy who had the audacity to do a scratch and sniff before winking at her.

"That should be a question on dating apps: *How often do you visit the student health center because your balls itch?*"

I was still laughing when the nurse called, "Jasmine Lozano and Alana Cameron?"

We both stood. Jasmine tossed me a grin over her shoulder.

"See? The universe wants us to become sister wives. We even get our coochies checked in sync."

"Just go," I snorted, nudging her toward the door.

I followed, pretending I wasn't two seconds from melting in this heat or that I hadn't checked my phone three times in the waiting room just to feel closer to Kais. My stomach flipped, subtle but insistent. Not anxiety. Just...something. Like the day was one degree off-center, a picture frame slightly tilted that no one had bothered to straighten.

"Bathrooms are down the hall. I'm sure you ladies know the drill about clean catch?" the nurse said, handing over two plastic cups with the enthusiasm of someone ten hours into a shift.

"Ah yes, I learned the clean coochie catch in med-surg," Jasmine replied without shame, already pivoting toward the bathroom.

I mouthed, I'm sorry, as I took the other cup from the nurse's hand. She gave me a look like she'd heard worse today. Probably had.

Kai Kai: Going into promo pictures now. Can I FaceTime you after?

Me: I'd be heartbroken if you didn't.

Kai Kai: Fuck. I miss you.

Me: Trust me. Next week can't come soon enough.

Kai Kai: Bathroom renovations at the house should finally be done by the end of the week, time to bring our toothbrushes?

> Me: Good idea, I'll pack my Reinhardt poster carefully.

The exam room door creaked open.

"Alana Cameron?" A med student stood in the doorway, barely looking up from her iPad.

"Hi, yes—it should actually be Reinhardt, not Cameron. I submitted the name change to the student center months ago," I said, finding it harder than normal not to sound irritated as I tucked my phone away. She gave a quick nod, fingers still flying over the screen.

"Got it. Just needs to be updated on our end, I apologize." More tapping. Still no eye contact. "Any other updates you want me to make to your profile while I'm in it? I don't see anyone listed from obstetrics. Who's following your pregnancy?"

The words barely landed at first. They sounded casual, like she was asking if I'd updated my insurance. I blinked, head tilting just slightly. *That wasn't for me. She must've meant the girl two charts ahead. This clinic was always behind.* Last time I came in, I was listed as someone named Timothy.

"I'm not pregnant," I said with a laugh that didn't quite reach my throat. A scoff, really.

She finally glanced up at me, brows knitting together. Then her eyes dropped again to the screen, scrolling fast. She rattled off my name and birthdate like she was troubleshooting a glitch in the system. I waited for her to catch her mistake. Waited for her to laugh and blame the long day and swap charts like they always did. Instead, her shoulders stiffened. A faint flush bloomed across her cheeks.

"Yeah, Alana Cam—Reinhardt." She corrected herself with a wince. "Your urine sample came back positive for pregnancy."

She froze, her face red the instant she realized what I hadn't.

"Oh. Oh." She whispered.

I stared at her. She stared at the screen.

"I'm so sorry," she said quickly, hand flying to her chest like she could catch the mistake mid-air. "I'm running on no sleep. Residency interviews are kicking my ass...". She held up a hand, catching herself again. "None of that's your problem. I should've asked, not assumed."

I said nothing. Just sat there, suspended, like my body and brain had temporarily lost contact with one another. "When was your last period?" she asked softly.

That probably should've been her first question.

I blinked, still lagging behind, "I haven't had one in about a year, maybe more... I've been getting the shot."

She nodded, eyes flicking over the iPad. "When was your last injection?"

"Um—April, I think. Last time I was here."

Another pause. More tapping. Then a slow exhale.

"I see. Have you been sexually active since then—well, obviously, yes. Sorry." Her cheeks burned red again. "It's just hard to pin an estimated gestation stage in this situation."

I closed my eyes and pressed the heels of my palms into them, like I could reset the moment. Or wake up from it.

"I was told it could take up to a year to even ovulate again. That I couldn't get pregnant until my period came back." She gave a low snort.

"Yeah, well... whoever told you that is running on less sleep than me."

My eyes flicked up at her with zero amusement.

"Sorry," she muttered. "I'm working on my bedside manner."

She cleared her throat. "When's the last time you were active? That might help."

I blinked again, like she'd asked me in another language. "A few weeks ago," I managed. "My husband's in London. It's not very often right now."

She nodded and glanced back at the screen. "Any symptoms?"

"Not that I've noticed, been too consumed with finishing out the semester" I groaned. "Just... bloated. Constantly. Even when I wake up. Is that bad?"

As the words left my mouth, panic quietly seeped beneath them like ink in water. My mind started backtracking, rewinding the last few months in rapid flashes. Every hard workout with Jasmine. Every skipped meal. Every glass of wine. Sushi. Cider. A dozen things I couldn't take back.

"Can I see?" she asked gently.

I hesitated, then lifted my gown. Her hand was careful, pressing carefully across my stomach.

"There's no way to know for sure without an ultrasound or bloodwork," she mumbled. "But if I had to guess... it's more than a few weeks." She looked up at me. "Could be months—maybe more. I can palpate your fundus, which usually means you're past the first trimester."

My heart thudded once, twice, and then dropped somewhere beneath the tile floor. I said nothing. I didn't even breathe.

"Would you like me to put in a referral to obstetrics?" she asked. "Or... would you prefer to talk through some other options?"

"Obstetrics," I said, my voice hoarse. "Please."

Tears stung at the edges of my vision, but I held them there, barely. She reached out and rested a hand on my knee. Not condescending. Not clinical. Just... human.

"I'm sure you know we can't do a pap today, but I'll get that referral started." She stood, already glancing back at the screen. "Congrats," she said quietly, and stepped out the door.

Just in time for a wide-eyed Jasmine to come flying in behind her. She burst into the room like a cyclone in sneakers.

"Oh my god. Oh my god. Oh. My. God." She paced like she needed to burn off adrenaline, hands flailing. "I heard that right? She said congrats? So not fucking gluten."

I shook my head slowly, reality pressing down like gravity all over again.

"Not gluten," I whispered with a small smile.

The next second, her arms were around me. "Oh my god, bitch, I'm going to be the hottest fucking Tía."

A laugh—thin, disbelieving—bubbled up from somewhere deep in my chest.

"Congratulations, Jazz. This is such a big moment for you."

She pulled back grinning, brushing a tear off her cheek like it was no big deal.

"Yes, thank you, it really is." We both laughed, too hard, too loud.

The kind of laugh you have when you don't know what else to do with the feeling rising inside you.

"You're going to be the best mom, Alana," she said suddenly, her voice going hoarse. "I'm so fucking happy for you." I wiped my cheeks with the back of my hand.

"Me too," I said.

And I meant it. But beneath the shock and the shaky joy, my thoughts narrowed to one person. Kais. His name pulsed through my chest like my own heartbeat. His face. His voice. The way he called me *Ya Amar* like it meant home. I imagined what he'd say in this moment. What his eyes would look like. I can picture how he would hold me and now I wish it was his arms around me instead of Jazzy's. I hadn't known for a minute and still my heart was clenching with a mixture of joy and guilt. I'm going to be a mom... he's going to be a dad.

God, I can't even imagine what it would've been like to have a father who was even half the man Kais is. But having him as a husband is more than I ever dreamed I'd be allowed to have.

Since I was a kid, I'd quietly imagined what it would feel like to have a family of my own. Back then, it was just about feeling loved —chosen. Like I could do everything differently than my mom. But being with Kais had already given me that.

And now, doing this—with him in a house he picked for us, where he stood in that nursery like it couldn't dare to be anything else…I don't even have the words for this feeling. And maybe… maybe he'd already known what was coming. The way he spoke to me lately. The way he looked at me, like he was preparing for something bigger than either of us could see. I don't know how to tell him yet. But I know he'd hold this the way he held everything that mattered to me. Like it was sacred.

MY MOM SAT STIFFLY in the passenger seat, cigarette already in hand—ready to light the second I pulled into the departures lane. She looked better now. Cleaner. Her frail frame had filled out slightly, but there was still no warmth in her eyes. Lunch had been awkward. Stilted. A few half-hearted jokes that didn't land, tangled between long stretches of silence and an all-out avoidance of anything real.

"How's your husband?" she muttered, eyes fixed on the slow crawl of traffic ahead.

"He's fine. I'm flying out to see him next week."

She didn't respond. She never tried—not once—to thank Kais for paying for her treatment. Hell, she's never even acknowledged it. She carries herself like it was owed to her somehow, like generosity is just another form of debt someone else is meant to pay off.

The car crept forward, inching through the line of vehicles like time itself had slowed in protest. It felt like a punishment, every second stretched too thin.

"Lisa agreed to let me see Macy next week," she whispered finally. "I can FaceTime you when I'm with her if you want."

I nodded slowly, my eyes fixed ahead. "Do you think she'll even recognize me anymore? She hasn't heard my voice in over three years. I've only seen her in pictures and videos."

"And whose fault is that, Alana?" she scoffed, not missing a moment to make me feel even worse.

I let out a dry humorless laugh. Of course. I should've known better by now—should've known not to expect softness. And yet, some part of me still waits for it. That little girl tucked deep inside, the one who still longs to be seen by this woman, still wants that impossible moment. Who keeps wishing for a real mother. The kind you call with good news. The kind who hugs you like you matter. The kind who'd hear I'm pregnant and cry for joy instead of finding a way to make it about herself.

But if I'm being honest? It feels a hell of a lot better now that I can remind that girl that we made it without her. That we didn't break. That we clawed our way out anyway and then found a king amongst men—and he throws every dragon this woman ever brought into the room straight into the sea.

Shoving that contempt back down took effort. I did it anyway.

"I'd love to talk to her," I said, mustering the most genuine smile I could as we finally reached the terminal. She slipped out of the seat without a word.

I met her at the trunk to help with her bags, lifting each one out in silence until only the last remained. As I set it down beside her, she stared at me, eyes squinting slightly, like she was studying something disgusting.

"Freshman fifteen's hitting you pretty late, I see."

I rolled my eyes.

"I'm just bloated. Too many sweet treats with my roommate last night," I lied, fast and flat.

"Better watch out, you'll lose that husband of yours quicker than you tricked him into marrying you," she said like it was a joke, but I know part of her meant every word.

I've never been worthy of much in her eyes, no matter how hard I tried. The prideful part of me wanted to boast, tell her I'm pregnant and that husband she's referring to will reorder the stars in the sky when he finds out. Tell her that I'm loved beyond compare to anything she's ever shown me. But I don't need to do that. I don't have a thing to prove to her.

Even when I feel hurt by her bullshit, I can still see that pain in her eyes. The pain that shaped her to be this way. My pride won't fix that, though I've always hoped me loving her would. But even if it did, there was no chance in hell I'd tell her before I told Kais— especially not when she had a gift for sucking the joy out of anything good in my life.

Still, I opened my arms for a hug. She hesitated. Then stepped in. Her grip was firmer than I expected, almost like she needed it. Like she didn't know how to ask for comfort but couldn't quite refuse it when offered. And just for a second, my heart cracked for her. Just a little.

"Come home and visit..." she mumbled into my shoulder.

The words wavered. Then she pulled back and dusted herself off, as if shaking off whatever that moment had stirred up.

"For Macy, you know. Maybe you could come to one of those jail-like visitations I get with her."

She adjusted her oversized sunglasses with casual deflection, her tone back to neutral, her armor back in place. But that scrap of softness—the hesitation, the almost-hug, the flicker of something real—felt like more than I've ever gotten from her. And that broke something in me all over again. I wiped the tears from my cheek before they had the chance to fall. I'm her daughter, after all. Shoving shit down is what I learned from her best.

"I will. Maybe when I get back from London in a few weeks."

A security officer waved us forward, motioning for her to head inside.

"Yeah, whatever. Just call me when you decide," she said, lingering a second too long before finally turning. Then she was gone, disappearing through the automatic doors with a simple 'Later', tossed over her shoulder like spare change. Not even a glance back. I wouldn't expect anything more.

Alana

-33-

VOICE MEMO, TIME STAMP 8:43 P.M.:

"Okay, so for tort reform—God, I sound tired already—for tort reform, the primary argument is limiting frivolous lawsuits in order to reduce liability costs for businesses, but the tradeoff is..." I paused to yawn, rolling my neck as I sank deeper into the couch.

Studying for my last final was brutal enough but now that I knew I was pregnant, I couldn't believe how loudly my body had been trying to tell me before my mind caught up. Voice memos helped me retain information, sure, but my mind wasn't here. It was somewhere across the Atlantic. With him.

Kais had gone to bed hours ago after FaceTiming me. Just a quick check-in, all soft smiles and heavier things left unsaid. I almost told him then. God, I wanted to. But he looked exhausted, his eyes rimmed with the weight of a thousand obligations. And if I told him, he'd be on the next flight before I even finished the sentence. I couldn't have that. Not now. Not when I knew how hard he's worked for this fight. What it had cost us in time and strain to get to this close to the finish line.

So, I told myself it could wait a little longer. I'd see him in one more week. One more breath. I'd tell him face to face, where there was no screen between us. Until then, I'd sit in it a little longer, this quiet, secret, strange little bud of joy tucked under my ribs, fragile and burning.

I hit record again.

"—but the tradeoff is limiting access to justice for individuals, especially those without the means to fight prolonged legal battles. The ethical implication—"

A pounding knock sounded through the front door. I didn't even pause the recording, just set my phone on the counter.

"Jazzy," I complained, pushing up from the couch with a faint smile. "You really need to start remembering your damn keys, girl. I'm not always gonna be here to save you from the wrath of Florida humidity."

I padded toward the door, bare feet brushing against the tile, and opened it without thinking. I froze.

Oskar Reinhardt.

He stood in the doorway like he had every right to be there: tall, lean, skin slightly sunburned, wearing jeans, a T-shirt, and a baseball cap like this was just some casual drop-in. Like he hadn't tried to publicly humiliate me the last time we met.

"Good evening, Alana. Aren't you a vision," he said, dragging his gaze over me like I was something to be inspected, picked apart.

My tank top and pajama shorts suddenly felt too skimpy, like they were giving him too much.

"Why are you here?" I didn't bother disguising my tone.

"I have something I need to talk to you about. May I come in?"

He didn't wait. Just pushed through the door like he always had a seat at the table.

"You've got some balls," I said, shaking my head with a breathy laugh. "I'll give you that much."

"That I do."

He didn't smile, just let his eyes roam the apartment, all judgment and calculation.

"What a stroke of luck you hit, marrying my son. And without a prenup, no less."

He clicked his tongue, taking slow steps toward the kitchen island. His fingertips brushed along the countertop like he was checking for dust, like this place wasn't good enough to share the same square footage as his last name.

"Thought I'd find you in South of Fifth. Seems more your speed these days. This place doesn't quite say Reinhardt, does it?" He turned, flicking his hand in my direction like I was something to be wiped off the marble. "But then again, that name doesn't quite suit you either."

I didn't move from my spot near the door. Not because I was afraid. Because I was trained not to. One thing I learned growing up with men like this—men who made threats sound like compliments—you never let them put their body between you and the only exit. You stay close to the door. You make sure they know you see every step they take. You give them nothing.

I couldn't deny what cracked through me in that moment. I wanted Kais. More than that: I wanted Kais to be here. To round the corner, to put himself between me and this man. To say my name, hold my waist and make everything still the way only he can. But he wasn't going to. Not tonight. Not tomorrow. Because he didn't know. Didn't know about the little surprise curled in my belly. Didn't know I'd spent the last week before I found out swallowing the urge to text him "come home" with nothing else.

I chose that. Because if I said those words, he would come. He would give everything up if I asked. Which is why I haven't. So now I'm standing here—protecting a child he doesn't even know exists, a child he doesn't know already needs protecting. And I have to do it alone. Because that's what this moment demands. So, I stayed exactly where I was. Grounded. Alert. And something settled inside me. Not fear. Not even anger. It was something older than both. A kind of knowing. A line drawn.

"You can skip all the bullshit, Oskar. Get to the point. My

roommate will be here any minute, so I wouldn't suggest you try anything stupid."

He laughed, deep and amused, leaning back against the counter like we were sharing some private joke. Arms crossed, icy eyes tracking every inch of me.

"Relax. I'm not here to fuck you. If I were, you'd already be bent over this counter." He knocked his knuckles against the butcher block with a slow rhythm, each tap loaded with implication.

My stomach turned. The chill that crept up my spine left something sour in its wake.

He walked up to me. "But that's too easy, isn't it?" he continued, gaze narrowing. "Although I'd love to see every way Kais would lose his fucking mind." He smiled, not an ounce of warmth in it. "No. You're going to do something for me instead."

I scoffed.

"I'm not doing shit for you. Please leave."

I gestured toward the open door, but he didn't move to the door. He stepped closer to me, close enough I could feel the warmth rolling off him and slid something into my hand. A stack of photos.

Heat crawled up my chest as I flicked through them.

Five in total.

Each one of my mother. Strung out. Begging. Gaunt.

The first four were time-stamped from before Alanzo found her over the summer. The last one—today. A blurry shot of her outside that same apartment in Fort Worth. Not even twelve hours out of rehab.

I inhaled a bitter breath, the air like fire in my lungs. My pulse spiked, but I didn't let my expression crack.

"Congrats, Oskar," I said cooly, flipping the last photo back into place. "You caught my mother relapsing. What the hell does that have to do with you?"

He tilted his head like he was expecting a scream. A breakdown. Anything bigger than this. But I held my ground. Because now I knew exactly what kind of game he was playing. And I was already preparing to beat him at it.

"It has nothing to do with me, *Tochter*," he said, that smirk curling with smug delight. "But the media might be interested in Kais Reinhardt's new wife's charmingly broken family. The sister you abandoned to trap my son..."

He took a step closer, tone dropping like a match.

"And if that's not interesting enough, we could always sweeten it with poor *Mutti* getting a bad batch. Fentanyl's all the rave where you're from, isn't it?"

He stepped back again, the threat cooling into something calmer—crueler. He studied me like he'd already won. I didn't move. Not because I was afraid. Not because I didn't have anything to say—I had plenty.

No.

I stayed frozen because just over his shoulder, I could see the edge of my phone on the counter. Still recording. Voice memo blinking red, like a tiny, pulsing life line.

Let's dance, Oskar.

I lifted my chin. "So, what is it you want in exchange for not killing my mother and blackmailing your son, Oskar?" I made my voice louder, clear—so the mic would catch every damn word.

He chuckled, dark and low. "I knew I'd get that fight out of you." His gaze dropped. "Though I'd rather have gotten it in... other ways."

Then he reached out. His finger grazed the top of my chest slowly, stopping just short of my cleavage. I've learned the thing that keeps me safe in a situation like this is to stay quiet about it, don't give them a reason to get angry, it only makes it worse. But something inside me snapped clean in half. Because if Kais knew this man had touched me—had even tried—he wouldn't stop until there was nothing left. It wouldn't end with Oskar. He'd burn through anyone who let it happen. And I couldn't let that happen. Not to him.

I hissed and batted his hand away. "Keep your fucking hands off me. Say what you came to say—and get out."

He smiled again, but it didn't reach anything human. His blue eyes were gone behind blown pupils, wide and glassy. Like he'd taken something, or maybe this was his high, watching people squirm.

"Settle down. It's simple," he said. He stepped back just slightly, giving himself the illusion of space, like we were just two civil adults discussing logistics.

"All you have to do is stop by your husband's office. Plug this into his computer," He held up a tiny black thumb drive, pinched between two fingers like a luxury cigar. "And it'll take care of the rest."

Then he placed it on the counter behind him with the same care you'd use to set down a bomb.

"What does it do?" I asked, though I already knew I wouldn't like the answer.

He scoffed like the question offended him. "That's not your business."

I kept my tone even, eyes flat. "If you want me to do it, it is."

He sighed. Not out of frustration but boredom.

As if all of this—the threats, the thumb drive, my life—was just an annoying errand he hadn't gotten around to yet.

"Kais' numbers are too high," he said, brushing a speck of lint off his sleeve. "And if they stay that way, the buyers start asking questions. The kind that hurt people. This just... keeps the playing field level."

"You mean it hides something."

His head snapped up, the veneer slipping for just a second. "It corrects something."

And there it was. The crack. The moment his mouth moved faster than his sense of self-preservation. I didn't blink. Just stared him down, letting that little voice in my head (the one that had sat through every criminal law lecture) start cataloguing terms: fraud. obstruction. tampering. conspiracy. It was the kind of phrasing you used when you were guilty. When you were already trying to rewrite your version of events.

He realized it too late. I saw it in the way his jaw clicked shut, a flicker of irritation behind his eyes.

"You're scared," I said, mostly to myself.

Oskar's smile returned, but it twitched at the edges this time. "No," he said slowly, "I'm pragmatic." He looked me over again, colder now. Like he was tallying my weight in leverage.

"You'll do it," he said. "Because deep down, you know my son isn't going to risk the good name of his empire for a junkie's daughter."

I didn't blink. Not because it didn't hurt. But because I refused to show him that it did. And still, he didn't stop. He checked his watch like he had somewhere better to be. Like this was beneath him.

"You have two days," he said, voice light. "Plug it in, and this all goes away. Kais never has to know."

He turned without waiting for a response. Walked to the door like he owned it. Like he'd made his move, and now the rest was up to me. He didn't look back. The second the door clicked shut, I felt it in my chest—tight, nauseating, like I hadn't been breathing the whole time.

I glanced at the counter. The thumb drive sat there like a loaded gun. And just past it, half-hidden behind a recipe book, my phone. Still recording. Still blinking red.

Immediately I stopped it and scrolled to my mom's contact. I pressed Call. It rang once. Twice. Straight to voicemail.

I stared at the screen, thumb hovering, before hitting Call again. Same thing.

No answer.

THE NEXT DAY, I got to campus a few hours before my last exam. Didn't matter that I wasn't scheduled for class. I just needed to be somewhere built on logic. Where people talked in terms of rules and consequences, not threats and innuendo. And I knew just who to go to. I waited outside Professor Daniels' office until the student before me left. Then I knocked and stepped in. She looked up from her laptop, blinking behind her glasses like she'd just remembered the outside world existed.

"Alana," she said, smiling. "Everything okay?"

I shut the door behind me. "Can I ask something? Hypothetically."

Her expression shifted, still kind, but alert now. "Of course."

I pulled out my phone and tapped the voice memo.

"Let's say someone gives you a thumb drive and asks you to plug it into a private computer connected to a corporate buyout."

She tilted her head. "Who's the someone?"

"Let's say... a former partner. One who's about to be cut out of the deal."

Her smile faded completely. I hit play. Just a few seconds. Enough to hear Oskar's voice, cold and certain: *If the numbers are too high, the buyers start asking questions. The kind that hurt people. This just... keeps the playing field level.*

I stopped it. Professor Daniels blinked once. "Depending on what's on that drive, you're looking at attempted fraud, possibly obstruction. Definitely corporate tampering. And if he's using you to do it—that's coercion. This is serious."

"Serious enough for investigators?"

She gave a small nod. "Definitely."

She didn't ask what I planned to do with it. She didn't need to. I remembered something from London after Kais fired Oskar, something he said to Lars in a low voice when he didn't know I was listening: "Hire someone neutral. Quiet. I want eyes on everything Oskar's touched in the last year." At the time, I thought it was just protocol. Just Kais being Kais. Now, I understood what it really was: my back door. An open line to the people already closing in. A lifeline that keeps my husband blissfully unaware and safe.

Outside her office, I called my mom again. Straight to voicemail. I'd have to handle her later, for now I needed to get to London without Kais knowing. This wasn't Kais' fire to handle. Not right now. Not when he was days from locking everything down with his merger and weeks from defending his title. Because if I gave him this now—if he heard what Oskar said, if he saw that thumb drive—he wouldn't rest. He wouldn't pause. He'd take Oskar out of the equation himself, and the fallout wouldn't be business. It would be war.

So I booked a flight to London. Round trip. No alerts, no texts, no hint of a visit. I'd go straight to whoever Kais put on the ground. Hand them the recording, the thumb drive, and come back without a squeak I ever left. Let the facts do what they were built to do. Kais always protected me like I was his whole world. Now it was my turn to protect him, because he was mine, too.

Kais

♫ 34

"You've reached the voicemail of Alana Cameron. I can't come to the phone right now, but leave your name and number and I'll call you back... Unless you're calling about my car's extended warranty—you can call me Bob, and I'm not buying."

I sighed.

She needs to update that bloody voicemail, not even her damn name anymore.

Second unanswered call today. Very fucking unlike her. The woman sent me voice memos just to tell me about her lunch, some dodgy thing her roommate said or to bark at some shirtless interview she saw of me. I fucking loved it. Lived on it. It was the only thing that's kept me even remotely sane while she'd been across the goddamn ocean. And now—nothing. Radio silence. For *sixteen* hours.

A flight to Miami was starting to look more reasonable than this press tour bullshit. Canceling the fight entirely wasn't off the table either. I don't even care how much that would cost me financially. Only thing stopping me was knowing she wouldn't want that. Wouldn't forgive herself if she thought I gave up something for her. It'd set us back ten steps from how far we've come, how far she's come to letting me be by her side. And that's the problem. She'd never ask. Even if she needed me.

I wiped a hand down my face, steadying the thought, then walked through the lobby of the firm for what I hoped was the last time. The lobby doors hissed shut behind me. Cold air, polished marble, the hush of money and menace everywhere. *Thank fuck I'm done with this place after today.* Just a few signatures, some forced smiles, and then I'd finally be free of this place, Reinhardt Capital and everything it had stood for. One less weight around my neck. One step closer to everything I actually wanted.

The elevator chimed.

"Kais." Lars stepped into my path just as the doors opened. "Need a word before we go in."

A breath dragged through my teeth. "If you tell me you're pushing for a higher valuation, I'm walking back out."

He shook his head, stepping into the elevator with me. "No. I'm good with where we landed. This is about Oskar."

The air around us shifted. Just slightly.

"What about him?" I asked.

"We got something. Someone met with the investigator this morning, gave them a drive and a full audio recording."

That landed. He didn't have to say it twice.

"It's the last piece we needed," Lars continued. "He's done."

"Do we know who came forward?"

Lars shook his head. "No name. They only agreed to share it if their identity was fully concealed."

I narrowed my eyes. "I don't love that."

No name? No trace? Anonymous evidence was a risk. Anonymous motives were worse. Still—if the recording was real, if it closed the loop—maybe it didn't matter who drove the last nail.

"But I guess it's not really our problem anymore, yeah?" I muttered, brushing past it. "Let's finish all this shit."

The elevator doors slid open. Light spilled in from the board-room ahead: lawyers, investors, photographers already gathering. Sebastian Voss already one step into his first HR violation as the new owner. Didn't matter. Just meant we were finally at the end of the rope.

"Kais, my boy!" Sebastian grinned, offering his hand. "A beautiful day to double your net worth, I must say."

I shook it, gave a polite nod, and said nothing. Because all I could think about was that recording and Oskar. *What the fuck is on that drive that closes the door for good?*

Everything after that passed in a blur. Speeches. Congratulations. Celebratory bullshit cloaked in six-figure suits. Every twat in the room acting like they'd been with me since the beginning. Like they helped build this thing from the ground up. They didn't. I did. At one point, this room would've meant everything to me. Reinhardt Capital was my whole identity.

Every breath I took, every hour I bled into this place—it was all just an attempt to make it something Oskar couldn't. And I succeeded. But it all meant fuck-all now. Because every dollar, every deal, every ounce of respect I earned didn't matter when everything I wanted was across the goddamn world and not answering her phone.

I moved fast once the final signature was dry. I wanted out. But Michelle Roman stepped into my path, extending her hand for a handshake I didn't have time for.

"Oh, Mr. Reinhardt, I've really enjoyed working with you," she said. "It's been a pleasure."

I nodded, shaking her hand. "You've always been a shark. A good one."

She hesitated, like she had more to say.

"I was sad to hear your wife turned down Oxford," she added. "I sat in on her interview, actually. She's remarkable."

I had no clue. But it didn't surprise me. Not after the way she looked at that nursery. Not after the way she talked about building something in our name, about soft things and second chances. About who she could be if she stopped surviving long enough to start living. She didn't say it then. But I heard it anyway. And now, hearing it out loud from someone else — made my chest go quiet. Full. Because even across the world, even while we were apart, she was still choosing this life. Ours.

I nodded coolly. "She's got her reasons."

That's all Michelle needed to know. For me, knowing Alana believed in what we were building to sacrifice her studies, that was enough too.

Michelle smiled. "Well, if she changes her mind, the door's open. She'd be an asset anywhere." Then her voice brightened like we were old friends instead of strangers tangled in closing paperwork. "You two should come out to celebrate tonight. I know a few people are heading to Mercer's—some press, some investors."

"She's out of town, but thank you," I said, figuring that'd be the end of it.

But Michelle paused, lips parting just slightly.

"Oh?" Her brow lifted. "That's strange. I thought I saw her this morning leaving the lobby."

What? *What the actual fuck is she talking about?* I blinked, held my expression tight.

"Must've been someone else," I said. But my blood was already running hot.

Michelle smiled.

"Well, if you change your mind, you know where to find us. Good luck to you both."

She walked off but I didn't move. Not right away. My mind was already spinning through possibilities, timelines, gaps. Alana had been off. Not just quiet—distant. Like she was holding something back. But one thing was certain: Alana was unmistakable. She wasn't someone you mistook for anyone else. Her long dark curls. The curve of her body. The way she walked into a room and even the air stilled. If Michelle saw her, she saw her. *So what the fuck is going on?*

I stepped into the hallway, spotted Lars still on the phone.

I mouthed the words before I passed him: "Get me that recording." Then I stepped onto the elevator, jaw tight. Already behind schedule. Already late for something else that didn't matter anymore.

THE GYM HAD BEEN CLEARED and converted into a press circus: spotlights, branded banners, folding chairs for the media, and enough heat from the camera rigs to bake a man alive. Montee stood near the ring a bright-eyed interviewer and a mic shoved into his face. Promo press. My least favorite part of the sport. I couldn't give a fuck about selling a fight. Couldn't give a fuck about explaining what makes me better than the man across from me. It was the silence that fueled me. The stillness of the ring. No thoughts. No emotions. It's precision and control that brings the victory. But that silence had been harder to find without Alana. And she knew that. Which is why she always called before these bloody circus shows. But still, nothing. I slid my phone from my pocket to text her.

> Me: Is your roommate acting out one of her murder mystery podcasts on you?

No reply.

Just an email notification from Lars.

Subject: *Oskar Audio.*

I nodded once to Montee. "Need to step out."

He waved me off without looking, still talking about my conditioning like any of it mattered. I ducked through the side corridor, earbuds already in, thumb hitting play. The audio started muffled —rustling, background noise, then Oskar's voice came through, crisp and close.

"Relax. I'm not here to fuck. If I were, you'd already be bent over this counter."

Who the fuck is he talking to like that?

Then—

"Although I'd love to see every way Kais would lose his fucking mind."

And I knew. I knew exactly who the shit-eating cunt was talking to. My fucking wife. Heat climbed my throat. My jaw clenched so hard I felt it in my temples. I listened—barely breathing—as her voice came through next.

"So, what is it you want in exchange for not killing my mother and blackmailing your son, Oskar?"

Then—

"Keep your fucking hands off me. Say what you came to say— and get out."

I didn't need to hear another fucking thing. The hallway vanished. No sound. Just blood in my ears and the cold, clinical voice of the man who had no idea how close he was to dying. I was already out the door. Didn't remember walking. Only the blast of heat, the roar of my own pulse. Montee caught me by the shoulder just before I reached my car.

"Oi, Reinhardt. Where the bloody hell are you going? Everyone's waiting," he called out.

"Get your hands off me, Montee." I shrugged him off and opened the door.

"Don't be a fucking twat. You'll breach your contract if you walk out now."

I shoved the phone into his hand and pressed play. He went silent. His face changed as the audio rolled through—his jaw tightening, shoulders drawing back. He didn't look at me when it ended. Just handed the phone back, slow.

"Kais—" He stepped in front of the door like he could stop a moving train. "Lad, you can't do what you're thinking of doin'."

Muscle locked across my shoulders. My body went still. Couldn't even hear him over the sound of blood roaring in my skull.

"That's my fucking wife, Montee." I said through gritted teeth. Then something in me snapped. "MY FUCKING WIFE!" The roar echoed through the carpark.

Montee didn't flinch. Just grabbed my shoulders, held me like he knew what came next. "Yeah, it fucking is. So what now? You go kill the man? Then what? Huh?"

He stepped in closer, grabbed my head with both hands like he could force my eyes to focus. "Then fucking what, Kais? You leave her to clean the blood off the floor? To watch you rot in a cell for twenty years while he wins anyway?"

I shoved him hard in the chest.

"Fuck you."

"Yeah, that's right. Fuck me. Be bloody pissed, Kais. Break somethin'. Break me." Montee's voice hit like a slap, but he didn't raise it.

He stepped in, close. Closer than anyone else would dare.

"But you're not that fuckin' street rat anymore."

I felt my pulse hammer behind my eyes. He didn't stop.

"And Alana? She probably fuckin' knew what this would do to you. That's why she didn't tell you. She knew you'd kill the man. So go on, then. Do the one thing she was trying to protect you from. Blow it all to hell. Let her watch you burn it down in her name."

My teeth ground together. Jaw like concrete. I stepped into him until we were chest to chest, fire pressed to kindling.

"You don't know shit."

My voice came out low. Shaky with control. One wrong breath and I'd swing.

He didn't back off. Didn't blink.

"Yeah? I don't know shit?" His eyes flashed. "I'm the one who found you, lad. Sixteen. Bleeding from the mouth. Fighting in clubs that reeked of piss and desperation. Taking beatings from men twice your size like you were askin' for it."

He shoved a hand into my chest—just enough to make me feel it.

"I'm the one who taught you how to leash the fuckin' dog." His voice cracked. "The one who taught you to control it."

My stomach clenched. I hated how right he was.

He shook his head.

"Don't throw it all away now. Not for that fuckin cockhead."

I exhaled hard. Shook my head. But it wasn't surrender. It was fury trying not to scream.

"It doesn't fuckin' matter anymore, Montee." My fists ached to hit something. "He touched her." The words tasted like blood. "Said he'd bend my wife over a fucking counter like she was nothing."

Heat climbed my throat.

Rage.

"And you think I'm letting that son of a bitch take another breath?" I didn't look away. Not this time. "You're out of your fucking mind."

"No, son. You can't," Montee huffed, "But I'm goin' take it. Not you."

That caught me. Everything stilled.

"Fuck no." My voice dropped low. Controlled—but barely. "This is mine to handle. Not yours."

He waved me off like the decision was already made, like the fire in my chest didn't matter. His eyes had gone cold, flat and dark, like he'd already stepped over whatever line I was still toeing.

"No, Kais. It is mine." He poked a finger into my chest, voice steady but rough around the edges. "You're like a fuckin' son to me, and I won't stand to see you throw your life away. Not when it's just fucking started." His chest rose with a breath he didn't seem to want to take. "I know how to get him."

He nodded toward the lot. "Just go finish your fucking press before you add another bloody problem you don't need to the list, yeah?"

Then he turned, stalked off to his car, shoulders squared, steps heavy, but steady. I watched him disappear, my heart hammering like I'd just walked out of a title fight and left the cage open.

Every part of me screamed to follow. To finish it myself. To do what I was built to do. But I didn't. Not because I wasn't going to. At this very second, Montee was right, as bitter as that thought tasted. Fuck the money I'd lose walking out of this press conference. That wasn't what stopped me. It was the legal hell that would follow. The headlines. The courtrooms. The distance. *I refuse to let another thing come between me and my wife.*

So I walked back in. Answered every question like I was made of concrete. Kept it short. Efficient. "No comment." "We'll see." "Let the hands do the talking." And the second the lights went out I was on a war path to find Oskar.

MY PHONE BUZZED JUST as I stepped onto the front porch of Oskar's house.

"Lars." I answered without slowing.

"It's happening tonight," he said. "Police are moving in. Full custody order. He'll be in holding before midnight."

I didn't respond. Just ended the call and slid the phone back into my coat pocket.

The front door was already ajar. No sign of a break-in. Just the kind of crack that says *we're expecting you*. Inside, the house was dim, lit only by the low flame flickering in the stone fireplace. Shadows stretched long across the walls, swallowing the furniture in undisturbed silence.

Three masked men stood near the hearth, dressed in black— sweatshirts, gloves, balaclavas pulled low. I didn't need to see their faces. I knew Montee by the way he carried his weight. Still as stone. He didn't say a word. Just gave me a nod, one I returned.

I moved across the room, unhurried, each step purposeful, the outcome had already been decided and I was just here to witness it. The fire cast dancing shadows along the stone, and Oskar lay crumpled beneath them like something discarded. He looked up as I crouched beside him, one eye already swelling, the other glassy with pain. Blood slicked his chin and teeth, and when he tried to spit it toward me, it barely cleared his lips.

"Fick dich ins Knie," he rasped.

I tilted my head, the corners of my mouth pulling into something that wasn't quite a smile.

"Go fuck myself, huh?" I repeated, huffing a laugh. "You seem to want a lot of people to fuck these days, *Vater*."

He tried to speak again, but a wet cough took him under. I didn't flinch. Just turned slightly and gave the man behind me a nod. Another blow landed hard, clean—straight into Oskar's ribs. He curled inward with a grunt, but the mouth kept running.

"Too much of a bitch to do it yourself, *Mistvieh*?"

I let the insult hang there for a beat before answering.

Then I clicked my tongue disapprovingly. "You're not looking so good. This"— I gestured to the blood, the bruises, the twitch of his fingers around his broken body— "doesn't quite say Rein-hardt, does it?"

Another nod.

Another strike.

He gasped, clutching his stomach, trying and failing to sit

upright. I stood slowly, brushing off my hands as if the filth might cling.

"Then again," I said quietly, "that name never really fit you, did it?"

I turned to go, already making peace with the idea that a broken rib and bruised ego would have to be enough. But then—

He laughed.

A low, hoarse thing, full of bile and rot.

"Should've fucked your wife," he wheezed, spitting blood into the ash by his boot. "The way I fucked the whore who had you."

Time didn't stop, but it tightened like tape around my hands before a fight. Everything in me went still. Clarity. There was no heat. No adrenaline spike. No roar in my ears. Just the lethal, precise focus of what needed to happen next.

I turned back toward him, each step measured. He tried to smile through the blood, but his mouth couldn't hold the shape. I grabbed him by his sweater and sat him up against the couch. Then, with the kind of control that I'd only learned from years of restraint, I drew back and hit him once.

The crack echoed off the stone of the fireplace. His jaw split under the force of it, collapsing in on itself like a dropped fruit. He slumped sideways, groaning something unintelligible, one hand clawing at the edge of the couch. I stood slowly, flexing my fingers, checking for damage. The ache in my knuckles pulsed, but nothing painful.

No breaks. No regret.

Sirens began to bleed into the night, distant but approaching quickly. I knelt once more, leaned in close enough to smell the metallic bite of blood on his breath, and gripped what was left of his jaw with my hand tight enough to make him whimper.

"Memorize her name," I said, voice flat and quiet. "Say it in every fucking prayer you make behind bars. Because she's the only reason you're still breathing."

I shoved his head back and stood. He crumpled backward

against the base of the couch. And I turned away, walking calmly toward the back door where Montee stood waiting, shadowed and silent as he's been since I was boy. We all slipped out into the night without a word, disappearing up the hill, through the alley where I'd parked.

I didn't look back. Just sat in the car, hands loose in my lap, watching the wash of blue and white light flood Oskar's house like a reckoning finally come. We sat in the car without speaking. Montee leaned forward, forearms resting on the steering wheel, eyes locked on the chaos below. Sirens wailed louder now, bouncing off rooftops and windows, scattering shadows as blue lights strobed across the alley. From this distance, it didn't feel real. Officers swarmed the house like wasps. Flashlights in every window. Voices echoing over radios.

And still, Montee hadn't said a word. He knew better than to break the silence too soon. I flexed my right hand in my lap, testing my knuckles again. Tender, but intact. The pain was dull, already fading. Not at all like the weight in my chest.

Montee finally glanced over. "How's the hand?"

I didn't look at him. Just kept my eyes on the flashing lights.

"Fine."

Not the truth, not a lie. Just a placeholder for all the shit I couldn't say. My phone buzzed in my lap before either of us could speak again.

Unknown number. Miami area code.

My stomach knotted immediately.

I answered without thinking.

"Alana?"

There was a pause on the line—one second, maybe two—but it felt like longer. Enough time for my brain to go chasing every version of this moment it didn't want.

"Hi, yes. I'm calling from the office of Dr. Miller, just confirming an appointment for next Monday?"

I closed my eyes, my entire body bracing against the rush of adrenaline. This wasn't what I thought it was. It wasn't her voice. It wasn't the call I needed.

"...Who are you looking for?" My voice came out rougher than I meant it to.

"Alana Reinhardt. This is the number she listed as a secondary contact. We haven't been able to reach her primary yet."

The ache behind my ribs deepened. It had been over a day since I'd heard from her—something that used to happen once an hour. My brain scrambled for logic, but nothing stuck.

"And what's the appointment for?"

The woman didn't hesitate.

"Her new patient visit," she said cheerfully. "To establish care for her pregnancy."

The word hung there.

Pregnancy.

All the blood drained from my face. The room. The night. The cops. Everything dropped away. I wasn't breathing. Wasn't blinking. I wasn't anything for a second.

She's pregnant. My wife is—

I stared at the windshield, watching blue lights reflect off the inside of the car like they were flashing through me.

"...Yeah," I said quietly, swallowing hard. "She'll be there." My voice barely sounded like mine.

"Great. We'll send a reminder a few days before. Congratulations to you both."

The line went dead.

I stayed completely still. My thoughts didn't race, they collapsed. Too many of them crowding the same space all at once. Alana. Pregnant. Alana, carrying our— The car felt too small. Or maybe I did. My lips parted, but there was nothing to say. Nothing that wouldn't split me wide open. Montee turned his head toward me. I didn't have to look at him to feel it.

"You good mate?"

I shook my head 'No' once.

It was all I could manage. Then I hit her name in my contacts and pressed call. She picked up on the third ring.

"Kai?"

Just her voice—just my name on her tongue—and my whole body snapped to attention. But something in her tone wasn't right. There was a tightness behind it. A shake she hadn't bothered to hide.

"Alana, what—"

She cut me off. There was a sob caught in her throat, quiet but unmistakable, like she hadn't meant for it to slip through.

"Kai... my mom." She sniffed, and it was the sound that wrecked me: small, broken, struggling to find oxygen in the wreckage. My whole chest tightened like it was being crushed from the inside.

"What happened?" I asked, barely able to get the words out. "Alana, what happened?"

She hesitated. Long enough that I could hear her trying to put herself back together, just enough to speak.

"She overdosed yesterday," she whispered. "She's gone, Kai." Another breath, unsteady. A sound that wasn't even fully a sob just a whimper that cracked down the center of my spine.

I didn't think. Didn't pause.

"I'm on my way." The words tore out of me.

Because fuck this. Fuck everything.

"No," she said quickly, the desperation catching up to her voice. "Kais, please don't. I'm heading to the airport now. I'm flying to Dallas. I can't... I can't take it. Having you there. Knowing what that costs you. What that will cost us." She trailed off.

"Alana, no." I wanted to argue. To fight her on it. But I could hear it in her tone—that secret unraveling at the edges. The grief already winning. The strength she was clinging to just to ask me not to come.

"Please," she said again, softer this time. "Just... *don't*. Not this time. I'll see you when I get back, okay?"

And there it was. The line I wasn't meant to cross. The one she'd drawn not because she didn't want me, but because she couldn't carry me too, not on top of everything else. My wife. My heart. My whole fucking world. Carrying so much on her own. Carrying our baby.

I swallowed hard. Could barely speak.

"Alanzo goes with you," I managed. "He doesn't leave your side."

There was no pause, no hesitation. Just that quiet grief behind every syllable.

"I love you."

She said it like it was the only thing she had left to offer me. And fuck, I could hear how much she meant it. How much it was killing her not to let me be there.

The call ended.

And I just sat there, staring at the phone in my hand like it might give me one more second with her. Like if I held it tight enough, I could still fix it. But there was nothing left to fix. No fight I could win. No enemy to break. Just the only woman I ever loved, in more pain than I could reach, carrying a child I didn't know we had, and asking me to stay away. And I knew what this was. Another locked door I wasn't allowed to break down.

I'd spent most of my life on the wrong side of those doors. Told to stay put. Stay quiet. Stay away. Even when every part of me was screaming to move. To fight. And now the one person who's ever made me feel like I belong—who's ever looked at me like I was something worth coming home to—was asking me not to open the door. Because to her loving me meant protecting me from the very thing I was built to walk through.

No one had ever loved me like that before. Not in a way that saw all the damage I could do and chose, instead, to keep me whole. Not in a way that didn't ask me to bleed for them just to prove I cared. I'd still do it for her anyway, for our family.

So, I let the phone fall into my lap. My head dropped back against the seat, eyes burning, chest splitting wide open from the inside. I've always known how to move through pain. But this—*this*—was the first time I had to sit in it. To let my heart go somewhere I couldn't follow her. And believe she'd come back to me.

And there, in the dark, with Montee silent beside me and sirens still echoing in the hills, I let it happen. Not the anger. Not the noise. Just the silence that comes after. The kind I knew far too well. Somewhere in that space between breath and heartbreak, I finally broke.

Alana

-35-

♪ 35

Dallas, TX

"Guests should be arriving any minute now. Can I help you with anything?" the funeral director asked gently, his hands folded in front of him as I finished adjusting the last of the flower arrangements.

I shook my head with a practiced smile. "No, I'm good. Thanks."

Why I insisted on doing the florals myself, I'll never really know. Maybe it was the motion of it—cutting stems, arranging petals, keeping my hands full so my mind wouldn't spiral into the emptiness of it all. Grief was too quiet when I sat still.

"Lana, where do I put this?" my cousin Penelope called from behind me, hoisting up a large, blown-up photo of my mom from her modeling days. It was my favorite picture of her: long before the drugs, before the chaos.

She looked like the version of her I clung to in memory. The one I needed today.

"There's an easel, ask Jazzy," I called back.

"She was moving it earlier. Thanks, Penn." She nodded and disappeared down the hall.

Penelope was the only family member I was actually glad to see: warm, funny, still exactly the same despite everything our family had put us through as kids. Having her and Jasmine here grounded me in a way I didn't realize I needed. But no one could fix the ache that came from not having Kais.

Over a month without seeing him, and it felt like my skin didn't quite fit right. I married the man in less time than that. This stretch of time apart had unraveled me in ways I didn't know possible.

"Baby doll, this looks fine," Jasmine said as she came up behind me, her hands resting gently on my shoulders. "You're picking because you're nervous. I'll be your Kais today." Her voice dropped to a low register, serious for a second before she lightened it again. "Now cheerio, let's go, you little bugga."

A breath of laughter escaped me accompanied by an eyeroll as she steered me toward the front doors of the funeral home. "He doesn't sound like that, you know."

She grinned.

"You're right. Let me channel my inner Jason Statham."

She closed her eyes like she was preparing for a possession.

"Oi, babe—let's go let these people in, yeah?" she said in the worst faux-British accent I'd ever heard.

I laughed, and it warmed something in me. Just for a moment. "Still not it. But I'll take it."

She smiled, then reached down and laced her fingers through mine, holding tight as I steadied myself in front of the chapel. Before I could pull the handle, she leaned in close and whispered, "Sister wives," right against my ear.

That alone gave me enough courage to open the doors.

People poured in—some familiar, most not—all claiming to know my mother. Each of them carrying stories or sympathy or some flimsy memory they thought I'd care to hear.

The room filled slowly but steadily. Penelope stood posted near the guest book, managing the flow of traffic like it was her job. Jazzy, on the other hand, muttered obscenities about every single person who passed. Kids included. It was wildly inappropriate. And exactly what I needed.

Everything in me felt tight, like I'd been bracing for impact for weeks and still hadn't unclenched. Cold. Numb. Like I'd left my body somewhere else entirely. I hadn't cried since the night I got the call. Even then, it wasn't the news that broke me—it was hearing Kais' voice and knowing I couldn't let him come. Asking him to stay away felt like breaking my own bones. But I had no choice. *I'll break me over and over before I ever break him.*

"We should start soon," the funeral director whispered at my side.

"Not yet," I replied, eyes still on the door. "My sister isn't here yet."

The crowd had thinned. Most of the guests had arrived, and the buzz of quiet conversation echoed softly through the chapel. But still no sign of Macy. Or Lisa. Or James. Half the room was filled with members of their family, faces I'd seen only in scattered memories, if at all. They came up to me one by one, smiling like I was some distant cousin they'd been rooting for from afar. "You were this high last time I saw you," they'd say, gesturing somewhere below their waist. I forced polite smiles. Thanked them. Nodded. But none of it landed. I can't say I remember any of them. Even so I wasn't waiting for their condolences. I was waiting for the only person coming here who mattered.

I spent most of my life in the house Macy was raised in. Victor, her dad, my step-father who was never a father to me at all. And Lisa—his mother—was the kind of woman who cooked dinner and kept a roof over your head but never looked you in the eye long enough to see if you were drowning. Turned a blind eye to bruises and cries for help. She gave me chores, not warmth. Expectations, not comfort. I lived there sometimes when my mom was too strung out, but I never belonged there.

The only one who ever made me feel like I did was James— Victor's father. *Pawpaw* as he made me call him. Summers in his garden were the only good thing I carried from that house. We'd dig through the soil together, hunting for worms and beetles while he told me their names and what they meant. His hands were always dirty, always steady. He made things grow. He made me feel seen. My blood wasn't his. But my heart was. At least... until the day in court.

Until the moment he stood on the other side of the room and chose to leave with Macy—without saying a single word to me. Not even a goodbye. That hurt almost as much as losing her. And now I'm here. Waiting. Hoping. Still aching for the only real family I ever had.

Music began to play softly—something instrumental and vaguely familiar—as a slideshow of my mom flickered across the TV screens around the room. Image after image. Younger versions of her, radiant and laughing, frozen in the moments that came long before the world ever broke her. I kept my eyes on the door. And then it opened. Lisa. James. And *Macy*.

She wasn't a toddler anymore. Not the round-cheeked, dimple-knuckled baby I remembered. She was taller now, with a gap-toothed grin and long limbs that didn't quite know what to do with themselves yet. A plaid dress puffed out around her as she moved, and the second her eyes found mine—

"Lana!" she shrieked, her voice bright and sure and everything I'd been aching for.

She launched herself into my arms, and I dropped to meet her like my knees had given out. I wrapped myself around her tightly, breathing her in, my whole body warming and trembling under the weight of how much time we'd lost. How much I'd missed. But I held it in. Because she didn't need my tears. She needed to feel safe.

"Hey, Mace," I whispered, pulling back just enough to look at her face.

"Someone stretched your legs out while I was gone. How old are you now? Twelve?"

She giggled, all soft curls and missing teeth.

"No! I'm six and a half."

I smiled through the crack in my chest. Even her voice was enough to undo me.

"That's right," I said gently, brushing some hair behind her ear. "I totally knew that."

When I looked up, Lisa was standing stiff as ever, her arms crossed tightly over her chest like she was bracing herself for a confrontation no one invited her to. James stood beside her, unreadable, his expression neutral but watchful. Older, maybe. Sadder, definitely. As I stood up, coming face to face with Lisa, Macy takes my hand and I hold onto it tightly.

"Sorry for your loss," Lisa muttered, stepping in for a stiff, one-armed hug that barely touched me.

I returned it with a polite hand on her back. "Thanks," I said softly, keeping my voice neutral, careful not to let anything she may hold against me slip out.

Behind me, Jasmine stood like a bodyguard made of sunshine and smoke, her eyes narrowing at Lisa with enough quiet fury to light the room on fire. Then, as if remembering she was technically a guest, she pivoted smoothly, crouching down to Macy's level.

"Hi, beautiful," she said, her voice warm and lilting.

"I'm Jazzy. I'm your sister's best friend. I've heard so much about you."

Macy looked up at her shyly, still holding tight to my hand, and offered her other one for a shake. Jasmine gave it a soft squeeze, then stood and extended her hand to Lisa and James without saying another word. I shot her a subtle look, eyebrows raised. Soften. Please. We're surviving this, not setting fire to it.

She rolled her eyes, barely restraining a sigh. "I guess we can start now," she said, clapping her hands once like she was corralling a wedding party.

"Grammy, can I sit with my sister?" Macy asked, her voice small but certain.

Lisa glanced down at her with clear hesitation.

"I guess that's fine," she replied, half-hearted and distant, already glancing toward the front rows like she wanted this over with.

I squeezed Macy's hand gently. "Come on, baby girl. I've got a seat for us up front."

She didn't let go of me. Not once. She stayed curled into my side the entire service, her little fingers twined with mine, anchoring me in place as much as I did for her. The officiant kept things light, like I'd requested in the email. No dramatic sobbing, no testimonials that painted my mom as someone she never was. Just music, a few quiet reflections, and a slideshow of who she used to be—who she might have stayed, if the world had been kinder.

Macy didn't cry. Not a single tear. But I saw the shift in her jaw when certain photos played. The way she blinked too fast when someone said our mom's name. She was hurting. Of course she was. But she wasn't scared. And more than anything, that mattered to me. She knew she wasn't alone.

The rest of the afternoon passed in a blur: hugs I didn't register, words I barely heard, people I hadn't seen in years offering comfort like it came with instructions. And then we were at the gravesite. Lisa made Macy sit with her and James. And as much as I thought I'd hate that, I didn't fight it.

I needed a minute. Just one. Between me and the casket. Between the little girl who used to braid daisies into her mother's hair and the woman about to watch a coffin disappear into the ground. It was a simple wood box. Pale. Unassuming. Like it didn't know the weight of what it carried. All her wasted potential. All her beauty. All her pain. All her love. And all her worst mistakes.

I stood still as people lined up, one by one, to toss handfuls of dirt into the grave. Like it was some kind of ritual cleansing. Like the act could tidy up what came before it. It didn't feel like peace. It felt like an insult. Like the final punctuation mark on a sentence I never got to finish. I hated it—hated that she let it come to this. That her story ended in a borrowed dress and a rented tent, with strangers throwing dirt over her body like she was a plot to be covered and moved on from.

It hurt for Macy, too. That this was all she'd get. That she'd never know the woman in the photo or the one who danced barefoot in our kitchen when I was little before the boyfriends came along. Only the fallout. Only the damage.

A soft hand smoothed over my back. Jasmine. No words. Just touch. Just the quiet kind of presence that says you don't have to hold this alone. And that was it. That was what undid me. Not the service. Not the dirt. Not even the casket. But her hand on my spine. I broke. Silently. Fully. For my mother. Not for what she was. But for what she could have been, if she'd just fought a little harder.

EVERYONE HAD CLEARED out of the tent. A light sprinkle had started up, nudging the rest of the guests toward the reception hall and leaving the cemetery quiet. I stayed. I wasn't ready to eat. To mingle. To hear more stories from people who hadn't spoken to my mom in years. I just needed a second to be still. To gather myself. The seat beside me was cold, and I missed Kais so bad it physically ached.

I rubbed slow, absent-minded strokes across my belly with the side of my thumb. Having a piece of him living in me helped, even just a little. I whispered something I don't even remember. Maybe it was a prayer. Maybe it was just his name.

"Do you know what you're having?" A deep voice came from behind me.

James Estepp.

I looked up and blinked—he looked the same, just older. Still tall, still quietly charming, with that dazzling smile that always made people trust him too easily. Even now, with his umber skin speckled by rain and his suit wrinkled from too much sitting, he looked like someone you'd believe.

"I do not," I said, taking a breath.

He sat beside me like he'd been doing it all my life.

"I'm really sorry about all this mess you've been through, Peach."

That name. It gutted me. He hadn't called me that since I was Macy's age. Since I followed him through his garden with sticky fingers and too many questions. And hearing it now, after everything, felt like opening a door I'd already closed.

"Yeah, well." I shrugged. "Now I guess you and Lisa don't have to deal with us anymore. That must be nice for you."

He exhaled heavily, nodding like the weight of that truth had been sitting on his chest for years.

"Yeah," he said quietly. "I guess I deserve your disdain."

He reached into his coat pocket and pulled out a yellow envelope. Held it out like it weighed more than it looked.

"But I came to make it right," he said. "At least... as right as I can."

My hands hesitated. "What is this?" I asked, already skeptical.

"An apology." He didn't flinch. "I should've stood up for you. I shouldn't have let Lisa control the whole thing with your sister the way I did. I was wrong. And I'm sorry."

His voice didn't shake. But I could see it in his eyes, that kind of regret that lives in the bones. He ran a rough hand over his salt-and-pepper scruff and looked away like he couldn't stand to see the disbelief on my face.

"We signed over visitation rights for Macy," he said. "Summers are yours. So are holidays, if you want 'em. And she's got a cell-phone now—she can call you whenever she wants. It's all in there."

My breath caught. I pulled the envelope open with trembling hands. Read the top of the document. Read it again. It was real. All of it. Just like he said.

I didn't mean to cry but the sob came anyway. Steady and quiet, like it had been hiding under my ribs all day. I wrapped my arms around him without thinking. And he held me the way he used to when I thought he was safe.

"You're an amazing daughter," he said softly into my hair. "And sister. And you're going to be the best damn mom, Peach. Don't let anyone tell you otherwise."

My voice broke on the words. "Thank you, Pawpaw."

And for the first time in years, he cried with me.

I sat there long after he left. The tent was empty now. The rain had thinned into a mist which clung to the cool air. The envelope sat in my lap, still warm, like it held something holy. Like it had freed something in me I hadn't realized was caged. I didn't move. Just breathed. Just let the stillness settle over me like a blanket. It wasn't peace, exactly. But it was close. Close enough for today.

Eventually, I stood. Brushed the damp soil from the hem of my dress and straightened my spine. The air smelled like wet grass and memory. From under the awning, I watched Jasmine and Penelope gather the last of the guests—herding people into cars, umbrellas blooming open in a field of gray.

Macy was already tucked into the backseat of James's car, her cheek pressed to the window, fast asleep in her little puffy dress. I let my eyes linger on her, long enough to memorize her softness. Her smallness. The miracle of her being here at all. Then I touched my belly, fingers splaying gently across the soft curve.

My voice was barely a whisper. "Time to go meet your dad, little one." And I turned toward the car where Alanzo waited for me.

♪ 36

MIAMI, FL

I couldn't get back to Miami fast enough. Jasmine did her best to distract me over the weekend, and I did my best not to let the baby news slip to Kais over FaceTime before I could see him. But every hour felt like I was holding my breath underwater, suspended in that space between knowing something life-changing and not being able to share it yet.

Then Monday came. And breathing got just a little easier—because tonight, I'd finally be in his arms again, I just needed to get through this check-up and I'd be off.

"You sure you don't want me to come in, girl? I am the *Tia*," Jasmine said, idling at the curb outside my doctor's office, one hand draped casually over the wheel.

"No. Kai has to be the first one at one of these." I tucked a curl behind my ear, trying to keep my voice steady.

She clicked her tongue.

"Aww, that's so sweet. Well, call me after touchdown in

London and you tell him, please. Obviously jump his bones first though."

I shot her a look, laughing despite myself.

"You're a menace." I rolled my eyes.

"And you love me." She leaned across the console, and I pulled her into a hug.

"Thank you, Jazz. For everything."

She rubbed my back the way she always does when she knows I'm holding too much.

"Of course. Now get your ass in there and check on my baby, please."

I smiled, blew her a kiss, and climbed out. At the curb, I lingered. Just for a second. One deep breath. One hand on the strap of my bag like it could steady the tide rising in me. But there was really only one thing that could do that. I pulled out my phone. Pressed Kais' name.

> Me: Hey, are you out of that press thing yet?

The typing dots never appeared. But a second later, my phone rang. I picked up on the first vibration.

"Hi," I said, breathless—from doing absolutely nothing but thinking about him.

"Good morning, Ya Amar." His voice was low. Rough. Like he hadn't slept.

"You okay?" he asked gently.

I swallowed. "Getting there."

The silence stretched—not awkward, just full. I wanted to tell him so badly I could barely breathe. The words sat in my throat like they were trying to climb out without permission.

"I've got a few errands to run here," I said, trying to sound casual, "and then I'm meeting Alanzo at the hangar this afternoon. Shouldn't be long."

Another silence. Then, "Okay. I love you."

It sounded like it hurt him to say just that and nothing more.

"I love you too." And God, I meant it. More than anything I'd ever said.

We hung up, and I stared at the black screen for a second, heart thudding against my ribs. I could've told him. Should've. But this wasn't news for a phone call. This was news for the second I saw his face. For when I could take his hands in mine and finally say it out loud: *We're having a baby.*

I'd held it in this long, through all Oskar's bullshit, through my mom's funeral. I could hold it in now for him. So he could focus, so he could breathe without another thing pressing down on him. I wanted this news to be good news, not something he already had to fight to protect. I pressed a hand to my belly. Let out a shaky breath. And walked into the doors of the doctor's office.

The moment the clinic doors opened, the world tilted.

I saw him.

And for a second—just a second—everything stopped.

My heart didn't just drop. It sank. Something inside me had been holding out, holding on, and the second it saw him, it finally let go.

There he was.

Kais sitting in the waiting room like he'd always been there. Like the world hadn't cracked open in his absence. Same soft blue tracksuit he bought to match mine in Morocco, only now it looked softer, lived in. His elbows rested on his knees, hands laced tight as if in prayer. His eyes were already on me. Watching me. Like he'd been doing it for hours. I couldn't move. Not at first.

I didn't answer the receptionist when she greeted me. Didn't try to smile. I just walked. Straight to him. No air, no thought, no plan. Just him. Just the gravity of what I'd been aching for since the moment I told him not to come and the shock of him quietly showing up for me the first moment he could. And the second he stood and wrapped his arms around me— *I exhaled.*

Weeks of tension unraveled in my chest. Tears ran hot down

my cheeks. My body folded into his like a missing piece clicking into place. I clung to him, fingers curled in the back of his sweatshirt, my face tucked under his neck, trying to breathe in every second we'd lost. He held me like he wasn't going to let go again. Like he'd chained himself to this moment and dared the world to try and move him.

I pulled back with a watery disbelieving laugh, just enough to see his face. To hold it in my hands like it might disappear if I blinked. And there they were.

Tears—slipping down his cheeks, soft and quiet. Like everything he hadn't said was pouring out the only way it knew how. I wiped each one away with my thumbs. Kissed them where they fell. Said nothing, because there was nothing I could say that would mean more than this.

He kissed me deeply, like I was the only thing keeping him breathing. And then he held me again, tighter this time. His hand curved over the back of my neck like he could keep the world out if he just held me close enough.

"Please don't ever push me away like that again," he whispered into my hair. "Please." His voice cracked on the last word.

And my heart didn't just shatter. It broke open. Because I knew exactly what it had cost him to say that. Because I had felt it too.

"I'm so sorry, Kai. I—"

He didn't let me finish. His mouth found mine again, soft and certain, stopping the apology before it could take shape. That kiss didn't ask for forgiveness. It gave it. When he pulled back, his voice was warm but there was something raw tucked beneath it.

"Don't," he said gently. "I know everything. All of it."

His eyes found mine then, steady and unflinching.

"From now on...it's just me and you, yeah?" He brushed a strand of hair behind my ear. "You don't get to do this alone anymore."

Something in me broke all over again—but this time, it didn't hurt. It was relief. I smiled through the tears still clinging to my lashes.

I shook my head, just slightly. "It's not really just me and you anymore, though."

I reached for his hand. Took it carefully with my nervously shaking hands. Then I pressed his palm to the small swell just beneath my shirt.

His breath caught. And for a second, he didn't move. Didn't blink. Didn't speak. Then— A laugh. Barely there. Shaky and wet and filled with something I couldn't name. His thumb stroked over my stomach, featherlight, reverent.

"No," he whispered. His voice broke like light through a window. "No, it isn't."

He didn't say anything else. But I could feel everything he wasn't, somewhere deep in my soul. In that place that speaks a language only he understands. He laced his fingers with mine— tight, sure—and walked me toward the check-in desk like he was already walking us into something new. Something permanent. Something that belonged to all three of us.

Kais

♪ 37

I GOT TO THE DOCTOR'S OFFICE TWENTY MINUTES EARLY. Fifteen of them, I spent watching the second-hand circle the clock. The last five, I spent bracing myself. Not because I didn't trust her. God, I do. But when you've spent your whole life waiting to be left, you start preparing for it. Even when the person you love most is the one who taught you what staying looks like.

The chairs in the clinic lobby were too small. Too stiff. The kind made for waiting. I sat on the edge of one, elbows on my knees, fingers clasped tight together to stop them from shaking. I hadn't told her I was coming. Just hopped on the plane after my last press conference last night and showed up—because I needed to be here.

For her. For this. I didn't know if she'd want that. If she'd turn around and walk out when she saw me. My whole body was too still, too tense, like I was back in the locker room before a title match. But this wasn't a fight I could train for. There was no opponent, no bell. Just the weight of everything I wanted finally stepping through the door.

And then she did.

She didn't speak. Didn't slow. Just walked right into my arms like she'd been holding her breath, too. And when I caught her, everything inside me fucking collapsed. She was here. She was real. And I was still hers. She was still mine. No explanation needed, no rehashing the storm of shit we just walked through just us.

Our family. Our life.

Sitting in this dark room with her now felt like a fucking fever dream. Not the kind of quiet I'd known before where silence was just a held breath before the hit. This was something else entirely. Soft. Clean. Weighted in a different way. The kind of quiet that came with closed doors and held hands. With lavender-scented soap and machines that hummed like they had nothing to prove.

Alana laid back on the exam table, her shirt rolled just above her belly, skin glistening from whatever lotion she uses. One hand rested on her chest like she was keeping her heart in her chest, the other tight in mine. Her knuckles had gone pale from the pressure. She didn't let up. I wouldn't. Not after everything.

I don't know how to explain it—what it does to a man to sit beside the person he thought he almost lost. To see the curve of her stomach swollen with a future you were never sure you'd get. My lungs couldn't find air. Like every part of me forgot how to function, watching her like that. So still. So brave. So fucking beautiful I could hardly stand it. That little swell of her belly...Christ, it wrecked me.

I'd imagined it, dreamed it, fought for it. But now that it was here, real and within reach, I didn't know what the hell to do with the feeling cracking open in my chest. It was too much and not enough all at once. Like trying to drink from a flood. I was terrified. And I had never felt more whole.

"You look beautiful like this," I said, watching her in awe.

She smiled softly. "A bloated crying mess?"

I shook my head, "A mother. The mother of my baby." My voice grew hoarse around the words.

MARIE ALLEN

She pulled our locked hands to her mouth and kissed my knuckles with shaking lips.

"Other than being your wife. I couldn't be happier wearing any other title," she whispered. "It's been like having a piece of you with me everywhere I go. I'd do this a million times over if you let me."

"You will, *Ya Amar*" I whispered, my voice catching. "And I'll spend every moment of it on my knees thanking you for it." I leaned over and brushed a kiss to her forehead.

The ultrasound tech came in a few minutes later, all smiles and gentle movements. She introduced herself—kind voice, careful hands—but I barely caught her name. Everything in me was trained on that screen. It felt as if I blinked, I'd miss it. Like this whole thing might disappear if I looked away for even a second.

She spread the gel across Alana's stomach. Made a bit of small talk we didn't answer. Then came the wand. A little pressure. Some static. A distorted whoosh. And then— *They* appeared.

Two of them.

My breath stopped. I sat forward, frozen, every muscle in my body pulled tight as wire.

The tech laughed softly.

"Wow, twins. Way to go, guys."

I didn't laugh. I couldn't. I was holding my breath against the sheer magnitude of what I felt, terrified that moving would shatter the moment.

"Twins," Alana whispered, tightening her hand in mine.

The tech moved the wand again, slowly this time, pointing out limbs and features like we were meant to take notes. Alana counted fingers and toes in a whisper, tears already streaking her cheeks.

Tiny hands moved on the screen—clenching and releasing like they were trying to grab the world already. One of them kicked. Hard. The other curled inward like they were saving energy. A spine. A ribcage. Two fluttering chests, rising and falling. And then

336

—*their hearts*. Beating. Right there in front of me. The steady thump filling the room. Fast. Alive. Unapologetically real. I still couldn't breathe.

Alana turned to look at me, her eyes rimmed with more tears that hadn't fallen yet. But mine hadn't stopped. I didn't even know when they started again. Something shifted in me. Broke free. Awe. I'd never seen anything so clear in my life. The ground under my feet finally made sense. She squeezed my hand tighter. Laughed through her tears.

God, she looked so fucking happy. Like her entire body was glowing from the inside out. That laugh cracked me wide open. Because that—that was everything I've ever wanted. To see her like this. To be the reason she smiled like that. To build a life that let her feel joy without having to apologize for it. And in that moment —watching her, watching them—I knew. There's nothing in this world I wouldn't do to protect that look on her face. Not a single fucking thing.

They were ours. Not a dream. Not some far-off possibility we whispered about in bed at 2 a.m. Ours.

I didn't speak. Didn't trust myself to. My thumb moved in slow strokes over her knuckles—the only part of me that could move. Everything else was locked down, frozen in place by the sheer weight of what was in front of me.

"They have your profile Kai, that's definitely your nose," Alana said, pointing to the soft grey profiles on the screen.

The technician said something. Words I didn't catch. My eyes stayed glued to the screen. As if I stared long enough, it might imprint on my bones. Then I caught part of it.

"Eighteen weeks, six days" she said gently. "Almost halfway there, Mom."

Halfway. To everything I never thought I'd have. To a future that didn't burn every time I reached for it. Then came the question.

"Do you want to know what you're having?"

I didn't look at the tech. I looked at Alana. Her eyes snapped to mine, wide and shining.

"This is yours to decide, babe," she whispered.

I brought her hand to my lips, kissed the space between her ring and her knuckles.

God, I love this woman. Love her so much it aches in places I didn't know had nerve endings. So much I'd kneel at her feet for the rest of my life if that's what it took to keep her safe. To keep her laughing. To keep her here.

I wiped my face with the back of my wrist. Cleared my throat like that would steady me.

"Yeah," I said, roughly. "I wanna know."

She smiled softly and nodded to the tech. "Me too."

There was a pause. The tech adjusted the wand. Clicked something on the monitor. Then, as if it wasn't already obvious on the screen, she said it aloud.

"Two baby boys," she confirmed, her voice warm. "Looks like they're sharing a single placenta, so maybe even identical."

"Perfect," Alana whispered, her voice wavering.

Two sons. My heart opened like it had been waiting for this moment all its life. Like something in me always knew them too. My Boys. Not one. Two. Both growing inside the woman I love like a fucking miracle wrapped in skin. Identical. Like they already knew each other before the world got the chance to. I stared at them, jaw tight with emotion I couldn't begin to name. Boys. Sons. My Sons.

There'd always been a door between me and whatever came next. But this moment—this woman—she opened it with both hands, threw away the key, and told me everything on the other side is mine. And fuck, I wanted it. All of it. Her. Our babies. The sleepless nights. The first words. The tiny hands gripping mine like I was their whole world. I'd taken belts, titles, companies. But nothing had ever been mine like this.

Alana looked up at me with those glassy eyes and trembling smile like she still couldn't believe this was real either. And maybe it wasn't. Maybe this was one of those dreams I'd wake from with blood on my knuckles and silence in my chest. But her hand was in mine. And two heartbeats echoed on the screen. And I didn't want to ever wake up.

The tech gave us both a warm smile, then stood.

"These are yours," she said, handing Alana a stack of pictures.

"Here, maybe put one of these on your desk at home." Alana said, handing them right to me.

"I'll give you two a few minutes to get cleaned up. You're all set to check out whenever you're ready." The tech said, then left quietly, pulling the door shut behind her.

The room felt even quieter now. Still, sacred. Alana's fingers reached for mine again. She looked up at me—eyes a little glassy, mouth curved with that faint, tentative smile she only gave me when she was a little unsure of her footing. Then, barely above a whisper—

"Can I come home?"

It wasn't dramatic. Wasn't some big, cinematic ask. But it stopped the entire fucking world. Because it wasn't really a question about geography. She wasn't asking to sleep in my bed. She was asking if she still had a place with me. If after everything she'd carried, everything she'd held back, everything she'd protected me from... if I still wanted her.

Christ, the fact that she even had to ask— that she didn't already know— ripped something I didn't know I'd been holding together. She could've screamed. Begged. Broken down right here in this clinic, and it wouldn't have leveled me the way that one quiet sentence did. Because she meant it. Not in the way people toss around apologies or ask for grace like it's owed. No. This was something different.

This was her peeling back every layer of armor she'd built just to get through these last few months and offering me the soft, unguarded center of her. The part that still wasn't sure if she was allowed to ask for love. If I'd still give it.

I looked at her—really looked at her. Hair still slightly out of place from the exam table. The remnants of dried gel on her stomach. That faint crease between her brows she got when she was trying too hard not to cry again. I'd never seen anything more beautiful in my life. And maybe this was the moment everything shifted. Not the wedding. Not Morocco. This. Her asking if I still saw her as mine. And me finally understanding that she always fucking had been.

I reached for her, placing my hand to the side of her face, my thumb brushing just beneath her eye to wipe her tears.

"You don't ever have to ask me that," I said, and it came out quieter than I intended. Because if I spoke louder, I might fall apart. "If home's wherever you are, then yes. Come back to me. Stay with me. Always."

She let out a breath then, like she'd been holding it for weeks. And when she leaned in, pressing her lips to mine. I felt it. The letting go. The returning. The quiet, sacred kind of staying that didn't need permission anymore. I pulled back just enough to look at her again. To memorize her, in this moment, to mark the first page of this new book.

Then I reached for the paper towel beside the exam table, gently wiped the gel from her stomach because it was sacred. She slid off the table, and without thinking, I sank to one knee in front of her. Pressed both hands over the soft curve between us. Not to feel a kick. Not to listen.

Just to be close.

"Welcome home, boys" I whispered, fingers spreading wide over her stomach. "I'm your dad. I've been waiting my whole life to meet you."

She touched my face again, fingers brushing through my hair, and I looked up at her. No fear. No question.

Just the woman I love, standing in front of me with everything we'd been too afraid to want finally within reach. I stood, laced our fingers together, pressed a kiss to her temple and whispered.

"Let's go home."

And we did.

Alana

38

"Right this way, Mrs. Reinhardt," Alanzo said, guiding me behind what had to be at least six security guards, all moving with military precision like I was the freaking President.

"Jesus," Jasmine muttered as she slid out of the backseat behind me, adjusting her tiny purse like it was a weapon. "Is this for us? Or are we smuggling the hope diamond in through your womb?"

I glanced over my shoulder, gave her a tight smile, trying to look more composed than I felt. My heart was already jammed in my throat, pulse ticking too fast. The noise outside was thunderous—Wembley at full tilt—and the closer we got, the more I wanted to throw up. There was nothing appealing to me about watching my husband step into a ring and let another man try to break his face. Jazz, on the other hand, was practically bouncing in her heels.

"Oh, come on handsome, I won't break it just let me call one tiny code blue." She teased the security officer next to her.

"Do you want to go see him before it starts?" Alanzo asked quietly, glancing over as we passed under a low archway lit with blue and white spotlights.

My whole body ached to say yes. Just to see him, touch him, borrow a fraction of his steadiness before everything kicked off. But I shook my head. I couldn't pull him out of that headspace. Not now. Not with the fight minutes away and the whole world watching.

"No," I said softly. "He needs to stay locked in."

We walked through a cold brick hallway, the kind that echoed everything back twice. Every step—my heels, Jasmine's heels, the shuffle of the security team—sounded like it didn't belong to us.

The roar of the stadium ahead bled through the stone like thunder behind a closed door. It was coming for us. Fast. As we passed a floor-to-ceiling mural of Kais (mid-fight, gloved fist frozen mid-air, eyes locked like he was seconds from a kill) Jasmine let out a low whistle.

"You'd think someone that pretty wouldn't make a career out of letting people swing at his face," she muttered, "Tragic waste of bone structure."

I huffed. "You need a new boyfriend. Post-breakup Jazzy is a menace."

"I'm sorry," she said, completely unapologetic. "I've been emotionally abandoned. My coping mechanism is thirst."

I rolled my eyes but let myself smile. My fingers were trembling, so I focused on fixing the hem of the powder-blue body-con dress that Kais specifically requested I wear—his reasoning, delivered with zero shame: *"So I can keep my eyes on the boys."*

It hugged my belly just enough to be noticeable, paired with the red bottoms that were already blistering my feet, a far cry from the sweatpants and Uggs I actually wanted. But when Jasmine stepped out of her room in stilettos and a leather dress, there was no way in hell I was letting her call me a librarian again. The doors opened, and everything hit at once.

The lights, the sound, the pulse of the crowd crashing down like a wave. Loud, unrelenting rap music blasted from speakers overhead. Lights strobed across the rafters. The air was crisp, open above us, the kind that felt too big for your lungs. *God. These boys are going to come out scrapping just like their dad.*

Two fighters were already in the ring, throwing punches like they'd been waiting their whole lives for this moment. The crowd around them shouted in every direction—beer cups raised, cameras flashing, security scrambling. But I didn't care about any of it. I was here for one man. And he hadn't walked out yet.

The moment we stepped into the light, the cameras descended like vultures. Flashes, lenses, shouts, none of it fazed me anymore. I did what Kai told me to do: smile, breathe, and—when necessary—whisper *fuck off* under my breath like a proper lady.

"Hey, mama," Jasmine leaned in close, lips barely moving. "I need to hit the bathroom. You go ahead, I'll meet you. I don't want you to miss anything."

I hesitated, eyes sweeping the stadium. "Are you sure?"

She thrived in crowds, but this wasn't a crowd. This was a sold-out arena. Noise and testosterone and sweat-soaked adrenaline.

She nodded once.

"She'll be fine. Some of the boys will go with her, Mrs. Reinhardt," Alanzo chimed in, already scanning the perimeter like he had the place mapped in his head.

"Gentlemen, shall we?" Jasmine teased, winking at me as she strutted off like she owned the damn stadium. Alanzo led me deeper into the chaos.

Every step closer to the ring felt like stepping into another world. Our seats were just behind the announcers' table, so close I could practically taste the heat radiating off the lights. The two commentators in front of us were already shouting— "He's down! He's down!"—as the match in progress ended with one man collapsed at the center of the ring, arms wrapped around his ribs like he was trying to hold himself together.

A chill rippled through me. I smiled for the cameras still trained on my face, but my hands were clenched tight in my lap, nails biting into the skin of my palm. The ropes. The lights. The noise. It was too much and somehow not enough to distract me. Because the man who taught me what safety feels like was about to walk into a cage designed to hurt him.

"Alana."

I turned at the sound of my name. Emilia was a few rows back beside Ollie, her honey-blonde hair twisted up, her hand resting on the back of her chair. "Congrats," she mouthed, eyes flicking to my stomach with a small, sincere smile. I nodded back, the noise swallowing my response.

The crowd shifted again, cameras turning toward the stage as the fighters from the previous match took the mic. That's when a heavy hand landed on my shoulder, followed by a bear hug that lifted me half out of my chair.

"*Lana mama*," James Del Toro grinned as he pulled back, his golden-boy smile damn near blinding under the arena lights. "You look incredible. Those boys are getting big." His eyes fixed on my belly.

"I just saw you yesterday, James." I rolled my eyes, grinning.

"Yeah, and I'm sure they already miss me." He nudged my belly like we were longtime co-conspirators. Then he dropped into the seat beside me with the kind of ease only James could pull off in a stadium full of screaming fans.

"You ready to see our boy work?"

I drew in a breath, the kind that felt too big for my already tight ribs.

"I don't know how I'm going to handle watching someone hit him."

He scoffed like the very idea offended him.

"Please. Kais is a surgeon in there, barely gets touched. You know he's the only man who can sell out Wembley in less than twenty-four hours, right?"

I nodded, still nervous. "I guess you two have that in common. Sold-out stadiums for him, Driver's championship for you. How will I ever compete?"

He leaned over, pinched my cheek. "You've got two of the best trophies riding shotgun. Game over."

It made me laugh, the kind that reminded me I wasn't in this alone.

"Who's your date tonight?" I asked, nudging the focus off of me.

"No date," he shrugged. "Just the stunning Oliver and lovely Emilia. Though... I'm pretty sure I met my future wife at the food stall."

I raised a brow. "You'll have to slow down to settle down, James."

He winked. "Yeah, I blame you Reinhardt's for rewriting every idea I had about love. Now I have no choice but to find my girl."

The lights above us dipped, the air shifting like the whole arena was holding its breath.

"Oof. Show time," James said, rising to his feet with a quick tap to my knee. "I'll catch you after."

And then he was gone, leaving the seat beside me empty again. But my chest was a little lighter than before.

"Defending heavyweight champion Kais Reinhardt, standing at six-foot-five, weighs in at 220 pounds—"

My breath caught. That was less than I remembered. He'd been cutting down for months. I knew that. But hearing it now—laid bare in numbers—it made my stomach twist. "—will fight at a slight disadvantage to Nicholi Sabach's six-foot-six, 274-pound frame."

A full fifty-four pounds heavier. My palms started to sweat. Kais wasn't small by any stretch, but beside a man like that? It was hard not to see him as outmatched.

Jasmine reappeared, slipping into the seat beside me and grabbing my hand like she hadn't just vanished into the madness out there.

"Did you miss me?" Jasmine grinned, dropping into the seat

beside me and grabbing my hand like she hadn't just disappeared into the belly of a sold-out stadium.

"Not even a little," I said, squeezing back.

"Good. That's why I didn't get your ass anything from the concession."

I side-eyed her. "Right, not at all because the snacks suck."

She rolled her eyes.

"Okay, that too. But it sounded better when I framed it as petty."

Before I could fire back, the lights suddenly dropped again. The announcer's voice boomed across the stadium, soaked in bravado.

"The time has arrived. The moment we've all been waiting for... let's bring the fighters to the ring. First up, making his entrance... Nicholi 'Murder Man' Sabach!"

A crack of fireworks shattered overhead. Then pop music so loud it made my teeth rattle. Out came a massive, bald man in a sequined gladiator skirt, stomping and screaming until his face turned purple.

"Wow. What a twat," Jasmine said, deadpan, leaning in close.

"You actually nailed that one," I mumbled, my eyes locked on the spectacle.

He was pounding his chest like a cartoon villain on steroids.

"Man, I really hope Kai beats the shit out of that guy." I muttered.

"Oh, he will," Jasmine said with a wicked little smile. "But just in case, I've got one shoe locked and loaded."

I snorted, my nerves buzzing just beneath the laugh. She didn't know it, but her humor was the only thing keeping me from falling apart right now. After the flames and sparklers burned themselves out, the stadium fell quiet, almost reverent, like everyone knew not to speak over what came next.

"And now..." the announcer's voice rang out, thick with theatrics. "Making his appearance in the ring... the reigning undefeated, undisputed *heavyweight champion of the world*. The Fighting Darling of London—*Kais Reinhardt!*"

A roar erupted. Deafening. Wild. Every screen in the stadium lit up with a silent montage of my husband knocking man after man unconscious—slow-motion punches, bodies hitting the ground, the unflinching stillness in his eyes. And then—

Silence.

A single violinist stepped onto the stage and began to play 'Clair de Lune'. It wasn't soft. It was haunting. The kind of sound that made your chest ache.

And then the live feed cut to Kais. My lungs forgot how to work. Something in me stilled, then surged all at once, like the gravity in the room had shifted to make space for him. He wasn't just my husband in that moment. He was something more—something mythic. Untouchable. Holy.

Every time I thought I'd seen the deepest version of him, he showed me something more. And tonight, I could feel it in my chest: what it meant to be his. To be loved by a man the whole world watched like a storm they couldn't look away from and still found a way to make me feel seen in it.

Then he appeared at the mouth of the tunnel like he was stepping out of another world. Cold. Composed. His robe and shorts were all black—no flash, no sparkle, no ego. Just two stark white sponsorship logos stamped over his shoulders. His hair was pushed back with a black headband, and even from here, I could see the lock that always fell in front of his eye. He was so beautiful it didn't make sense. Not in this arena, not in this bloodsport. He didn't belong to this world. He just ruled it.

The violin stopped the second he reached the stage. And then, as if it were rehearsed, the entire stadium erupted into song—tens of thousands of voices in perfect rhythm:

"Woah, woah, Reinhardt.
Woah, woah, Reinhardt."

Fireworks exploded again, louder this time, as Kais stepped down the aisle—his walk measured, untouched by the chaos around him. The chants carried him forward like a war anthem. He looked carved from ice.

"Fuck, he's scary as hell," Jasmine whispered beside me.

"Is it bad that I'm turned on?" I muttered.

She huffed a laugh. "Girl, I think you might be just as crazy as him."

And then, his eyes found mine. Just for a second. That deadly stare broke, and he winked. One subtle flick of acknowledgment. One silent reminder he was mine. And then he was gone again, climbing into the ring like he was stepping into the operation room.

The announcers rattled off stats and commentary, the crowd a living beast all around us. But I couldn't hear any of it. The only thing I could hear was my own heartbeat, counting down to the bell. And then—it rang.

The other guy came at Kais fast and cocky—but Kais had clearly seen it coming. It was like watching someone solve a puzzle in real time, tracking every twitch, every angle, already ten steps ahead. Sabach looked massive next to him, all muscle and bravado, but Kais was quicker. More tactical and lethally precise. They circled each other in silence, gloves tapping once in that ceremonial pause before the violence. Neither of them swung.

They just moved. Two predators waiting for the other to blink. Then Sabach rushed, driving Kais back toward the ropes, throwing a wild right. Kais slipped it like it was nothing, ducked low and glided back to center. That must've rattled the sparkly bastard, because he started blowing kissy faces like a toddler having a tantrum. Kais didn't react. Just extended his left, measured the distance—

And cracked him.

A clean, jab right to the nose that sent the man stumbling backward and straight to the mat.

"Oh shit!" Jasmine snapped beside me.

"Oh! Sabach went down!" the announcer shouted, his voice splitting through the roar.

The ref began the count as Sabach dragged himself upright, nose already red, eyes wide like he'd just seen a ghost. Kais stood silent in his corner. Calm and unreadable.

They met in the center again. This time, Sabach charged in dirty, throwing a brutal combo of body shots that slammed into Kais' ribs. My whole body tensed. I felt the air knock out of me. But Kais didn't flinch. He stood there, took it, moved with it like his body had already done the math.

They locked up in a clinch, swaying shoulder to shoulder until the ref broke them apart.

"Who knew boxing was so intimate?" Jasmine muttered. "Maybe I should rethink nursing, clearly this is where all the affection is."

I didn't answer. I couldn't. My pulse was racing too hard.

"Reinhardt is a master of patience," one of the commentators said, just feet away. "Sabach wants a reaction, but Reinhardt is bloody unshakeable."

A flicker fluttered low in my stomach: soft, quick. I couldn't tell if it was nerves or the babies kicks. Maybe both. I didn't move. Just watched Kais like he was knitting my entire world together, praying nothing broke him.

They circled again—seconds ticking like thunder—and then the bell rang. Kais turned back to his corner. Calm. Controlled. A weapon to some.

The entire universe to me.

39

"WAKE THE FUCK UP, LAD!" MONTEE SNAPPED THE second I hit the stool.

His palm smacked the side of my head—not hard, but loud enough to make the crowd fade for a second.

"What the fuck was that? You're lettin' that big bastard push you around like you ain't the one with the goddamn crown!"

I didn't speak. Didn't blink. Just let the water drip down my back and kept my eyes locked on Sabach, who was bleeding from the nose and breathing heavily already.

"He's slow. He's sloppy. You let him get one in because you're waitin'. For what?" Montee snarled, grabbing both sides of my face, locking me in.

I spit into the bucket and stood before the bell even rang. Montee didn't move out of the way. Just leaned in closer, voice guttural.

"Where's that fire you had in ya at Oskars?" he growled. "Wake that fuckin' beast up. You're Kais Fuckin' Reinhardt. Put his head on the bloody mantle."

The bell rang.

I was already moving. Sabach lumbered forward, fists high,

breathing through his mouth like he didn't know this round was his last. I slipped the first jab—barely turned my head—then answered with a quick shot to the ribs. Just a test. He flinched.

Good.

He came back swinging too wide. I ducked the hook, stepped left, and caught him clean in the jaw with a right that snapped his head sideways. The crowd roared. I barely heard it. He stumbled, recovered, threw again.

Sloppy.

I buried a left into his side, then followed with a right uppercut that clipped his chin. He dropped his guard: instinct, panic. That was all I needed. I launched forward, full body behind the hit.

One-two. Temple. Jaw.

He fell back onto his ass. The stadium vibrated in a chant. I stepped to my corner watching as the ref counted him up. Sabach's lips were slick with blood, breath too labored.

One. Two. Three. Four. Five. Six. Seven. Eight.

He rose to his feet.

His eyes wide and bewildered, shaken. He nodded to the ref and it was time to end it. I moved in quick, stepping with my left and cleaning his jaw with a single right hook. He crumpled like a fucking building, knees giving out before the rest of him even registered the fall.

Down cold.

Everything around me erupted with screams, lights, fireworks, Montee. I didn't celebrate. Just stood there as the ref pulled me back and waved it off.

TKO. Second round. Just like I said it would be.

My chest rose once. My gloves came down slowly. And then I looked for her. The crowd blurred. Lights bled. But I found her—right there behind the ropes, hand over her heart, tears on her cheeks, belly swollen and a smile that made everything inside me steady again.

The post-fight swarm hit the ring like a tidal wave. Hands were on me, cool towels, camera flashes, someone patting my shoulder, another reaching for my wrist. I barely registered any of it. Montee shoved through the chaos and started tearing at the laces of my gloves.

"You sure about this?" he asked, low enough that no one else could hear.

I gave him a single nod. He let out a long exhale, like he'd been holding it for years.

"Go on then," he muttered, yanking the last glove free. "Do what you came to do, lad."

That was all I needed.

Sabach was still slumped against the ropes, surrounded by medics. I didn't spare him a second look. Not my business anymore. My business was one row back, heart in her hands, eyes never leaving mine.

I jumped the ropes, landed with a thud on the outer platform, and made my way toward the announcer's table—ignoring the barrage of noise, the people trying to stop me, the hands trying to steer me elsewhere. She stood again the second she saw me coming.

"Come on," I called over the roar of the crowd, waving her toward me.

"What? *Kai*!" she laughed, clearly stunned, already half-moving.

I didn't wait. I reached the barricade, wrapped my arm around her waist, and lifted her clean over it. Security opened their mouths, but the look I shot them said enough. I'd just put a grown man to sleep—no one was about to fucking tell me no.

"Come with me," I whispered into her hair, the scent of her pulling me down to earth in the best way.

She nodded without hesitation. I hoisted her into the ring then I climbed back in, lifted her into my arms wrapping her body with mine. Sweat and all—because why the fuck not? She didn't flinch. Didn't care that I was soaked in adrenaline and blood and everything in between. Her arms came around my neck like she'd been waiting to breathe, and her lips—soft, cool, sweet—found mine.

I kissed her once. Then again. Then again. Until she laughed. *That sound*. The one I'd chased through dreams. The one that made everything slow down.

"Kai," she breathed, brushing her nose against mine, "don't you have to talk to these people behind you?"

I didn't even glance back.

"Nothing comes before you, *Ya Amar*."

She smiled, eyes glassy with disbelief and joy all tangled up. I took her face in both hands and kissed her again, slower this time. Like a vow. Like a fucking prayer.

"I love you," she whispered against my lips.

And that was when the ref stepped in, grabbing my wrist and raising my arm into the air just as the announcer roared my name. I didn't look at the cameras. I didn't flex for the crowd. My only win tonight was right here. Pressed against me in a blue dress, carrying the only other two people who made this whole thing worth walking away from.

Sabach declined to shake my hand after. Like the proper fucking cunt he is. And then, right on cue, a mic was shoved in my face. A short man in a decent suit stood at the other end of the mic, grinning like he had just knocked someone out.

"The Fighting Darling of London, Kais Reinhardt. The youngest undisputed heavyweight champion in history. Undefeated time and time again. Absolutely brilliant." His voice dripped with elation, like the win belonged to him too. "How does it feel coming off what many are calling the best performance of your career?"

I didn't look at him. My eyes were on Alana, still right there, hands resting on the curve of her stomach, her ring catching the lights above us. Montee stood a few feet off, nodding like he already knew what was coming.

"Yeah," I said, breath heavy. "Styles make fights. Mine just happened to be the answer for the lad. I'm pleased with the outcome."

The interviewer smiled, waiting for more. Didn't get it.

"You've never been a man of many words, Kais—but the fans love you. You show up. Every time. So... what's next for you?"

Alana's eyes met mine again. Soft. Proud. Like she already knew what I was going to say before I did. And just like that—I knew. There wasn't a single part of me that wanted to be anywhere else. I kept my gaze on her as I spoke.

"This is the end of the road for me, mate."

The mic dipped slightly. The crowd shifted. Alana's brows lifted—just a little—but her hand didn't move from her belly.

"You're breaking a lot of hearts tonight, Reinhardt. And at what most would say is the prime of your career."

I nodded once.

"It's no secret you've had a big year," he went on. "One of the main points of chatter being your recent exit from the finance and dating markets." He chuckled. "So is this a newlywed sabbatical, or a final farewell to England's darling?"

"It's a farewell," I said plainly. "My focus is on growing my family and building something for the next generation of fighters in our community."

He blinked. "Well, I'll be honest, I'm stunned. And I imagine most of England is too after a night like this."

"I don't take it lightly," I said. "I've been boxing since I was a boy. If it weren't for Montee Aitken, I wouldn't be here. In the ring or otherwise." I glanced his way.

He nodded once, jaw tight.

"And I sure as hell wouldn't be where I'm going without the love of my life—my wife, Alana."

I looked back at her. Tears welled in her eyes, threatening to take her makeup with them.

"I'm grateful to all of you," I said into the mic. "But it's time for me to go home."

I shook the man's hand, already moving back to her before the next question could leave his mouth. A flood of other interviewers swarmed, voices rising, cameras flashing, hands reaching—but I didn't see any of it.

Only her. In seconds, she was in my arms again, tears streaking down the cheeks I loved more than my own breath. She held onto me like she didn't care we were still center ring, like the world had already fallen away.

"Kai..." Her voice broke slightly as her hands pressed against my chest. "Doesn't this feel crazy? You don't have to do this."

Her eyes searched mine, wide and wild, like maybe she could still talk me down from the ledge. But I was already flying. I brushed my knuckles along her jaw, kissed her lips slow, and pulled back just enough to say—

"Does it feel crazy to you, Ya Amar?"

A soft laugh broke through her tears. She shook her head, eyes shining. "I don't know, Kai Kai," she whispered. "You could convince me to do all kinds of crazy things when you call me that."

We smiled at each other then—quiet, breathless, steady in a way we hadn't been at the start. We knew where we began. Strangers in passing. A moment that should've meant nothing. And here we were. A lifetime later. Or maybe only a second into it. Because everything after this— *was just the beginning.*

Epilogue

"Alana"

ONE YEAR LATER....

"Will you call me when you get home from school? Don't forget your art project—I want to see how it turns out," I whispered into the phone, tiptoeing down the stairs, careful not to wake the boys from their nap.

"I won't forget, Lana. Will Zayd and Rafi be up then?" Macy asked, her face crowding the screen as she leaned closer to the camera.

"They should be if you call right after the bus," I said, slipping into the kitchen. "Do you remember how far in the future we live?"

"Six hours!" she declared proudly.

I smiled.

"Still the smartest girl I know."

I watched her one last time as she headed toward her stop, wind catching the ends of her braids.

"I gotta go, the bus is here. Love you!" she said, voice echoing just slightly as she held the phone far too close again.

"I love you too, baby girl." I ended the call and set the phone down gently on the counter.

Kais stood shirtless at the sink, washing bottles in the afternoon light.

"She sounds bright today," he said over his shoulder.

I stepped behind him, wrapping my arms around his waist, pressing a kiss between his shoulder blades.

"She is. She had a really good summer here. It'll be nice when she comes again after Christmas."

I rested my cheek against his back, listening to the steady rhythm of his breath.

He turned off the tap and faced me, looping his arms around my middle, eyes searching mine. "We can live in Texas for a while, if you want, *Ya Amar*."

"I know." I nodded, threading my fingers behind his neck. "But I like it here. I love our house. Your gym, the work you're doing with the outreach program and the shelter. This is our life now."

He watched me quietly.

"And being in Texas doesn't change my visitation. You know how Lisa is." I shrugged.

"It's fine. I'm happy."

I picked up the baby monitor from the counter, eyes softening at the sight of our boys curled into each other like puzzle pieces: two exact replicas of Kais, down to the lashes, beauty mark and pouty mouths.

"They look so perfect when they sleep like this," I said, softly. "So innocent."

Kais glanced over my shoulder, his smile lazy and full of quiet affection. "Yeah... until they wake up and find five new ways to try and kill us."

I snorted.

"I love them though."

"Me too." He took the monitor from my hand, setting it

gently back on the counter like even that deserved care. Then his hands found my hips, tugging me into the splay of his legs.

I barely had time to catch my breath before he pressed me flush against him, the hard ridge of him already straining through his sweats. I gasped, my palms flattening against his chest, heat curling low in my belly. Every time. Every time, it felt like the first time. His hand slid to the small of my back, keeping me there, his other trailing slowly over my hip. A smile pulled at my lips.

"We've got, what... a solid thirty minutes?" I purred, letting my fingers trace the curve of his bicep. "I was going to make breakfast, but—"

His hand slid down my torso, rough palm grazing the silk of my robe before parting it open. His fingers dipped between my legs, right over the ache he'd caused, and my breath caught hard in my throat. God. Just the heat of his hand there unraveled something in me.

"Kai—" I barely managed before his mouth captured mine, all groan and hunger, like he'd starved for this. For me.

My hips rolled into his touch, needing the friction, needing him closer. I reached down, my fingers brushing his. Bold. Sure. I pushed the fabric aside and let him feel how wet I already was. Then I slipped my hand into his sweats, found the thick weight of him, and stroked slow, teasing him with the wetness he'd drawn out of me so easily .

"Fuck," he hissed, his voice breaking apart as his hand fisted in my hair, forcing my gaze to his.

"I need you," I whispered, my mouth hovering just over his. "All of you."

His eyes burned, restraint teetering on a knife's edge.

"Can you be quiet for me, *Ya Amar*?" he asked, voice dark and rasping.

I shook my head, grinding into his touch without shame.

"No, Kai. Don't make me be quiet." It came out as a moan.

His fingers slipped past my panties and pushed inside me,

coaxing a whimper from my throat that he swallowed with his mouth. Tongue tangled with mine, his free hand anchoring my hip as I moved in time with his rhythm—chasing it, needing it. But it wasn't enough. Not this. Not when I had him to myself. All of him.

"I don't want to come like this, Kai," I panted, my body starting to pulse around his fingers, the wave rising fast.

He slowed, mouth trailing hot over my jaw as he whispered, "What do you want, my love?"

I pulled back just enough to see him. His pupils blown wide, his lips parted, breath coming ragged. And I knew. He'd give me anything. Everything. I cupped his jaw with one hand, let the other trace the hard etching of his stomach. My voice was low, nearly trembling.

"I need to feel you inside of me," I said, honest and raw. "Nothing else will do."

He stopped. Just for a second.

Then he lifted me like nothing, my legs wrapped tight around his waist as his mouth crashed into mine. His hands gripped the backs of my thighs, fingers digging in like he couldn't get enough of me, couldn't get me close enough. The second my words left my lips he was already acting on them, as if the decision had never been up for debate.

I gasped into his mouth, fingers tangling in his hair as I kissed him deeper, took more of him: his tongue, his heat, his everything. He bit down gently on my lower lip before dragging his mouth down my neck, teeth grazing the sensitive line of my pulse. Then he laid me out on the couch like something precious. I reached for the tie of my robe, but he caught my hand firmly.

"You know better." He growled. "You're mine to undress. Understand?"

I nodded, breath catching.

"Yes, sir. I know." I whispered, a mischievous smile tugging at the corner of my lips.

He studied me for a moment, jaw locked tight, eyes burning. Then he turned, grabbing a blanket and spreading it in front of the fireplace—methodical, in control as always, even as need flickered like fire beneath the surface. He set the baby monitor on the coffee table, the quiet hum of the twins' room crackling faintly through the speaker.

"Come here," he said, and I did, because I'd literally do anything the man tells me to.

He wrapped his arms around my waist and guided me down onto the blanket, his palms warm against my skin. Then slowly—so fucking slowly—he untied my robe, slipping it from my shoulders like it was the most sacred thing he'd ever touched.

Only my panties remained. He knelt between my legs, his every muscle carved and golden in the firelight, skin gleaming like honey, that hard ridge between his hips catching the glow in a way that made my mouth water. *God, I could come undone just from the way he looked at me. From the way he always has.* He slid two fingers inside me again—slow, precise. I arched into his touch, hips chasing more, needing him.

"Kai, please," I gasped, eyes fluttering shut.

He leaned down, kissing the swell of my chest, his mouth hot and teasing. Then his tongue flicked over my nipple. Slow at first, then firmer, teasing. My hips rolled instinctively against his hand, his thumb moving in torturous, coiling circles over that aching, swollen flesh that already pulsed for him. Every nerve lit up beneath the heat of his tongue until a drop of milk broke free.

"Fuck, Kai," I groaned, my voice cracking as I felt it. As he saw it.

He hovered his mouth above mine, breath labored.

"You're going to come for me just like this, baby," he rasped, voice thick with need. "And then again. And again. Until you can't anymore."

But my body faltered—just for a second. "Kai... I don't want you to see me like this." I gestured to my breasts, to the leak I couldn't stop. "Like my body's not mine anymore."

He stilled. Kissed me. Slow, aching, knowing. Then he pulled back just enough to press his forehead against mine.

"Look at me," he said, soft but firm.

I did.

"I love you." His voice didn't waver.

His jaw was tight. But behind his eyes—God, behind his eyes was everything. He took my hand and laid it over his heart, covering it with his own.

"My soul is your soul," he whispered, kissing the place where it beat steadily beneath my palm. "Your body is my body," he said, before bending down, running his tongue gently—methodically—over every trace of what I'd tried to hide from him. Worshiping me in the language he spoke most fluently: devotion. I couldn't breathe. My body was already breaking.

"You're so fucking beautiful," he said against my skin, then took my other nipple into his mouth—warm, slow, claiming—and I shattered.

My release tore through me, hot and quiet, my body spasming under the weight of his mouth, his hands, his love. I choked back my cry, clinging to him, undone and holy in the firelight.

He moved carefully, guiding me to my side, settling in behind me like he was built for this. For us. Then he filled me in one slow, deep push, sinking into the pulsing heat of my release.

"Fuck," I gasped, breath hitching as my vision blurred. "Thank you," I whispered.

His arm slid around me, hand wrapping gently but possessively around my throat, turning my mouth back to his. His thrusts came slow, measured, claiming.

"I know nothing but this, Alana," he whispered against my ear, his breath hot. Then his mouth found that tender spot at my neck and sucked softly, sending a jolt through my spine. "Is this what you wanted, Ya Amar?"

"Yes, Kai," I breathed, barely able to speak. "I just need you."

"There is no me—only us," he groaned, thrusts deepening, pace building in rhythm with my need. "You're so buried in me, I'm only yours. Eternally."

He hooked my thigh higher over his hip, dragging himself into the hilt with a rough, guttural sound. Then he stilled. Just for a second. Just long enough to bring his lips to my shoulder.

"You're everything, Alana," he said against my skin. "My body. My every breath. My life. All yours."

Then he moved again—hungrier, deeper—like the words themselves had snapped the final thread of his restraint as much as mine. His every word was an ecstasy all its own, not because I've developed a praise kink since being with him— *I have*— but because he fucking means it. He shows me everyday without fail. My body hummed responding to his every movement with a tight build of pressure that saw behind my eyes.

"You're about to come for me again."

"I—Kai, I—" I whimpered, body already locking down on him, the pressure unbearable.

"I know, baby. Don't hold it back. You're safe," he whispered, matching my desperate rhythm with his own.

I came again with a choked cry, clinging to him as he spilled into me—his release breaking free in shaking pulses and low German curses that vibrated against my back. My legs were jelly beneath me, trembling and useless—but he held me. Then lifted me like I weighed nothing and laid me carefully over the arm of the couch, face down, flushed and wrecked, both of us slick and panting.

He reached from behind, sliding a pillow beneath my hips— angling me just right. Even like this, when he was starving for me, he still took care of me. Every time.

His voice came low and hot against my spine. "Do you want more?"

I nodded, dazed, breathless.

"Yes, sir. But—" I panted, arching toward him, voice hoarse with need, "Stop holding back. Fuck me, Kais."

He chuckled darkly. "Cry into the pillow when you need to, Ya Amar."

Then he grabbed the tie from my robe—warm from the fire—and bound my wrists behind my back with ease.

I gasped, cheek pressed to the couch, watching through half-lidded eyes as he pressed a soft and devout kiss to my wrists. A second later, his hands clamped down on my hips with bruising force—and he drove into me. A brutal, beautiful intrusion that stole every last ounce of breath from my lungs.

My body lurched forward, then reeled back into him on instinct because the stretch, the pressure, the overwhelming full-ness of him unleashed was everything I'd been aching for. Again. And again. Each thrust cracked through me like thunder, shaking the ache loose from the pit of my stomach and dragging it to the surface. My muscles burned, trembling from the inside out as I clenched around him, greedily trying to hold him there.

"You want to be fucked like this, Mrs. Reinhardt?" he growled, voice fraying at the edges, wrecked and barely human.

I whimpered—tried to nod—but before I could, his fist wrapped in my hair, tugging just enough to tip my head back. The other hand gripped the tie at my wrists, yanking me into him with every savage thrust. I could feel the slick heat of us between my thighs, the strain in his arms, the wild need coiling tighter and tighter.

The tie around my wrists tightened as he used it to draw me back onto him, deeper with every punishing thrust. My insides seized and fluttered with every push, so close I could barely think. Each motion forced a cry from my lips, raw and involuntary.

"Don't stop—please," I choked out, hips rocking back into his, chasing every devastating inch of him.

He released the tie with a snap, spun me to face him in one clean motion, then hooked his arms under my thighs and lifted me, my back meeting the wall with a rattling thud, the force vibrating through my spine. I gasped, clinging to him, arms around his shoulders, legs locked around his waist as he filled me again.

A display of his power and of my worship. Every drive of his hips dragged a helpless cry from me, every angle stroked that aching, needy place inside me that only he ever found. My head dropped forward against his, breath hot between our lips.

"You're close again, aren't you?" he snarled, voice raw with need. "Come on, baby—show me."

"Yes, sir," I whimpered, barely able to speak through the unrelenting pressure coiling inside me.

His tone dipped, darker now. Possessive. Filthy. "Good girl. Mark what's yours. Make a fuckin' mess for me, baby."

"F-Fuck, Kai—" My cry broke wide open as he drove into me harder, deeper, grinding against every nerve until the world tilted. My body convulsed around him, clenching tight, trembling violently as pleasure detonated from the inside out. My vision went white. My limbs locked. My whole being shattered into splinters of light and heat and him.

"Come for me, Kais—please—" I begged, breathless.

He let go. His whole body tensed—one quick, shaking breath before he plunged in deep, his voice a torn, reverent growl as he came for me. My name broke from his lips in German, in English, in a low litany of devotion that came straight from the core of him.

Our breath came in ragged, staggered pulls. My limbs trembled, body still pulsing from the aftershocks. He stayed inside me, holding me against the wall like he didn't trust gravity not to take me from him. His forehead pressed to mine, sweat-damp and warm. He was still panting, chest heaving against mine, but his hands—his hands were tender now, one cradling the back of my head, the other smoothing down my spine like he was making sure I was still real.

"Alana," he whispered, voice cracked and raw, "Mein Herz. My fucking heart."

My chest cracked. He didn't have to say more, I knew. Knew he was feeling the same aching pleasure and pain I felt that came from a love like ours. Too painful to contain, too painful to not let burn you alive. He kissed me then, not hungry, not desperate, just home. Like the world had stopped and this was all that existed.

"My heaven is whatever room you're in," he muttered against my mouth. "In this life you let me have with you. I don't want air if you're not breathing it too."

I blinked up at him, throat tight, heart wide open.

"Kai..." My voice barely worked, thick with everything I didn't know how to say. I pressed my forehead to his, our noses brushing. "You are my fucking air."

I kissed him slowly, longer this time. Letting him feel it. The feeling I felt in my chest—in my bones—his kind of love. The kind that ruined me for anything else.

A soft rustling came through the baby monitor: quiet whines, a faint shuffle of limbs against the mattress. I exhaled, exhausted, my body still slack against Kais' chest, pressed to the rise and fall of his breath. His hand moved slowly along my spine, anchoring me in the stillness. Then my phone buzzed against the coffee table.

Kais didn't flinch. Just looked over his shoulder before he kissed the crown of my head, then muttered, "That's your girl."

I didn't even need to look. That low, persistent vibration at this hour was definitely Jasmine calling. The monitor crackled again, this time followed by a tiny, pitiful squeak.

"Sounds like we've got about two minutes before your sons stage a prison break," I mumbled, voice hoarse as I peeled myself off him.

"I'll get them up," Kais said, pressing a kiss to my shoulder before gently guiding me to my feet. "Take the call. Then go shower."

"You sure?" I said, wincing. He gave me that look, the one that said *there's nothing I wouldn't do for you*.

"I've got them. Go."

I nodded, reaching for my phone just as the boys' voices lifted in twin cries through the monitor. I swiped the call with a smirk.

"Good morning, Jazz."

Her voice came through, hoarse and ragged all at once, "That fucking asshole is sleeping with my Pilates instructor!"

My arms froze halfway into my robe. "Milos? How do you know?"

"I just walked in on them—on top of each other—in my bed." Her voice wavered as wind whooshed through the speaker, footsteps quick and uneven like she was pacing. Or running.

"Fuck. What a goddamn asshole. I thought you weren't back from California yet?"

"Assignment ended early. I thought I'd surprise my boyfriend, who's been texting me like he's dying without me." A brittle laugh slipped out, then turned into something darker. "*Fucking pendejo.*"

She rolled into a streak of Spanish curses so fast and scathing I half-winced, half-cheered her on. Then she stopped—dead quiet, breath caught like she was trying not to fall apart.

"What do I do, Alana?" she said, softer now. "I can't stay here. It's technically his and Penelope's place, and I just—I don't want to be here."

I exhaled, already climbing the stairs. "Come here then, Jazz."

There was a pause. Then, "What? To London?" Her voice cracked.

I stepped into the bedroom, where Kais was changing the boys, sleepy and wiggling on the bed.

"Yeah," I said, flipping on the shower. "You have another contract lined up?"

"No. I'm burnt, Lana. Like I thought I'd take a couple weeks off but now with this—" her voice wavered again, "I don't even know."

I looked over at Kais.

"What about private nursing?" I offered. "Kais has a friend—got in a bad accident a few weeks ago. He needs a live-in nurse. His assistant's not cutting it, and I bet the pay's solid. Plus, it's low pressure. Quiet. A break from the hospital grind."

Kais looked up, brow raised. He mouthed, *I'll call him,* and gave me a subtle nod.

"You know what? *Fuck it.* Yeah—if they want to hire me, I'll take it. I just need the hell out of Dallas. I never should've moved here," she said, frustrated.

"Consider it done. I'll text you the info and a plane ticket as soon as I'm out of the shower."

She sighed. "I can—"

"I know," I cut in gently. "You can buy your own ticket, Jazz. But you'll talk yourself out of it before you do."

A soft, almost sheepish chuckle slipped through the speaker.

"I was going to say I can still be your sister wife, if you want me to be."

I rolled my eyes.

"You're my sister wife for life. But you still can't have my husband, Jazz."

"Stingy bitch," she muttered, then softer, "Thank you."

"Not necessary. I'll see you soon. Love you."

"Love you too," she said—quieter this time. Like it almost broke her to say it.

The call ended. I set my phone down on the counter, the bathroom mirrors already white with steam. I pressed my palms to the sink and exhaled a slow, steady breath. Kais pushed the door open a second later, warmth following him in like a second sunrise.

"Green light from James," he said. "Tell her to call Loretta for the details. He's still pretty out of it."

I nodded.

"Thank you, Kai-kai." I smiled up at him.

He crossed to me, Rafi in his arms, still flushed from sleep.

Zayd crawled in behind him, fast and determined, the way he always was. Kais leaned in, brushing a kiss to my lips just as Zayd pulled himself up using the hem of my robe, his chubby fingers gripping tight. I scooped him into one arm, kissed his cheeks, then leaned over to kiss Rafi where he rested against Kais' chest.

He watched all three of us with a soft, amused smile before whispering, almost too quiet to hear: *"Mein Herz."*

And we were. His heart.

His home.

Just like he was ours.

That was the thing about love like this. It didn't need a reason —it just always knew where it belonged.

Just like the moon has always known the sun. A love older than time itself, where the sun dies every night just to let the moon shine... and the moon lingers each morning, holding on for one more second of his light. Until the two eclipse. And everything else falls still in their wake. An unyielding love, quiet, written like fate.

♫ 39

THE END

Cant get enough?

The *Unchained* series continues with:

James ♡ Jasmine

in

Chicane

www.Marie-Allen.com

About Marie

Marie Allen writes swoon-worthy romance with emotional grit. Known for her perfectly imperfect heroines, unapologetically possessive heroes, just the right amount of spice, and found families you'll want to be part of.

Based in the Rockies, she's a first-generation organic farmer who believes love stories don't need perfect people—just the right kind of messy. When she's not writing, you'll find her planting something, building the perfect playlist, or daydreaming about her next fictional crush.

 x.com/AuthorMarieAllen

tiktok.com/@AuthorMarieAllen

youtube.com/AuthorMarieAllen